THE DREAM MAKER

Jean-Christophe Rufin

THE DREAM MAKER

Translated from the French
by Alison Anderson

Europa Editions
214 West 29th Street
New York, N.Y. 10001
www.europaeditions.com
info@europaeditions.com

First Publication 2013 by Europa Editions

Translation by Alison Anderson
Original title: *Le grand Cœur*

Library of Congress Cataloging in Publication Data is available
ISBN 978-1-60945-142-4

Rufin, Jean-Christophe
The Dream Maker

Cet ouvrage a bénéficié du soutien des Programmes d'aide à la publication
de l'Institut Français.
This work, published as part of a program of aid for publication,
received support from the Institut Français.

Book design by Emanuele Ragnisco
www.mekkanografici.com

Cover image: Jean Fouquet (c.1420-80), *Virgin and Child* (Melun diptych),
Royal Museum of Fine Arts, Antwerp. Giraudon/The Bridgeman Art Library

Prepress by Grafica Punto Print – Rome

Printed in the USA

We were two, and had but one heart.
—François Villon

CONTENTS

THE DREAM MAKER

I.

In the Land of the Mad King

I know he has come here to kill me. He's a stocky little man, and he does not have the Phoenician features of the people from Chios. He hides as best he can, but I have noticed him several times in the narrow streets of the upper town, and down in the harbor.

The nature is fine on this island, and I find it impossible to believe that such a setting could be that of my death. I have been so afraid in my life; so many times have I feared poison, accidents, and daggers, that I now have a fairly precise image of my demise. I have always imagined it would happen in semi-darkness, at dusk on a damp and gloomy day of rain, a day like that of my birth, a day like all those of my childhood. These enormous prickly pear trees, swollen with sap; these purple flowers hanging in clusters along the walls; this still air, quivering with heat like a lover's hand; these herb-scented paths; these tile roofs as round as a woman's hips: how could all these tranquil, simple splendors act as instruments to absolute, eternal night, to the violent chill of my death?

I am fifty-six years of age. My body is in perfect health. The torture I suffered during my trial has left no trace. It did not even leave me filled with disgust for my fellow human beings. For the first time in many years, perhaps the first time ever, I am no longer afraid. Glory, unimaginable wealth, and the patronage of the powerful have stifled whatever ambitions I might have had, along with my fervid impatience and vain desires. If death were to strike me today, it would be more unjust than ever.

Elvira is at my side and knows nothing. She was born on this Greek island and has never left. She does not know who I am, and that is what I love about her. I met her after the departure of the crusade ships. She did not see the ships' captains, or the knights dressed for battle; she did not see the pope's legate conveying to me their affected respect or their hypocritical praise. They believed me when I claimed to be in pain, to have the flux in my belly, so they agreed to leave me behind on this island in order to recover—or, more likely, to die. I begged them to find me lodgings at an inn near the harbor and not in the old podestà's citadel. I had told them I would die of shame if that nobleman of Genoa, upon returning from his journeys, were to learn I had forsaken war . . . In truth, I feared above all that he might find out I was in perfect health. I did not want to be under any obligation to him that might allow him to prevent me, when the time came, from leaving the island and regaining my freedom.

It was a ridiculous scene, with me lying in bed, my arms outstretched on the sheets, sweating not from fever but the stifling harbor air that entered the room. Jostling one another for space at the foot of my bed, and all the way to the wooden stairway and down to the lower hall beneath us, was a group of knights in their coats of mail, of prelates wearing their finest chasubles (unearthed from the chests on board the ship and still creased from such long compression), and captains with their helmets under their arms, drying their tears with their fat fingers. Each of them thought his awkward silence absolved the cowardice of abandoning me to my fate. My own silence strove to be one of absolution, of fate accepted without a murmur. When the last visitor had left, when I was certain I could no longer hear from the street the clanging of armor or the slap of boots and iron against the cobblestones, I exploded with irrepressible laughter. And laughed for at least a good quarter of an hour.

On hearing me, the Greek innkeeper initially thought my dying moments had put on a hateful mask of comedy. But after I pushed back the sheets and got to my feet he understood that I was simply happy. He fetched some white wine and we raised a toast. The next day I paid him well. He gave me some peasant's clothes and I went for a walk through the town to prepare for my flight from the island. It was only then that I spotted the man who wants to kill me. I did not expect to see him. I was filled more with dismay than with fear. Alas, I am only too well acquainted with such threats, but they had almost completely disappeared over these last months and I thought I was free of them at last. Being followed again disrupted my plans. It would be more complicated now to leave the island, and more dangerous.

First of all, I must avoid staying in the town, where I might easily be unmasked. I asked the innkeeper to rent a house for me hidden in the countryside. He found one the very next day and showed me the way. I left at dawn, a week ago now. I did not find the house until I was already upon it, because it is protected from the offshore winds by thorny hedges that conceal it from outside gazes. I arrived at the hottest hour of the morning, soaked in sweat and covered with the fine dust of the limestone path. A tall, dark-haired woman was waiting for me. Her name is Elvira. The innkeeper must have thought what I had given him was a considerable amount of money, and he believed it was in error. So that I need not come and correct it, he had enhanced the service provided by adding a woman to the lease of the dwelling.

Elvira, with whom I could only communicate through facial expressions, welcomed me with a simplicity I had not known for many years. For her I was neither Argentier to the king of France, nor a fugitive protected by the Pope, but simply Jacques. She learned my family name when I took her hand to place it on my heart. The only effect this confession had was for her to take my hand in turn, and for the first time I felt her round, firm breast in my palm.

In silence she had me remove my clothing and she washed me with lavender water, warmed by the sun in an earthenware jug. While she scrubbed me gently with fine ash, I looked at the steep, gray-green slope of the coastline in the distance, covered with olive trees. The crusade ships had hoped for the meltemi to leave the port. They were slowly moving away, their sails slack in the sluggish breeze. How could this final nautical excursion still be called a crusade, so far from the Turks? Three centuries ago, when knights and priests and the poor were rushing to the Holy Land to find martyrdom or glory, the word had a meaning. Now that the Ottomans were victorious everywhere and no one had either the intention or the means to fight them, now that the expedition was limited to encouraging and arming with fine words the few islands still determined to resist, what an imposture it was to qualify this journey with the high-flown name of "crusade"! It was merely a whim on the part of an aging pope. Alas, that old pope had saved my life, and I, too, had joined in the masquerade.

Elvira picked up a sea sponge swollen with water. She rinsed me off methodically, neglecting not a single patch of skin, and I shivered at the touch of the sponge, its rough caress like that of a cat's tongue. The ships looked sullen on the blue shield of the sea. They rocked to and fro, hardly moving, their masts tilted like a cluster of invalids' canes. All around us the crickets chirred, expanding the silence and filling it with waiting. When I drew Elvira to me, she resisted and led me into the house. For the inhabitants of Chios, as for all the peoples of the Levant, pleasure is for shadows, in cool enclosures. Full sunlight, heat, and space are unbearably violent to them. We stayed in bed until nightfall, and that first evening we supped on black olives and bread on the terrace, in the light of an oil lamp.

The next morning, wearing my disguise, my face hidden in the shadow of a broad-brimmed straw hat, I went with Elvira to the town. At the market, behind a display of figs, I saw again the man who is here to kill me.

There was a time when such a discovery would have compelled me to act: I would have tried to flee or to fight. This time, withholding any decision, I was paralyzed. It is strange how, instead of propelling me into the future, danger now takes me immediately back to my past. I cannot see the life I will lead tomorrow, only my life today and, above all, yesterday. The sweetness of the present moment calls back the phantoms of memory, and for the first time I have felt an intense need to capture these images on paper.

I believe the man who is on my trail is not alone. As a rule, these killers work in groups. I am sure Elvira will be able to find out a great deal about them. She anticipates my every desire. If one of those desires is to stay alive, she will do everything to satisfy it. But I have told her nothing, given her no hint. It is not that I want to die. I have a confused feeling that my death, when it comes, will be in keeping with my fate, and what matters above all is to understand it. This is why all my thoughts take me into the past. Fleeing time has woven a tight web of memories in my mind. I must unravel it slowly, to discover at last the thread of my life, so that I can understand who, someday, is to cut it. That is why I have begun to write these memoirs.

Elvira has placed a wooden board beneath the trellis on the side of the terrace where, by morning's end, there is shade. From morning to late afternoon that is where I write. My hand is not accustomed to holding a quill. Others did that for me for many years, and more often to line up numbers than words. When I discipline myself to make sentences, force myself to make some order of what life has thrown at me at random, in my fingers and my mind I feel a pain that is very close to pleasure. It seems that, in a new way, I am attending the difficult birth through which what has come into the world goes back into it, in writing, after the long gestation period of forgetfulness.

In the blazing sun of Chios, everything I have known becomes clear, colorful, and beautiful, even the dark and painful moments.

I am happy.

*

My oldest memory dates back to when I was seven years old. Until then everything is vague, obscure, uniformly gray.

I was born at the time when the king of France lost his mind. I was told very early of this coincidence. I never believed there might be the slightest link, even a supernatural one, between Charles VI's sudden madness, which came about as he was riding through the forest of Orléans, and my birth not far from there, in Bourges. But I have always thought that the light of the world went out when the monarch lost his reason, as if it were the eclipse of a planet. And that was why we were surrounded by horror.

At home and abroad, all anyone spoke of was the war with the English, which had been lasting for over a century. Every week, sometimes every day, we heard tell of a new massacre, of some infamy suffered by innocent people. And we were fortunate to have the protection of the town. The countryside, where I did not go, seemed to be prey to every manner of vile deed. Our serving women, who had family in the nearby villages, came back with horrendous stories. My brother and sister and I were kept away from their stories of rape, torture, and burning farms, and of course we had no greater desire than to hear them.

All of this against a backdrop of dreariness and rain. Our

fine town seemed to float in an eternal drizzle. It grew slightly darker in winter, but from the beginning of autumn until the end of spring the town knew every nuance of gray. Only in summer might the sun prevail, and then the heat subjected the town to a harsh treatment for which it was not prepared, and the streets filled with dust. Mothers grew fearful of epidemics: we were kept locked at home, where the closed shutters again brought shadow and gray, to such good effect that we never forgot what it was like.

I had acquired the vague conviction that the only reason the world was like this was because we lived in the cursed realm of a mad king. Until I was seven, it never occurred to me that this misfortune might be avoided: I could not imagine such a thing as elsewhere, worse or better but certainly different. There were the pilgrims on the Way of St. James, who had set off for faraway, almost mythical lands. I would see them coming up our street. With their satchels by their side, and their sandals in their hands, they would cool their feet for hours in the Auron where it flowed below our town. It was said they were going to the sea. "The sea?" My father had described it to me, a vast expanse of water, as big as an entire countryside. But his words were confusing: it was easy to see that he was merely repeating what he had heard from other people. He himself had never seen the sea.

Everything changed the year I turned seven, on the evening I first saw the creature's red eyes and tawny fleece.

My father was a furrier. He had learned the trade in another small town. When he had become skilled at handling the simple skins of foxes or hares, he moved to the big town. Twice a year at the major fairs, wholesale merchants sold the rarer pelts of vair or gray squirrel. Unfortunately, the dangers of war frequently made the trip impossible. My father had to count on petty tradesmen to bring him the skins from the wholesalers. Some of those merchants were hunters and had trapped the animals themselves, deep in the forest. They would head off using the skins as currency; they exchanged them on their way for food or lodging. These men of the forest generally wore fur themselves. But they wore the pelt on the outside, whereas the craft of furriers like my father was to turn the skins so that the fur was on the inside, to keep one warm, only slightly visible at the cuffs or the collar. For a long time this was my only way of distinguishing the civilized world from barbarity. I belonged to a society of men who had evolved, and every morning I put on a doublet lined with invisible fleece. A savage man was like an animal, and could still be seen covered in fur. It mattered little that it was not his own.

Piled in the studio that opened onto the courtyard at the back of the house were bundles of several qualities of vair, martin, and sable. Their gray, black, and white tones were just like those of our stone churches and our slate roofs turned purplish black by the rain. The ginger highlights of certain pelts made one think of autumn leaves. Thus, from our homes to the deepest forests of faraway lands, the same monotonous colors reflected the melancholy of our days. People said I was a sad child. In truth, it was rather I was disappointed that I had come too late into a world from which the light had departed. I nurtured the vague hope that someday the light would return, because I did not feel I was truly disposed to melancholy. All that was needed was a sign for my true nature to be revealed.

That sign came one evening in November. Vespers had rung at the cathedral. In our new house, made all of wood, I shared a room with my brother on the third floor, beneath the eaves. I was playing at tossing a ball of wool to my mother's dog. What I liked best was to see him dive into the steep stairway, his tail in the air, when I threw the ball. He would come back up holding it proudly in his jaws, then growl as I took it from him. It was a dreary evening. I could hear the rain pattering on the roof. My mind was wandering. I threw the dog his ball of hemp, but I had lost interest in the game. Suddenly an unexpected calm fell upon the room: the dog had scrambled down the stairs but had not come back up. I didn't realize at first. When I heard him yapping on the floor below, I realized that something unusual must have happened. I went down to find him. He was standing at the top of the flight of stairs that led to the ground floor. Nose in the air, he seemed to have smelled something downstairs. I sniffed, but my human sense of smell did not detect anything unusual. The odor of baking bread, which the serving girl made with my mother once a week, covered the fustiness of fur we were all used to. I shut the dog in the storeroom where my mother kept linens and cushions, and went quietly down the stairs to see what was going on. I was careful not to make the steps creak, because my parents did not allow us into the downstairs rooms without a good reason.

A glance through the open door was enough to ensure that there was nothing out of the ordinary in the kitchen. The courtyard was deserted. I went over to my father's workshop. The shop workroom that gave onto the street was closed, as on every evening, by panels of solid wood. That meant that the journeymen had left for the day, after the last customers. Yet my father was not alone. From where I hid by the door that led to the courtyard I could see a stranger, from behind. In one hand he was holding a burlap bag in which something was moving. The silhouettes of my father and the visitor stood out against the white background of a wall hanging made of squirrels' bellies that was being assembled. A torch cast a bright light into the room. I should have gone back upstairs right away, as my presence there—during a visit, especially—was strictly forbidden. But I had no desire to leave, and besides, it was too late. Everything happened very quickly.

My father said, "Open it," and the man let go of the neck

of the bag. The animal that leapt out of it was the size of a small mastiff. A collar held it to a chain. The chain suddenly went taut when the beast pounced toward my father. It gave a stifled sound then arched its back. It looked in my direction, then with its mouth wide open, gave out a hoarse roar such as I had never heard. I abandoned all caution, stood up straight and went to stand in the doorway. The animal was looking right at me, and its eyes were a porcelain white fringed with a sharp line of black fur. It was standing at an angle to me and I could see its haunches. I had never seen such a color, and could never have imagined a coat like that existed. In the light from the candlestick its fleece was golden, and scattered against this background of motionless sunlight were round spots shining like dark stars.

My father initially seemed cross with me, then just as I realized the folly of my behavior, he reassured me.

"Jacques," he said. "You have come at the right time. Come closer and take a look."

I took a hesitant step forward and the animal reared up, straining against the chain, which the man held tight in his fist.

"No closer!" cried the stranger.

He was an old man, his thin, wrinkled face tarnished by a short, scruffy beard.

"Stay where you are," ordered my father. "But take a good look, you may never see another. This is a leopard."

My father, with his marten fur cap on his head, gazed at the feline as it blinked slowly. The man smiled, revealing his toothless mouth.

"It come from Arabia," he whispered.

I kept my gaze fixed on the animal. Its golden fur merged with the word I had just heard for the first time. And the man sealed this union even tighter by adding, "Is desert there, sand, sun. Always hot. Very hot."

I had heard of the desert at my catechism, but I could not

imagine what that place must be like, where Christ withdrew for forty days. And suddenly that world had come to me. Today I can see it all, but at the time there was nothing that clear in my consciousness. Particularly as the animal, which had been standing calmly, almost at once began to roar and pull against his chain, knocking my father backwards into a bundle of beaver skins. The stranger took a stick from his tunic and began to beat the creature so hard that I was sure he had killed it. When the beast lay lifeless on the ground, he grabbed it by the paws and stuffed it into his bag. I saw no more, because my mother had laid her hands on my shoulders and pulled me away. She told me later that I had fainted. The truth is I awoke in my room in the early morning, certain it was all a dream until my parents, at breakfast, spoke to me about the incident.

In hindsight, I know exactly what that visit meant. The man was an old gypsy whose trade was to show his leopard wherever he went. There were times when he was received at castles by lords eager for distraction. More frequently, he haunted fairgrounds and village squares. He had bought the animal from a merchant on the byways of the Holy Land. Now the gypsy was getting old, and his leopard was sick. If I had had more experience, I would have seen that the animal was weak, toothless, and malnourished. The gypsy had tried to sell it to another traveler, but no one wanted to give him a good price. That was when he came up with the idea of selling the animal for its skin. He had happened by my father's workshop and suggested it to him. But no sale took place and I never found out why. In all likelihood my father had no customers for such a piece. Or perhaps he felt sorry for the animal. For though my mother was a butcher's daughter, my father never dealt with anything but an animal's remains, and he did not have the soul of a skinner.

It was an isolated episode. It did not matter if it never happened again: it had left its indelible mark on me. I had glimpsed another world, a world that was here on earth and alive, not the hereafter of death which the Gospel promised us. A world that was the color of the sun, and its name was Arabia. It was a fragile thread, but I clung to it stubbornly. I questioned the priest at the chapter of Saint-Pierre, our parish. He told me about the desert, about St. Anthony and wild animals. He told me about the Holy Land; his uncle had been there, because he was from a noble family and acquainted with knights.

I was still too young to understand what he was telling me. But he did confirm that my premonition was well-founded. There was more to the world than rain, cold, darkness, and war. Beyond the land of the mad king there were other places I knew nothing about, but which I could imagine. Thus, the dream was not merely a gate to melancholy, a simple absence from the world, but much more: the promise of another reality.

One evening a few days later, my father, in a low voice, told us some terrible news: the king's brother, Louis of Orléans, had been assassinated in Paris. The uncles of the mad king were intent on killing one another once and for all. John, Duke of Berry, who lived nearby and whose courtiers made up the bulk of my father's customers, would not be able to remain neutral among his brothers for very much longer. Now war was breathing on us with its pestilential breath. My parents were trembling with fear, and not long before I, too, would have yielded to panic.

Just when the world was too full of pain, the animal had leapt out of his bag and stared at me with a roar. It seemed to me that if everything went dark, there would still be time for me to escape toward the sunlight. And though I did not understand what it meant, I said that magical word over and over: Arabia.

*

It took five years for the war to reach us. When it touched our city, I was no longer of an age to fear it; rather, I desired it.

I was twelve years old that summer when, allied with the Burgundians, the army of the mad king marched on us. The Duke of Berry, our good Duke John as my father used to call him, with a sorrowful smile, had been prevented from entering Paris, where he had a residence. Obliged to abandon his usual caution, he had sided with the Armagnacs. "Armagnacs," "Burgundians": I heard these evocative, mysterious names at the dinner table when my parents conversed. Outdoors, in our games, we took turns pretending to be a hero from one side or the other. We, too, fought among brothers. While we could not understand the politics in detail, we thought we had at least grasped some of its inner workings.

Rumor from the countryside had it that the Burgundians were coming closer. On her way to see her parents our serving girl happened upon a company of soldiers. Several villages around their own had been burned and pillaged. The poor girl wept as she told us of her family's misfortune. She needed to confide in someone, so I let her talk.

While these events had happened very near to us, they aroused in me not fear but rather intense curiosity. I wanted to know everything about the soldiers and, above all, the knights. Our serving girl's stories were very disappointing in that respect. The plunder in the countryside had been committed by vulgar ruffians; at no time did her parents see any real soldiers of the kind I had imagined.

My passion for the Levant meant I had heard many stories about the crusades. At the Sainte-Chapelle I got to know an old man who was a deacon, and who in his younger days had gone to the Holy Land to fight.

Thus, I shared the passion of many of my companions,

although it was on the basis of a deep misunderstanding. They were yielding to their interest in weapons, horses, jousts, and every sort of violent deed or exploit considered prestigious among young men. For me, chivalry was rather a vehicle to the enchanted world of the Levant. If I had known of any other way to be transported to Arabia, it would have been equally fascinating. At the time, I was convinced that the only way to get there and to vanquish all the obstacles on the way would be astride a leather-clad steed, wearing a suit of armor with a sword at my side.

There were a dozen or so of us, all children of the same age, born in the same neighborhood of town-dwelling parents. The offspring of servants or peddlers occasionally joined us; the sons of noblemen ignored us. I was somewhat taller than the others but I had a fragile constitution. I spoke little and never really let myself go when playing. Part of me remained aloof. My detached attitude must surely have seemed superior to them. My presence in the group was tolerated. However, when the time came for secrets or naughty stories, my friends arranged to leave me out.

We had a leader. He was a fat boy called Éloi, a baker's son. His curly, coarse black hair made me think of sheep's wool. His physical strength was already impressive, but his power over the group was principally due to the fear his verbal boldness and bragging inspired. He was sure of victory before even beginning to fight, simply by virtue of his reputation.

At the end of June the Burgundians were at the walls of the town. We had to prepare for a siege. Herds were hastily brought within the walls. Every square was covered with barrels filled with salt meat, wine, flour, and oil.

Summer came early and was miserable. At the beginning of July the storms began. Pounding rain caused the drainpipes to overflow, adding to the chaos and panic. To the delight of our gang of kids, the streets filled with armed men, who began to prepare our defense. The court of Duke John had always paid more attention to art and pleasure than to combat. Nobles never went around dressed for war. Now the threat hanging over the town changed everything. Noblemen once again adopted the accoutrements that, in a bygone era, had signaled that their ancestors were entitled to the rank of count or baron. And one day, for the first time in my life, I saw a knight up close.

He was riding at a trot up the paved street leading to the cathedral. I ran to his side. It seemed to me that if I jumped up to ride pillion with him he would take me all the way to Arabia, to the land of eternal sun, with the vivid colors of the leopard. The horse was covered with a gilt-embroidered blanket, armor-clad feet in the stirrups. Inexplicably, I felt nothing for the man hiding beneath this carapace; what fascinated me more than anything was the way in which his armor had been designed to make him invulnerable—the hammered steel that went to make up the suit, the shining paint on the shield, the thick fabric covering the horse. A man in simple clothing on an ordinary horse would not have had the fabulous powers I granted this knight.

I was, alas, doomed to dream, for it seemed impossible that I might one day leave behind my station as a simple burgher, something I had only just begun to be aware of.

My father took me more and more often to the Duke's palace when he had business there. He did not hope to make a craftsman of me, because I was extremely clumsy. He saw me, rather, as a tradesman. I loved the atmosphere of these visits—the rooms with their high ceilings, the guards at every door, the luxurious wall hangings, the ladies in their brightly-colored gowns. I loved the jewels in their necklaces, the shine of the pommels on the gentlemen's hips, the light-colored wood of the parquet floors. My interest increased still further when my father explained, during a long wait in the antechamber of one of the Duke's relatives, that the very particular perfume in these halls derived from diluted essences from the Levant.

These visits to the palace, however, had quashed for good any hope I might have of entering their world. My father was treated with despicable scorn, and he tried hard to teach me how to put up with it. In his opinion, it was an honor in itself to sell something to a prince. Nothing was too good for such a customer. Every gift, every effort, the nights spent stitching, cutting, designing models—none of it had any meaning or value until a rich customer voiced his satisfaction. I remembered the lesson and accepted our fate. I learned to find my courage in renunciation. When we left the palace, after a visit where my father had been coarsely treated, I was proud of him. I would take his hand as we walked home. He was trembling, and I now know it was from humiliation and rage. However, in my eyes, the patience he had shown was the only form of bravery allowed us, since we would never be called on to bear noble weapons.

Among my mates I maintained a distant reserve, following my father's example. I rarely spoke, I agreed with what they said, and I played a modest part in the adventures that others conceived. They tended to scorn me, until something happened that changed everything.

In the month of August of the year I turned twelve, we had finished preparing for the siege of the town. We were indeed surrounded. The oldest residents recalled the English sacking half a century earlier. Stories of those ghastly deeds were making the rounds. Children in particular delighted in them. Éloi impressed us every day with horrible tales that customers left behind in his father's shop along with their change. He had set himself up as our captain because, according to him, under these new circumstances we were now a body of troops like any other. He had great ambitions for this little army, starting with procuring weapons. In the utmost secrecy he organized an expedition. For several days he held clandestine meetings, sharing his knowledge and his orders with the members of the group, the better to keep control of it. Shortly before the great day, one of his muttered conversations must have been about me, because everyone but me took part. Éloi came at last to deliver the verdict: I could be one of them.

Under normal circumstances, summer was a time of freedom for the schoolboys of the Sainte-Chapelle. The war was yet another reason to set us free. We spent our days together, idle, sitting outside our houses. We were not allowed out at night, and the soldiers on watch would arrest anyone wandering in the streets. Therefore we would have to carry off the exploit in broad daylight. Éloi chose a hot, stormless afternoon, conducive to siesta. He led us down into the tanners' neighborhood, and from there, by crossing a grassy slope, we came to a swamp. He had located a flat-bottomed boat, its pole hidden not far away. There were seven of us on board. With the pole, Éloi pushed the boat, and we drifted slowly out into the stream. The cathedral rose in the distance, towering above us. None of us knew how to swim, and I'm sure the others were terrified. I was afraid until the boat was well away from the shore. But once we were slowly making our way through the algae and the lily pads, I was filled with an unexpected happiness. The sun and the heat of August, the mystery of the water on whose surface all roads are possible, and the reverberant flight of insects all made me believe we were on our way to that other world, even though I knew it was incomparably far away.

The boat slid into a cluster of reeds. Éloi, still standing, leaned over and motioned to us to be quiet. We were still drifting down the narrow inlet bordered with the velvety tips of the stems when suddenly we heard voices. Éloi pushed the boat over to the riverbank. We jumped on land. I was given the order to stay and guard the boat. From behind a hedge we saw in the distance a group of men lying on the ground. They were surely *écorcheurs*[1] from the army of Burgundy. A dozen or so soldiers sprawled in the shade of an elm tree, near another bend in the river, most of them asleep. The grunts we had heard were what passed for conversation among those still awake. Their campsite was in full sun, and at some distance from the men. It contained an untidy collection of fur blankets, satchels, water skins, and weapons, spread around the charred circle of what had been a campfire. No one was guarding the camp. Éloi ordered the three smallest among us to crawl through the grass to the weapons, steal as many as they could carry, and then come back. The children did as they were told. They threaded their way to the campsite and noiselessly filled their arms with swords and daggers. Just as they were about to head back, one of the *écorcheurs* stood up unsteadily to go and relieve himself. He saw the thieves and raised the alarm. When he heard the shout, Éloi set off at a run, followed by two other boys who never left his side.

"They've got us!" he cried.

He jumped into the boat with his two right-hand men.

"Come on," he commanded.

"And the others?"

I was standing on the bank, still holding the rope that served to tie the boat.

"They'll catch up. Come on, now!"

As I stood there without moving, he grabbed the rope from my hand and with an abrupt shove of the pole, pushed the boat out into the reeds. I heard the stems snapping as the boat moved away.

A few seconds later, the other three showed up, sweating profusely. Each of them had made it a point of honor to keep

[1] The *écorcheurs* (literally "flayers of dead bodies") were armed bands who desolated France during the reign of Charles VII, stripping their victims of everything, often to their very clothes.

one or two of the trophies they had stolen from beside the campfire.

"Where's the boat?" they asked.

"It's gone," I answered. "With Éloi."

Today I think I can safely say that it was at that very moment that my fate was sealed. I was filled with an astonishing composure. For those who knew me, there was no change with respect to my usual demeanor, that of a phlegmatic dreamer. But for me, it was very different. Habitually, my dreaming took me into another world, whereas now, I was truly in this world. I was acutely aware of the situation at hand. I could sense the danger, and identify all the protagonists of the drama. The privilege of knowing how to act like a bird of prey, overlooking everything, gave me a perfectly clear vision of both the problem and the solution. While my companions looked all around, trembling and distraught, without seeing a way out, I said, as calm as could be, "Let's go that way."

We ran along the narrow bank. The soldiers were calling out, their voices thick. They were not yet very near. They had to wake up, first of all, size up the situation, and agree among themselves, and in all likelihood these mercenaries did not all speak the same language. I saw clearly that our salvation lay in our small size and agility. I led my troop along the riverbank and eventually found, as I had sensed I would, a narrow wooden bridge to cross the inlet. It was a simple, rough-hewn tree trunk, already worn and sagging. All four of us stepped lightly across it. The *écorcheurs* would find it more difficult to cross and, with a bit of luck, it would break beneath their weight. We continued our flight and I kept up a steady rhythm, slower than my companions would have liked. It was out of the question to run until we were exhausted. It might be a long ordeal; we had to preserve our strength.

I will not go into the details of our misadventure. We made it back to the town after two days and one night, crossing canals astride floating tree trunks, stealing another boat, and making our way past a troop on horseback. We arrived home as night was falling, our skin covered in bramble scratches; we were famished but proud. At no time did I lose my composure. My companions had followed my orders to the letter. I had insisted on their keeping the weapons they had stolen. Thus, we were not only safe, but also victorious.

In the town there was considerable talk about our adventure. On the basis of the heroic self-aggrandizing tale Éloi had spun, everyone had thought we were dead. He claimed he had followed us to try to hold us back. "I wanted so badly to save them, alas . . . " and so on. Our return suddenly brought the truth to light. He was punished severely, and, above all, his prestige evaporated instantly. He became the first of many enemies I would make throughout my life, simply by virtue of having exposed their weakness.

My parents had wept so bitterly at my disappearance that they could not scold me when I turned up. Moreover, the Duke had gotten wind of our adventure and had personally congratulated my father.

The other three survivors were responsible for my reputation. They described, in all honesty, their own helplessness and my clear-sightedness. Henceforth, although nothing changed in my behavior, everyone began to view me differently. I was no longer taken for a dreamer, but a thoughtful boy, not timid but reserved, not indecisive but cunning. I did not refute these new opinions, but grew accustomed to eliciting admiration and fear with the same indifference that had enabled me to endure scorn and distrust. I gleaned useful reflections from those opinions. Éloi's defeat allowed me to perceive the existence of a form of authority other than mere physical superiority. Through our entire adventure I had not displayed any particular resilience; several times over my companions had even had to hold me up or help me to my feet. However, I had never stopped being their leader. They deferred to my decisions and did not question my orders. So, there was power and there was strength, and the two things were not always one and the same.

Strength came from the body, whereas power was the work of the mind. And while I did not clearly distinguish these concepts, I did explore them a bit further, and my thoughts led me, in a way, to the edge of a precipice. While I may have seized power during our adventure thanks to my mind, it was not owing to any particular knowledge. I did not know where we were, nor had I ever been in a similar situation, nor were my decisions based on reason, except perhaps to make us choose the paths that were inaccessible to the roughnecks stalking us. For the most part I had used my intuition, that is, by finding my way through the usual world of my dreams. So, it was my experience of something that did not exist that had enabled me to act and take command in the real world. In a word, dream and reality were not completely separate. This conclusion made me light-headed, and at the time I took it no further.

At the end of the month, a truce was called and the siege was lifted. Our town breathed deeply. Life could go on as before.

*

While the war may have spared us, it was still being fought elsewhere. I had no idea what other towns were like, particularly the one known as the capital. Paris seemed to me to be a great tormented body. All one ever heard were tales of murder, massacre, and famine. This curse, in my opinion, could only be explained by the city's proximity to the mad king who lived there and spread his insanity all around him.

Oddly enough, it was my mother who gave me the opportunity to get a more precise idea of Paris, and yet she was a timid woman who hardly ever left the house and had never ventured outside our town. She was tall and extremely thin. Averse to drafts, cold weather, and even light, she lived in our dark rooms and kept the fires going all year round. Our wooden house was tall and narrow and served as the décor to her days, providing her with any number of plans which she implemented as the day went by. Her bedroom was on the second floor. She stayed in bed until fairly late then dressed carefully. The courtyard and the kitchen occupied her for the rest of the morning until it was time for lunch in the adjacent room. In the afternoon she generally went to see my father in his workshop to help him with the bookkeeping. Then, when the canon arrived, she went upstairs to take mass in the small chapel she had arranged on the top floor near our bedrooms. Our house was built in the fashion of the era: each floor spread wider than the one below, in such a way that the room at the top was also the biggest.

It was a reclusive life, and it seemed infinitely monotonous to me, but my mother did not complain. I learned much later that she had been a victim of violence in the best years of her youth, perpetrated by a gang of lepers and *écorcheurs*. They had plundered the village where my grandparents lived, and my mother, who had only just gone through puberty, was taken hostage by those thugs. She had come away with a deep horror of war and at the same time a great interest in it. Of all of us, she was always the best informed of the situation. No doubt thanks to visitors, she garnered precise information about the latest events in the town, the neighboring regions, and even beyond. She had a vast network of informants, because through her father she belonged to the powerful butchers' brotherhood.

The memory I have of my maternal grandfather is of a man of refined manners, his nose red from perpetual rubbing with the cambric handkerchief he held clutched in his fist. He was always elegant, and gave off a scent of perfumed oil. No one could ever have pictured him splitting the skull of an ox. So, while he might have been resigned to doing so in his youth, for many years he had had at his disposal a host of apprentices and slaughterers who took care of these chores for him.

The butchers' guild was strictly organized, and not just anyone could join. The representatives of this chapter corresponded with butchers in other regions, and this enabled them to keep abreast of news. Although they conducted their business in town, the butchers also knew the countryside, because that was where they bought their animals. And so they were informed of the slightest event even before it reached the ears of the king's entourage. This world of the butchers' trade was ordinarily a discreet one. Other burghers looked down on them, so the men who traded in meat sought honorability by forming alliances with more highly respected guilds. My grandfather was pleased that his daughter had not married a butcher, but he was of the opinion that my father's trade still smelled too strongly of animals. He liked me very much, no doubt because I had a more delicate constitution than my brother, and was, therefore, naturally destined for a profession of the mind. His greatest joy would have been to see me become a man of law. To him I owe the debt of my years of schooling—although to his death we hid from him the fact that I had rebelled against Latin.

Late in the year that followed the siege of the town, I heard my parents speaking in hushed tones of grave events: Paris was a bloodbath. The butchers had rebelled, led by a certain Caboche, whom my grandfather knew well. Encouraged by the Duke of Burgundy, they had risen up against the excesses of the court. A learned assembly of jurists had drawn up an ordinance of reform. Under the pressure of the butchers and the rebellious population, the king was made to listen to the one hundred and fifty-nine articles comprising the new constitution, and approve it. At that point he was in a period of lucidity, and had clearly found it most unpleasant to be faced with his subjects' censure. The reaction came swiftly thereafter. The Armagnacs now claimed to be the defenders of the peace, in opposition to the unruly butchers—it was their meat, henceforth, which hung from the gallows in the streets of Paris. Those who escaped the massacre had fled. One of them reached our town. As butchers were under suspicion, my grandfather sent the fugitive to us for refuge.

The man's name was Eustache. We hid him at the back of the courtyard in a shed where goatskins were stored. In the evening he sat outside the kitchen, and when we came home from school we gathered around him to listen to his stories. We found him very entertaining, because the way he spoke was different from us and he used very colorful and unfamiliar expressions. He was, in fact, a mere shop boy. His work consisted of unloading the meat driven every morning by cart to the kitchens of the great houses. Although he had probably only ever seen the servants' quarters, Eustache gave us a detailed description of the princely residences in Paris—the hôtel de Nesle, which belonged to the Duke of Berry, its doors and windows wrenched off by the crowd to prevent him from staying there; Artois, which was the property of the Duke of Burgundy; the hôtel Barbette where the queen lived, and on whose doorstep Louis of Orléans had been assassinated. His eyes glowing with hatred, Eustache delighted in describing the luxury of those houses, the fine furnishings and china, the beauty of the tapestries. His descriptions were meant to make us feel indignant. He always insisted on the poverty that surrounded such places of luxury and debauchery. I don't know what my brother thought; as far as I was concerned, far from making me feel indignant, these tales served to fuel my dreams. With regard to wealth, the only example I had was the Duke's palace in our town, and I admired it. Every time I went there with my father, I was fascinated by the luxurious décor. Our condition as modest burghers condemned me to a life in a lopsided house. I was not unhappy there, but my dreams carried me into more brilliant dwelling places, where there were walls decorated with frescoes, and sculpted ceilings, and vermillion serving plates, and tapestries embroidered with golden thread . . . I shared none of Eustache's hate-filled indignation about princely dwelling places.

On the other hand, I did listen sympathetically when he spoke bitterly of the way the powerful treated the other castes—the burghers, workers, and servants, without whom they could not survive. Thus far I had accepted the painful lessons my father had given me on each of our visits to his rich clients. Nevertheless, I was appalled by his submission to their scorn and insults, and the constant blackmail when they did not feel like paying. My outrage was buried deep, embers beneath the ashes of filial love and obedience. It was enough for Eustache to blow on those embers for my rage to flare.

Shortly after the fugitive arrived in our home, my father took me with him to the home of a nephew of the Duke of Berry to deliver a large coverlet of white marten. The young man was scarcely twenty years old. He made us wait in the antechamber for two long hours. My father had worked part of the night to finish the order. I saw him reeling with fatigue yet unable to sit down, for lack of a seat. When at last the young lord bade us come in, I was shocked to see he was receiving us in his nightshirt. Through the door to his room, we could see a naked woman. He adopted an ironic tone in speaking with my father, calling him emphatically "the Honorable Pierre Cœur." With a nod of his head he reached for the coverlet. Then he stiffened and motioned to my father that he could leave. My father would have obeyed, the way he always does, but this time he was in urgent need of money in order to pay for a large order of pelts he had just received. Fighting his nature, he got up the courage to demand payment for his work. The Duke's nephew walked back up to him.

"We shall see to it. Send me your invoice."

"Here it is, my lord."

With a trembling hand my father held out the invoice. The young lord scanned it, displeased.

"It is very expensive. Do you take me for a fool? Do you think I don't know your pathetic tricks? You expect me to pay full price for something stitched not from the animal's belly but from several pieces from the back."

My father's lips were twitching nervously.

"These pelts, my lord, are all of the best quality . . . "

I knew that my father took particular care in choosing his suppliers and their merchandise. He absolutely forbade himself from taking any of the shortcuts that other, unscrupulous craftsmen resorted to on occasion. Alas, paralyzed by the respect he thought he owed the whippersnapper, he did not know how to defend himself.

"Forgive me for insisting, my Lord. But I must rely on the generosity of your Lordship kindly to pay me for the item today because—"

"Today!" said the duke's nephew, looking around him as if he had a room full of witnesses.

He gave my father a stern look. As I observed him, I understood that he would have liked to maintain his insolent stance, but that something had suddenly given him pause. Perhaps he was afraid his uncle might reproach him. The old Duke was not kindly, but he paid well. It was his policy to foster a circle of craftsmen and artists in his town, in order to enhance his reputation as a man of taste and patron of the arts.

"Well then, so be it!" said the young man.

He went over to a dresser and opened the drawer. He took a few coins and tossed them on the table in front of my father. At a glance I totaled five *livres tournois*. The coverlet was worth eight.

My father picked up the coins.

"There are five here," he said in an unsteady voice. "We are missing—"

"We are missing?"

"Your Lordship must have misread my invoice. The item is worth . . . eight."

"It might be worth eight *livres* if there were no flaws."

"What flaws are there?" protested my father, sincerely concerned that he might have let an imperfection slip by.

The young man grabbed the blanket and held it out.

"What, can you not see?"

My father stretched his neck to inspect the entire fur. At that very moment, the two fists holding the coverlet moved apart, and with a sudden snap and a ripping noise, the seam joining the two skins gave way. My father stepped back. The Duke's nephew let out a loud insolent laugh.

"Can you see it, now?" he exclaimed with a sneer. "Bastien, see these gentlemen out."

Still laughing, he returned to his bedchamber.

As we went home in silence, I felt my anger welling up. Once I would have admired my father for his self-control. But Eustache had taught me to see that my indignation was legitimate. I was no longer alone in thinking that work must be respected, that there are limits to the power given at birth, that the arbitrary rule of the nobility was no longer justified. Caboche's men had fought for these principles. As I did not know the details of their struggle, nor did I fully understand it, the feelings that had once been a source of guilt were now shared and reinforced.

As we walked home I opened my heart to my father. He stopped and looked at me. I saw in his eyes that he was more upset by my words than by the insult he had just received. I know now that he was sincere. He did not think any other attitude was possible with regard to the powerful, in the world as it was. He had raised me with one goal in mind: to enable me, when the time came, to survive.

He immediately made the connection between my rebelliousness and the inflamed talk Eustache was spreading through the house. At my father's request, no later than the following week the butcher was found another hiding place, and shortly thereafter he left town.

In truth, my father had nothing more to fear in that respect: the harm had been done. Eustache had given me permission to voice the ideas I already had. As for following his example and, more generally, that of Caboche's rebels, that was out of the question. As the son of a furrier, I was used to classifying human beings as if they were animals, according to their pelts, and I had noticed that Eustache had the same curly, wiry head of hair as Éloi. Both of them were advocates of reckless brute force, the exact opposite of weakness, but in the end it was of the same kind—that is, primitive. I was not tempted in the slightest to yield to it. There were surely other methods we could use to force the nobility to respect us, to make them reward our work and give a place in society to those who were undistinguished by birth. My aim henceforth would be to discover those methods, or to invent them.

*

Girls of my age—my comrades' sisters, neighbors, or churchgoers from the same parish—were of little interest to me. I left it to Éloi and his kind to tell tales of conquests where fantasies rivaled sordid encounters. With regard to this subject, as to others, I preferred to daydream. The little people whom as children we saw among us and who were called girls were devoid of any interest to me. Propriety maintained that they must stay silent. Their bodies did not have a boy's strength, and in any case, they were not allowed to join in our games. Their resemblance to actual women—our mothers, for example—was vague, if not downright nonexistent. If these incomplete creatures were worthy of any feeling, it must be compassion.

Then came a time when, suddenly, one of these girls would leave her chrysalis, and a new body would come to life. Her waist grew longer, her breasts and hips grew rounder. Her gaze, above all, lost the humble modesty to which she had been condemned by so much silent waiting for this apotheosis. All of a sudden there were women among us. They studied us in turn, scrutinizing our smooth cheeks and our narrow shoulders with the same pity we had shown them and which they now reserved for us in plentiful supply.

However, once they had taken this minor revenge, they deployed their newfound power more judiciously than we did. The attention they hardly paid to boys in general was counterbalanced by the vivid interest they showed some of them in particular. With a great deal of sensitivity, but not so much so as to make these nuances unintelligible to us, they would designate one or the other as their favorite. These games of desire placed us, and them as well, in competition.

The subtle hierarchy that had been established in our group of boys had been turned on its ear. It was now also subject to the ranking that the girls established from outside. Fortunately, there were times when our rankings coincided. And that is what happened to me.

Since my adventure during the siege of the town, I had gained the respect, if not the friendship, of my comrades. Two of the survivors of the expedition, Jean and Guillaume, came out and said they were in my debt, and they complied with my slightest request. All the others were afraid of me. My silence, my absence, the calm and thoughtful way I expressed my thoughts gave me, wrongly, a reputation for wisdom that I was careful not to contradict. Such wisdom could not, at our age, be the fruit of experience: it must come from somewhere else. Judging by some of the fearful or even suspicious gazes people cast at me, I understood that many of them thought I had supernatural powers. In another era I would have been accused of witchcraft. Very early on I was able to gauge to what degree human qualities conceal danger, and how reckless it can be to flaunt them. All my life I have experienced this. Talent, fulfillment, and success will make you an enemy of the human race: the more it admires you, the less it finds itself in you, so it will prefer to keep you at a distance. Only crooks, given the mundane origins of their fortune, acquire that fortune without severing ties with others of their kind; they might even win their friendship.

However, the esteem I enjoyed among the boys did have its advantages—in particular, that of making me interesting to girls. Jean and Guillaume brought me daily reports of what this or that girl had said in her brother's presence, proof of their interest in me.

The year I turned fourteen, I shot up. I now had a scraggly beard that was brown like my hair, and I had to shave three times a week. The strange deformity on my chest that had been visible from birth became more pronounced: it was as if someone's fist had punched a hollow in my chest. And while this abnormality had no effect on my breathing, the doctor recommended I avoid any physical effort, and I must never run. These instructions gave me an additional reason to have my right-hand men carry out any tasks that fell to me.

The girls seemed to appreciate my slowness and immobility. The strength one derives from one's power over others is incomparably more efficient than the one that comes from within one's own body. Physical power can arouse animal desire. It is precious for a lover. But at an age where another person's attraction is measured by the ability to endure (even eternally, when marriage is at stake), a man's authority is more attractive than his strength. Thus my hidden weakness, this bodily defect I concealed beneath padded doublets and flowing shirts, merely increased my restraint and the flattering reputation that ensued.

I did not pay a great deal of attention to these issues until I, too, was stricken with love and a passionate desire for conquest.

In our new neighborhood, a short way from our house, there lived a family whom my parents looked up to. Over time, I was beginning to realize that not all burghers had similar fortunes. In spite of the admiration I had for my father, I was forced to conclude that he was by no means in the upper ranks of our class. Drapers, such as Guillaume's father, Messire de Varye, were more illustrious. Certain tradesmen, particularly those who dealt in wine and grain, had built houses that were far bigger and more luxurious than our own. Higher still were those whose profession was money. One of our neighbors was a moneychanger; his wealth had enabled him to acquire the position of valet to the Duke. He did not merely go to the palace, like my father did, in order to solicit something and be treated rudely. He had an official place, albeit a modest one, in the Duke's entourage. This was enough, in my opinion, to give him considerable prestige.

The man was a widower. He had three children from his first wife. A daughter was born from his second marriage, and she was roughly two years younger than me. She was a sickly girl who went around with her eyes cast down, and she seemed to be afraid of everything. The only memory I had of her was of seeing her scream with terror one day, when a huge black Percheron horse snapped the shafts of his cart after slipping under the weight of a load of wood.

She disappeared for several months after that. It was said she had fallen ill and her parents had sent her to the countryside to recover. When she came back she was no longer a child. I remember very well my first sighting of her new appearance.

It was a day in April when the sky hesitated between cloud

and sun. I no longer remember what dream I was chasing; in any case, I was lost in thought and hardly looked around. Guillaume was with me, and we were slowly walking somewhere. As usual, he was talking and I wasn't listening. He did not immediately notice that I had stopped.

We were on our way up from the Place Saint-Pierre and she was crossing the street slightly farther up. Behind her, the freshly painted wall of a house under construction sparkled with whitewash against a patch of sunlight. She was wearing a black houppelande with a hood against her neck. Her blonde hair curled rebelliously against the chignon that was supposed to keep it in place, and it danced in the sunlight. She turned her head to us and stopped for a moment. The features of the child had yielded to the pressure of an inner strength that had molded her forehead and cheeks and infused her lips with blood, enlarging her eyes around blue irises that I had never seen before, because her lids were always lowered.

I immediately thought of her name. Not her first name, which I had forgotten, and which I would later repeat so often and cherish so much. It was her family name that came back to me in a flash: Léodepart. This strange name was Flemish. It is, apparently, a distortion of Lollepop. We spoke about it one day at table with my father. In that instant, Léodepart betrayed all at once its relation with "leopard." The two words, so similar, had burst into my life with the same force, and perhaps the same significance. They were linked to beauty, to light, to a certain brilliance of the sun upon a blonde creature, to dreams of elsewhere. The leopard had gone back into its bag, leaving behind this stuff of dreams, and a name, Arabia. Mademoiselle de Léodepart, although forged from a different essence, was clearly from the same world as the leopard.

Her Christian name was Macé. I heard it from Guillaume, and that was my first step toward her that day. The weeks that followed were filled entirely with my desire to get closer to her.

I led this campaign with the same apparent calm I had displayed during our escapade, but deep inside I was devoured by a far greater fear. By dint of cunning and false pretexts, I managed several times to cross her path. I was determined to speak to her, but every time I felt the words catch in my throat. She walked by without looking at me. One morning, however, I had the extraordinary impression that she had smiled at me. On the days that followed, she was as cold and absent as ever.

I was desperate at the thought of everything that separated our two families. Previously I had ignored any differences between my father's condition and that of other burghers and their families, but now I could not help but exaggerate them. Our house, at the corner of two streets, seemed narrow and ridiculous, whereas Macé's house seemed scarcely less vast and luxurious than the Duke's palace. I wore myself out trying to come up with a trick to get myself invited to her house. Nothing worked. Macé's brothers and sisters were much older and I did not know them. We had no friends in common. Our parents did not visit each other. There were times when we were together at a service at the Cathedral, when the bells rang out a holy day. Alas, we were always far apart.

These material obstacles were driving me mad. I began to envision the most desperate solutions. I observed the locks on the Léodeparts' house, and the number and habits of their servants. I imagined stealing into the courtyard one night, going upstairs, and declaring my love to Macé, abducting her if I had to. I wondered how we would live, whether my friends would agree to help me, and how my parents would react. Not for a moment did I doubt her feelings. In hindsight, that is what seems most extraordinary. We had hardly set eyes on each other, and we had never spoken. I had absolutely no idea of her opinion and yet I was sure I was right.

The matter came to a head one autumn morning I will never forget. The chestnut tree on the small square outside our house had turned yellow, and passersby walked through the leaves scattered on the ground. We were waiting for a delivery of fox pelts from the Morvan region. Suddenly, the tall figure of Messire de Léodepart filled the doorway to the workroom. My father rushed to greet him. I stayed back and could not hear their conversation. It seemed probable that he had come to buy a piece of fur or have something made to measure. The only thing out of the ordinary was that he should come in person. Our customers, for the most part, were women, and most often they merely sent their servants. A mad theory raced through my mind, but I banished the thought as a manifestation of the lovesickness that was eating away at me, and which, by reasoning with myself, I was gradually curing. I went up to my room and closed the door. A new little dog, which my mother had acquired at the beginning of the year, had come in with me. I played at teasing him, caressing him roughly. He nibbled at my fingers and gave out shrill little yelps. Therefore I did not immediately hear my father calling me. I hurried down the stairs. When I came into the parlor, I found Léodepart standing silently next to my father. They were both looking at me. It was an ordinary workday, and I had not taken any particular care with my appearance.

"Say hello to Messire de Léodepart, please," said my father. "He has just taken office as provost, and we craftsmen must show him our respect."

I greeted him awkwardly. Léodepart motioned to my father that he need not continue with that subject. He seemed eager to attenuate anything that might increase the distance between them, and his demeanor was one of good-natured simplicity. He was looking at me with a strange smile.

"You have a fine boy, maître Cœur," he said, nodding his head and smiling.

The introductions went no farther, and he took his leave.

After seeing him out, my father remained silent and gave

me no explanation. My mother came back from a visit shortly before the midday meal. They sat together for a long time behind closed doors, then sent for me.

"Do you know Léodepart's daughter?" asked my father.

"I've seen her in the street."

"Have you spoken with her? Have you sent her messages through a servant, or by any other means?"

"Never."

My parents looked at each other.

"We will go to their house on Sunday," said my father. "You will try to be well-groomed. I shall finish the new fur tunic I promised you by then and you shall wear it."

I thanked him, but my desires were elsewhere and I could not resist asking the question.

"What do they want, exactly?"

"To marry the two of you."

And so it was, thanks to a few words my father uttered through his teeth, that I was told of my destiny. I had been mistaken about everything, except the most important thing: Macé shared my feelings. She had succeeded where I had only come up against the wall of my circumstances. I later learned that she had been interested in me for a long time, even when she was still a child. She been charmed by the story of my adventures during the siege of the town, and had discreetly obtained information about me through her friends who had brothers my age. Obviously she had seen my confusion when at last I did notice her, and yet she had enough composure not to let anything show. As soon as she was sure of my feelings, she took charge of things, with a view to making both of us happy.

First she had convinced her mother. Then together they had besieged the provost. He had other plans for his daughter, but all with a view to her happiness. If she made another choice and persisted with it, despite his words of warning, he would not have the heart to force her against her will. Léodepart had imposed his ambition upon the three eldest children: they were all well married and unhappy. So he had agreed that the youngest could opt for happiness, at the risk that the object of her love might be good for nothing. Even if I was not a fine match, at least our family was honorable. No one could call it a misalliance.

We were engaged three months later. The wedding took place the following year, the week of my twentieth birthday. Macé was eighteen. The Duke sent two gentlemen to bless us on his behalf. It was, it seemed, a brilliant wedding. All the merchants and bankers in our town, and even several noblemen who were among my father-in-law's clients (and who, in truth, were in his debt), followed the procession. I hardly had time to enjoy myself, because all I wanted was for the crowd to vanish and leave us alone at last.

It had been agreed that we would move into the Léodeparts's private residence, where we would occupy a suite on the upper floor of the left wing. The apartments had been carefully prepared, decorated with furs from my father. We arrived late in the evening. The wedding party was still in progress in the hall my father-in-law had rented on the outskirts of town, near the mill by the Auron.

Everything I knew about physical love I had learned from observing animals. I had not gone with my comrades when they visited the whores, and they were too afraid of my opinion to tell me what they did there. And yet I was not worried. It seemed to me that Macé would guide us, that she would express her desires and anticipate my own.

Our uncertainty gave our bodies a shivering restraint which enhanced our pleasure. I could already tell that Macé was as taciturn and dreamy as I myself was. Our gestures, in the silence and nakedness of that first night, evoked the masked dancing of two ghosts. The instant I possessed her I also realized I would never know anything about her. In the same instant she revealed what she would always give me—her body and her love—and also what she would withhold—her dreams and her thoughts. It was a night of happiness and discovery. Upon waking, I felt the slight bitterness, as well as the great relief, of knowing that there would always be the two of us, but that each of us was alone.

*

In my new family I discovered an activity I had known nothing about: the commerce of money. Hitherto I had never taken the slightest interest in those little discs of bronze, silver, and gold that circulated among the merchants in exchange for their services. I viewed money as an inert thing, and, had they been rarer, the white pebbles in the garden might just as easily have replaced those coins.

Through Léodepart I learned that money is a thing apart and, in its way, it is alive. Those who deal in it learn the complicated rules governing its exchange, for money is a common species that can be subdivided into innumerable families. Florins, ducats, and *livres* bear the mark of their birth. They are stamped with the effigy of the sovereign who reigns over the land where they were minted. Then they go from hand to hand and into strange countries. Those who encounter them question their value, as one does with servants when deciding whether to employ them or not. Those who work with money—metalworkers, bankers, changers, lenders—constitute an immense network, spread all over Europe. Unlike my father, who was skilled in one particular trade, men who work with money touch no single product but can acquire them all. Those shiny little coins, worn smooth by the rubbing of eager fingers, contain an infinity of possible worlds. One ducat, if the person holding it so desires, can turn into a feast, a jewel, an ox, a carriage, happiness, revenge . . .

Money is pure dreams. To contemplate it is to cause the endless procession of the things of this world to parade before one's eyes.

My father-in-law tried very patiently to teach me the art of exchange. Very quickly he reproached me for not being sufficiently attentive to what I was doing. With money, as if I were staring into the fireplace, I tended to let my mind wander. For such a precise, meticulous activity as an exchange transaction, a disposition to daydreaming is not an asset: I made mistakes that could cost dearly. Even though my father-in-law handled important business, his margins were slim. The slightest negligence when weighing the metal or calculating proportions could severely affect his profit.

But he was a good man, and indulgent. I was his son-in-law. He saw my faults but did not withhold his trust. It was his conviction that each of us is capable of discovering the employment that suits him, provided he knows exactly what his aptitudes are. Mine would certainly not make me a moneychanger. It remained to be seen whether I would be good at anything else.

On thinking back on this era, I tell myself that it was dark and painful, yet fruitful. I was not getting on in life. In the opinion of my fellow citizens, I owed my position to my in-laws and not at all to my own merit. My father-in-law had settled us in a house he had expressly built for his daughter. Our first child was born the year after our wedding. He was a fine boy whom we called Jean. Three more were born in turn. Macé was happy. In our house, which still smelled of cement and fresh wood, the children's cries and the servants' chatter drowned the silence between Macé and myself. We loved each other sincerely, with that rather sad distance that both unites and separates people who lead lives of the mind.

I was full of doubts, plans, and hope. Many of my ideas were mere daydreams, but some of them would determine my life later on. Those years between the ages of twenty and thirty were a time when my idea of the world and the place I hoped to have in it would be decided, laboriously but forcefully.

As I made my way in my father-in-law's milieu, I began to have a broader and clearer view of the state of the country and those who exerted power. Prior to this, given my father's humble position, I had known only people whose lot it was to be submissive. The vagaries of war, the conflicts among noblemen, the uprisings among the people, were events we never perceived as anything other than the result of a destiny to which we had no choice but to submit. The Lords asserted that their power was God-given, as it had been with their ancestors in the days when a laborer entrusted himself to a knight for his defense. They were still arrayed in the immense prestige of the crusades, which had returned the true Cross to the heart of Christianity. My rebelliousness in the face of the humiliation my father was forced to undergo was mere schoolboy childishness: I knew, even though I did not accept it, that in becoming an adult I would also have to bow my head. The order of things seemed immutable to us. But as soon as I was at my father-in-law's, I understood that fear and subservience need not be inevitable.

When I went with Léodepart to visit nobility, I was able to see the difference between the treatment they reserved for him and that which was given to a simple furrier. My father-in-law was a link in the solid chain of money, however invisible. The noblemen feared him and were careful not to humiliate him.

I had been married for two years when at last the mad king died. His passing did not bring peace; on the contrary, it seemed as if his madness, which he had held captive in his person, was now spreading throughout the country. The nobility fought among themselves more than ever. No one seemed capable of assuming the sovereign's legacy. The Dauphin, Charles, stood by as John the Fearless, Duke of Burgundy, was assassinated; he was hounded, fought by all, including his own mother. Shut away in her Paris mansion, she schemed with her son's enemies to entrust the throne of France to a three-year-old English sovereign.

One day I traveled with my father-in-law to Anjou, on a matter that required his presence. This was the first time in my life that I was leaving our town. I was horrified by what I saw. Just as glass, when it shatters, spreads over a large surface far beyond the point of impact, the quarrel among the noblemen had fragmented into innumerable local quarrels, ravaging the country. We went through entire villages in ruin. It was impossible to count how many barns, stables, and even houses had been burned to the ground. Famished peasants tilled tiny plots at the edge of the forest where they could hide at the first alarm. It was late autumn and the air was already cold. One day our horses were stopped mid-morning by a troop of several hundred wandering children; they were infested with ringworm and barefoot in the icy mud. They aroused less fear than pity. A bit farther along we met a minor lord and his troop who were equipped for hunting. From the questions he asked, we understood that he was after those children, they were his prey, and he hoped to bag the greatest number of "pieces" possible. He spoke of them as if they were wild boars or wolves. The human race had vanished from this realm; there were only enemy tribes who could not even concede to others the dignity of being a creature of God.

Traveling with us were four men-at-arms, and we had refrained from carrying anything valuable. We slept in small towns or fortresses where my father-in-law was known. There were times when we arrived at the expected place and found nothing but ruins.

I returned from that trip with the smell of death burning in my nostrils. At least now I knew the state of the realm. My mistrust of princes in particular and all lords in general went from instinctive to rational. What I had seen of them in the antechambers where my father used to wait had surely taught me their true nature. The era of chivalry was over. Not only did that caste no longer protect anyone, as they had in the time of my ancestors, but, on the contrary, they were now the source of all danger. Was the king's madness the cause or the consequence of so much unrest? No one could say. In any case, nothing was as it had been. Honor had become a pretext not to respect others but to crush them. The superiority of birth no longer gratified those who were so honored with a sense of duty; they seemed to think it gave them the right to look down on anyone inferior, to treat them like animals, even dispose of their lives.

Worse yet, as if it were not bad enough to be bringing the country to ruin, the lords were incapable of defending it. At Agincourt, the year I was fifteen, they had gone once again into battle, and their only concern was to strut about, show off their lineage, obey the rules of chivalry, wield their spears with dexterity, and parade their heavy, caparisoned chargers with elegance. Subsequently, though the English had only a third as many men, their simple archers and villeins, who had no honor but were clever and quick, were able to annihilate the French forces. And now that they had been defeated they were hailing a foreign king and placing the country under the thumb of an English regent whose only ambition was to humiliate the populace and pillage the land until there was nothing left.

When we reached our town it felt as if we had left hell behind. Bourges was certainly no paradise. The city was grayer than ever, living according to its lifeless rhythm. It was far from being the city of my dreams. But at least it was at peace. The wise old Duke had saved it from ruin. After his death, he had left his property exclusively to the Dauphin. Which meant that Charles, now king, stayed on there, and, for lack of anything better, made Bourges his capital. I had the opportunity to go to the palace on several occasions, but did not see him. It was said that since fleeing Paris at the time of the great massacres he stayed huddled in rooms without openings, and gave audience to no one. In any event, he did not stay in the same place for long, and he obliged his diminished court to travel from château to château like hunted prey.

No one knew what would become of this sovereign without a realm, at war with his entire family. At the time, and despite the role he would play later on in my life, he was in my opinion nothing more than one prince among others, and I placed no faith in him. When the Dauphin Charles became King Charles VII, my father died. The poor man just managed to tell me I must acknowledge the king's authority. Right to the end, he worried about the traces of rebelliousness he sensed in me. And it is true, in spite of the affection I bore my father, his subservience seemed to belong to another era.

My father-in-law's method seemed far more attractive. He had no sincere bonds with those he served, be it King Charles or his enemies. He merely got from them what he could. And because of his financial power, and the need for his services, he was always held in high esteem.

I endeavored to follow in his footsteps. For several years I managed without deriving a great deal of satisfaction. I did not realize it, but there is an age when you can force your nature with sincerity, and with each passing day convince yourself that you are following the path you must take, when in fact it is leading you away from your true wishes, setting you adrift. The most important thing is to preserve enough energy to be able to change the moment this disparity begins to make you suffer, once you have understood your error.

Therefore I decided that, of all the trades available to me, I would work with money. In those days it was a rare substance. The quantity of currency that was in circulation was hardly enough for the exchange. Many transactions, for lack of cash, had to resort to payments in kind or letters of credit. The most common coins were made of silver, the more valuable ones of gold. Of all the obstacles that stood in the way of trade, the lack of liquidity was one of the most significant. Those who dealt in money occupied a coveted place. If they were able to lend or send money to a faraway creditor by avoiding the vagaries of transport, they had great power at their disposal.

Initially I thought this power would satisfy me. My modest success went to my head, and, with the small amount my parents had left me as well as Macé's sizeable dowry, I had acquired the flattering reputation of a young man of fortune.

Adulthood had turned me into a tall, thin fellow; I puffed out my chest to make up for my birth defect—although Macé had taught me how to consider it without horror. I strove to be elegant at all public functions. I had set up an exchange workshop at the back of our courtyard and I had a vault where I was able to store items of value. I was consulted by the grandest houses in the town. A number of noblemen had been sufficiently humiliated in my presence for none of them ever to imagine treating me in any other way than with respect.

I fulfilled my Christian duties scrupulously, but saw this as nothing more than an obligatory custom. I cannot say when I stopped believing in God. In truth, since our escapade during the siege of Bourges, I had been addressing my prayers to a higher force that I did not locate in the usual images of Christ or God the Father. It seemed to me that one could only communicate with this invisible power through a rare, indescribable agency that was available only to the few. It would be impossible, for example, for an imbecile like Éloi, with his boastful manner, to communicate with God or even have an idea of his existence, despite the fact that he spent his Sunday mornings wearing an alb that was too small for him, circling around the priests at the cathedral and performing more genuflections than the liturgy required.

Macé's piety was more moving to me, although no more convincing. I watched her spend long hours on her knees, her face in her hands in prayerful attitude. But those images she worshipped, in particular a Holy Virgin in painted plaster, which had been cast for her from a statue in the Sainte-Chapelle, were unimaginatively human and inert, regardless of the artists' talent. It seemed clear to me that, in spite of her efforts, Macé could not communicate in this way with any of the true powers that radiated their will into our world. When we spoke, however, I could see in her the independence of dreamers, that consciously cultivated intuition that comes of being constantly in the presence of invisible realities and supernatural forces.

I do not have a very detailed memory of those years. They seem to form a block made from an alloy of equal parts routine and happiness. Children were born and grew; the house was full of them. They were well-fed and beloved. I was earning my living in an honest manner, and my business did not take me far beyond the town and its surroundings. The news that came from afar made us bless every day the happy fate that kept us sheltered from war, famine, and plague. We heard muffled rumors of the conflict between King Charles and the Englishman who claimed to reign over France from Paris. The Loire River marked the border between the two royal domains. At times peace seemed within reach, but no sooner did we believe it so than the battles had already resumed somewhere.

To put it bluntly, the situation was getting worse and worse. With my little trade in money, my little fortune, and my little family, I could only hope for relative prosperity, local and provisional. We were at the mercy of the slightest change in circumstances. I had grown accustomed to the situation as it stood; my only ambition was to go on occupying my modest, comfortable spot. On the surface I had given up on changing the world, let alone trying to discover a better one.

And yet my childhood ideas had not completely disappeared. They were buried in my head and sometimes came back to torment me. They were certainly the reason I suffered from migraines now and again. Bright colors would shine before my eyes, and a few seconds later half of my skull would be throbbing like a cathedral bourdon. I now know that this was a sign. My hopes and dreams came clattering back to me in the form of these flashes; they tore the fabric of the simple, familiar things that surrounded me. The leopard, if I helped him, could still leap out of his bag.

For a long time I did not understand these calls. When the catastrophe arrived, I was no longer able to ignore them.

*

I had kept my childhood friends. Most of them were married. Their children played with mine. The subtle hierarchy that had been established during our adventure at the time of the siege continued to suffuse me in their presence with authority and mystery. But these qualities exerted no more than a modest influence over our lives, since they were led separately and our relations were limited to family visits.

That is why when I first met Ravand, I could not turn to my usual points of reference. The friendship we forged was not at all like any of those I had known up to then. In his presence I had neither prestige nor power. On the contrary, it seemed to me that I had everything to learn, and my position was one of admiration, which quickly bordered on submission.

Ravand was two years older than I, assuming that he knew the truth about his birth. His parents, he said, were Danish. That explained his height, his near-white hair, and his blue eyes. His appearance alone would have sufficed to make him stand out in our Celtic country, where people's skin and eyes are an autumnal hue of browns and reds. Added to that were his astonishing history and personality. He settled in our town at the end of one winter as it turned to flood. Everything was wet and gray. Ravand's blue eyes were like the promise of a clear sky we had never hoped to see again. He arrived from the north in grand style, with five valets and ten men-at-arms, none of whom were from the same place or spoke French. He required no more than two weeks at the inn; fetching the gold from his carriages, he paid cash for a house, which one of our friends had just built.

He furnished it very simply. The entire town was curious about him. I overheard talk but paid no attention. So, my surprise was all the greater when, a few days after his arrival, he sent me an invitation.

His house was not far, so I went on foot. It was located on a winding street that led up to the cathedral. Two men were stationed at the street entrance and kept an eye on the passersby. At the door, two more men stood guard, clad in leather and coats of mail; they looked like *écorcheurs.* Such manners were not typical among merchants. Inside, there reigned the atmosphere of a fortress. The rooms downstairs, heated by a blazing beech wood fire, were veritable guardrooms. Some of the men slept on the floor, like soldiers on a campaign, while others came and went, speaking loudly. In the courtyard behind the house two ginger-haired fellows were washing immodestly in a barrel of rainwater, chests bared. I went upstairs by a narrow stairway similar to the one in my childhood home and came out into a vast room lit by two tall windows of white stained glass. Ravand greeted me, taking my hands and looking me straight in the eye with an expression of recognition and enthusiasm.

And yet one felt that, if he so decided, all warmth would drain from those eyes and they would become cruel, cold blades. I immediately expressed my gratitude to Ravand for his welcome, the way a traveler might thank a highwayman for taking all his worldly belongings but leaving him his life.

The room was furnished with only a table and two fluted chairs. The table was piled high with pewter dishes that were still dirty with the remains of various meals. Pools had formed where glasses had spilled. Three or four porcelain pitchers stood surveying this battlefield. I had never seen such a household, particularly as it was set in a building almost identical to the one in which we lived, and which our womenfolk were careful to keep harmonious, comfortable, and clean.

Ravand offered me a drink. Before he served me, he inspected the bottoms of a dozen or so glasses before he found one he concluded was not as dirty as the others.

"I am pleased to make your acquaintance, Jacques."

Neither Master Jacques, nor Messire Cœur. He spoke to me as a friend, but the friendship was that of a soldier, used to measuring a man against courage and death.

"So am I, Ravand."

We clinked glasses. I saw that a midge was floating on the surface of my wine, and yet I drank it down in one gulp. Ravand already had me in his power.

He explained that he had come from Germany, where he had been in the employ of several princes. The size of their state did not match his ambitions; he had come into France from the north, after encountering the English and working for them. After several years spent in Rouen, he had taken to the road again, determined, this time, to serve King Charles. He did not tell me the reasons for this change, and I did not feel bold enough to ask him. What ensued would prove I had been wrong not to.

Ravand talked about King Charles as if he were a prince with a great future ahead of him. This was rare enough to surprise me. Ordinarily the king's name was only spoken in order to comment on his defeats.

"Might I ask, please," I ventured to say, "what is the nature of your talents?"

In truth, until then I had thought he was the leader of a group of mercenaries. The country was infested with these itinerant gentlemen who placed both sword and retainers in the service of those who offered the best wages and the most tempting plunder.

"I am a minter," said Ravand.

Minters are those who forge precious metal. Their art derives from the Chthonic mysteries of fire and the mine. Instead of hammering ploughshares or knifeblades, they manufacture the tiny pieces of gold or silver that will spend their lives traveling from hand to hand. The path of currency is an unceasing adventure, with sojourns in pockets, forays into the marketplace odors of hay and cattle, and jingling together in a banker's overstuffed coffers amidst solitary intervals in a pilgrim's satchel. But at the origin of all these adventures is the minter's mold.

To discover Ravand's profession was all the more astonishing in that Macé's late grandfather had also been a minter. I had known him for a few years before his death. He was a discreet burgher, levelheaded and somewhat timid. He had practiced his profession in our town thanks to a license from King Charles V. It was difficult to imagine two more dissimilar characters than that plump notable with his carefully groomed hands and the coarse Scandinavian with his mustache dripping with wine.

At the same time, this confession enlightened me as to the reasons behind Ravand's desire to meet me. Nor did he hide the truth from me.

"A minter must be rich," he said. "I am rich. But for the king to give me his trust, he must know me. And he does not. You were born here, in his capital. Your family is honorable, and through your wife you are related to the last minter of the town. I suggest we form an association."

Ravand was not the type to take a fortified town by means

of a long siege. He favored a quick, frontal assault. As far as I was concerned, he was right. Had he employed more subtle means to convince me, while beating around the bush, he would have aroused my suspicions and reinforced my resistance. Whereas by casting his pale gaze upon me in that deserted hall where the floor had not even been planed, he immediately won me to his cause. I heard myself agreeing to his proposal, and I went home feeling somewhat giddy for having plunged into these unknown waters, not knowing where I might end up, out at sea.

The fortune Ravand had brought with him, along with my credit in the town, quickly ensured us of success. We did not see the king, but his chancellor made it known to us that he approved of our undertaking. We built a workshop on some land that had come with Macé's dowry. Ravand's assassins made it their entrenched camp. Stacked in sealed coffers on the walls were precious metals, gold and silver, entrusted to us in the form of ingots. Other safes contained the pieces Ravand melted in great quantity. Later on I would be called an alchemist, and that was one of the many explanations people gave for my fortune. The truth is I never made gold with anything other than gold. But Ravand taught me the best way to make a profit from it, which is also the worst.

The king, upon the recommendation of his councillors, decided on the proportions we were to use for our alloys. From a certain quantity of silver—which, as everyone knows, is counted in marks—we were obliged to melt a given number of coins. The purer the alloy, the fewer the coins we produced; if there was less of the alloy, then the coins were also worth less, and there were more of them for one mark.

The room where the alloys were made was the heart of our activity. Ravand watched over it in person, equipped with mortars and assay balances. He needed only one man to help him: a thin old German, covered with scurf. His many years breathing the noxious fumes of mercury, antimony, and lead had poisoned him, and indeed he died a few months later.

Ravand taught me everything, with patience and enthusiasm. In the beginning, the adventure went to my head. The red flames of the forge, the hot gold bubbling in marble crucibles, the shine of pure silver and its capacity to resist alteration from other metals by imposing its color and brilliance, even when it was in great minority—all of this caused a new heart to beat in the anemic body of our town. From here departed the streams of coins that would go on to circulate throughout the realm and beyond. It was as if I were the keeper of a magic power.

And yet it took me only a few weeks to discover the truth. It was not as shiny as the new coins that jangled as they fell into our coffers. The breadth of our activity concealed the meanness of our methods. For at the heart of the manufacturing secrets that Ravand revealed to me was another secret, even more closely guarded: we were deceiving the king. When he ordered us to cast twenty-four coins to the mark, we made thirty. We delivered the twenty-four coins as ordered and kept the rest for ourselves. It was easy and very profitable.

Oddly enough, I had never dealt in crime until then. My father had always made it a point of honor not to cheat his customers, although they suspected him of it all the same. Everyone, in fact, would have found it perfectly normal for him to get rich in this way. His satisfaction came from never selling his work for more than its just value. His profit was purely moral, and his only reward was the pride of knowing he was an honest man. As for Léodepart, he was too wealthy to run the risk of resorting to villainous methods. In short, I assumed that dishonest means were expedients to which only the destitute or chronically impoverished would resort. And now Ravand was showing me another world: one could be involved in matters of great importance, minting the money of the realm, and yet still indulge in the base practices of scoundrels of the lowest sort.

And when I did express my surprise, he explained that it was common practice. Thanks to Ravand, I discovered there was a war being fought among the minters working in neighboring regions. In Rouen or Paris, on behalf of the Englishman who claimed to reign (as in Dijon, where the Duke of Burgundy on his vast lands depended on no one), coins were minted that were intentionally of a very low standard. When these coins came our way, to the lands that were faithful to King Charles, they were exchanged against our own, which had a much higher content of fine metal. With these superior coins the merchants returned to their own lands, richer at our expense. By minting coins of too high a standard, we were impoverishing the kingdom and allowing precious metal to pass into the hands of the very princes who were at war with our king. Ravand managed to persuade me that by resorting to fraud to enrich ourselves at the king's expense, we were actually doing him a favor, albeit he had entrusted us with this employ. And I believed him, until that spring afternoon when a detachment of ten of the king's men-at-arms came to arrest us in our workshop and throw us in prison.

Ravand greeted this judgment with great serenity. I would subsequently learn, too late, that he had been at risk of arrest on numerous occasions. It was in order to avoid a heavy sentence that he had fled from Rouen and ended up in our town.

For me, this imprisonment was a harsh ordeal. Hardest of all was the shame, of course. We hid it from my children, but their playmates answered their questions soon enough. I was in despair at the thought that the entire town now took me for a thief. Much later I would learn that, on the contrary, this ordeal had merely added to my prestige. In the eyes of the majority, it was as if I had undergone an initiatory rite: I had looked straight at the black sun of power, close up; I had felt its heat and stolen its secrets. With my in-laws the damage was much greater: from the start my father-in-law had viewed my alliance with a stranger as foolhardy. With my imprisonment foolhardiness had become sin. I was convinced that on leaving this place—if I ever left this place—it would be difficult, if not impossible, to find an honorable position in the town that had witnessed my dishonor and my fall. I could not conceive of any future other than flight.

As for the discomfort of detention, I bore that more easily than the torment of moral scruples. I was taken to a cell in the Duke's palace. It was, naturally, dark and damp. But I had had my fill from birth of darkness and dampness, and so the prison seemed no more than a simple extension of my gray, rainy destiny. I did not suffer from the destitution; on the contrary, I came to realize that comfort, a wealth of fine fare and clothing, the ministrations of numerous servants, and everything I had thought was important was, in fact, a needless burden. Prison, for me, was an experience of freedom.

I was treated well, or not too badly. I was alone in my cell, and I had a table and chair at my disposition. I was allowed to write to Macé and even make arrangements for my business. Above all, I had a great deal of time to meditate, and I drew up a lucid evaluation of these early years of adulthood.

I was already over thirty. There were not many moments that stood out from the ten years that had just passed, other than moments of happiness, such as the birth of our children, or certain hours spent in the countryside with Macé. On several occasions we had gone alone on horseback to the ring of villages that surrounded the town and which were known as La Septaine. It was rather unwise of us, because nowhere was safe in the kingdom. Gangs were known to go as far as the edge of town. But we enjoyed the risk, which, when all was said and done, was moderate. My father-in-law had bequeathed us a country house in the middle of a birch forest where we left a few guards. We went there to sleep and to share our love.

The rest of those years did not leave any outstanding memories. This was cruel proof that my desires and deeds were hardly ambitious. I had undertaken, indeed hoped for, only minor affairs, on the scale of our small town. Capital by default of a king without a crown, the town acted as if it were important, and in that way I resembled it. Even my association with Ravand, in which I had placed such great hopes, was nothing but an illusion. Reality was far less colorful: we were petty crooks. We were obtaining personal profit through betrayal. We had been entrusted with a mission and we chose not to fulfill it as we should have. This meant we were despoiling not only our king, but the entire populace. I was acquainted with the work of a monk, Nicolas Oresme. He had shown that bad coinage enfeebles trade and ruins kingdoms. Thus, not only had we tried to serve ourselves by pilfering from the common wealth, we had also broken the wheels of the carriage we had been asked to drive. We were miserable wretches.

Fortunately for me, Ravand was locked up in another cell and we were not in contact. This allowed me to think on my own and draw my conclusions before he was able to influence me. For when we were released, I found him smiling, full of optimism, and ready to start all over. According to him, the situation was far more complicated than I realized, and far better. He had obtained our release by paying the king's men. To hear him talk, our only mistake had been to forget a few highly placed personalities when distributing our bribes. He tried again to convince me that adulterating the coinage was a profitable business for everyone. We were the first to benefit, but all those whom we paid to close their eyes, beginning with the princes, were eating at the same table. I would later have cause to remember this lesson.

For the time being I remained convinced, however, that I had committed a grave crime, and that my sin was one of both mediocrity and a lack of honor. With hindsight I can affirm that this conclusion was my salvation. It gave me the will to conceive a radical solution. Without it I would not have come so easily to my decision. Instead, I remained faithful to the oath I had taken in the silence of my jail cell: as soon as I got out, I would leave.

The necessity of departure was not solely the result of the shame I felt. It had been there long before—perhaps it had always been there. For as long as I could remember, I had always wanted to leave this land where I had been cast by birth, where only grayness, fear, and injustice reigned. The mad king might be dead, but his curse continued to afflict the country. While in prison I learned that a new manifestation of his folly had recently appeared. My jailers told me that a young girl of eighteen, a simple shepherdess in a village in the borderlands of the East with neither fame nor education, had commended herself to God to save the realm. And the sovereign, driven to defeat and on the verge of losing Orléans, had placed this woman called Joan of Arc at the head of his armies. The father's madness had certainly spread to the son, so much so that he was calling upon succubi, entrusting them with the fate of the realm . . .

To flee this madness! To cast off the chains that bound me to the fate of a country ravaged by lunacy. Chivalry had left behind the ancestral framework which had once ensured it of a wisdom shared equally with laborers and priests. Now brute force knew neither limits nor reason.

I had enough information to find my way out. The Levant that I had long envisioned: I knew of ways to get there. Perhaps this was the only advantage of the early years in my trade, that I had heard innumerable travelers' tales. In that peaceful time I may not have been able to imagine anything other than putting down roots where I was, but a part of me continued the quest for the unknown. The leopard I had seen so long ago had not been reincarnated either in Léodepart or in Ravand's melted gold. It continued to show me the road to Arabia. Nothing could stop me from taking that road.

*

After the ordeal of my incarceration, Macé was subjected to the ordeal of my departure. I had thought about it for a long time. I felt it was absolutely necessary to leave, and, determined to tolerate no obstacles, I would crush them all. The most difficult one, however, was the silence my wife and children set before me. Not for a moment did Macé show any sorrow to see me abandoning her for a journey from which I might not return, nor did she oppose me. It was one of her greatest qualities that she devoted herself not only to love, but also to the man who was its object. Macé loved me when I was happy. When I was free. She loved me alive, vibrant with plans and desires. I had been telling her about the Levant for a long time. I spoke to her about it in the evening, in the springtime, during the walks we took in the country, by the shore of the pond. I spoke to her about it in the depths of dark, muddy winter, in the cold air as we listened to the sinister bourdon of the cathedral. I spoke to her about it as a dream carried all through childhood, but which I had grown accustomed to seeing as something that would stay forever in the confines of my imagination. It is quite possible that I communicated my passion to her. She was, as I have said, a silent woman, attentive to others, with the reserve and detachment and faraway gaze that showed how absorbed she was, in herself, by all sorts of thoughts and images that she did not share.

When on leaving the prison I informed her that I would be leaving the next month for the Levant, she stroked my face, looked deeply into my eyes, and gave me a smile which at no time seemed pained. I even wondered for a moment whether she would suggest coming with me. But our children held her back, and she was not the kind of person who would want to put her dreams to the test of the world at any cost. To be sure, she envied me, and she was too wise not to know that my absence would be painful to her. But deep within I remain convinced that she was happy for me.

We prepared my journey in secret. We could not alarm the children, nor provoke a commotion in the family. To safeguard their future, Macé urged me to take care not to arouse any additional anxiety among our business relations.

We discussed together what sort of dispositions I must take for the journey. She was in favor of the presence of an armed guard at my side. Still, according to the travelers' tales I had heard, if I took the road from Le Puy-en-Velay then went along the wide Rhone valley as far as Narbonne, I would have nothing to fear. It is true that there were gangs of *écorcheurs* who sometimes went that way. But an escort might merely attract their attention and arouse their greed, without being sure for all that of protecting me from assault. A modest tradesman going to visit a relative would make a less interesting victim. Therefore I set off with only a valet for company. I left on horseback, a robust but rustic mount, something of a workhorse, which would not attract the attention of thieves, either. Gautier, my servant, rode behind on a mule.

We left one morning at dawn, the week after Easter. The festivities of the resurrection were filling people's hearts with hope. Although my own heart had never been very open to faith, I shared the general cheer as a favorable sign. The time of the resurrection is also that of springtime. The longer days, the purity of colors, the rising sap might have been so many reasons to hold me back. Yet they had the opposite effect, hastening my departure. The children found out at last that I was leaving, but they were too young to appreciate the length of time they would be deprived of my presence. Macé and I had made our long farewells during that last night. I promised her

I would be careful; I promised her my love, and she responded with similar vows.

Gautier and I stopped at noon to share some bread by the side of the straight road, as it headed due south. We had not yet turned to look behind us. When we cast our gaze in the direction of the town, we discovered that it had already disappeared behind the rolling fields covered with wheat in the blade. Only the cathedral towers were still visible. Through the entire journey, this was the only time I succumbed to tears.

The rest of the way through the mountains of the Auvergne was tranquil and lovely. These regions had not suffered as greatly as the north of the country, where there was fighting with the English. Only the occasional armed gang had passed through, causing damage here and there. We met no one, but at the farms where we stopped we sometimes heard terrible stories. The gangs were often led by lords who had placed their swords in the service of princes. The men joined those who paid best, and changed their allegiance according to the conditions offered. These knights without honor had their entrenched camps where they stayed with their mercenaries and stashed the plunder of their campaigns. Some of these lairs were veritable fortresses, where warlords held court and indulged in every excess without fear of incurring the slightest punishment. In my opinion, this was additional proof that the world had gone mad. At the same time, I would have liked—though I did not wish it for all that—to be able to see with my own eyes what these depraved warlords were like. It seemed to me that in the lives of these brigand knights there was a will to be free of discipline and destiny that was not completely unlike my own ambition. But we reached the Rhone without meeting a single one.

Our town is at the confluence of streams, and I had never seen a great river. As we rode along this one, on the Regordane Way, I could not take my eyes from the powerful waters. It was as if they were already giving me an idea of what the sea must be like. Spring had come early and it was warm. The riverbanks were bright with blossoming fruit trees. Soon we saw species that were unknown in my region, or found it hard to grow there: cypress trees, planted in meadows like little green steeples; oleander, and olive trees, of a green paler than that of the trees at home; bamboo, growing to considerable height . . . Everything was different from my homeland, the Berry. The forests were not dark; insects, in the meadows, were noisier than birds; the moors were not overgrown with fern and heather but with dry clumps of fragrant herbs. The people we met spoke an Occitan dialect, which was very different from our language, and we could hardly understand them. Like elsewhere, war had spread mistrust and fear of misfortune. And yet the inhabitants' smiling good nature had been preserved.

The farther we rode, Gautier and I, the more alike we became. The heat had made us take off our warm clothes, and we were like two brothers in our shirtsleeves. But for the difference in our mounts, nothing would have distinguished servant from master. We were mostly silent along the way, because Gautier was not particularly talkative. Lulled by the horse's gait, I turned my thoughts over and over in my mind, at random. When I considered the first thirty-two years of my life, I was astonished to see how little they resembled the man who was discovering himself with each step of this journey. Stripped of everything in this scorching landscape, I felt within me an appetite for freedom, which made it all the more astonishing how little freedom I had enjoyed up until then.

I had only ever known the people from my own town, except for Ravand and a few rare merchants. I knew their background, their family, their position, and I could guess their thoughts. Before my departure I would have said that such references were necessary for human exchange. And yet now, as an anonymous voyager, with no external marks of fortune or position, fearlessly and with great curiosity I went up to the people whom chance placed on my path, knowing nothing about them. These exchanges between stranger and stranger turned out to be infinitely richer than the usual commerce between people who already know everything about each other.

I had always slept in the shelter of thick walls and closed doors; I had been born in a carapace of a town, one which seemed necessary to survival. Now, in the warm regions we were passing through, despite the cool nights we adopted the habit of sleeping outside. I discovered the sky. Back at home, stars were hidden by clouds most of the time. I used to gaze at them for a moment after supper on a summer's night before going back into the enclosure of a house. On my journey, I surrendered to the night. Once our campfire had died, leaving nothing but embers, and the earth was completely dark, the stars called to us, blindingly bright against a black sky free of clouds. I felt as if I had broken out of my shell. I might have been the last of those stars, the most insignificant and ephemeral of all thoughts, but, like them, I was drifting in a vast space without boundaries or walls. When we rode into Montpellier, I had become another man: myself.

In this town I could have made use of numerous contacts, in particular in the circles of moneychangers and other agents of trade. Sooner or later, people would find out who I was and it was not my intention to hide it from them. But I did not want to give a first impression based on who I used to be. My aim was to start all over, to wipe the slate clean. We took lodgings at an inn. As I talked with strangers, I learned a great deal about the town and those who traded with the Levant. A "muda" of Venetian ships came through each year and called at Aigues-Mortes. For the last two years the Venetians had not shown up, and word had it that this year again they would not come. The town was divided in its opinion as to the reasons for this defection. The only thing of which they were certain was that products from the Levant were already in short supply, and their prices had gone sky-high.

I used these days to tour the region and get an idea of the disposition and relative wealth of each town. It was during one of these trips that I first saw the sea.

The landscape was flat, trees were rare, and groves of bamboo rustled in the wind that brought strange smells. We had lost our way, and our horses advanced slowly along a narrow path of sand and white pebbles. At one point a knoll of earth covered in succulents and clumps of herbs hid the horizon. We climbed the knoll and suddenly saw the shore. All the years that have passed have never made me forget that first moment. In the distance a haze of sunlight and water mingled sea and sky. A wide strip of fine sand separated the last outpost of land from the assault of the waves. Thus, as my dreams had foretold, I had proof that the solid world where we lived our lives did not cover the entire Earth. It ended in this place and yielded to an immense wave from which other realities could emerge. I was eager to rush forward and greet them. At the same time, had I not heard of ships and sailors I could never have believed it was possible to defy this liquid space, thrashed by wind, shaken by waves and swell, seductive and hostile like death.

We stayed for a long time on the shore that first day, so much so that the sun burned our faces. We saw sails go by some way off from the coast, and I watched this miracle and found it more astonishing than the sea. Of all human activity, sailing seems to me the most daring. To ride the waves, and trust one's destiny to the wandering of the wind and the turbulence of water, to head off in the direction of nothing, filled all the while with the hope, or even the certainty, of finding something there. The calling of a sailor seemed to be the fruit of dreams even more insane than my own.

We returned to town. From that moment on I had only one desire: to board a ship, head out to sea, and, since the skill of captains made it possible, sail to the Levant.

My valet, Gautier, had been very discreet during our journey. He had left me alone and I was grateful to him. But it was only fear and a certain timidity that had induced his silence. It was not his true nature. He was, in fact, rather talkative, and he made friends easily. This quality did not depend on language. In this region where he could hardly make himself understood, he had long conversations with everyone we met. I made the most of his talents to make him my informant. In Aigues-Mortes, he forged friendships with fishermen and all sorts of seafarers. Thus, he learned that an expedition was being mounted to the Ports of the Levant. A galley was being loaded in the port, and it belonged to a merchant from Narbonne by the name of Jean Vidal.

I went to see the vessel. It was much larger than the fishing boats and even most of the commercial ships. From the wharf it seemed as tall as several houses. A painted wooden panel at the rear blazoned its name: *Notre-Dame et Saint-Paul.* The hull was made of the same wood that had gone to build the roof and walls of my childhood home. But these beams, instead of being placed on solid ground, rose high in the air and danced to the whim of the waves. Men were unloading bales of cloth from a cart and preparing to stow them in the hold. They informed me that the ship would soon be sailing. We hurried back to Narbonne. In my baggage I had a folded velvet suit and the accessories required should I need a burgher to recognize me as one of his own kind. Gautier went ahead to introduce me. Jean Vidal received me amiably. He was a man my age, with a sharp gaze and the small mouth of someone who weighs his words, guarding them in his mind with the same caution reserved for the money in his coffers. He was pleasant and well disposed toward me. He informed me that the ship was already fitted out. A group of Montpellier merchants had bought shares in her; the cargo was full. I insisted on buying a share. When I had made my introduction, I emphasized the office of minter I had occupied in Bourges, and we had spoken the names of several prominent merchants of the Languedoc with whom I had been in business. Vidal showed great respect for our city and viewed it, quite justifiably, as the new capital of the realm. These connections left him favorably inclined, and he sought to please me. We agreed to that I would board the vessel with my valet, but that my share in the cargo would be purely symbolic. I accepted his terms, all the more gladly because I had brought only money with me, and very little in the way of goods (in all, a bale of precious fur which I intended to use along the way to acquire what we might need).

Thus, less than a week later, I climbed the wooden gangplank and boarded the galley. I met a dozen other passengers. They had said their farewells to their families and were now in that exalted, worried state of mind which always precedes departures. They spoke loudly, laughed, called out to people on the wharf to hand them one last letter, or convey a last recommendation. I understood that most of them had never been to sea. The ship's captain, Augustin Sicard, walked among the voyagers, trying to calm them with reassuring words. With his healthy complexion and round belly he looked like a laborer. No doubt I had been mistaken about sailors. I had pictured them as visionary dreamers. Sicard made me think that they came, rather, from an ancient race of peasants. Frustrated by the limits of their fields, they had decided to expand the furrows ordinarily traced in the soil to the surface of the water.

The oarsmen at their benches were not that different. They had the resigned air of men who work in nature. Their calloused hands curled round the wood of the long oars in the same way they had once held the polished handles of their hoes. We sailed at dawn. Most of the passengers stood by the stern, waving and gazing at the city fading into the distance. As I had no one to wave to on the wharf, I stood by the prow, breathing in the sea air. Everything was new, terrifying, and full of promise: the creaking of the wood, the motion of the deck as it went up and down according to the surface of the sea, the sun appearing in a gap between clouds and water. The wind brought the smell of the sea and droplets of salt water, whereas below deck the ship smelled of sap and sweat, victuals and pitch.

Nothing could bring me greater happiness than this birth into an unknown life, promising both beauty and death, hardship today and wealth, no doubt, tomorrow. The life of adventure that lay ahead, unlike the burgher's life and its security, might augur the worst but also the best—that is, the inconceivable, the unexpected, the fabulous. I felt alive at last.

II.

The Caravan to Damascus

The day before yesterday I went with Elvira to the town and was almost found out. The man who is looking for me was in the midst of a heated discussion with two other men who seemed to be strangers as well. I observed them from a distance as I leaned against the wall of the harbormaster's office. Suddenly, I saw them start in my direction. I had been distracted by the maneuvers of a ship in the harbor and by the time I realized they were headed my way they were already quite near. I had not noticed that at this midday hour there were fewer people about. The strangers no doubt needed some information. They wanted to come up to me because I was the closest person, and one of the only ones not hurrying off to his lunch. Fortunately, my hat hid me well and I was still in the shade of the wall, whereas they were hampered by the dazzling sunlight as they walked toward me. I do not think they recognized me. When I fled, they laughed loudly and did not give chase. No doubt they took me for a poor peasant frightened by their rich merchants' finery.

Still, I came close to being unmasked and captured. After this alarm I have decided not to venture into town for the time being, but to try and make myself scarce. I will stay in the house and limit my walks to the immediate vicinity.

In the morning our terrace is in the shade, and the lingering chill of night prevents me from staying still. This is the time when I go for a walk along the path that leads down to the sea. The nature here does not waken with the dawn. On the contrary, it is in the evening that the colors blaze and all the fragrances rise. With the appearance of the sun, the plants seem to curl in on themselves, grow pale and motionless in anticipation of the sun's pounding, until sunset. The early morning is an inquisitive moment when one can watch the preparations for this vigil. The sea itself, at this morning hour, hardly moves, and the lapping of little waves against the sharp rocks produces a regular murmur, as calming as a lullaby. I take these soft hours to let memories of the past rise up. When I am full of them, so much so that I no longer pay attention to what is around me, I go slowly back up through the bushes of oleander and ilex and settle beneath the trellis, now warm, to write.

There are many houses like ours on the island, and I hope that my pursuers will grow weary of exploring them before they find me. Through Elvira I sent a note to the innkeeper who found me this hideaway, to ask him to spread the rumor that I embarked on a vessel bound for Rhodes, or Italy. To my message I added a sum apt to persuade him to do my bidding.

Although there is nothing to justify it, I feel confident. I have been hounded for so long that I have come to know my pursuers' methods. They throw themselves on the clues they are given with very little discernment. All I have to do is wait.

But this alters the atmosphere of my time here. I had come to Elvira's with the idea that I would stay for only a few days. Now I will have to reckon in weeks, or even months. The sweetness I have found in her presence is no longer merely a passing comfort. Our silent affection has acquired the strength of a veritable attachment. I do not know what she feels, but for me something is being born which looks not yet like love; perhaps, simply, it is like happiness.

I am more and more occupied with my writing. Ever since I began the story of my life, my greatest desire, every day, is to immerse myself in the past as if it were a clear, warm pool.

I had begun telling of my journey to the Levant, and the setting in which fate has placed me at this time is by far the best I can imagine to inspire me. Chios, with its heat and its colors, already belongs to the Levant . . .

*

It was an extraordinary voyage. I have preserved such a detailed, precise memory of it that it would be possible for me to tell you about it for days. At the time, however, the wealth of the experience first seemed to me like a chaos of novelties, troubling my understanding. I do not exaggerate when I say that it has taken the rest of my life, and so many other experiences, to put some order into what was initially a shock that left me almost without consciousness.

On board ship, our days were spent in the heat on deck. The labored cry of the oarsmen, the creaking vessel, the seasickness and muted throbbing of headache troubled my mind. My companions were no better off. Those who had been proud burghers on departure had now stowed their fine clothing in the chests in steerage, and spent their days flat on their backs all around the railing, livid and filthy with vomit and excrement. As a result, we forgot about external danger, in particular the corsairs. On several occasions Augustin Sicard changed course to head into port, or had us anchor to leeward of an island that would conceal us while a suspicious sail crossed the horizon. We took in water at Agrigente, then in Crete. Finally, after a long, ultimate, and perilous crossing on the open sea we reached Alexandria in Egypt. Part of the cargo was unloaded there. Some of my companions took the opportunity to travel by land to Cairo, where the Sultan reigned. In spite of my desire to join them, I had to stay on board with two other passengers who were suffering, as I was, from fever and the bloody flux.

The galley, now almost empty, would continue its voyage to

Beirut, and then come back to Alexandria to fetch the others who had disembarked there. Those who were sick stayed on board for the short crossing. My condition gradually improved. I had regained my wits, and during the brief journey I questioned the crew about the Holy Land. A few sailors who had already been there told me about what I might find. They all insisted on the fact that I would be filled with wonder. And the moment I stepped ashore in Beirut this was indeed the case. But mingled with this admiration was a curious feeling. I was surprised by my own wonder. I found it difficult to discern what, exactly, was so worthy of praise in this place.

To be sure, there were the colors of the steep coastline: the sea takes on an emerald hue, and in the distance, steep hills covered with dark green patches of cedar forest overlook the city. The site is splendid, but other ports of call had already shown us such beautiful sights.

Beirut is an open city that preserves some traces of the edifices built by the crusaders, but most of them have been destroyed. This sign of ruin, sadly, resembles that which afflicts a great number of towns and villages in France. And as in France, one sees rich and poor side by side, notables and common folk. It does not seem that the lives of the unfortunate are any more enviable in the Levant than in our towns.

Nor did my sense of wonder come from references to the Gospel. The pilgrims I met in Beirut lived in a state of perpetual turmoil as they made their way from one holy place to another. A barren plot covered in pebbles put them into a trance the moment they thought they had found the place where the adulterous woman had been stoned. But I have already confessed to my lack of appetite for such celestial fare.

My companions were principally merchants, and they were most affected by what we discovered in the bazaars. The city was overflowing with precious goods: varnished pottery from Martaban, silk from Asia Minor, porcelain from China, spices from the Indies . . . These treasures, however, were not produced locally. In the city one could find artisans who enameled glass, inlaid cedar wood with mother-of-pearl, or hammered copper, but their crafts were, all in all, quite modest. As for the countryside around the city, baking with heat, it looked like anything but a garden of the Hesperides. One had to face facts: the Holy Land was not a paradise. So what was it that gave this land its particular character, which commanded admiration? I understood only after a week had gone by.

The last of the cargo had been unloaded from the galley. Sicard replaced it with goods bought locally to be shipped to Cairo. The vessel left again for Alexandria. The plan was that it should come back within a month. I decided to stay on land with a few companions. We would re-embark the next time it called. In the meantime, I wanted to go deeper inland and penetrate the mystery of the Levant, with its strange charm.

We hired donkeys from a muleteer and set off toward Damascus. The road wound its way through the mountains. In spite of the heat of the day, the nights were freezing. We would awake covered with a heavy dewfall, moisture sliding down our necks and into our collars. Then we traveled down a broad valley, which the pilgrims called the valley of Noah. They believed that it was in this very place that Noah built his ship while waiting for the flood. We rode along gorges that led to a vast expanse of desert outside Damascus. It was here that an encounter showed me what I was looking for.

A camel caravan was arriving slowly from the east. Made drowsy by the majestic swaying of their animals, the camel drivers hardly looked at us. The animals were laden with enormous hampers in which one could see earthenware jars, carpets, and copper plates. The muleteer said that the caravan had come from Tabriz, in Persia, carrying goods from all over Asia. The caravan passed slowly by, and suddenly I understood what was so magnificent about this place: it was at the center of the world. In itself it did not possess any exceptional qualities, but history had made it the place toward which everything converged. It was here that the great religions were born, where the different peoples you met in the streets could mingle: Arabs, Christians, Jews, Turkomans, Armenians, Ethiopians, Indians. Above all, this place attracted all the wealth of the world. The finest objects made in China, India, or Persia joined the best productions of Europe or the Sudan.

This discovery fed my thoughts as we continued on our way to Damascus. It completely overturned the image I had had of the contemporary world thus far. If the Holy Land was the center of the world, that meant my native France was relegated to its very edge. The interminable disputes between the king of France and the English, the rivalry between the Duke of Burgundy and Charles VII—all these events which we viewed as essential were mere unimportant details, and actually had no reality when considered from the place where we now were. History was written here; we discovered traces of it at every moment, in the form of temples covered by the sand. The crusaders had thought they could conquer this land. They had been defeated after so many others, and their ruins were added to those of other civilizations drawn to the center of the world, and which had perished here.

I was pleased that I had managed to unravel the wool of my thoughts. But to what conclusion did it bring me? Had I, for all that, found what I had come for? My melancholy was proof that I had not. This Levant was still too real, too similar. When I discovered the desert with its golden hues, I thought once again of the leopard from my childhood. He had come from this place to show me the direction I must follow. Shortly before we reached Damascus, I went through a crisis that my companions failed to understand.

We had broken our journey at an oasis where another caravan stopped, an immense caravan incomparably richer and greater in number than all those we had seen thus far. It was a veritable world unto itself. There were over two thousand camels, richly equipped. They were kneeling, saddles removed, when we arrived. Spread all across the oasis and even as far as the surrounding desert, they formed a motionless mass, swarming not only with camel drivers but also women and children, busy around the fires which smoked from pits made in the sand. When at dawn the signal was given, the multitude awoke all at once to prepare for departure. It was as if an entire city was rising to its feet, getting ready to set forth. Laboriously, the animals assembled in groups according to family and tribe, and took their place in the procession. At the head of the caravan were drummers, pounding on their enormous drums, while behind them came men-at-arms on horseback. I was told that their destination was the desert of Scythia. There they would meet up with other convoys going as far as China.

I felt a call deep inside to join that caravan. I am not mystical by nature; it is my habit, rather, to remain master of my feelings. And yet this time I was overwhelmed. It was my conviction—and nothing had prepared me for it—that in that very moment I had met my destiny. I had already sacrificed a great deal to reach the Levant, the place of all possibility, the promised land of my dreams, but I was only halfway there, so to speak. I could still sever the last ties which connected me to my former life—abandon the galley, leave for the unknown and surrender to its decrees. This caravan, all of a sudden, had come to show me which way to go.

I wandered among the camels, grazing their manes with my fingertips; I was subjected to terrible temptation. I went deeper and deeper into the compact mass of animals as they stamped the dust, impatient for the departure signal. It would be given at dusk. All day long my companions looked for me, for our little troop was due to leave at the same time for Damascus, which was not very far away. When they found me, initially I refused to follow them and remained deaf to their questions. They thought some mysterious ailment had deprived me of my reason and perhaps my understanding. In the end I stayed with them, but I lay motionless for many hours, distraught, lost in thought, my face distorted in a grimace of pain.

Finally the memory of Macé and our children prevailed, and I gathered enough strength to cast off the temptation to leave, never to return. My companions rejoiced to see I was once again myself and had finally agreed to go with them. But they had no inkling of the conflict that had taken place inside me. How could I explain to them that I had just rejected the myriad lives I could have lived, in favor of the one life to which my prospects would now be limited? Inside I was suffering, mourning for those imaginary destinies. I had left for Damascus, my desires countless, and now I would arrive there stripped of those promises. There was only one thing left to do: to take the only life given me and strive to make it rich and happy. That would already be a great deal, but it would be so little.

I had put the leopard back into his bag for a long time.

*

It was my good fortune that this crisis occurred at the outskirts of Damascus. To enter such a city at a time when I felt I was beginning a new life that was deprived of all the others was a consolation and a joy. What I hadn't felt in Beirut was even more obvious in Damascus: this city was truly the center of the world.

And yet it had suffered serious destruction, not merely as a result of the wars against the Franks but also of Turkish incursions. The most recent of these, a few years before my visit, was that of Tamerlane: he had torched the city. Ebony beams and sandarac varnish had gone up in flames. Only the great Mosque of the Umayyads had survived the disaster. The city had not yet been completely rebuilt when I arrived there. And yet it exuded an impression of power and unequaled wealth. It was the primary destination for the caravans, and its markets were overflowing with all the wonders that human industry can produce. The mixture of races was even more astonishing than in Beirut. It was said that the Christians had been put to the sword by the Mongols until there were none left. But many Latin merchants had returned and could be seen about the streets. Franciscan monks from France, the Cordeliers, welcomed us at a monastery they kept at the disposal of pilgrims and Christians passing through. Damascus was linked to Cairo and many other towns by a service of rapid couriers mounted on camels. We received news of our companions who had stayed in Egypt and were able to send them our news.

Above all, Damascus had a wealth of fabulous gardens. This art, taken to the most extreme refinement, seemed to me on a par with architecture as the sign of a great civilization. The noblemen in our parts, locked away in their fortresses and constantly threatened with plunder, did not have the leisure to arrange the earth in the way they arranged stone. We knew only two worlds: the town or the country. Between the two, the Arabs had invented the ordered, welcoming place of enclosed nature that is the garden. To do this, they had simply reversed all the qualities of the desert. They had replaced its vast openness with the protection of high walls; burning sun with cool shadow; silence with the murmuring of birds; drought and thirst with the purity of cool springs flowing in myriad fountains.

In Damascus we discovered many other refinements—in particular, the steam bath. I took one almost every day and experienced an unknown pleasure. Never, until then, had I allowed myself to think that one's body could, in and of itself, be an object of pleasure. Since childhood we had been accustomed to keeping our bodies covered and hidden. The use of water was a painful obligation in a climate like ours, because most often it was cold, and our baths were rare. Contact between the sexes always took place in the obscurity of canopied beds. Mirrors reflected only the finery covering clothed bodies. In Damascus, however, I discovered nudity—letting oneself go to the heat of air and water, to the pleasure of time devoted solely to doing oneself good. Since I had only one life, it might as well be filled with happiness and sensual delight. I realized, as I sat sweating in the bath of perfumed steam, how new this idea was to me.

This was perhaps the most astonishing particularity of Damascus, and it rounded out my understanding of the Levant: this city was the center of the world, but it used this position to increase not only the power of those who lived there but also their pleasure. The purpose of these caravans converging on the city was trade, to be sure. Goods were imported, exported, and exchanged, and they brought profit. But the city took its share of anything of value and this was for one purpose alone: to serve its well-being. Houses were adorned with precious carpets. People dined on rare porcelain. The sweet odors of myrrh and incense drifted everywhere; food was chosen carefully, and chefs employed their art to compose their meals with expertise. Scholars and men of letters studied in freedom and in their libraries could consult books from every land.

This concept of pleasure as the ultimate goal of life was a revelation to me. And still I was aware that I had not taken the full measure of it, because as a Christian I was not allowed contact with those individuals who were both the supreme beneficiaries and the givers of these pleasures: women. We were closely watched in this respect, and any attempt at an intrigue with a Muslim woman would be grounds for beheading. We did, however, catch glimpses of them. We saw them in the street, we met their gaze through their veils or the latticework of their windows, we could make out their shapes, smell their perfume. Although they were reclusive, they seemed to us to be freer then our women in the West, more devoted to sensuality, promising a pleasure that our unclothed bodies in the hammam gave us the audacity to imagine. We sensed that the intensity of such pleasure could fuel violent passion. Strangers shared bloody tales of jealousy leading to murder and sometimes massacre. Far from inciting revulsion, such excess only fuelled desire. Several merchants had paid with their lives for their inability to resist temptation.

When I found myself alone I was inhabited by the memory of my only woman; she who was the frequent object of my thoughts. I imagined her sharing these delights with me, and I promised myself I would carry home with me the instruments of pleasure. I bought perfume, carpets, and bolts of bocasin, a cloth similar to silk which the local craftsmen wove with cotton.

A month went by in this way, and we were about to leave again when we had an astonishing encounter. We were lying on leather cushions, tasting sweet cakes of every flavor, when our guide, a Moor who had been with us since Beirut, announced the visit of two Turks. He uttered these words with a laugh, and we did not immediately understand the reason for his irony. The mystery dissolved the moment the Turks in question appeared. They were two tall men with unkempt hair, their faces covered with neglected beards. From the way in which they wore their clothing, it was only too obvious that it did not come naturally to them. The moment they opened their mouths, there could be no further doubt: they were two Franks in disguise.

The elder, a man with thinning ginger hair, introduced himself with the sort of haughty pride I had been familiar with since childhood, from the hours spent waiting with my father in the antechambers of nobles' houses.

"Bertrandon de la Broquière, first esquire to his lordship the Duke of Burgundy," he said.

We were mere merchants, and he invoked his right to inform us of his name and title in a lofty manner. However, his outfit was so ridiculous, and our informal attitude, which we had not altered since his arrival, colored his self-assurance with a certain awkwardness, even fear. We introduced ourselves in turn, not deferring to him in any particular way, and he and his companion sat down on the cushions reluctantly.

We were waiting for the sorbet our errand boy had ordered for us. A discreet servant with a grave manner placed a finely carved copper tray before us. We offered some to the esquire, but he refused.

"I will never eat such rubbish! You are taking a great risk, mark my words."

And he explained how the snow used to prepare the sorbet was brought by camel from the mountains of Lebanon.

"I have heard that they send it as far as Cairo," I exclaimed admiringly.

Our interpreter confirmed this. Previously the snow was shipped by boat to Alexandria, but now the Sultan Barsbay had established order on his roads, and small caravans of five camels could transport the precious ice cream to the capital.

"It is astonishing that it does not melt . . . "

"In every caravan, there is one man who is instructed with the technique to keep it intact during the voyage."

We marveled at this additional proof of the Arabs' expertise. But Bertrandon shrugged his shoulders.

"Nonsense! They lose three-quarters of it and the rest is contaminated. It is pure disease they are transporting, not ice cream."

He gave a coarse laugh. Yet he had not managed to put us off our sorbet. Mine was perfumed with orange flower water.

While we were delighting in our treat, the esquire began to pontificate. However, he occasionally shot a dirty look at the Sarrasin who was our interpreter. With a great deal of tact, the

Sarrasin claimed he had an errand, in order to leave us alone. Now the esquire no longer withheld his virulent criticism with regard to the Arabs. He exalted their treachery, their violence, their immorality. The effect of his sermon, and no doubt the aim of it, was to make us feel what wretches we were, to enjoy the company of such savages.

"Then why," I dared to ask, "are you wearing their clothing?"

After all, we may have been seduced by the charms of life in Damascus, but at least we still had the courage, through our finery, to proclaim that we were Christians.

The esquire lowered his tone and, leaning closer, confided that this travesty was necessary for him to carry out his plans. We understood at that point that he must be on a secret mission on behalf of his master, the Duke of Burgundy. This putative discretion was all the more ridiculous in that, from the moment they saw him, the Mohammedans could hardly ignore whom they were dealing with. Nevertheless, on the strength of his supposed invisibility, Bertrandon was gathering as much information as possible on the countries that hosted him. He asked many questions about the towns and villages we had gone through. He insisted, without the slightest shame, on the military details: Had we met any troops? Who was guarding this bridge or that building? How many men-at-arms were accompanying the great caravan? (I refrained from telling him that I had almost joined it.) As the interrogation progressed, we understood more clearly the nature of the mission with which he had been entrusted. Their aim, no more and no less, was to prepare a new crusade. Of all the princes in the West, the Duke of Burgundy was the one who continued to make the most concrete plans for a reconquest of the Levant. Had he not financed an expedition several years earlier that had ended in failure?

As soon as I was aware of Bertrandon's true intentions, I saw him differently. What I had found entertaining was now appalling. There we were, the six of us, comfortably reclining in this garden whose colors, shade, and cool air harmoniously converged to please our senses. We were tasting divine sorbet, one of the most ingenious human inventions, said to have given rise to so many others. Our clothing was new, stitched in the bazaar according to a model we had brought with us, and made of finely woven cloth printed with subtle designs. Our skin exuded the perfumed oil with which our daily bath anointed us. And now here before us was this greasy-haired oaf, scratching the vermin beneath his scruffy clothes and, despite the distance between us, gratifying us with the stench of his body and his breath, all the while proclaiming his aim to wield fire and sword in order to bring civilization to this place.

Never before had I been given the opportunity to contemplate a specimen of knighthood in his natural state and removed from his familiar environment. Having once been our glory, the knights were now the instruments and symbols of our ruin. Their ancestors had thought of God; these men thought only of themselves, of the honor that was bequeathed to them and which they cherished more than anything.

Their only desire was to fight, but they had proved themselves incapable. They had lost all their battles, for they had no care for discipline, strategy, or victory. Their death brought glory, and that was all that mattered. They cared little for their imprisoned princes, the ransoms to be paid, the forfeited lands, the ruined people. They cared little for anything except feeding their warmongering indolence, they cared not that the burghers had been bled dry, or that the peasants must fast, or that the craftsmen must work at a loss. In France, this stubbornness was held to be the sign of a noble soul.

But in this garden, in the presence of these two vulgar individuals stripped of armor and prestige, who picked their teeth with the sharp end of their dirty fingernails, the truth was dazzling. One thought went through my mind, which in France I would have banished with horror, but which now appeared to me as indisputable proof: it was fortunate that the crusaders had not managed to conquer the Levant. And it was vital that they never should.

In contrast, our position as merchants—which, like the nobles, I had always viewed as trivial, material, and without honor—now seemed quite different to me. We were agents of trade, not conquest. Our vocation was to bring to all the best of what others produced. We too, in our way, entertained the ambition of appropriating other civilizations, but in exchange for what they might desire from ours. Destruction, pillaging, and enslavement were foreign to us. Our aim was to capture only living prey.

After having wormed out of us everything he could, Bertrandon began to discourse endlessly on the situation in Constantinople—the city had been reduced to nothing, from paying tribute to the Turks—on the Ottomans, whom he respected and who opposed the Arabs, whom he loathed; on the politics of the Latin cities of Venice and Genoa, whose rivalry did not prevent them from encroaching every day a bit more on Byzantine territory and Arab possessions.

I stopped listening. This meeting, however unpleasant it might have been, had taken me back to the West. In any case, our stay was coming to an end. We had two short days before we must leave for Beirut and embark on the galley.

Before our meeting with Bertrandon, I would have been sorry to leave. Now I was glad.

The return was a joy. Every day that took me closer to home was a precious gift. The journey, however, was far more difficult than it had been going the other direction. There were terrible storms that severely tried our ship. Finally, just off the coast of Corsica, one last squall drove us onto the rocks. I almost drowned, carried away by the waves. As I struggled in the foaming breakers, I struck my left hand against one of those sea creatures covered in spines that are to be found in abundance on the seabed and the rocks. Several dozen tiny black spikes entered my flesh. We were assisted by the inhabitants of the island, only to encounter still greater misfortune. A so-called prince, a brigand without honor who reigns over this coastal region, seized all our possessions and threw us in prison. We were kept there for several weeks while we waited for Vidal to pay our ransom.

Finally we arrived in Aigues-Mortes at the beginning of winter. My hand had swollen and was becoming infected. At one point I thought I might lose it, might even lose my life. When eventually I recovered, I understood that such fears had attenuated the regret of having been robbed of everything. Before Christmas, Gautier and I set off toward home on the road along the Rhone; I was penniless. Vidal hoped to compensate for our losses through a letter of marque and reprisal. As soon as he obtained it—and he did obtain it—privateers would be allowed to attack the ships belonging to the nation that had robbed us. The booty would serve as compensation. It was an efficient procedure, and served to reduce the dangers inherent in navigation. But it was slow, and did nothing to alter the fact that for the time being we were ruined.

The strange thing was that, far from afflicting me, this destitution filled me with unexpected pleasure. I felt as naked as a newborn baby. And, indeed, I was being born into a new life. I had finished mourning for my dreams and had replaced them with memories. I was returning with a host of ambitious projects, richer than if I had brought bolts of silk or bales of spices. My wealth was still invisible, potential. I held this precious treasure well concealed, as if I had not yet determined what I could buy with my gold. But I was filled with confidence.

I had sent a courier ahead from Montpellier with a message for Macé. I knew that she was waiting for me. These last weeks,

I had been consumed with desire for her. My hands stippled with scars served to remind me that I had caressed the devil; the thought of my ordeal made the prospect of the sweetness to come all the more precious. I cried out in my sleep. My good hand reached for Macé's soft white skin, trying to escape the hurtful fur of the beast that pursued me in the waters of dreams.

We were headed into the wind as it blew across the plain, and our horses struggled at a weary gait. Our homecoming was an endless trial, for it seemed as if the cathedral, although its towers were visible above the horizon, would never come any closer. At last our steps rang out in the dark and empty streets; we knocked on the door, the spyhole slid open, and there were tears and cries and caresses. The night was full of such long-awaited pleasure that it was almost painful.

It took us almost a week to weave our lives together again. I told all my story and Macé brought to life for me the myriad events of the motionless little world that had been waiting for me.

*

I did not recognize my town. My memories were of a gray and gloomy place, perpetually in the darkness. I had arrived one day at the end of spring, and it was luminous and full of sunlight. Added to the brilliance of the sun was a teasing humidity that gave the warm weather in our parts a quality that was very different from what it was in the Levant. The word "soft" immediately came to mind to describe this sunny well-being.

Those first days, as I prepared to confront the town, I took long walks through the marshland. I saw this as a way of gently finding my footing in the town again, of growing accustomed to it. As I wandered through the shade of the weeping willows, among the black boats, I saw the light dancing on the flowing stream, long clusters of algae swaying like pennants beneath the surface of the water. Before returning to my house and family, I needed to become reacquainted with the land where I was born, to feel the need to stay there, until I was grateful to Providence for having brought me into the world.

After my arrival and the outpouring of emotion, the true effect of the journey became clear: everything was familiar and yet it seemed hardly recognizable. Nothing was self-evident. In spite of myself, I began comparing. Our houses, for example, of which I had once been so proud, as any inhabitant of this major town would be, now seemed small, cramped, rudimentary. The corner pillars, exposed beams on the façades, and diamond patterns on the wood gave something of the primitive cabin to our homes. In the Levant I had seen palaces made of stone, and densely inhabited towns where narrow streets wound their way with difficulty through tight clusters of multiple-storied houses. Our wealth seemed very poor to me indeed.

Another reality that had come to light during this journey was the long presence of time. Before now, all I had ever noticed around me were the traces of a relatively recent past. The cathedral and the principal monuments in our town were no more than a century old, or two at the most. In the Levant I had encountered far more ancient vestiges. In Palmyra I had the leisure of visiting ruins left by the Romans, and on several occasions during the voyage I had seen Greek temples. Now that I was home, I noticed for the first time that our town did have its ancient relics scattered here and there; the most impressive of these were the ramparts that surrounded the hill where the cathedral stood. I had walked a thousand times beneath the tall towers erected here and there, but I had never connected them to those same Romans the Gospel spoke of. This discovery, however insignificant, had a great impact on me. I had only ever conceived of elsewhere as being in space:

to see things move, one must move oneself. I now understood that time also affects things. By staying in the same place, one could be present at the world's transformation. Thus, the ramparts that were reputed to be impregnable had eventually been conquered; now there were streets running along the base of them, and the neighborhoods of new houses built at their foot spilled downhill to the streams below. And someday, perhaps, these houses too would disappear, or would be dominated by taller buildings. This was called time, and when one played a part in it, it became History. It was up to each of us to play our part. No one knew whether the palaces I had discovered elsewhere might someday be built here. In short, I had left this town thinking of it as an unchangeable heritage; and now that I had returned, I could see it was the raw material of a history that depended solely on human beings.

There had been much talk about my journey, and I received many invitations to share my story. A number of merchants of varying importance expressed their desire to join me should I—as they imagined I should—venture to repeat the experience. I did not accept any of their proposals. My thoughts were strangely clear. I knew what I wanted to do and how to do it. The problem, above all, was to determine with whom I should do it.

To attain my goal I needed to associate myself with others. But the secret of my ambition could only be shared with someone I could trust entirely. I went through my acquaintances, but could find no one whose support I could rely upon without reticence. But then I thought of our band of children during the siege of the town; perhaps it was superstition to remember that episode which had shown to me and to others who I truly was, but I felt I ought to seek out those comrades who had been with me during the adventure, and who had subsequently shown me their unfailing loyalty.

I went first to see Guillaume de Varye. He was living in

Saint-Amand, and he had not contacted me since my return. I could understand why. He was ashamed. His cloth trade had suffered severe difficulties. Several convoys had been pillaged, a warehouse had been destroyed by fire, a major client had been killed by an armed gang and now his widow refused to pay . . . Business was going very badly. Guillaume welcomed me to a home that was starving. His wife was coughing, gaunt, and pale. You could see in her eyes that she knew she was dying. Her greatest fear was not knowing whether her children would outlive her. Still active, serious, and indefatigable, Guillaume told me of all his efforts to thwart fate. But no matter what he did he seemed to be forever heading into the wind. Just the day before, he had found out that an affair he had placed great hope in had fallen through. I observed him as he spoke to me, his eyes lowered. He was still a small man, thin and nervous. The energy he had bottled up inside could find no other outlet now than despair or sickness. He was like the country around him: full of courage, talent, and goodwill, but circumstances made all such qualities futile. I was no different, save for one thing: I knew that elsewhere conditions existed that could allow talent to prosper.

I suggested to Guillaume that we work together, and as his first salary I offered to pay off his debts then and there. He began trembling from limb to limb. Had it come from anyone but me, he would have feared such an offer, would have hesitated to surrender to the will of someone he did not know well. But I had saved him once, and he had not forgotten. All this meant was that we would set out again together, as at the time of our adventure. He stood up, embraced me, and then went down on one knee before me like a lord swearing allegiance. Chivalry, in those days, was still our only reference. When at a later time we would think back on this first contract, it made us laugh. The fact remains that it was stronger than a signature, and no one ever contested it.

The second man I needed was Jean, whom we called Little Jean, his real name being Jean de Villages. This would require still greater tact. Jean was younger than I. He had belonged to that troop of boys who were enthralled by Éloi, our former comrade who claimed to be the ringleader. Our adventure during the siege of Bourges may have put Éloi out of the picture, but it meant that Jean was left to seek out even less commendable role models. Initially Jean turned to me—unfortunately, in those days I had no inclination to dictate the conscience of others, and I had refused. I sensed a bad energy in him, a destructive enthusiasm that compelled him to attack any form of authority. He was a rebel by nature. He was one of those people—and I would meet several like him later in life—in whom an invisible wound had never healed, a wound sustained in childhood through the violence of someone close, and which would cause this person to scream with an indistinct hatred all through his life. No matter how violent they are, the result is the same: violence ends up unleashing the bad temper painfully accumulated in their wounded souls. At the age of fifteen he killed a man for the first time.

It was during the turbulence of war, on behalf of his captain, and no one held it against him. He had followed a gang leader and joined the army of King Charles. He was seen in Orléans when the Maid Joan reconquered the town, and he was present at the king's consecration in Reims. The very next day, as if he found it loathsome to serve a man who was now a legitimate monarch, as if he could only find his place in resistance and lost causes, he left the army. It was rumored that he had returned to our parts. He started a wine business and sent several convoys to his former companions-at-arms to quench their thirst. Then he disappeared. Guillaume, who had remained his friend—and this was one of the first instances where he would prove himself useful—had reason to believe that Jean had gone to work for a mad lord in the region of Lyon by the name of Villandrando. He had been wounded in the thigh and come back to the Berry to recover. He lived under the protection of the lords of Aubigny, for whom he rendered services too shameful to mention. I went there to meet him. Guillaume had warned him of my visit. I expected to find an *écorcheur* and, to be honest, I was afraid that the drink and debauchery so common to men of war would have ruined him.

To my great satisfaction, I found a man who was in perfect health. He was a head taller than I. His body, in his close-fitting smock, was slim and muscular. A life in the outdoors had tanned his skin and on his cheeks were the shining traces of a blond beard. The wound in his leg was almost healed and he limped only slightly. All that remained of the child I had known were his blue eyes, full of joy in that way of people who suffer and who are troubled in body or soul. I knew that the first minutes of our meeting would be decisive: either we would find we had become strangers, and I would have nothing to expect from him; or, as I had imagined, our former friendship would be intact, and he would be the right man for me.

A servant woman hovered nearby. Jean spoke to her gently and I saw this as a favorable omen. Nothing would have disturbed me more than to find him gruff in manner, the way soldiers can often be.

"So," I said, "you have become a warrior?"

"It is what I wanted, Jacques, it is what I wanted," he replied pensively, with a constant smile in his sad eyes.

He described at length his time fighting with the French troops. Only the noblemen had a role to play; they decided everything, even if it meant imposing their mistakes. The others were mere carcasses, fattened for the sacrifice.

Unlike other commoners, whom I would meet later in life, he had no liking for the art of war.

I understood that Jean had been looking for a leader and

had never found one. He told me about the siege of Orléans, the only fray where he had been able to use his energy to the full. He had fought under Joan of Arc, about whom he knew nothing other than that she claimed to have been sent by a God in whom he did not believe. He had seen her in the camp when they were removing her armor; he had seen her thin, bare leg, and she had lowered her eyes. I understood that he would have been capable of following her to his death. He liked leaders who were weaker than him. With anyone else, sooner or later he would direct his violence against them; he left so as not to tear them to pieces.

I sat down opposite him, to seem even smaller, and spread my white hands on the table. My nails were always well groomed, and I had been told I had a woman's hands. Now I was disarmed, and as I sought to have a hold on him, these hands signified my weakness.

He came closer and grabbed them. His face lit up and I thought I could see tears welling from his eyes.

"Jacques," he said, "Providence has brought you to me."

Our childhood friendship was intact, the same friendship that had defined our roles once and for all. He was ready to follow me, now and forever. I had won him over.

*

The next two years were strange. Inside myself, I knew exactly where I was going, and never doubted the success of my undertaking. And yet, viewed from without, my situation was most precarious. I had been to prison. Then, with no explanation, I had left everything behind to go to the Levant. My only excuse might have been that I had gone there to make my fortune; I had come home penniless. I was over thirty years of age, and I had accomplished nothing on my own. It was not that anyone ever called me a "good for nothing" to my face, but I could sense that the words lingered in the thoughts of those around me—with the exception of Macé, who, in her silent and absent way, always trusted me. She sincerely hoped for my success, even if I suspect she had always known that success would take me away from her. She told the children marvelous stories where I played the hero. But my son Jean was already thirteen, and he could judge for himself. And when, in spite of his natural reserve, he asked me questions about my life, I had the distinct impression that he had his doubts about me.

My father-in-law was aging well. Although he complained incessantly, deep down he was happy that he was still—perhaps for a long time yet—the one on whom the family's survival depended. I was sufficiently sure of my ground not to fear his judgment. I just wanted him to agree one last time to lend me the money I needed to launch the enterprise I had in mind. I gave up trying to convince him of the legitimacy of my endeavor. No matter the argument I set forth, his mind was made up: he expected nothing but failure on my part. I asked Macé to intercede on my behalf, and at last he yielded.

We rented a warehouse in the tanners' district. Our first meeting was held in the middle of June on a day of extreme heat. The smell of the hides came in through the open casements and we understood why the rent we had obtained was so cheap. Around a cheap pinewood table, sitting far back for fear of splinters, Guillaume, Jean, and I surrounded the young notary who had drawn up our first contract. We signed it, and the lawyer, who had been holding his breath ever since he arrived in the room, hurried away, choking. Our meeting lasted until late at night. Jean went out to fetch some wine and supper. I did almost all the talking. All the notes, references, and ideas I had stored up during my months of travel now emerged all of a sudden. Time had put them in order and given them a shape. My companions adopted the project as it stood. Their only questions were of a practical nature. Who would do what? And how? And with what means? The complementary nature of their characters immediately guided the distribution of tasks: Guillaume would take care of the administration, paperwork, and accounts; Jean would be the one to take to the road, to convince our partners, and, if need be, to break down barriers.

What was the nature of our business? Quite simply, it was a trading house. It would specialize in the Levant, yet be open to all of Europe. At first glance, this was nothing original. After these years of war and insecurity, to want to buy and sell in faraway places was simply proof of honest optimism. I had taken notes all through my journey. I had recorded the names and addresses of all those who might be useful to us. The Corsican ruffian who had robbed us after the shipwreck had not found it worth his while to make off with my scribbling. In addition to the notes regarding the activities of Mediterranean ports, there was a vast amount of information I had collected during my less glorious years. Starting with my father-in-law, then Ravand, and even in the depths of the jails where I had been confined, I had been constantly listening, questioning, and learning.

Now it all made sense. Instead of conceiving a modest activity which fortune, perhaps, might gradually enhance, my plan was to establish, right from the start, a network on the scale of France, the Mediterranean, and the Levant. If I wanted my catch to be miraculous, I must first spread my nets very wide, very quickly. This would require an enormous effort of organization, and my two comrades understood this. Unlike the ordinary merchants who had offered to go into business with me in hopes of gaining from my experience, Jean and Guillaume were not prosperous burghers. They had everything to gain and nothing to lose. Above all, they were of a nature to be exalted by the sheer size of the task.

The only time I feared they might lose heart was when I revealed the exact amount I had at my disposal to start the business. But I had foreseen their objections. We would not proceed like other houses, opening branches or appointing representatives. We would only ever sign provisional contracts, contingent on a current transaction and terminating with that transaction. If there were people who wished to join us and act as agents in the towns where we traded, they were free to do so, but they must not count on us to pay them. They would find compensation in the business they brought to us. In short, the most important thing was to establish our name wherever we went, to inspire trust, to build a reputation that would, at first, be largely overrated. As the number of those willing to place their trust in us grew, our reputation would become solid. Jean was very enthusiastic about this aspect of the business. He was someone who loved to talk, charm, and show off, and this was a part made to measure for him. He began describing the wardrobe he would need and I commended all his suggestions. I had traveled humbly, the better to observe those around me, but I knew that when the time came to implement our system, we would often be required to forego modesty, and seek to impress by any means at our disposal.

Therefore we agreed that Guillaume would leave quickly to settle in Montpellier, where he would organize the expeditions to the Levant. To begin with, we would have to rely on those merchants already trading, and use their ships. As soon as Jean had his gentleman's wardrobe, he would head for Flanders, which belonged to the Duke of Burgundy. He would see if it was possible for us to import cloth. Part of his shipment would be sold there and then, in the king's territory, the profit of which would go to finance the transport of what remained to the east. As soon as he could, Jean would go to Germany and even to Rouen, the last region in France that still belonged to the English, in quest of the goods on the list we had drawn up together. Then he must head for Lyon without delay, where important fairs were held, in order to secure the cooperation of a local agent.

Jean emphasized the need to recruit an escort to assist him in these undertakings. A gentleman could not travel alone, still less if he was transporting goods. Guillaume, already acting the accountant, protested that we did not have the means to pay the wages of armed escorts. Jean rather scornfully demonstrated to him that he was better acquainted with such people than Guillaume was. To hire them, it was not necessary to pay them up front; the gangs that were ravaging the country on behalf of princes and noblemen of every stripe were only remunerated on the basis of future booty. Their members often waited for a long time before obtaining their share. But expectation sufficed, provided that when they went to sleep at night, drunk, soothed by a whore, they could dream about whatever Providence, always kind to simple hearts, might have in store for them.

"And what sort of spoils would you offer our men?" objected Guillaume.

"A share of our profit, once we have it."

I felt that they had already established a rapport of emulation and jealousy, of brotherhood and mutual incomprehension, which would make them irreplaceable as a team. Without ever deliberately trying to divide and rule, I have always held the union of contraries to be the secret of every successful undertaking.

When it came time to define my role in the business, I simply declared that I intended to resume my trade as a minter. Our commerce, like all commerce in those days, would be perpetually hindered by the lack of precious metal within the realm. As long as we did not have enough goods in reserve, we could not resort to barter; we had to be able to control the circulation of coinage and dispose of credit with all the money-changers in France. This would be my task.

That is what I told them, and they agreed. But they knew very well that there were other things I was not telling them. The first of these required no explanation because it was self-evident: I would be their leader. The establishment would bear my name. When dealing with others they would evoke it as if it were a sort of Open Sesame, a divine formula uttered respectfully in hushed tones. It went without saying that from that day on, in our shared interest, their task would be to contribute to the creation of my legend, to making my name a mark and a myth. They would be for me what Peter and Paul had been for Christ: the subservient creators of his universal glory. I fully appreciate how ridiculous and grandiloquent such a comparison is, and I would like to reassure anyone who might be tempted to think I was taking myself for a god that we were fully aware that the entire enterprise rested upon a fabrication. We knew better than anyone how weak, mortal, and fallible I was. However, our activity must be seen as more than mere trade, as something vital, but without glory or expectations. We wanted our business to be inspired, to have scope, to envision horizons in keeping with an entirely new purpose. To this end, our enterprise must not appear to be merely a merchant's property, but rather the sect of a prophet. And that prophet, since we must have one, would be me.

It was evening and we were still at work. We had rolled up our sleeves, our brows were pearled with sweat. Through the open casements we had heard the bells ringing vespers from two neighboring clock towers.

There could be no greater divide between our ideas and projects and our actual situation. What characterized us best at that time in our life was failure, and perhaps that was also what united us. Those who looked on us with the pity one reserves for losers would shrug their shoulders if they overheard us weaving our wild dreams. Because I knew that deep down they were aware of the ridicule we might inspire, I abstained from sharing with my associates the true dimension of the plan that haunted me. They knew me well enough, since the siege of Bourges, to realize that in addition to our practical measures, and the enterprise I shared with them, I certainly had other ideas, a loftier vision of the goal I sought to attain. They did not question me further. Perhaps that element of mystery was necessary for them to convince themselves I was truly the prophet whose message they would be carrying out into the world. Perhaps they knew, above all, that it was pointless to try and make me say any more about it than I was prepared to.

And indeed, my attitude would not have changed, even if they had questioned me. For I was convinced that there was only one person to whom I could reveal my deepest thoughts. For anything to be possible, everything depended on that person, and if he did not agree, it would be pointless to make my intentions public.

That person was King Charles.

*

For two years I tried relentlessly to obtain an introduction to the king. The obstacles facing me were of two kinds. First of all, he never stayed in one place. The peace negotiations with Burgundy and the English demanded much of his attention. But in spite of all that he did not refrain from following his armies into the field. From what I understood, he kept the possibility of negotiation open, while exerting uninterrupted military pressure on his adversaries. Scandalmongers viewed these contradictions as the effect of his indecisiveness and the conflicting advice lavished on him by members of his entourage. I preferred to see this as proof of his cunning and political savvy. Whatever the case may be, the sovereign's perpetual movement made an encounter difficult. I came to the conclusion that the best thing would be to stay in one place and wait for him to come through our town before seeking an introduction. I had some support in that domain, and though my existence might have been insignificant, it was not completely invisible.

It remained to be seen how I might obtain an audience alone with the king, an essential condition if my plan were to succeed. Should I reveal the nature of it to those who could help me meet him? Or should I use a different pretext—but in that case, what? The only time the sovereign had ever placed his trust in me, albeit without knowing me, was something I remembered with horror: my wretched experience minting money with Ravand. At first I thought it would be better not to mention it. But as I could not come up with anything better, I concluded that the coinage affair was perhaps the best way to introduce myself, particularly as I hoped eventually to act in that capacity again. I went to see Ravand.

He was living in Orléans, where he had been practicing the same profession since the liberation of the town. It was immediately obvious that he was prospering. He had put on weight, and his cheeks and nose had begun to acquire red blotches. Still, his energy was intact, drawn from the heat of the forge.

I shared with him my scruples about resuming my position as a minter after the scandal of our fraud and conviction. He had put the event so far behind him that he had to pause and think for a moment to grasp what I was referring to.

"Bah," he exclaimed, slapping his thighs, "that's part of the trade! A minter who has never been to prison is like a riding master who has never fallen off his horse. He cannot be trusted."

Once again he went through the things I had not wanted to hear three years earlier. And this time, I listened. According to Ravand, a minter was paid to do the opposite of what was purportedly expected of him. He was there to guarantee the content of the coins he was making, but everyone knew he actually manufactured them using a lighter alloy. Such a fool's bargain was possible because the minter was paying. He shared the profit of his fraud with all those who were in a position to indict him. In a way, he took responsibility for a collective sin. He guaranteed the order of things. If, through some misfortune—and this did happen from time to time—the rivalry of his protectors led them to quarrel, he would suffer the consequences. He would be arrested, all profits would cease, and very quickly the very same people who, because of their quarrel, had had him thrown in jail would decide it was preferable to get along, and bond together to have him released.

"The safest way to avoid such a misadventure," he concluded, "is to ensure one always deals with someone whose power can never be questioned."

"The king?"

"Of course!"

He smiled and raised his glass. I was glad he had broached the topic so quickly, because that was precisely where I was headed.

"That's just it, Ravand, I would like you to obtain an introduction for me . . . "

The Dane narrowed his eyes. He took a moment to evaluate the quantity of deceit in my proposition. Was I about to double-cross him? Might I not be seeking to obtain some advantage from the sovereign at his expense?

I waited, extremely calm, my eyes wide open. He convinced himself that nothing was troubling the combination of naivety and sincerity of which he believed to me to be made.

"You want to see him . . . in person."

"In person and alone."

"What the devil!"

A man of fire and metal was not afraid of swearing.

"And so he receives me," he continued. "But he has known me for a long time. The problem, you see, is that he is suspicious. Even if someone comes to him warmly recommended, until he has sniffed him out himself he remains wary. And when I say sniffed out . . . you shall see."

We sat down to dinner even though it was very early. When the serving woman put the dish down in front of us, I understood that for Ravand it was always dinnertime, that he never refused the food she brought up from the kitchen by the hour.

"Do you know where he is at present?" I asked, to defer the moment when I would have to bite into a greasy chicken leg.

"It is difficult to say. He has been leading the talks with that scoundrel Burgundy. It seems he has brought together all his former companions, even those who were disgraced. I've known him to be surrounded by a number of different clans, depending on the era. Someone might be at court today and in prison tomorrow, or even stitched up in a sack and thrown into the water. But at the moment, there is a general amnesty. Charles wants to put an end to it. If anyone is left out, they could be bought by Burgundy or the English. The king wants no more traitors."

Ravand spoke with his mouth full. My appetite, already poor, abandoned me altogether when I saw his chipped teeth.

"I have been told that he is continuing to wage war—"

"Scarcely. He is torn between negotiation and combat. From what I have heard, he is meeting with his counselors in Tours at the moment. Sooner or later he will head east again. He might come this way, or through Bourges."

"Can you get a message to him?"

"In writing, certainly not. For what I have to tell him, it would be preferable to leave no trace. However . . . "

He was hesitating. Was it over which piece of meat to pick up next, or the words he intended to say?

"I have to see him, in any event. I am reaching the end of the mission he has entrusted me with, and we must discuss the next stage. Peace has a heavy price, but war an even greater one. He needs the profit I make on the currency more than ever."

He stood up and wiped his hand with his black fingernails on the fabric of his doublet.

"You've helped me make up my mind, actually. And I thank you. I'm going to leave tomorrow for Tours, while he is still there. And I'll let you know whether he will agree to meet you."

"Alone, you understand?"

"Yes . . . yes, alone."

He grabbed me by the shoulders and embraced me. Ravand burned through life the way he melted gold. Into the combustion he recklessly tossed food and drink, women and danger. But what gave it all taste was friendship, carefully gathered in small quantities, because it was a rare and precious thing, a spice of which he could never get enough.

Ravand was as good as his word. One of his guards came to our town to deliver the good news. The king would be passing through Bourges and would receive me. He would arrive on Holy Thursday, would attend Easter Mass at the cathedral, and leave again on Monday. His people would inform me of the day and hour for our audience. I must stand ready day and night during his entire stay. The sovereign was known to send for his visitors at a late hour, and would not tolerate tardiness.

Thus, there were two days until the king's visit. The time seemed both very long and extremely short. I had to think of everything, foresee everything. I was fully aware that my entire life would depend on this interview. It would be no ordinary audience. What I had to say would not be limited—as the sovereign must surely imagine—to some minor petition requesting a favor or an office. I hoped, moreover, that he would allow enough time for me to set forth my proposal. In any event, I had to be sure of his attention right from the start, and hold him captive with my words.

Whenever I thought of it, I could easily convince myself that I had no chance of success. But the moment I stared such despair in the face, I was filled with great serenity. I became master of myself, lucid and determined. I was scrupulously observing Lent, along with any other activity likely to convince others of my faith—something I no longer had—and this, too, proved how insignificant I was. I was nothing. I had nothing to lose. But if I did gain something, it would be everything.

The king arrived on the appointed day and settled in the Duke's palace. I was ready. Macé, who had been informed of the matter, was particularly attentive. Between my return from my journey and all that was to follow, this was indisputably the happiest period in our marriage. Now I regret that I was so absent during that time, as all my attention was on what I hoped to accomplish. Macé sensed that I was not really there, and she must have suffered greatly. We never spoke of it.

At night I went to bed fully clothed, like a monk who must respond at any moment to the final call. I listened for footsteps in the street, for a sound in the house. It was a damp and perpetually dark month of March. Icy rain fell at dawn.

The message I had been waiting for came at daybreak on Saturday. Three men came to the house and pounded on the door. It was as if they had come to make an arrest. However, no condemned man had ever been so eager to give himself up. In an instant I was downstairs.

I followed them through the rain. Cold drops trickled down my back and I preferred to think that they were the cause of my shivering. It must have been five o'clock. We met the watchman on his rounds, overwhelmed by fatigue, but otherwise the streets were deserted. At the Duke's palace, however, several windows were brightly lit. It was impossible to tell whether they had just been lit or whether the candles had been burning all night long. I wondered whether it was the first audience of the morning, or the last one of the night, that the king had reserved for me. In the first case, he might have trouble staying awake; in the second, his only wish would be to sleep. I forced myself not to see it as a bad sign.

I was led through rooms I had visited back in the days of Duke John, when I used to go to the palace with my father. But now the guards took me deeper into the palace. I discovered stairways, corridors, and countless antechambers. The king's retinue had occupied the premises in great disorder. The hallways were filled with chests, from which hangings or dishes had been hastily removed. Valets slept in corners. On the floor were trays piled with the remains of the supper the courtiers had eaten hurriedly in their rooms. We went up a flight of stairs and along a narrow passageway to a low door guarded by two young soldiers. They conferred with my escort. One of them opened the door, went in, and closed it again behind him. After a long while, he came back and motioned to me to stand ready to enter. One of the guards offered to take my drenched cloak and I gratefully accepted. Finally, the door opened and, bowing my head slightly, I went in alone.

*

My first impression was that I had been projected into an alternative space. I had just entered a dark room, with neither boundary nor point of reference, the only exception a table in the middle where a single candle was lit. The weak light it cast faded into the obscurity. From a certain quality of silence and the resonance of my footsteps I understood that the room must be enormous, but deserted.

My father had often spoken to me of a ceremonial hall that could hold the entire population of the Berry. It had caused much admiration at the time of its construction, because the builders had to use exceptionally tall tree trunks to carve the ceiling beams. I peered into the darkness but my eyes could not make out a thing. The room was silent. I went up to the table and into the halo of candlelight. I stood there and waited. Papers were spread on the table; I resisted the temptation to look at what they might contain. If the purpose was to disconcert, I had to concede that disconcert it did. I felt like an unarmed man walking through a dark forest, not knowing which way the danger lay. I continued to wait for several long minutes. Suddenly, behind me, although I could see nothing in the darkness, I heard a faint sound. Then I heard it again a moment later. It was a sort of breathing, or, rather, a repeated inhalation. The foolish thought came to me that a mastiff might be hidden in the thick shadow. The sound came closer. And suddenly I heard Ravand's words again: "When I say sniffed out . . . you shall see." When I turned in the direction of the sound, I recoiled with surprise. A man was standing at the edge of the gloom. A few shards of light, lost in the dark space, bounced off him and sculpted his shape against the black background, like a bas-relief carving in the fireback of a hearth. The motionless man was staring at me, and it was he who had been making the sound that had alerted me, with his short intakes of breath.

He came forward and stood in the light. According to the description I had been given, this was the king. My surprise was such that I found it difficult to believe what I knew, or to persuade myself of it. What held me back was neither the extreme simplicity of his attire, nor his ugliness, nor his fearful manner. I had simply not expected to meet a man of my own age.

"Good evening, Cœur," he said softly.

"Good evening, Sire."

He went to sit on a wooden chair behind the table and motioned to me to sit opposite. He was careful to keep well back from the table, so that I could see all of him. He waited for a while, as if to give me the leisure to allow this vision to penetrate my brain and draw my conclusions. Now when I think back on this manner of his, I can easily conceive the reason for it. Charles VII, better than anyone, knows how to make his appearance speak louder than his words. By showing himself in full to his interlocutors, he immediately establishes his authority over them, an authority of a very particular nature. I have met so many men of power in my life, and I know that they can be divided into two categories. There are those who impose their authority through the strength they emanate—these men are often warlords or leaders, but there are men of the church among them as well. The energy, enthusiasm, and boldness which inform their personality give all those who come in contact with them a desire to leave everything behind and the courage to confront anything, provided it is in following them. Their strength is their power. But there is a second category, much rarer and above all much more formidable, who find power in their weakness. People of this sort come across as weak, vulnerable, or wounded. Placed by destiny at the head of a nation, an army, or an ordinary undertaking, such men confess, through their appearance, that they are helpless to carry out their task, but cannot be resolved to abandon it. Their self-sacrifice is so obvious that it triggers admiration in others and a sincere desire to serve. The weaker they are, the more strength they recruit around them. Everyone makes a great show of bravery to satisfy them, and they accept this homage without ever abandoning their wretched demeanor. These weary kings are the most dangerous.

I did not know all this back then, and I had never yet had the occasion to be in the presence of such a man. The trap worked perfectly and I pitied him immediately.

What struck me, and made him pleasant to me, was his great simplicity. In this very place I had met nobles who were far less illustrious, yet made an odious use of the superiorty their birth gave them. Charles, however, seemed to have received his titles of Prince, Dauphin, and King as curses. They brought him some distinction, to be sure, but also a great deal of jealousy, hatred, and violence. He saw his royal role as a fatality, almost a weakness. He would only be rid of it when he was rid of life, and in the meantime, it deprived him of life itself. What I knew about him illuminated this curse, painfully so. He had watched as his mad father reigned over the country; his mother had yielded to the extreme pressure of her enemies, to the point of embracing their interests and rejecting her own son; a foreign king fought him for his crown in his own capital—no destiny could be as tragic as his. This crooked little man, whose only weapon was the long nose he used to sniff out his visitors and locate his enemies among them, now elicited a surge of total devotion in me. The little smile at the corner of his lips should, however, have warned me. He was stronger than he was prepared to let on, like a hunter disguised as prey, always glad to find a new victim caught in his snare.

The king was also silently examining my own person. His calm and silence were disconcerting. I was accustomed, in critical moments, to asserting my authority over others by stepping back and displaying a coldness that contrasted with their excitement. With a character such as the one I had in front of me, this method would not work. For a moment I was tempted to reverse the roles and act in a voluble and passionate manner. But that was not my true nature, and by improvising such a transformation I ran the risk of falling flat, or even making a regrettable impression of falseness.

I emptied my mind, took a deep breath, and waited. As Charles was not very forthcoming, the conversation began with a long, drawn-out silence. Finally, very cautiously, he moved the first pawn.

"So, I hear you have come from the Levant?"

I understood that Ravand had used my voyage as bait. If you said "Levant" you actually meant "gold." Many tales had gone to enhance the notion that the lands of the Levant were overflowing with gold, so much so that it was worth less than silver in our parts.

"Yes, sire."

This short but solid defense seemed to disconcert the sovereign. He wrinkled his nose and made a gesture with his curved forefinger as if he wanted to straighten it. I would soon realize that this gesture was merely one of the numerous tics that afflicted him.

"It would seem my uncle Burgundy is preparing to launch a crusade?"

This was a long sentence for the amount of breath he seemed to have available. He ended it in a murmur, then inhaled deeply through his mouth, as if he had almost drowned.

"Indeed. In Damascus I met his first esquire, who was gathering information for that purpose. He was disguised as a Turk."

"Disguised as a Turk!"

Charles burst out laughing. His laugh was tortured, like all the rest of his expressions. In truth, one might have thought he was writhing in pain, and the sound which came from his clenched teeth had something of the cry of a partridge rising in fear from a field of wheat. His eyes were weeping. It was painful to watch him. Still, I was pleased to have a reaction from him, perhaps against his will.

"Do you think he will succeed?"

"I hope he will not, sire."

"What do you mean?"

"There are many more things to be done in the Levant than to instigate crusades that are no longer necessary."

Charles narrowed his eyes. My boldness seemed to frighten him. He glanced hastily from left to right. I wondered if anyone else were there in the room. My vision had gradually adjusted to the darkness and I could not see anyone. But perhaps in the darkest recesses there were invisible people observing us.

"Do you not think it is necessary to restore the true faith to the Holy Land . . . and to make the Mohammedans . . . who are imposing their law . . . show respect?"

He had uncoiled his sentence in spurts, laboriously. His shortness of breath was not the only reason for this slowness. He was searching for words as if he were reciting a lesson. I concluded that these ideas were not his own, and that he was encouraging me to contradict them. At the same time, it was a risky wager. Although I could not evaluate the extent of my host's perversity, I was beginning take the measure of it, and the mortal danger implied by any direct exchange with him.

"It seems to me that nowadays our attention must first be given to Christian lands. Two centuries ago, we were building cathedrals, the countryside was rich and our towns were prosperous. We had the wherewithal to send expeditions to the Levant to restore the true faith. But today our first duty as Christians is to restore the prosperity of our people. Perhaps a day will come when we will be powerful enough to resume the conquest."

The king froze and for a moment I thought I had said too much. All his tics vanished while he stared at me. He was not smiling, nor did he seem indignant. It was just an icy, avid stare. Much later I would learn to recognize this expression. It appeared on his face whenever his gaze happened upon something that aroused his covetousness—an idea he wanted to appropriate, a woman he desired, an enemy he had just condemned, a talented person he judged necessary for his service. I remained motionless, trying to hide the doubt that was stifling me. Finally, the tension relaxed quite unexpectedly: he yawned noisily.

A jug of water and a glass stood on the table. He helped himself, took two swallows then, oddly, passed me the glass.

By then I was seeing traps everywhere, and this caused me to hesitate a moment too long. Which was worse, to drink in a king's glass or refuse his offer? I saw him smile and so I opted for fraternity. Basically, here was a man my own age offering me something to drink, and I was thirsty. He seemed pleased to see me take the glass. Later on, I would have the opportunity to observe how naturally he shared everyday gestures. This simplicity was the consequence of a harsh, impoverished upbringing. At the same time, I have seen him condemn a man for having taken liberties with him that were far less obvious.

"And how," he continued, "should we proceed to restore, as you say, the prosperity of our people?"

He had uttered these words with an infinite sadness that seemed sincere. Some invisible suffering made him swell his chest and gave him the strength to continue in a voice that was almost loud.

"Have you traveled in my kingdom? . . . Ruins . . . Villages burned, war. Death. The English, pillaging us. Burgundy, who has taken the best part for himself . . . Those who serve me rape and kill wherever they go. Yes, I do agree . . . You are completely right. There is nothing for us in the Levant. But here. In this very place. How can we restore wealth? Wealth! What am I saying? How can we feed everyone? Just that. How?"

He slumped on his chair, exhausted by his disjointed tirade. The question again crossed my mind: had he already slept, or was he receiving me before going to bed? And suddenly, seeing him collapsed on his seat, I thought that my question could only make sense regarding someone who lived a normal life. For him, there could be no sleeping hours, nor such a thing as wide-awake. His life must unfold in that state of anxiety that combines wakefulness and rest. On that point at least, I was not mistaken.

He picked up the jug from the table, poured some water into his palm and splashed his face. Then he seemed to emerge completely from his torpor and he looked at me eagerly.

"Well, what say you?"

"You are the one, sire, who will bring prosperity to your kingdom."

It was important that I begin with something obvious. The memory of Joan of Arc had been present in my mind since the beginning of our interview. This same man had questioned her, just as he was questioning me. Like me, she had no titles to inspire his trust, and yet, he had listened to her. Why? Because she had touched in him the chord of pride and weakness, the hidden, mysterious spring which made this strange man believe that he was everything but that he could do nothing. She had said, simply: you are the king of France. And that simple fact had led them to Reims, and to his coronation.

"Yes," I said again, "you will bring prosperity to this kingdom."

I paused for a moment, in silence. The king swallowed noisily, as if he had just absorbed the balm of my words and was waiting for it to take effect. I saw him sit up straight, stare into the darkness ahead of him, and with the tone of someone who is already headed toward his dreams he asked, "How?"

And so I explained it to him. I told him everything I had concealed from my partners, because they were helpless to change anything in these matters. I spoke to him about France being split in three—the lands of the Englishman which included Paris, those of the Duke of Burgundy, and his own lands in the Berry and the Languedoc. Each region turned its back on the others and there was no movement of men and things among them. He was the only one, by accepting peace, who would be able to reestablish communication among these three pieces of France. The country would then be open to trade again, and products from the entire world would converge toward France, from Scotland and from Florence, from Spain and from the East.

"This war has been lasting for more than a century, sire, but you will put an end to it. This will not simply be another truce. Peace is not merely a suspension of war. Peace means the industry of mankind, the movement of goods, the blossoming of cities and markets."

"You speak like the merchant that you are," he interrupted, suddenly scornful.

For the first and only time, I showed my temper.

"But I despise merchants, sire! They think only of their own profit under any circumstance, and they are comfortable with poverty for as long as it raises their prices. What I want is abundance. I want to create wealth through movement and trade. I want caravans bringing the finest creations from every land on earth to converge upon France."

He slumped again on his chair, adopting the sullen air of a scolded schoolboy. He wrinkled his nose and scratched it with his fingertip.

"At present," I continued, "those caravans all go to the East. I have seen them. The wealth they have brought has created a refined civilization. More refined than our own. And those knights of ours, rotting beneath their filthy suits of armor, have failed to understand this."

"'Rotting beneath their filthy suits of armor.' Ha, ha! Well said."

I was no longer paying attention to the king's reactions. I had to go on to the end.

"They went there to take, though they would have done better to learn. The Levant is rich in both wealth and knowledge. We could gain by imitation. It is not merely a question of being equal: we can do better. I am convinced that the Levant is in decline. It is going nowhere in its prosperity. If we were to study its methods, bring back its techniques and knowledge, and if we maintain peace, I have no doubt we could surpass them."

In spite of myself I had become excited, and the king felt it necessary to curb my enthusiasm.

"Messire Cœur, what exactly have you come to propose to me?"

I placed my hands on my knees and took a deep breath.

"I have set up a trading house with the Levant. We have relays in a number of regions, including Burgundy, Flanders, and as far as Rouen. Let peace come, and the difficulties of communication will subside."

"That is all very well, but how does it concern me, apart from the question of peace, of which I am very well aware?"

"Sire, this house is yours. Give it your protection and it will grow to the dimension of the realm. What we are doing on a small scale, you would give us the possibility to accomplish on a grand scale."

The king sneezed and wiped his nose on his cuff. His eyes were shining, and I could not tell whether it was the mention of profit that excited him, or whether he was mocking me in a nasty way.

"In short, you want me to become your associate?"

"No, sire, my intention is solely that your Majesty should live without going to war."

This argument had its effect—I could tell from the shadow that briefly darkened his gaze. The king was in a position to know better than anyone what war brought him. It was in order to wage war that he required his lords and the cities of the realm to pay their bitterly negotiated contributions. But he also knew the cost of peace. Deprived of those exceptional contributions, he would have very few resources, particularly as in declaring himself king he had decided, to please his princes and induce them to fight alongside him, to abolish taxes. He was caught in a terrible dilemma: perpetual war, or poverty. Suddenly I had shown him the possibility of another source of income, one which could be obtained through trade. Hitherto it had taken the form of taxes that were difficult to raise. What I was suggesting was to involve the State in these activities, to control them, expand them, practice them himself. The instrument I was devising with Guillaume and Jean was not destined to remain our property. I saw it rather as the embryo of an organization which would be the king's property and to which he would bring his power.

My intuition was clear in principle but there were still many points to clarify. What would be the link between the sovereign and my plan of action? Who would administer the network? How would the profits be divided among the different agents required?

During a long silence, I could sense he was considering these difficulties, and no doubt drawing up a list of issues to be resolved. As always when the solution to a problem did not appear clearly to him, or when he needed help in obtaining what he wanted, his expression became wretched. His features fell, and it seemed that even his eyes were not looking in the same direction. He slumped forward, touched his fingertips together; his bony hands looked like two spiders. It was impossible for anyone in his presence not to be moved by this vision of weakness, uncertainty, and suffering. And I like a fool hurried to his assistance.

"You must know, sire, that I will be entirely devoted to this undertaking if your Majesty sees fit to endorse it."

He blinked as if in warning but perhaps it was just fatigue overcoming him. Suddenly he changed the subject.

"You are seeking to become a minter again, or so I have heard?"

Ravand must have provided this detail when presenting my request for an audience. It was a good thing but trivial in comparison to the grand prospects we had just been entertaining.

I was tempted to avoid the question, but I felt that the king would not continue our previous conversation. I might as well try to obtain something.

"That is true, sire."

"Such a position can bring in a great deal, particularly when practiced in the manner you once adopted."

"Sire, do believe me when I say that I regret—"

He raised his hand wearily, unable even to spread his fingers.

"What matters is how one's profits are put to use, is that not so? I have no doubt that this time you will be more sensible."

He may have stated his point allusively, but it was clear nevertheless.

"Your Majesty can always rely on me."

At that very moment, as I bowed my head to accompany my words, he stood up.

"Goodnight, Messire Cœur," he said, from the edge of the shadow, turning his head to gaze at me one last time.

He looked exhausted. In the vast hall his silhouette was tiny and the darkness immediately swallowed him up.

I felt saddened and helpless, like someone abandoned by a friend. Dawn was breaking, smudged with gray, when I went home.

*

I was puzzled by our interview. When Macé asked me how it had gone, I did not know what to tell her. I constantly reexamined the words we had exchanged and reproached myself a hundred times over. It was obvious that I had been too abstract, too passionate, and above all too direct. The king had surely been displeased to hear me lecturing him in that way.

But the most troubling thing of all was the absence of any conclusion, the way the sovereign had departed abruptly at the end of the interview, without letting any of his opinions about me show.

Nevertheless, these fears were tempered by a few encouraging realizations. First of all, the king had received me alone, which was extremely rare. Thus I had been given the opportunity to see him without his usual courtiers at his side answering in his place. The moment he appeared in public with them, the king had a self-effacing, almost fearful attitude. His tics did not help matters. He rarely came out with an idea of his own, and merely consented to those expressed by his counselors. As they were often contradictory, he had acquired an unfortunate reputation for indecisiveness. He was held to be weak and easily influenced, and in fact, there were not many who believed he governed on his own.

To me he had shown another face, his own face, with his doubts and questions and inner struggles regarding the world around him. I would learn my lesson from this, and never allow myself to see him as a puppet. The other favorable sign, although it was difficult to interpret, came from Ravand. He told me a few weeks later that the king had questioned him about me for a long time before agreeing to meet with me. Knowing the king as I do now, I can tell what he had in mind. His subservience to the clans surrounding him was only equaled by the brutality with which he cast off his favorites and withdrew his trust from those who had taken the liberty of abusing that trust too generously. In order to prepare for such reversals, Charles observed. He was curious about new people and set about, in the utmost secrecy, putting them to the test. What Ravand had revealed to me gave me hope that this had been the case with me. But as the days went by, then the months, and there was nothing, I concluded that I had not passed the test. When I thought back on our nocturnal meeting I reproached myself a thousand times over, and was convinced that I bore full responsibility for my failure.

Fortunately all my energy was consumed with starting our business and I was left with little time to brood over my errors. Jean sent me messages through the men in his group, and Guillaume had set up a veritable private postal service between Montpellier and Bourges. Eager not to overlook any possibility for enrichment, he had made it quite profitable by agreeing to carry letters for rich clients from the Languedoc.

The enterprise was rapidly taking shape. After so many years of devastation, there were shortages everywhere. The first shipments, sent to inaugurate the network we were creating, yielded considerable profit. Guillaume was able to participate in fitting out a ship for Alexandria as an important shareholder.

Prospects were all the more favorable in that the king had finally signed a peace treaty in Arras with his uncle the Duke of Burgundy. This news turned my thoughts to him. As odd as it might seem, for we had met for scarcely an hour, I missed the king. I felt a deep bond with this unhappy little brother.

Peace with Burgundy greatly facilitated trade with the Duke's territory. Unlike those regions with which Charles had had to make do, those of Philip the Good were prosperous, and had largely been spared by the gangs. The imperial provinces controlled by the Duke, Flanders, and Hainaut were extremely industrious. As the war had deprived them of convenient outlets, they proved to be favorably inclined toward those who, like my partners and myself, offered to sell their products in new markets.

I was very busy in those days and took no notice of the fact that I was becoming rich. It must be said that the business swallowed everything. Every sale led to a new purchase, a new trade, a new gain, and every gain, immediately reinvested, then became part of the constantly moving cycle which we were setting in motion. The lack of cash and the rapid growth of our activity did not allow us the somewhat useless luxury of building up capital. Sometimes, when convoys went through our town, I would help myself to items of silk or gold to give to Macé. It was as if I were stealing from our own pocket, and we enjoyed it all the more. Later on, when wealth made permanently available to me more precious objects than I could ever have desired, I sometimes looked back fondly on those early days of prosperity. They went hand in hand with a sort of incredulity, almost a culpability, which made the acquisition of objects even more delightful than ownership.

I traveled often, and my first long absences date from those early days. Very quickly there came a time when my presence at home would be exceptional. I often deplored this, but in the beginning everything was still a source of pleasure, risk, and discovery.

A year and a half had passed since my meeting with the king, and I had received no news from him, either directly or through Ravand's intermediary, though Ravand had seen him several times since then. We were overwhelmed by the business, and I had eventually put the king out of my thoughts, even if in some corner of my mind I still hoped for something from him. It was upon my return from a journey to Angers that I found his messengers.

There were two of them, and they had ridden strictly for this purpose from Compiègne. They introduced themselves as the king's men but nothing, apart from their arrogance, substantiated what they said. I was tempted for a moment to contest their identity, but one of them said to me with a laugh, "Upon my word, you are more awake than the other time!"

He was one of the guards who had led me to the audience at the Duke's palace.

From then on I no longer had any doubt.

"What message does his Majesty have for me this time?"

"No message," answered the guard with an insolent smile. "You are to pack your trunk and follow us, that is all."

"It is packed, I have just come from a journey."

"In that case, we can leave at once."

I scarcely had time to embrace Macé and the children before riding off with the two men. On the way, they gave me some news of the situation. Paris now supported the king. Those burghers who only yesterday had sworn their loyalty to Burgundy had attacked the English garrison and opened the gates to the king of France. He had not yet entered the city himself but was preparing to do so. I wondered what role I might obtain in such a play. For the three days of the journey, I sometimes felt like a prince being followed by his escort, and sometimes like a prisoner between his guards. In truth, I have always greatly enjoyed such high points in life when one does not know which way fortune will lead. And if I had not had a liking for such balancing acts, I should have fallen much lower and above all much sooner.

Autumn came late that year and although it was already the end of October, the trees still had their leaves and were only just beginning to turn red. As we drew closer to Compiègne, we met more and more people on the roads. We could tell that the war was still raging nearby, because there was a constant coming and going of armed troops. At the same time, from their casual, nonchalant air, and the joyfulness of the civilians—men, women, and children, for the first time in many years, were getting a taste of the heady freedom of being able to move about without fear—it was obvious that the time for peace had come.

The king's army was camped beneath the walls of Compiègne, at the very place where Joan of Arc—unwise, or betrayed—had been captured. The king and his court were hidden away in a palace in the town. We entered through two wide open gates, where an old guard with a good-natured manner kept casual watch. My escort was waiting for orders and visibly did not know what to do with me. I followed my guardian angels to one house after the other. Each time, one of them waited outside with me, while the other went to inquire within. Night had fallen. Sleeping arrangements were made in a private house. The owner was a stern burgher whose loyalties were divided between joy over the royal victory and concern for his property. Incessantly frowning and scowling, he led us to a loft, where wood had been piled for the winter. There were rustling sounds and murmurs and stifled laughter as we climbed the stairs, and we understood that he had hidden his womenfolk—his wife, his two daughters, and the serving girls—for fear of an attack. The next day, as I was washing in the courtyard, I pretended not to notice the little pink face watching me from a narrow window in the stairway. Our presence kindled their curiosity. I had always been faithful to Macé, but now I felt the stirrings of desire, which fear and uncertainty enriched like powerful fertilizer. If we had stayed longer, I do not think our host would have been able to protect the virtue of his brood. Alas, or fortunately, on the second day my guards received the order to take me to the palace.

I did not know the reasons for my summons, nor the rank of the person who was to receive me. I had not given up hope that it would be the king himself, and this was confirmed to me when the messengers handed me over to a guard wearing royal regalia. This time, there were no dark corridors or secret doors. I went up wide stairways full of people, resonant antechambers echoing with noisy conversations. At last the guards showed me into a vast hall, though its proportions were smaller than the hall in Bourges. Two chandeliers, all candles ablaze, dissolved the darkness of late afternoon and cast their brilliance on the suits of armor. The crowd in the room consisted of many captains and knights in coats of mail, their weapons at their side. I also noticed a group of prelates, evocative of a large bouquet consisting of violet corollas and purple skullcaps. Surplices of lace, watered silk hats, sleeves lined with fur visible at the cuffs: one's eyes were dazzled by luxury, but no semblance of order allowed one to arrange these impressions into an intelligible whole. It was a brilliant chaos that nothing seemed to restrain. And yet there must have been some hidden logic apparent to those who were used to it, for my presence did not go unnoticed. Although I had dressed carefully in such a way that I would not stand out, the majority of those present immediately identified me as a stranger. Conversations stopped as I walked by, and curious gazes, more hostile than anything, followed me as I went with the guards farther into the room. And the farther we went, the denser the crowd of people clustered together, moving reluctantly aside to let us pass. Finally we went through a last row of people and came out into a narrow circle, almost deserted, occupied by a platform. On the platform was a wooden armchair with a high straight back carved with fleurs-de-lis. The king was hunched over in this seat. It was obvious how uncomfortable he was, as witnessed by the angle his crossed legs made with his torso, while his shoulders sloped to the left, obliging him to hold up his head with a weary hand. This was no longer the man I had seen in Bourges. Mute, his eyes half closed, struggling in vain against the nervous tics which distorted his face, he was the very image of suffering and debility. The previous day I had had the leisure to overhear the rumors in town celebrating the sovereign's heroism during the capture of Montereau. The legend had spread in order to arouse the people's admiration. But the reality I had before me was very different. More than ever, the king continued to reign through his weakness. He had gathered around him all the influential people who, at one time or another, had advised his rule, but he was increasingly besieged by this ghastly company. In a way, they held him hostage. In any case, he enjoyed making them believe this was so.

I had unwisely thought that the king would address me.

After I had greeted him in an appropriate manner, I kept my face turned towards him, in expectation of what he might choose to say. A lord whose name I did not know, and who stood leaning toward the king with one foot on the platform, called out to me.

"Are you Jacques Cœur?"

"The same, my lord."

"The king has called you here to go with him to Paris. We shall set off tomorrow."

I bowed respectfully to mark my total submission to this command. All around me, people regarded me haughtily. By confirming my name, I had revealed that I was a burgher and a tradesman, and these grand nobles paid me with a weight of scorn equal to my value.

"As soon as we reach Paris, the king would like you to take charge of administering the taxes in the city."

I could not help but glance over at the king. He gave me a look of recognition, so fleeting that only I could see it, then again assumed his absent, mournful air.

The lord with whom I had been speaking turned away and began to converse with other people. I understood that this was the sign to leave. I bowed to the king and went out again, following the guards.

*

As soon as I was outside, I inquired how I might expedite messages to Montpellier and to Lyon, where Jean was staying. We had to evaluate as quickly as possible the consequences of my new responsibilities upon our enterprise. I also asked my associates to put money aside for me in order that I might equip myself appropriately for my new dignity. I had sufficient means to buy a horse and hire two valets. I went back into the house where we had slept in order to gather my belongings, and my sudden entrance caused the brood of pretty women to hurry away, leaving me with the painful sweetness of their perfume.

Until then, great changes had been prepared in dreams and silence; now the time had come for the metamorphosis. It was no longer enough for me to *imagine* my undertakings or to hope for an event: now it would be granted me to *experience* them. This unknown factor aroused several reactions in me, some familiar, others new. Among those to which I was accustomed, there was this almost icy calm, which made me see myself and everything around me as though from the lofty altitudes of a bird of prey. Among the new sensations was a sensual appetite that had never seemed so strong. My carnal relations with Macé had been softened by tenderness. We approached each other only in darkness, not confessing to any desires other than those modestly expressed by our bodies. Now, in this commotion of malodorous men and war horses, in the confusion of the court as it made ready to visit its capital once again, I felt a crucifying need for a carnal relation, in broad daylight and in the open air, as if my body had absorbed all the anxiety my mind had expelled. Perhaps the violence of my new condition demanded above all an appeasement of equal strength, something only a woman could procure for me. The situation, however, while making such a passion infinitely desirable, absolutely prohibited me from surrendering to it for the moment. I took leave of our host and departed with the great convoy of the court.

We entered Paris several days after All Saints' Day. I was not near the front of the procession, far from it. So I did not see the celebrations that the populace of the capital had prepared for the king they had opposed for so long. I heard talk of an official ceremony to hand over the keys to the city, and of songs and dances organized on the squares. When I arrived, there were still here and there groups of men and women in disguise, heading home dejectedly. The festivities, in truth, were primarily a way of appealing to the mercy of their new master. They forced themselves to laugh, for fear of having once again to suffer and weep.

The sight of Paris distressed me. I felt the same shock as when, on my way to the Levant, I had passed through the devastated regions of the Midi. And even then, the countryside between the ruined villages at least offered a restful picture of nature, once again grown wild but bursting with life. The wounds of Paris were gaping and barren. Riots, pillaging, fires, epidemics, and successive mass departures had violated the city. Many houses were abandoned, and refuse had accumulated on empty lots. Half the shops on the Pont-au-Changes were closed. The dark and narrow streets were still cluttered with everything the people had thrown at the English to make them leave, and pigs rummaged in the debris, eating their fill. The king moved into the Louvre. I found accommodation at an inn on the rue Saint-Jacques, while waiting to find out the location of the mint, which was now my responsibility.

My situation was paradoxical. At court I knew no one, with the exception of the king himself, whom I could not approach. By gathering information here and there I learned that the man who had spoken to me in Compiègne was called Tanguy du Châtel. This was a renowned name, for he was Charles's oldest companion, from the time they were children. It was he who had wrapped the future king in a blanket and hastily taken him away when the Burgundians occupied the capital twenty years earlier. His return was a brilliant revenge, and he had insisted on resuming his former title as provost of merchants. In this time of reconciliation, he was in the way. He was accused—without proof, but there were strong suspicions against him—of having held the dagger that had killed the father of the Duke of Burgundy on the bridge of Montereau. Only at Arras was this stain removed, when the king, who shouldered the blame, was humiliated. No king could favor a former criminal without provoking the anger of his new allies. I learned that Tanguy du Châtel, despite the restoration of his title, had not been allowed to move into the Châtelet. In short, he was being hidden away. I finally found him in the innermost recesses of the Louvre. He was holding an audience in a vaulted room, a damp crypt whose walls, facing the river, were covered in saltpeter. He received me in a most inconsiderate manner, and I understood that my appointment as *exchequer* had been imposed on him by the king. He asked me if I had any talent in the matter and I replied that I had been in charge of the mint in Bourges for several years. He did not seem to know that I had fallen foul of the law. He handed me a letter which he had dictated to a secretary and which authenticated my new position.

With this accreditation in hand I walked to the coinage workshop. It was at the back of a courtyard and consisted of a series of four rooms, almost empty. When fleeing, the enemy had taken not only all the cash, leaving the coffers gaping open, but also all the tools, and they had smashed the molds.

One old craftsman, too old to flee, was sitting in a corner eating walnuts. I recognized on his face the traces of the damage caused by metal vapors. He explained that the workshop had never been very active, as the English preferred to mint their coins in Rouen, and the Duke of Burgundy in Dijon. The quality of the coins produced in Paris was mediocre and, toward the end, they produced nothing but blackish billon coins—which sufficed amply, because in any case there was nothing for sale.

I went back to the inn feeling quite dejected. It was already cold, and in spite of my promise to reward him generously, my landlord had not found any good firewood. The fire burning in the only working hearth produced more smoke than flames, and heated nothing.

The next morning, in the hope that I might approach the king, I went to linger at the Louvre. With my official letter I was allowed into the rooms where the courtiers gathered. I did not see a single familiar face, and wandered aimlessly among the different groups. At least it was warm, and I stayed there for a while until my hands, blue with the chill of the icy wind, had regained their color. I was standing by a window blowing on my fists when a youngish man came up to me. He was tall and held himself somewhat bent over, as if leaning down to examine me. He was friendly enough for all that, and had the simple manner of a soldier. He had heard that I had been entrusted with the mint, and that I was a merchant.

I immediately understood that his solicitude was self-interested. No doubt he needed money and was counting on me to procure services or things for him that he would not have to pay for. This was a practice I had been familiar with since birth. And it still seemed to be the order of things, though to a lesser degree than before. After all, he was a nobleman. For the time being, in any event, I was destitute and could not do anything to help him. He could help me, however. I asked him about the court, about the political situation in the capital, and about the progress of the war. He explained that the English had not gone far, that they had attacked Saint-Germain-en-Laye and there would surely be more fighting. His opinion of the capital was quite severe, and he did not seem sensitive to the pity which, in my opinion, the martyred city deserved.

"They are going to pay now," he said, referring to the Parisians.

As for the political situation, it filled him with bitterness.

"Now we are friends with the Burgundians," he scowled. "All is forgotten, don't you see? Even my father's murder."

At that moment I realized that he was the son of Louis of Orléans, whose murder my father had described the winter of the leopard.

"My brother is still in the hands of the English, but no one seems in the least concerned."

Charles of Orléans had taken up arms to avenge his father and he had been held prisoner ever since the debacle at Agincourt.

Thus the man whose acquaintance I had just made was the famous bastard of Orléans, Joan of Arc's companion and a valiant captain whose feats of arms were renowned throughout the land. I liked his blue eyes, his youthful air. There is always something very direct about soldiers, which may be due to their familiarity with administering death. To strike someone, even in battle, one must cast off the weight of a civilization that confines most of us to falseness and forced gentility. Once this screen is removed, man's true nature is revealed. Most of the time, only coarse men emerge from this bur, with the violent nature of roughneck soldiers. But now and again, stripped of any social artifice, a simple, almost tender nature can appear, a pure soul with the sensibility of a child, and the tactful manners ordered by a sincere respect for others. This was the impression made on me by the young man who, for some time longer, would be called the bastard of Orléans. When he took his leave I felt as if I had discovered a precious stone in the mire of that court.

*

But I was no further along for all that. Once the time for celebration was over, life in Paris once again became what it had been all during these last years: violence and hardship. Everything was rare and expensive, starting with food, and all the more so because there was still fighting around the capital, as the bastard of Orléans had informed me. I had written to Ravand to ask him to send me what I needed for coin making, but I had not yet received any response. I hoped at least to have some time before the first monetary production was demanded of me. One morning, no more than four days after I had moved into the workshop, two carts stopped outside, escorted by the provost's guards. They were filled with objects to be melted. There were cartloads of candlesticks, dishes, and jewelry, and the guards were piling them in the middle of the courtyard. A cluster of onlookers, their faces hostile, were watching this delivery. I learned somewhat later that the king, in thanks for the triumphant welcome he had received, had ordered that the confiscations take effect immediately. Churches were looted, private homes were raided, and anyone caught trying to hide their wealth risked their head.

All I could hope was that the battered city would not have much left to be requisitioned. As for everything that had already been taken and piled up at my workshop, I must set about melting it as quickly as possible.

Fortunately it turned out that Roch, the old worker, was a skilful foreman. He knew many of the former employees of the workshop who had deserted for lack of work. By the end of the week there were over a dozen of us, including the apprentices and guards. We made use of the old molds, by altering the inscriptions: Charles VII replaced Henry VI. Our makeshift effort resulted in *Chenrl VII*, but in all likelihood no one would take offense.

Our alloys were not very precise and the coins we produced did not look like much. As a merchant I would willingly have attempted to manufacture a higher standard of currency. I was convinced that the quality of its coin was necessary for a country to inspire confidence and attract the best merchandise. But du Châtel had implied that he hoped to see the profit of this activity without delay, and I could not meet his expectations without resorting to Ravand's underhanded formula.

By the end of the month my workshop was functional. I delivered sizable quantities of coins to the royal treasury, and kept enough to pay my employees and myself. I had become a person of some importance. I avoided going to court, where I would have been overwhelmed with requests for loans or assistance. That did not prevent people from visiting me for the same reasons.

Never had I seen so much wealth and poverty side by side as in Paris. Aristocrats felt obliged to show off, because the city now had the honor of being the capital. In spite of the filth and poverty all around, they continued to live in grand style in those palaces which Eustache had described to me all those years ago. But in order to receive guests in style with torchlight and chandeliers, they would go five days a week without supper. The women had more face paint than food. Starving carcasses were clothed in silk and velvet. In spite of the appetite this lifestyle was beginning to awaken in me, I effortlessly turned away any number of opportunities. All I had to do, when I saw a woman headed eagerly my way, was to see her withered bosom, her missing teeth, the scurf on her décolleté covered in powder, to feel all temptation vanish. Never had I known such a strange mixture of extreme luxury and utter decline. In Bourges we were more or less well off, but no one would have endangered his health for the sole benefit of superfluous appearances.

Thus, in spite of myself, I quickly acquired a reputation for virtue.

Roch, my old foreman, did not leave the workshop. He slept in a shed at the back of the courtyard. And yet, inexplicably, he knew everything that was going on in the city. He was the one who, one morning, brought me the latest rumor: the king was going to leave again. The people of Paris did not know what to make of this decision. On the one hand, they were proud to be the capital once again, proud to have their monarch staying there. On the other hand, Charles and his entourage had treated them not as loyal subjects but as a defeated populace, with a harshness even the English had not shown them.

And as for me, I did not know either what this departure implied. Was I to follow the king? And if so, where? Or should I remain alone in this hostile city, where I felt like a stranger? I had gone no further in my conjectures when, one evening shortly before nightfall, I received a visit from a strange character. He was a hideously deformed dwarf who went about in carnival clothing. He was followed by a horde of children who jeered at him. He sent for me, and introduced himself with astonishing self-confidence for someone who had been so afflicted by nature. In truth, if one disregarded his size and his deformity, he lacked neither daring nor nobility. I had heard about these royal dwarves who lived in the society of the highly ranked and adopted their manners, but this was the first time I had been granted the privilege of meeting one of them. He told me his name was Manuelito, that he came from Aragon, and after having served several masters he was now in the personal service of King Charles. No doubt his mission was to distract the king, but he spoke gravely to me. He hoisted himself onto a chair and we had a very serious conversation.

He started by announcing the most important thing: the king wished to see me again, that very night. Manuelito insisted that his master wanted this audience to remain secret. He was surrounded by noblemen who, under the guise of serving him, were actually keeping him prisoner and scrutinizing his every act and deed. He explained how we would proceed so that no one would know of my visit.

We then spoke about Paris, and he confirmed that the king intended to leave the city. He had never liked it there. He continued to be haunted by the memory of the ill-fated night when he had had to flee to escape slaughter by the Burgundians. Ever since he arrived in Paris he hardly slept and was prey to debilitating anxiety. Manuelito then took great liberty in describing the court to me. He explained that the princes were now demanding retribution from the king for their support. If they had helped him to defeat the English it was first and foremost for their own benefit. If the king were to grant them what they wanted, the kingdom he had just reunited would immediately be dismembered. These feudal lords wanted to be their own masters, and the king would be subject to their will.

"And what does the king want?"

"To reign."

"But he is so weak and indecisive."

"Don't be mistaken! He may be weak, and even that is a subject for debate. But he is not at all indecisive. The man has a will of iron. He is capable of overcoming all obstacles."

I was grateful to Manuelito for confirming what my intuition had begun to suspect. To conclude, he urged me to defy everyone. I do not know whether this devilish man had his spies and knew something. He was referring to the noblemen who would surely come to solicit me, and warned me against any temptation I might have to help them.

"Anything that reinforces them weakens the king. If they are in such a needy position today, it is because they are preparing to attack him."

I had a clear conscience and replied calmly that I would refuse to entertain any dishonest compromises. He nodded silently.

That night, at the appointed hour, I went to the Louvre, crossing the Pont-Neuf. I walked along the gutter until I reached the door Manuelito had indicated. The guard let me in without asking anything. My walk through the palace was short. The king was waiting for me in a small room near the entrance. It was in an outbuilding of the guard room, heated by the back of the big fireplace on the other side. There was no furniture in the room, and Charles was standing. He squeezed my hands. He was the same height as me but seemed smaller, because in his close-fitting garment his legs were twisted and remained somewhat bent.

"I am leaving, Cœur. You must stay."

"As you desire, sire. But—"

He waved his hand.

"I know. I know. It won't last. Wait. Be patient. I am no more satisfied than you are to see the way things are going. The fact remains that for the time being I must deal with what is most urgent. I need a great deal of money. I must not depend on them any longer."

From the knowing way he had said these last words, it was clear he knew that I knew about the princes. Manuelito could only have spoken to me on his orders.

"You are doing a dirty work, I am aware of that. Later, for the kingdom, if God grants me the strength, I will proceed differently: we will have a strong and stable currency. For the moment, if I am to survive, what I need is to get out of this city that I despise and which returns the sentiment for all it is worth. You must continue. Do not yield to threats. You will have news from me in due time. Farewell, my friend."

Again he squeezed my hands. I had the impression that he was on the verge of tears. Regardless of what Manuelito might have said, I was still convinced, at that time, of his weakness. And this weakness was all the more repellant to me in that his will, as the jester had said, was strong. I would have given anything to protect him, to provide him with the means to resist and overcome. Thus, I agreed to stay in Paris despite his absence.

*

The king and his retinue departed from the city the following week. He left a small garrison behind. But it was clear that, in the absence of the sovereign and his army, those who represented him in Paris were in great danger. The city was subject to riots, to great popular uprisings and intrigue among the burghers, and periods of calm were always precarious and deceptive. My position aroused individual envy, and collectively it marked me out for general hatred. Was it not to my workshop that every day the bounty seized from the city in the name of the king was delivered? I was obliged to reinforce the guards around the workshop and arrange for heavily armed escorts to accompany the coin-filled coffers I sent to the king. We had to fight off an attack in the middle of the night, and never discovered who had planned it. I had no difficulty finding a house near the workshop to rent, given the number of empty, boarded-up ones in the vicinity. I engaged an aging cousin of Roch's to serve me. Two mastiffs in the courtyard tasted my food to thwart poisoning.

I had time to take stock, painfully, of my present situation, and a surprise visit from Jean de Villages further stimulated my thoughts. Between two missions he came to Paris to bring me news of our business, which was prospering. Jean had appointed agents or simple correspondents in fifteen towns or more. He managed to ship cloth, gold, leather, and many other goods throughout the realm, as far as England and the Hanseatic League. Guillaume had sent a second shipment to the Levant, and was expecting the return of the first one soon. Our profit was considerable. The agents, once they had taken their own pay, were ordered to reinvest the surplus. Jean was suntanned from riding from town to town. I could see the adventure thrilled him—the element of risk, the success. In spite of the uncertainty of the highways, he had lost only one delivery, and even then, with his mercenaries, they had given chase and recovered from the thieves a booty equivalent to what had been stolen. I gave him all the surplus cash that our coin-making activities had allowed me to put aside, in order that he could use it to increase our purchasing power, and he went on his way. He left me feeling very dejected. I felt as if I had made a fool's bargain. My aim in approaching the king had been to place our enterprise under his protection, and allow it to flourish according to my own ambitions for it. Instead, the king had granted me a partial favor, which, even if it was provisional, nevertheless took me away from my own business. While my partners could enjoy the wind on the road or the salt spray on the sea, I was shut away in a pestilent city melting spoons and sharing my food with mastiffs.

And I was far away from my family. Macé wrote to me; she was totally absorbed by the children, and she gave me their news. I made sure she always had plenty of money. This was the beginning of an unequal and fatal exchange: for my absence and distance I paid a price that seemed sufficiently high to atone for my sins. Thus, material consideration gradually replaced feeling. But while the weights might be comparable in quantity, in quality they were no such thing. And yet even at the time I realized this, and I felt guilty. As time passed, and other presences came to make up for the absence of my family, however imperfectly, I would be less concerned.

I have already said that there were ample opportunities to betray Macé. And I was not lacking in desire. But the two never came at the same time. Until the day I had a visit from Christine.

She had come upon the workshop by chance, or at least that is what she said. Her story was heartbreaking. The daughter of an excellent family, well-educated, she had found herself orphaned after the epidemic of smallpox that had stricken the city a few years earlier. In despair, she had yielded to the advances of one of her distant cousins who wanted to marry her. She consented, although she did not like him. She referred to her own taste by lowering her eyes in a charming way, and blushing. To confess that she might have preferences in the matter was to reveal that she had desires, and the nuns had convinced her that this was evil . . .

The couple settled into a house in the street next to my

workshop. Alas, her husband had greatly compromised himself with the English and so he had fled with them, but not before promising to send help. He asked her to stay in Paris to keep an eye on their property. She would quickly discover that he had lied. Creditors came to her door, and she could not honor their demands. Her house was about to be seized along with all her belongings. She told me all this with great dignity, or should I say, in hindsight, with great mastery. I thought she must be no more than twenty years of age. Her beauty was perfect, humble, and modest, but when she looked up, and deep into my eyes, she lit a fire which my vanity drove me to believe was shared.

I was occupying an entire house on my own. I stammered a suggestion that she move into the upstairs while waiting for her situation to become clearer. She accepted after an appropriate hesitation.

Two days later, a late winter storm shook the house at night. The wind blew open the windows and hurled tiles into the street. In the middle of the night, Christine let out a scream. I thought something terrible had happened and I rushed to her room. I found her lying on the floor, trembling, prey to an intense terror. Sobbing, she explained that the thunder brought back terrible memories. I stayed with her. Unaware of the fact that she was making a great effort to convey as much to me, I assumed she would only find peace in my arms. Like most men, I was eager to find it natural for a woman to desire my protection, and from this vanity I drew the strength to comply. The moment I put my arms around her, Christine calmed down and her breathing became more regular, until a new source of agitation seized her. Filled with ridiculous pride at having rescued her, I was overcome with desire. We became lovers, and although there were no more storms, I returned nightly to her bedchamber.

Through this relation I discovered a carnal pleasure I had

never known with Macé. The clandestine nature of our situation surely had something to do with it. But it must be said that Christine, despite her young age, seemed to possess a level of experience which Macé, married as a virgin to me when I was equally inexperienced, could not hope to attain. In addition to sensual delight, Christine also brought a great deal to stimulate my mind. Until then I had been filled with grandiose dreams, but they were only dreams; as for myself, I was nothing, and I was aware of this. From the beginning, my in-laws had made it clear that they were reluctant to consent to our marriage, and that my condition was inferior. Nothing I had accomplished thus far would ensure me of the distinction that could have offset the deficiencies of my birth.

And now, for the very first time, with my return from the Levant, the creation of our business, and the king's favor, another destiny seemed possible—one which, without yet assuming the grandeur of my dreams, could nevertheless tear me away from the modest condition of my early life. I began to notice a new consideration in the eyes of all those who had never acknowledged me, and who now approached me in Paris. Christine incorporated this admiration into my private life. With her youthful simplicity, she applied herself to making me understand how much she respected me. There was nothing, not even my lack of experience in love, that she did not manage to turn to my advantage, by praising my rapid progress and the natural instinct that allowed me to fulfill her most secret desires. In short, I was happy, or at least I believed myself to be. Thanks to Christine, I forgot the tedium of my chores, and was able to put up with the city and all its inconveniences. I found the energy to turn down all the self-serving invitations I received. In a word, I had the impression that of all of the benefits that good fortune had begun to bestow on me, Christine was the most precious.

The situation altered abruptly because of an event that had

on the surface seemed minor but had turned out to be highly significant: I hired a new valet. Since returning from the Levant, I had no personal servants. I had hired guards, a cook, and chambermaids, but a valet—who shares one's everyday life, knows one's most intimate secrets and takes charge of delicate errands—I had not had such a servant since Gautier's departure. The good fellow considered that he had done enough traveling, and had gone back to his village. I needed someone new. As usual, I consulted with Roch, my foreman. He gave it some thought and recommended Marc, one of his nephews.

The aforementioned Marc showed up one morning, his eyes puffy and his complexion waxy. It was obvious that he had not spent the night in a totally honest manner. I have never been satisfied with first impressions, particularly when dealing with rascals. They are a varied species, and, if one pays attention, one can find in them all the best aspects of humanity. The world of crime concentrates a great deal of intelligence, boldness, loyalty, and, dare I say, idealism. Provided these qualities are not spoiled by too great a portion of lying, violence, and fabrication, they can prove extremely useful. For myself, I have been better served in life by people I dug out of the lower depths than by any number of allegedly honest individuals: only cowardice kept them from committing the worst sorts of crime, and often their only merit was to temper vice with fear.

Marc did not even try to hide the fact that he had an introduction to all the *écorcheurs* in town. The only true question was why he wanted to change his station in life. I asked him. With an obvious knack for saying the right thing, he explained that times had changed. Paris was no longer a place for riots, massacres, and usurpation—from this I gathered that he did not hold the English in high esteem. Henceforth, in the capital, there would be more to be gained by being honest. He implied that in his opinion I represented the sort of new fortune one could aspire to, through royal power. I might have every reason to fear that he only wanted to enter my service to rob me. After all, if he was still connected to a group of thugs, he could be their man on the inside and open every door. I wagered the contrary, and told myself that if he had truly decided to swear allegiance to my person, he would go about it with all the conscientiousness of his bandit soul and I could not dream of a more loyal servant. As it turned out, my wager was well founded. Marc would stay with me until my escape, and if I owe him my life today it is because, in order to save me, he forfeited his own.

I took him into my service that very day. Christine did not let anything show on first encountering him. But that evening, as soon as we were alone in her room, she begged me not to hire him. To convince me she cried and wept, perhaps too much, and this excessive display made me think that she must have other grievances against this stranger that she preferred to keep secret. I decided for once not to give in to her. Marc stayed.

I would have many years ahead to observe him and understand him. His acts were always appropriate, his judgment was clear, and his hunches correct. But I gradually discovered that all of these qualities stemmed from an extremely simple vision of the world. In Marc's opinion, men were men, and women were women. What I mean is that he thought there could be no man, no matter how serious or powerful, who would not lose his head over a pretty girl, provided she knew which weapons to use to reduce him to her mercy. And there could be no woman, no matter how honest, faithful, and virtuous, who was not capable of the worst folly for a man, if she thought he could awaken in her that volcano of desires which she must cover with ash against her will. This certainty gave him his own vision of the human race, seen through their weaknesses and desires. He never based his opinions on appearance alone, and was rarely impressed by the ramparts of gravity or virtue which people could raise around themselves. I deduced that in his former occupation he was probably neither a brigand nor a robber, but in all likelihood had been specialized in the commerce of young women.

From the moment he saw her he detected in Christine everything my foolishness had blinded me to, and she sensed the threat. I waited to see what would come of their confrontation. Each one led his or her own inquiry, and in the days that followed revealed horrible things to me regarding the other. Christine attacked first, and gave me precise information regarding Marc's former employ. She said she had obtained the information by bribing the wife of an innkeeper in the neighborhood, whose establishment turned into a gaming house at night. Everything she told me about my valet was entirely true. But he had already confessed as much to me. She was very disappointed to see that my opinion about him did not change.

It took a bit longer for him to tell me about her. What I learned was grave, but the fact that she had hidden it from me was graver still. According to Marc's inquiries, Christine was not the daughter of a family of means, but a duke's bastard. She had been raised by her mother, who was in service as a chambermaid to the duchess of Burgundy, and through imitation she had acquired the manners of a world to which she did not belong. After her mother's death, she had preferred to make use of her charms rather than go into service. She had fallen under the influence of a scoundrel with whom she had a daughter. The child was with a nurse in Pontoise. Her youth, beauty, and education enabled Christine to hunt for prize game. In the beginning, her protector had offered her to rich men who used her in full awareness of her station, and paid for her. Later on, she found it more lucrative to hide her true identity, and to simulate passion for men who were capable of ruining themselves for her. A magistrate from the Parliament had hanged himself two years earlier, leaving her a considerable sum of money. Thanks to the turbulent times, she always managed to disappear, only to return under a new identity. Her real name was Antoinette.

This revelation was like a thrust from a dagger. It is hard for me to say what was most painful—to find out that I had been betrayed? To see the metamorphosis of my beloved? To discover the banal nature of a story I thought was unique? Or perhaps, above all, to endure the disappointment of watching the self-esteem that love had given me disappear for good?

My first reaction, obviously, was to cast doubt on Marc's defamations. He was expecting this.

"Do not humble yourself by seeking to verify what I say," he advised. "It is all true. If you really want to know who you are dealing with, there is a very simple way."

To be clear in my mind, at his suggestion I conceived the ultimate test, which would enable me to obtain a definitive judgment regarding Christine-Antoinette. I informed her that I would soon be leaving on a short journey for four days. She asked me a few questions about the house, and I left her all the keys, including those to the coffers. This was a somewhat perfidious way to tempt her, but I wanted the test to be thorough. In order to give her free rein, I informed her that Marc would be going with me. And while I did indeed go as far as Versailles, my valet stayed behind to set the trap. The second night after my departure, Antoinette's protector arrived with a cart and three armed men. Marc had set a guard all around the house and, confident for once of his rights, he had placed the public watchmen on the alert. They waited until the coffers were opened and the first money boxes removed before they intervened. All the brigands ended up in jail. But at my request, Marc regretfully arranged things so that Christine could disappear without being harassed. After that, he invited his companions to drink to my health.

I never saw Antoinette again.

III.

Argentier to the King

That is how my adventure with Christine ended, a tragic farce. But she left a greater mark on me than I would have thought. I came away with an instinctive and enduring mistrust of women. I had always thought I despised the ones who sought me out for venal reasons; now I preferred them. From now on, nothing seemed more suspicious to me than disinterested love. I had to accept the facts: my prosperity, particularly in an era of great poverty, had made me an object of desire and intrigue. Anyone who tried to delude me into believing the contrary would only arouse my lasting hatred and mistrust. This was unjust, no doubt, to several of the women I met throughout my life whose feelings for me might have been sincere. However, the pain I inflicted by rejecting them always seemed less severe than that which I would have suffered had I allowed myself to be taken in by a new Christine.

There was another lesson I learned, which caused me to pause for a moment on the cusp of the future and compelled me to question my plans: as long as I had lived in my dreams, I had been safe from any mediocrity. I had only the highest ambitions, and as I calculated the way to go about fulfilling those ambitions, my strength was even greater. Ever since I began to convert my dreams to reality, I had become accustomed to wading through the mire of the everyday, through murky swamps of jealousy and covetousness. Jean and Guillaume shouldered their share, and very generously, but I was still left with many of these constraints. I felt a great urge to give it all up and return to the humble life alongside my wife and my children, which, when all is said and done, I deserved.

In truth, what I wanted above all was to leave the capital and the duties that held me there. But to do that would have been to betray the oath I had given the king, and thus to expect nothing more from him other than spite.

So I waited. Christine had merely provided me with additional reasons to despise Paris. Like the city, she was a mixture of refinement and brutality, pleasure and danger, beauty and betrayal, civilization and filth. To be free of the city, I no longer left the workshop, and was completely absorbed by my work. I ordered the king's quartermasters to bring increasing amounts of metal to be melted, although I was well aware that this meant more and more pillaging throughout the city, more tribute seized from the inhabitants, more wounds to the city's already tortured body. And this pained me, in spite of everything, for I could no more find it in me to regret having known Christine than I could help but feel a vague and paradoxical tenderness for this city I wanted so much to leave behind.

If I did not want to endanger my sanity, the situation must not continue as it had. Fortunately, at the beginning of the month of June, a message from the king came to inform me that he was appointing me "steward to the Argenterie," the royal fund for the king's expenditure. I had to leave for Tours at once. The good news was that I would be leaving Paris. It mattered little that it was in order to occupy an unknown and probably subordinate position. By seeking royal favors, had I not embarked on the path of submission? For a moment I was tempted to reject the offer and return to my partners. But an intuition compelled me not to break off relations, and to wait. After all, the king knew my situation and my plans.

Eight days later, I left Paris through the Porte Saint-Jacques. I took two guards as an escort, and Marc. He was afraid of nothing, except horses. It was truly a pleasure to see him pale and trembling, and clinging to the pommel on the saddle the moment his mount began to trot.

I took my time to reach Tours, where the Argenterie was located. I even took the opportunity to go through Bourges. Macé and the children welcomed me tenderly. Jean had grown a great deal. He was pious and extremely well-mannered. He had already decided to take holy orders. Obviously this was his mother's influence, voluntary or not. It was not from me that he inherited such a flawless, complete faith, which lent him a serious air. He had a perpetual little smile, both kindly and haughty, at the corner of his mouth. It was neither the ecstatic grin of saints, nor the absent dreaminess I knew so well, but rather the charitable and scornful grimace worn by religious dignitaries. It was no doubt to obey that same intuition that Macé had decided, if possible, to make a bishop or even a cardinal of him. Over time and with my absence, she had changed. Like a young wine that can either improve with age or turn to vinegar, that side of her that had been secret and taciturn was now neither goodness nor simplicity but rather all social pretension and vanity. My position in Paris, the money I sent her which was now flowing in, the profit from both my royal mandate and the activity of our enterprise—Macé transformed it all into emblems of dignity and success. There are pleasing and generous aspects to success and the way one can display it, with finery, feasts, and excellent fare. But that was not the path Macé had chosen. She was altogether on the side of gravity and austere rigor. Luxury for her meant celebrating mass, going to funerals in full mourning, and at Easter or Christmastime to have boring or wealthy people parade before her, in the secret hopes that she would seem equally prosperous to them, and even more sinister.

She was corresponding with my brother, who had taken orders at last and was in Rome pursuing a career to become a bishop.

I realized how greatly my life of toil in Paris had distanced me from my family. With hindsight, my adventure with Christine seemed more and more beneficial. She had opened my eyes to another world, a world where luxury was allied with pleasure to form an ephemeral couple, both delightful and guilty. It was not that I missed Christine, but rather what she had brought me now provided a permanent counterpoint to what I could see in my good town. In short, a spring had broken: for a long time, Macé and her parents had shown me the road to follow. And I had obeyed their decrees without question. Since my voyage to the Levant, and above all my stay in Paris, that fascination had vanished. It had yielded to a lucidity so sharp it was almost painful. Macé, with her ambition, her desire for respectability, her claims to virtue and honor, now struck me as ridiculous and drearily typical of her class.

At the same time, such needs were easy to satisfy. What mattered to her was that I continue my career in society so that she might aspire to the titles with which fortune would adorn me. And, naturally, money must enable her to display the various stages of our ascension. She wanted houses and servants, gowns and votive offerings, positions for our children and masses sung for her salvation. In return for which she tolerated my absence, more easily in any case than my return. Our carnal ties, which had never been very solid, had practically ceased to exist. If on occasion when passing through Bourges I tried to approach her, I found her more absent than ever. Worse than that, it seemed to me this time that her silence masked prayer, and naturally this chilled my desire. Without going so far as to try the novelties that Christine had led me to discover, even the simple register of ordinary tender gestures between a wife and her husband seemed sinful to Macé, requiring contrition before God. I did not insist. In spite of the discreet sense of guilt that I carried within—because it was my fault, after all, if I had abandoned her—I refused to wallow in regret, still less to change and become, like her, a pious upstart. Thus, I did not extend my stay longer than two brief weeks.

I felt lighthearted on leaving our town. It was as though I had been relieved of a burden. Macé had found her way, which was not mine. But our efforts were complementary. I had left to pursue my dreams, and I produced material goods in spite of myself. Macé transformed them into respectability and a future for the children. Basically, everything was going well.

I had given Marc leave during my stay in Bourges, and now I found him in a cheerful mood. He had made numerous conquests among serving women and streetwalkers. It was as if he were describing another town to me, one I had never had the leisure to explore, a town of sleazy taverns and bordellos, of drinking bouts and promiscuity.

We arrived in Tours in the middle of August, just after the Feast of the Assumption. The city was baking in the heat. I had some difficulty finding the Argenterie. It was a small, windowless building located behind the cathedral. Two soldiers were on guard, dozing in a spot of shade, their shirts open. They sullenly informed me that the Argentier was out of town. In spite of the letter appointing me as steward to the Argenterie, they refused to open it for me.

I took a room in an inn on the banks of the Loire and waited. I was beginning to wonder what the king intended to do. Why had he appointed me to this strange position, which seem to be completely dormant? After gathering some information in town, I learned that this Argenterie served as a warehouse used to store items that were necessary to the court—cloth and draperies, furniture, domestic tools—a royal intendancy of sorts. Having said that, the reality was far less brilliant. Several burghers to whom I had introduced myself and who knew my family told me in confidence what the institution actually represented: the Argenterie was poorly managed, poorly supplied, and rare were those at court who deemed it useful to avail themselves of its supplies. Most of them preferred to buy what was needed—not to mention what was superfluous—directly from merchants. I knew all about this, having been so often solicited for loans.

For lack of anything else to do, I dispatched letters to Jean and Guillaume to ask them to meet me in Tours. It was time to take stock of our situation. I now felt ready to invest wholeheartedly in our business.

While I was waiting for them, the Argentier returned. He was an amiable lord from Tours with a red face. I learned that he had a property near Vouvray and was more interested in his vineyards than the Argenterie. He was not pleased to see me there. He did not want someone coming to nose around in his business. The office to which the king had appointed him was certainly very lucrative. In any case, he had obviously opted to promote his own interests rather than those of the Argenterie's putative clients. When he gave me a tour of the warehouses, I was able to judge for myself how low in stock the place was, and how poorly managed. He was initially unwilling to let me inspect the books. While accountancy has never been my profession, I knew enough about it to realize that there were some serious irregularities. Messire Armand, for that was his name, explained unconvincingly that the war had ruined the Argenterie and made it impossible to renew supplies. When an item was available, one must purchase it no matter the price. This was how he justified buying everything at such a high cost.

He told me all this with a smile and a sidelong glance. Visibly he was trying to explain his system to me and to make me go along with it—that way we would share out the profits from his little arrangements. He did not like the idea, but he preferred it to the prospect of losing everything if I were to reveal his misdeeds.

I observed all this with more pity than covetousness.

The weeks that followed were very calm. During the August heat activity had slowed everywhere and at the Argenterie more than anywhere else. Nothing happened in September, either. Messire Armand tended to his vineyards, and then he enjoyed the prime hunting days. The king and his court were far away, and nothing indicated that they would be coming anywhere near Tours anytime soon. Thus, winter would not be very active either. I spent my time going for long walks along the river. Now I knew that all this water led to the sea, and the sea led to the East. Standing by this liquid expanse, I felt a communion with the entire world. It was a welcome pause after the turmoil of the previous months. I spent many hours in the warehouse, most of the time alone. Under the pretext of doing an inventory, while I went through moth-eaten bolts of cloth or dried-out leather hides, I pondered what might be done to gain something from this Argenterie. It must have been useful at one time, in an era of greater splendor. Could it not be so once again? Perhaps that was the king's secret intention. The more I thought about it, the more it seemed that something might be possible. At the very least, supposing I were to become the Argentier, the Argenterie could be a client of prime importance for the trading house we were still in the process of building. And I felt it must surely be possible to go even further.

*

Guillaume arrived in early autumn and Jean joined us a week later. I rented a house for the three of us on a hillside among the vineyards. The Touraine, with its clear skies and legendary rolling landscape, was conducive to long strolls, interminable meals, and evenings spent chatting with our feet stretched toward the fire made with vine branches that Marc lit for us.

I quickly realized that my companions took a different view of the situation. They only knew the commercial aspect of our endeavor, and were unaware of the more extensive plans I had conceived. They could not understand exactly why I had approached the king, and they interpreted it as a desire to found our monetary capacity on a solid basis of coin-making. Whatever the case may be, I did not enlighten them, but informed them that I had acquired an exchange bureau on the Pont-Neuf. It was the truth, but it would take years before it actually became operational. I insisted on the present difficulties of life in the capital, and my intention to regain my liberty with regard to the king. They saw this as good news. For as far as they were concerned they had not known any of the hardship that had been my lot in Paris. That was why they were optimistic, and even content. Guillaume had established a very solid commercial base in the Languedoc. He was trading overland with Catholic Catalonia and Spain, with Savoy, and with Geneva. By sea, he was shipping cargo to the Levant and, more regularly, trading with Genoa and Florence. He gave us a detailed account of our assets in the Mediterranean. The merchants in Montpellier and the entire region had grown to know this hardworking, audacious little man from the Berry. Everything was ready, henceforth, for us to start building our own ship. Guillaume had been counting on our meeting to gain our approval for this important decision.

As for Jean, he arrived in the oddest style. The brigands who composed his guard had tied him to his saddle so that he could stay on without having to move his legs. He had received a bad blow to his thigh during an ambush, and his wound was still oozing pus. This incident had not slowed him down; on the contrary, he drank and ate slightly more than usual. His meals would have made any other man gain weight. But he burned it up with his incessant activity. Even in his sleep, when he was resting in the room next to mine, I could hear him move around and call out. The results he obtained were in keeping with his efforts. On every road there were carts transporting the goods he had picked out. He now had correspondents and suppliers in all the major production centers.

Since the Treaty of Arras, the atmosphere of freedom and enthusiasm that reigned in France facilitated commerce. The war had lasted so long that each region had set about manufacturing what it needed. Wherever you went—taking the good years with the bad—you could find food, clothing, and drink. But there was an immense desire for things that came from far away. Women were weary of seeing everyone clothed in the same locally manufactured fabrics, and dreamt of something different. When an item of food or clothing came from somewhere else it was immediately in demand.

France, particularly in the north and the center, was still a war-ravaged country. It was still swarming with armed gangs who looted the countryside and held the towns for ransom. The situation had not returned to normal, far from it. And the populace, in truth, had almost forgotten what the word "normal" meant. War had gone on for so long that it was part of everyday life. All it took was for the conflict to die down for a while and even the slightest improvement was experienced as well-being, almost mistaken for happiness.

Many of the merchants had understood that the situation was now much improved. However, most of them were still discouraged by persistent difficulties. In general they were content to deal with one product or another, but very few had decided, as we had, to exchange everything that could be bought or sold. I was fairly proud of my intuition. It was clear to me that what mattered was to create a network, with relays and roads, and through this network to transport everything that might find a buyer. Jean had shown insight in relying on armed force to ensure the safety of our shipments. Guillaume's contribution had been to link the north to the south of the realm, and to prepare an opening for the future throughout the Mediterranean and the Levant. As for me, I had put at their disposal the network of moneychangers with whom my name would open every door. The first stage of our project was a success.

During those September days, we made some vital decisions. I convinced my partners that we must concentrate our efforts in the Levant. Guillaume had prepared the conditions for our presence in the eastern Mediterranean. Yet the region remained dangerous. Safety was the final obstacle to overcome. We agreed that Jean should go to Montpellier and arrange for his soldiers to protect the cargo. In an initial phase, we would send our ships no further than Italy, but then gradually we would extend their navigational range to include the ports of the Levant.

Meanwhile, during this time Guillaume would head north to organize the network of convoys that Jean had made possible, thanks to the contacts he had established and the escorts who now ensured the safety of the roads. I intended to join them soon, and to devote all my time to our enterprise. But first of all I must approach the king one last time to ask him to release me and assure him of my fealty.

Jean and Guillaume went their way. I addressed a request for an audience to the court and began to wait. It was a pleasant winter, the last one which I would spend if not in idleness at least in anonymity. Much of the time I was in nature. Almost every day I went for long, solitary walks through the forests and vineyards. I had never before had the opportunity to live like this in the country. By observing nature, I understood what had hitherto been a mystery to me. Why did I like luxury? For what deeper reason had I been fascinated for so long by the decoration of fine homes, the shimmering of cloth, the harmonious arrangement of palaces? These attachments were not the result of necessity. I did not care where I lived, and I felt at home in the humblest house. The moment I no longer had to put on airs, I removed my luxurious clothing and dressed in a simple homespun tunic. So if I liked luxury and admired the skill of craftsmen, architects, and goldsmiths, it must be for a more subtle and less visible reason. In truth, I like and admire everything the human mind creates to allow our dwellings to resemble nature. The gold of autumn leaves, the blackish brown colors of plowed fields, the whiteness of snow, the infinitely varied blues of the sky are taken away from us by walls; we are deprived of them by the covering of our roofs, the barrier of our wooden shutters, the curtains that hem us in. Art is the only way we can restore to our confined decor these riches that nature gives for free, and from which we have become detached.

This was what I discovered, and I felt reassured. In short, I believed in humankind, in its capacity to provide us with new creations that paid tribute to those originally given to us by nature. The talent of artists, the art of architects, the skill of craftsmen all find their highest expression in luxury, and their potential for growth in wealth. These are not, for all that, futile passions. On the contrary, they constitute mankind's highest achievements, the ones which make us equal to gods, by making us masters, creators of new worlds. After so much suffering and destruction, the time had come to favor this other aspect of humankind, which can be as creative as it is destructive. Without realizing it, I had imposed this very orientation on our enterprise, and my partners now considered it to be self-evident: we might be merchants, but we were not dealing in everyday products. You would never see us transporting flour or selling cattle or cheese. The only foodstuff that might interest us—and we had talked about it—was salt, and we had to view it as symbolic. We were interested in those additional little things that give taste to what is bland, anything that would differentiate a human feast from an animal one. The salt of the earth . . .

Everything else we transported across the surface of the globe would be the best human creativity had to offer. Silks from Italy, wool from Flanders, amber from the Baltic, gemstones from Le Puy, fur from cold forests, spices from the Orient, porcelain from Cathay: we would be the priests in charge of a new form of worship celebrating the genius of humankind.

As I walked along the rough trails on the chalky hillsides overlooking the Loire, I was absorbed more than ever by my dream. That dream, however, now took on the vivid hues of real objects, as though, through our endeavor, they might stride right out into the world.

*

The signal I was waiting for came at the end of winter. The king summoned me to Orléans, where his States-General were being held. No one would miss me in Tours. While I had been staying there, my somewhat vague identity had not enabled me to find my place among the various clans in the town. The noblemen still looked on me as a burgher, and the burghers were wary of those who held royal office, no matter how humble. Had I been more powerful, no one would have taken these differences into consideration. I would have ample opportunity to realize this at a later point. But my private wealth and my duties at the Argenterie were not in harmony. My wealth was already considerable, though not very visible. My royal office was quite obvious, but showed that I was subordinate. I did not mind the mistrustful quarantine imposed on me by the nobles; it allowed me to mingle with the peasants whenever my strolls outside the town led me past farms or hamlets. I occasionally spent entire afternoons in the company of bevies of young girls as they washed the laundry, their bare feet in the cool waters of a brook. I watched as they wielded the wooden carpet beater. I liked to see their strong teeth, the pink glow of their youthful flesh. No matter how high I would rise later on, I always knew I belonged to the common folk, that I shared their thoughts and suffering, but also their health and life force. God knows how many palaces I have seen in my life, how many sovereigns I have visited. These were mere polite calls, like those one pays a stranger when one is eager to go home. And for me, home meant the people, the herd of simple folk.

I let Marc intervene on my behalf, and extended these outings to purely carnal adventures with peasant girls. They behaved very naturally in my company. I attained my greatest victory and the certainty of greatest pleasure when, completely forgetting my fortune and connections, they joked with me as with a comrade. Wiser for my misadventure with Christine, I sought only pleasure and amusement, and no longer invested in any of the illusions of love.

I left all this regretfully, fully aware that soon a page would be turned that would make another man of me, and for a long time.

Orléans was in turmoil with the crowd of delegates gathered for the States-General. I found the king on the second floor of a large building opposite the cathedral. The changes in him were striking. He seemed to have cast off the solitude that had surprised me during our previous meetings. The first time, it was an absolute solitude, in the obscurity of an empty hall; the second time, it was the pathetic isolation of a man encircled by an invasive, obsequious yet hostile court. In Orléans, there were none of the persons of rank I had seen in Compiègne. They disliked the atmosphere of the States-General, redolent with the vapors of the common people, the burghers, and the petty nobility. And the mistrust which had come between the king and the princes incited them to stay on their estates, to prepare, perhaps, to confront him. Or at least that is what I thought the moment I noticed their absence.

Yet the king was not alone by any means. The court still buzzed around him, but it was composed of new people. These were younger men, less bellicose, and most of them were burghers by birth. They did not wear that expression of aggression, indignation, and scorn which the great lords deemed indispensable if they were to demonstrate their difference from the rest of the human race. The atmosphere that reigned in the king's rooms was lighter, happier. I would not have been able to say how I could sense this change, but it was clearly perceptible. Far from looking at me as if I were an intruder, the men I met on my way to the audience greeted me amiably. They were dressed in civilian clothing, with none of the symbols of military or ecclesiastical rank that the great lords never failed to display. As a result, it was impossible to know what anyone did. It was like a gathering of friends who refrained from imposing any reminder of their position or duties on others.

The attitude of these men toward the king resembled my own feelings with regard to him: neither servile submission, nor a desire to dominate in the manner of the great lords. The king reigned over them through his weakness and inspired in them the same urge to serve and protect which I myself had felt at our first meeting in Bourges. I had observed the sovereign's conduct with others, and that enabled me to better understand my own reactions in his regard. His lopsided walk, the hesitant, awkward movements of his long arms, the expression of painful weariness on his face—his entire attitude might be interpreted as a call for help. When one of the men in his entourage pulled out an armchair for him, it was not an obsequious assault; rather, the gesture was a sign of sincere pity, a charitable eagerness, of the kind one feels when responding to the shouts of the drowning by holding out a board for them to cling to.

What was new for me was that as I observed these reactions

in others it became blindingly clear to me how much the king enjoyed provoking them. To be sure, he was by no means vigorous or serene by nature. But with a bit of effort, he could have proven himself respectably average with regard to his physical capabilities and sangfroid. I was convinced now that it was through choice that he had decided not to compensate for his flaws but rather to accentuate them. Convinced he would not be able to reign with force and authority, he had chosen the rigorous option of striving to do so through weakness and indecision. In themselves, such traits of character were unimportant. However, I immediately saw the inherent danger. His pretensions to fragility and the appearance of fear so knowingly cultivated on his face stemmed from a constant effort. Charles put as much energy into seeming weak as others did to maintain their reputation of invincible strength. This meant two things, equally dangerous. First of all, he was not fooled by the attentiveness shown him. He knew how artificial its origins were, and could conceive of nothing but scorn for the men on whom he imposed an image of himself that was so contrary to the truth. Secondly, in order to remain in character and ensure his constant respect of such a restrictive vow, he had to exert extraordinary resolve. Anyone who can be so cruel to himself is bound to be equally cruel to others. He had shown in the past—by having his favorites eliminated, by covering in disgrace the very people who had served him most loyally—that he was capable of the most unexpected changes of heart. Naturally, he had passed them off as acts of weakness, letting others think that he lacked the energy to oppose those who plotted against him. Now I was certain that in fact he had conceived of them himself. I no longer doubted that it was as dangerous to serve him as to navigate among shoals. In spite of everything, the day I arrived in Orléans, when at last he turned his weary blue-eyed gaze to me, and called to me, holding out his hands, I hurried over, utterly disarmed, already eager to obey his will, as helpless as all the others in the presence of such weakness, although I was the last man to believe in it . . .

The king had me sit near him. He introduced a few people to me. Most of them were the new stewards to his reign, men with whom I would share for years the daily duties of affairs of state. And they certainly already knew this, but I did not. I saw only a succession of new faces and names that were still unfamiliar to me. The only one whom I recognized was Pierre de Brézé, who was already renowned in his youth as Joan of Arc's comrade-in-arms, the right-hand man of the former constable. Rumor accused him of having belonged to the little group that had abducted the king's counselor, La Trémoille, a sensual and amoral man. I immediately liked Brézé for his simplicity. No doubt he looked younger than he actually was. He was slim, and only his strong joints—in particular his wrists, scarcely noticeable above his long square hands—denoted the warrior. I recognized in him an eagerness to serve, a pride in defending the weak, and a propensity to defy the powerful, which must have made him easy prey for the king.

Suddenly, the king stood up, and before walking on he grabbed my arm to take me with him. I was startled by the familiarity of his gesture. At the same time, just when I might have thought that by clinging to me the king was giving yet another proof of his weakness, I felt his fingers squeeze my elbow like a vice. Limping and swaying, he dragged me to one side. We took a staircase with worn steps and came out at the back of the building into a service courtyard. Two chained dogs leapt up on seeing us. The king had me sit on a stone bench in the shade of a fig tree. He seemed to enjoy watching the huge hounds struggling against their chains, trying to attack us. The chain broke their momentum and they dropped to their paws, tongues slavering. Their barking, the clanging of their chains, their threatening fangs all seemed to amuse the king and even excite some cruel, brutal strain in him. At the opposite end of the small courtyard two washerwomen, arms bared, were struggling with piles of laundry. Charles stared straight at them, and the sight of the dogs had filled his eyes with a brutal desire. The poor girls looked down and concentrated on their work, giving the king the spectacle of their outstretched rumps and tensed muscles. It is no exaggeration to say that I felt my presence was inconvenient.

The king, however, did count on my presence. However much pleasure he might have derived from contemplating the scenes around him, he maintained sufficient self-control to go on speaking to me gently and questioning me like a sovereign. I would have innumerable opportunities in the years to follow to explore the paradoxes of his tormented nature: even today I still wonder if I truly hate him. At the time, I went no further than to think in passing that it might simply be unwise to love him.

"France is a pigsty, Cœur. What say you?"

He sniggered.

"There is a great deal to be done, sire," I said, loudly enough to make myself heard over the barking dogs.

The king nodded.

"Everything. We are going to do everything, believe me."

The mastiffs grew calmer on hearing our voices. To my astonishment, I saw that the king was tapping his feet, urging them to continue.

"The States-General are asking me to rid the country of the *écorcheurs*. It is a good initiative, what say you?"

"Yes, that would be useful."

"Of course, they did not come up with this on their own. I suggested it to them. But now that they have requested it, I shall be obliged to go through with it. Too bad for our dear princes, who will have to do without their mercenaries . . . "

One of the dogs, exhausted by rage, dropped heavily to the ground and howled in pain. Charles slapped his thighs as he shot ever bawdier looks in the direction of the washerwomen. I had heard a great deal about the king's sensuality, his propensity to accumulate mistresses of all backgrounds. I found it hard to grasp that such nervous weakness could also harbor this carnal appetite. Witnessing this disturbing scene, I understood that the king's tormented nature could lead him to both a terrified immobility, where he shook with the tics he affected in the presence of princes, and a lubricious excitement where violence rivaled vice, as in the behavior he was displaying before me at that moment.

"I am going to reform the Council," he continued. "They will no longer reign in my stead, of that I can assure you."

"They" meant the princes, I understood as much. There was nothing to say. I nodded.

"They have begun uniting against me. Last year, I had my way with them. But they will start again, and this time my son will be sufficiently scatterbrained and ambitious to join them. It does not matter, I shall break them."

A thought occurred to me, which I banished instantly. Noise and violence were Charles's everyday world. While my dreams were calm and spacious, his must be possessed, full of brutality and hatred. The tics that deformed him when he remained still were surely echoes of the storms ravaging his mind. This was why he felt so at ease amidst the barking hounds. However intense their howling might be, it probably never attained the intensity of the howling he heard inside. I was drifting away on these thoughts when he suddenly turned to me.

"We will need a great deal of money, Cœur. Much more than the small profits the mint could ever bring. Do you understand why I have appointed you steward to the Argenterie?"

My plan was to explain to him how the Argenterie and my own enterprise could complement each other. My discussions with Guillaume de Varye had convinced me that with our network of suppliers on the one hand, and orders from the realm on the other, centralized at the Argenterie, we could build an intensely powerful enterprise. But everything we professionals had laboriously imagined, Charles had already seen distinctly long before.

I had not been sure whether he had listened to me during our first meetings or not. Now I saw that not only had he listened, but he had drawn conclusions that far exceeded in boldness anything the men in his entourage might have been capable of conceiving. Thus, just as my pity was beginning to yield to other feelings, where a diffuse fearfulness prevailed, admiration leapt ahead and showed me why I was bound forever to this strange and fascinating king.

"First of all, I appointed you steward so that you could examine everything discreetly and make your plans. Have you done so?"

"Yes, sire."

"In that case, as of today I appoint you Argentier. The good man who currently holds that office will not be pleased, but that is his problem. He did not want to exercise it; he viewed it as a distinction that flattered his honor. As do they all, from finance to the things of war: they do not serve. They serve themselves. All of that is going to change."

I felt like crying out for joy. For I could see that this sudden conclusion would be a point of departure for everything to follow. It's absurd to say this, and perhaps you will not believe me. My spirits soared, as if I had suddenly taken flight. I was filled with great serenity; I was far away from the dogs, the washerwomen, the States-General, and even the king. I could see the caravans altering their route and turning for France. My country would become the center of the world, richer, more prosperous, more enviable than Damascus.

I hardly know how this conversation ended. I think someone came to fetch the king. He left the courtyard skimming the perimeter of the dogs' chains; their jaws were snapping not an inch away from the sovereign's legs. I could hear his laughter as he went up the echoing stairway. I was dead to my first life, and now as I watched the sun filtering through the thick downy leaves of the fig tree I felt like a newborn opening its eyes onto a new light.

*

In the sun of Chios my skin has turned brown. Elvira came back from Easter Mass this morning full of joy. On this Greek island that knows no winter, Christmas is hardly a festivity. Resurrection, however, sets hearts ablaze.

During the long nights we spend without sleeping, Elvira has taught me a few words of Greek. These seeds may have fallen on a mind long fallow, but they have caused some very old seeds to sprout, seeds planted long ago by our teacher of catechism at the Sainte-Chapelle in Bourges, so that now I am beginning to understand and express myself.

Only two days ago, I would have said that this was happiness. Alas, yesterday everything changed in an instant.

At the end of the morning, while Elvira was at the market fetching our weekly supply of lemons and garlic, a man came to the house. Fortunately, I saw him from a distance. I had just enough time to hide under the roof where Elvira dries the herbs she picks from the hillside. The man walked around the house. He called out to see if anyone was at home. I was slightly reassured to hear him speaking Greek, because my pursuers, whoever they are, have no reason to know the language. But he might also be an accomplice, recruited on the spot.

He went into the house and began walking around the room, opening the cupboards and moving things. I was afraid he might see my writings and take them away with him. But if he saw them, he was not interested; I found them where I had left them.

When Elvira came home, I was still somewhat stunned by the visit. She calmed me down as best she could. And somehow managed to explain what the visitor wanted. Because she had met him on her way back and spoken to him. He was an emissary from the podestà of Genoa who governs the islands. Upon his return from a voyage, the old man had got wind of my presence on the island and subsequent disappearance. The innkeeper had not felt bound by his promise of silence, since he was answering to the master of the island. When he found out where I was staying, the podestà sent his messenger to inquire after my health.

I don't believe a word of these explanations. It is surely a trap. Those who are looking for me must have found a way to convince the podestà to hand me over. If, as I suppose to be the case, my murderers are the envoys of Charles VII, I do not doubt that the good king has deployed every means at his disposal to capture me. Yet I was the one who, once upon a time, brought him the alliance with Genoa. He will know how to reactivate it to have me eliminated. I recognize his absence of scruples, the ardent hatred that I had learned to tolerate. I adapted to such perversity for as long as it targeted other men. Who would ever have thought that one day it would be my turn to be its victim?

But Elvira had a happy surprise in store for me: she had the presence of mind to tell the messenger that I had died. What I fear is that the podestà might send his people to verify what she said; in any case, since now anyone can find my hiding place, I am no longer safe. At least Elvira's lie will have allowed me to gain some time.

This morning she left for a village on the western coast, isolated in a small bay surrounded by cliffs, where one of her cousins lives. She will try to see with that fisherman how I might sail with him to another place. I have heard that a day's sail from here there are two small islands that belong to Venice. I would be safe there, provided there is enough fresh water to survive. Ever since Elvira spoke to me of these havens all I dream of is settling there. I have been the richest man in the West. I have lost count of the number of castles and estates which are still my property, yet I have but one concern: to find out whether there is enough fresh water so that I might live naked on a desert island . . .

Elvira made me promise to take her with me. I don't know what she imagines. No doubt she sees this flight, after all, as the first stage of an escape. I wonder whether, on carrying out the errands I ask of her, she has not learned too much about me. I greatly preferred the time when she looked on me as an unfortunate fugitive. I would not like the notion of my wealth to disturb the simple happiness I feel here with her. Life has taught me that money can transform even the simplest creatures. Nothing and no one can resist it, except perhaps those who, like myself, have surrendered to it completely and have seen its charms fade. Only money can deliver one from money. Elvira, as she has been getting to know me, has started having dreams that she does not share but which, I am sure, lead her toward dangerous desires for finery and worldly goods.

How can I explain to her that, while I might want to go on living, I no longer have the strength to recapture a place in the world? In truth, I am not seeking to escape. How can I explain what I feel? This unexpected stop at Chios has transformed me. On disembarking on the island, my intention had been to continue on my way. These days of writing and idleness have completely removed any desire to go further. My only hopes and fears concern this story of mine: I'm afraid I might not be able to finish it. If I am trying to save something, it is neither my life nor my future, but this work I took up quite by chance, and which now seems to me the most necessary task.

Given the point I have reached in my story, one might think it is futile to go on. After all, the day the king appointed me Argentier and named me to his court, my life became public. All my deeds were performed before witnesses, and those witnesses, summoned by the prosecutor Dauvet in preparation for my trial, have told all they know. My business, down to the slightest details, is a matter of public record: the immense success of the Argenterie, my three hundred agents all across Europe, the silver mines in the Lyonnais, the galleys which in my name have exchanged so many goods in the Levant, the commerce in salt, the estates bought all over the realm, the loans I have granted to people in high places, the friendship of the Pope and the Sultan, my sons' episcopal sees, my palace at Bourges—it is all known and acknowledged and recorded. I could stop my story here because from this point on my life speaks for me.

But what I feel is just the opposite. During the entire trial this was my greatest despair: to see my life reduced to numbers, property, stones, honors. It was all factual and yet none of that was *me*. Material success was only one aspect of my life. It is not of success that I wish to speak, but of that which troubled my soul for all those years: the passions, the people I met, and the fear, which from that day in Orléans has never left my side.

*

As the sole master of the Argenterie, I gave myself, body and soul, to the work. I wanted to prove myself worthy as purveyor not only to the king, but also to the entire court. The Argenterie must have everything that was needed in store and, above all, everything that was superfluous. I sent orders to all our branches and enjoined Jean and Guillaume to devote themselves for a time to this activity alone. I hired a lot of people. The warehouse in Tours, its doors and windows now flung open, was a beehive of activity. I acquired two more storehouses, one of which I equipped for arms and leather, the other for spices, and I kept the first warehouse for cloth. I worked with my employees from morning to night, in my shirtsleeves and sometimes even, when the heat obliged me to, bare-chested.

One afternoon without warning, the bastard of Orléans came into the leather warehouse. He found me sweating at the top of a ladder and burst out laughing when he saw me. But he was one of those noblemen who prefer the battlefield to the court. He was sharing the life of his men in camp. He concluded I must be doing the same and he treated me like a soldier on campaign. I clothed myself and invited him for a drink in the upstairs rooms of a tavern where I took my meals.

He surely had his own purpose for the visit, but I did not care; I was pleased to see him. Apparently he had come specifically to see me. The conversation was going round in circles, like the initial phases of a battle, and then, finally, he got to the point.

"I came to warn you in person, Cœur. The princes have had it. They ensured the king's victory over the English and now he despises them and treats them without respect. They are going to rebel. And I am going to join them."

"I thank you for your warning," I said tentatively.

He leaned closer and looked me deep in the eyes: "Join us! We need a talented man like you. And we will know how to reward you."

In the words of the bastard of Orléans there was a touching mixture of enthusiasm, as always when he sensed the possibility of battle, of the doubt one could sense behind his too obvious certainties, and of sadness, because he sincerely loved the king. I understood that he was waiting anxiously for my reply, not only because in joining them I would reinforce the camp he had chosen, but also because my decision would shore up his own or, if it was negative, undermine it.

I have never practiced treason, but I have only condemned it weakly, for I know how close it can often be to loyalty. There are moments in life when, faced with the enigma of the world and of the future, any human being can feel torn between a cause and its contrary. The step from one to the other is so small that in an instant one can jump from one side to the other with the ease of a child hopping across a stream.

To relieve him of his difficult identity as an illegitimate child, Charles VII had recently named him Comte de Dunois. The only grievance he had against the king was the monarch's lack of inclination to pay the ransom of his half brother, Charles of Orléans, who had been held prisoner by the English since Agincourt. Dunois, in all honesty, had no liking for his half-brother, who, had he been free, would have looked down on him. But that is the way bastards are: the difficulty of their condition incites them to try everything to obtain recognition from the family in which they were born. Charles of Orléans was writing poetry in London, and Dunois, deep down, did not feel sorry for him. The admiration and recognition he showed the king far surpassed the displeasure he felt on seeing him abandon his half-brother. And yet, out of loyalty to a family that did not love him, he was now preparing to betray his king.

Dunois informed me that the Dauphin, Louis, had joined the conspiracy, as his father had predicted, out of spite at not being granted any privileges. I had not yet met him. One day, in Blois, I had seen his tall, pale-faced form walk across a salon, with a cluster of noisy, boisterous young men in his wake. He cast looks like daggers all around him. It was said that he was a roué, both vain and dissembling, and had since childhood shown signs of the most alarming cruelty.

Dunois insisted on my joining their cause, as it would add

greatly to the conspirators' legitimacy. He complacently drew up a list of their members, which included the majority of the great lords, princes by blood, and dignitaries of the realm. Convinced they had saved the king, they now intended to assert their power by bringing him to ruin.

Dunois's open face awaited my response, eyes wide open, the corner of his lips agitated by a slight tic, which betrayed his impatience. From behind him, through the open window, there rose the smell of hay from a cart that had stopped in the street. It was high summer, a time when nothing seems serious, for it is as if the heat and its attendant pleasure were destined to last forever. I squeezed his hands.

"No, my friend, I cannot bring myself to abandon the king. I have decided to stay loyal to him, whatever the cost."

And I added with a smile, and as much softness as my voice could hold, that I understood him, that I remained his friend and wished him well. He left me, looking vexed, with a warrior's embrace.

In Dunois's presence my resolution had been firm. When I found myself alone, it was another matter. Thus far, there had been times when I was closer to the king, but never so much so as to compromise myself. After my journey to the Levant, I had maintained various friendships that enabled me to hope I might survive and even prosper, no matter the political situation. By accepting the office of Argentier and above all by refusing to join in the princes' rebellion, I had thrown in my lot with the sovereign. But now the conflict that was brewing promised to be as difficult as the one he had fought against the English. He was already in a very bad position, because now he would be fighting the very same men who had made that victory against England possible.

The highly placed individuals who had gone to make up the king's council were now his adversaries. Once again Charles was alone, betrayed by his own people. The situation, which might have discouraged others, was so natural to him that he seemed to adapt to it without a second thought. He immediately appointed a new council, and, to my great surprise, it included me.

The first meeting was held in Angers in a room on the second floor of the château. The atmosphere was strange. While most of the participants were visibly ill at ease, this diminished my own malaise. We could not count on the king to dissipate it. Sitting at the end of the table, his hands clenched, no doubt to hide the trembling, he opened the session, and contrived to bring about long embarrassed silences. There were no princes around the table, and only a few less illustrious noblemen, their first rank including the Constable de Richemont and Pierre de Brézé. The rest were burghers, the very men who, as I had noticed of late on arriving in Orléans, had filled the void around the sovereign. Their expressions were attentive and anxious. One could tell that no hereditary titles legitimized their presence in this place, that they derived that honor solely from their own merit, a quality which, at any moment, they might be called upon to prove. A prince does not have to justify who he is: centuries of history testify on his behalf. He can allow his gaze to wander through the casement, to dream of his mistresses, to think about his next hunting expedition. A burgher must stand ready to prove his usefulness. Next to me, the Bureau brothers were visibly in such a state of mind. They were joking in a low voice, smiling as men who for several months now had been used to being part of this inner sanctum, but their sharp gaze never strayed from the sovereign for long. When he questioned them, their answers came in clear voices. I tried to model my attitude on theirs. This went some way toward helping me forget the tinge of disappointment I had felt when coming in. Once again, when confronted with reality my dreams lost their lightness and mystery. So this was supreme power—this assembly of shabbily dressed men sitting sideways on uncomfortable chairs and trembling in the presence of a leader who had neither grace nor charisma?

And yet over time and my continued participation, the council began to seem different. Its true grandeur lay not in ourselves but in the decisions we made. Something mysterious, which is called power, transformed our ephemeral words into concrete acts with enormous consequences. In the space of only a few months, we made capital decisions. The king intended to make the most of his freedom and of the competence of this new council to implement broad-reaching reforms throughout the kingdom. He followed a methodical plan destined to destroy the power of the princes once and for all, and establish the authority of the monarchy at last.

The first thing to be done, to ensure the effectiveness of our decisions, was to win the war. Hence our priority was to give substance to the permanent army the king had created for himself. If he was to be free of his dependence on the great lords, or the contributions both in kind and in cash which the various regions agreed—or did not agree—to grant him when he was at war, he must have his own army, and be sole master of it. I set about financing and equipping these *compagnies d'ordonnance*.[2] The privilege of these armies, composed of simple peasants, was that they could use weapons that knights considered unworthy. Thanks to their archers, the English had defeated us time and time again; we now tried to organize a corps of archers, although with less success. Above all, Gaspard Bureau developed a new weapon, which had until then been little used, or used badly, an arm whose power no one had yet imagined: artillery. For the nobleman, this weapon

[2] The *compagnie d'ordonnance* was a military unit, the late medieval forefather of the modern company, built around a center of knights, with assisting pages or squires, archers and men-at-arms, for a total of 700 men.

of war was anything but honorable. An instrument made of metal and chemistry, used to strike someone from a distance, had no place on the fields of honor. That some miserable wretches could drag a cannon or brandish a culverin, that was one thing. The knights placed these methods on the same level as the machines that had been used from time immemorial to launch assaults on city walls. But to win a war by using artillery would have seemed disloyal and even ungodly to them.

We had no such qualms. We had to win. Our fate was intimately bound to the king's. If he perished, we would be sacrificed along with him. This was why we were so completely mobilized for victory.

In the beginning our fear was great. We observed the king and most of us doubted he could win, even with good armies. But as time went by, doubt gave way to admiration. My own confidence grew as I observed the way this secretive man admirably hid his hand when at council. The list of the measures he undertook to reform the realm clearly proceeded from long reflection. And to this intellectual capacity he was able to add great determination in his deeds. The princes' revolt had been named the Praguerie, in reference to the events that had ravaged Bohemia. In order to get the better of this Praguerie, for four years the king resorted to strength as much as to negotiation; he knew when to be merciless in his condemnation and when it was necessary to forgive. He played the common folk and petty nobles against the aristocracy. Everything unfolded as if, after the long prelude of the English war, his reign had begun at last. The child king who had had to be protected from the assassin's blade, the poor Dauphin rejected by his mother, the king without a realm of the early years, was suddenly taking his revenge against misfortune.

He did not, for all that, allow his contentment or his ambition to show. For while he may have gained self-confidence and authority during these years, he never abandoned his weak and fearful manner. As a result, it was left to us to express our joy in victory and our gladness of success.

For me, these four years were spent in exhausting work, permanent travel, and incessant concern. However, there was no sorrow to it, for I was carried by a deep joyfulness. During those four years, my endeavors met with success, projects came easily to fruition, results were obtained quickly and were in keeping with my expectations. Everything fell marvelously into place, as fluid as a dream. I was almost under the illusion that such harmony could last forever. In hindsight, I know it is quite impossible, but I am glad that I had the privilege to know such happiness, while it lasted. And I enjoyed it all the more in that, in those days, my work was my life. I was alone, Agnès had not yet appeared on the horizon, and without that altogether too absolute comparison, my happiness seemed truly complete.

*

The Argenterie was not simply one institution of the realm among others. What the king wanted was for it to play a very special role, and I gradually discovered what this was. Initially I had viewed this royal service merely as a market providing me with a secure outlet for the products we were trading. Henceforth, we could take major risks and invest considerable amounts in the purchase of costly goods; provided we chose those goods well, we could be sure of finding buyers who would ensure our wealth. The trading company still bore my name. As it grew, the need for a simple, familiar brand became more and more obvious. And as the number of our agents increased, it became vital to find a common term with which to refer to them. Jean and Guillaume, without consulting me, had generalized the use of the expression "Maison Cœur." Since my appointment to the Argenterie, the activity of my trading company had been inextricably linked to that of the royal house. In other words, we were purveyors to the court. It was convenient, however, to go on separating the two. After all, our company must not refrain from having other clients; it must even include other sovereigns among them. And thus the parallel development of two entities began, and I was the only bridge between them. On the one hand the trading company, on the other the Argenterie.

Among the first clients of the Argenterie were naturally the king and his close circle. When serving as his purveyor, I was able to apprise myself of the king's rapport with material goods. I became fully convinced that he took no pleasure in the pursuit of finery or precious objects. He gave me many opportunities to observe him in his natural state—when traveling, for example—and I concluded that he needed little to be satisfied. His impoverished childhood and the long persecution he had undergone had left him able to endure deprivation, perhaps even like it. But now, particularly since his victories, he had begun displaying a great appetite for luxury. He dressed in costly garments, covered the walls of his apartments with tapestries and furs, and above all delighted in giving gifts of great price. It did not take me long to grasp that his attitude was political and not epicurean. On this subject, as on others, the king had thought things through without confiding in anyone. The conclusions he reached were never the object of any speech or confidence; they were merely translated through behavior, which we were obliged to decipher. And in this respect, his opinion was simple and luminous: luxury, for him, represented power. His appearance was modest, and his nature gave him little with which to exercise power over his fellow man, so in its place he wielded the pomp of his attire and ceremonial décor. He compensated for the love he had never felt for Queen Marie d'Anjou with the generosity of his favors. As for his successive mistresses, while he offered them little in the way of warmth or even attention, he redeemed these failings with the magnificence of his gifts. So much so that once they were intimate with him, and at a time when they would have been most tempted to doubt his grandeur, the extreme refinement of his attentions forced these mistresses to acknowledge that they had, indeed, however laboriously, been sleeping with a king. I added fuel to the fire by supplying silks and sables, gold-embroidered cloth and softest leather. Through the efforts of my agents, jewels, precious metals, tapestries, perfumes, and spices came from all across Europe to end up in the king's frail hands; and he conferred on them their full value.

Everyone in the kingdom who was the least bit vain or ambitious—a population never in short supply—had begun to covet the same objects the king valued. Everyone rushed to the Argenterie: the burghers to forget that they were not noble, and the nobles to emphasize the fact they were not burghers. I sometimes found it difficult to keep up with the demand. While at the beginning these shortages distressed me, I quickly realized I must make the most of them. For they made the prices rise, carried desire to its height, and cast me in the enviable role as the man on whom everything depended. People thanked me for agreeing to sell items at three times their value. Those who made me rich were grateful to me, and wherever I went there were people in my debt.

I was not the only merchant, but I was the king's merchant, and he was the best propagandist for my talents. In addition, I used a method I had intuited years earlier, which on this scale worked wonders: I agreed to make loans. It had always seemed to me that finance and commerce ought to be connected. This idea, which came to me through my acquaintance with the Léodeparts, was initially not very widely held. I had seen it as a means of circumventing my difficulties where cash was concerned. As master of the Argenterie, I could now evaluate the true usefulness of also being a banker. By agreeing to credit, I gave buyers access to something that other merchants only offered at an exorbitant price. With my method, purchase became painless.

However, by resorting to loans, my clients put a noose around their necks: it might be slack at first but it would gradually grow tighter. This danger did not concern the burghers, because they had enough to pay cash. But nobles and even princes borrowed widely. The king himself encouraged the practice, and he had offered me his guarantee in case of any difficulties in recovery. He knew what credit was. In the old days, during difficult times, he had resorted to it himself, to such a degree that at times merchants no longer trusted him and refused delivery of goods. Engaged in his merciless struggle with the princes, he had understood what a formidable use he could make of this tool. Those who laid down their arms and joined him were shown extreme generosity. They were allowed to make use of the services of the Argenterie, initially in the form of gifts given to place a seal on their reconciliation. Then came a time of purchases, and soon, to preserve their rank at court, there were loans and debts. Before long, the proud ally was in my clutches—in other words, in the king's. I admired the skillfulness with which the monarch transformed his enemies into his debtors, without ever leaving off his air of weakness, in such a way that it never occurred to them to hold him responsible for their helpless situation.

The overlapping of my business with the king's dates from this era; later on, others, including the king himself, would reproach me for it. At the time, our interests were complementary. While he was reconquering his kingdom and wrenching those who were in league against him from the Praguerie, I was endeavoring to neutralize them, and attach them to him by ensnaring them in their own desires. For example, the king encouraged me to sell a costly chivalry harness to any prince or lord who requested one. In addition, he gave the order to increase the number of tournaments that would offer them the opportunity to display their skills. Thanks to the profit from such prestigious sales, we were able to finance the equipment of the *compagnies d'ordonnance.* By making the princes pay an exorbitant amount for the maintenance of a chivalry that was useless and outmoded, the king ensured himself of the means to replace it with a modern army which belonged to him alone, and which would enable him to fight them.

We proceeded in similar fashion with all the other reforms that the king undertook to consolidate his power. I made a profitable use of the task he ascribed to me to levy taxes on salt. As I was trading this product and was responsible for the taxes, I made a considerable profit, which I shared with the king. He also made me responsible for several fortresses, and later gave me subsidies to build ships that would serve my maritime commerce. All his assistance was repaid a hundredfold. Unlike the princes, who made use of their royal position for the sole purpose of increasing their power and facilitating their disobedience, I received favors from the sovereign solely in order to make them yield a profit for him. In this way he was able to constitute a veritable royal treasury, and acquire the means to reign effectively.

He thanked me for my contribution in various ways, first of all by ennobling me. This was a way of helping me in my commerce with the princes. The lords could now use the pretext of my title to leave off their haughty manners in my presence. In fact, the true reason for their amiability was not my new status, which hardly impressed them, but my wealth, which they envied, and which they greatly needed.

For, while I had been making a fortune for the king, I had also been ensuring my own. I hope I will be believed if I say that this was not my intention. The fact remains that the results seem to imply the opposite. It matters little in the end whether it was what I sought or not: the fact is that in this short space of time I had become rich.

It is difficult to grasp the degree of one's own wealth when one does not make use of it. I was constantly traveling on business, hurrying to the court as the king moved about on campaign, and I was far more accustomed to military camps and seedy inns than to palaces. Marc did his best to make sure I always had the appropriate garments. But on more than one occasion I was obliged to hide my dirty shirt beneath a ceremonial chasuble. One day, on a road in the Saintonge, we were stopped by thieves, and only with great difficulty did we find a few billon coins in our saddle holsters, which almost failed to satisfy them. They finally let us go, railing against the ill fortune that had placed such impecunious people in their path.

I liked this simplicity that bordered on deprivation. I liked the lightness of taking to the road without any baggage. The increasingly tangled skein of my business demanded constant care. In a way, I was in the service of my wealth, just as one can be in the service of a fine animal on whom one lavishes all one's attention, for the sole pleasure of knowing it exists, and is growing and becoming more handsome by the day.

Above all, my condition as an itinerant rich man gave me the privilege of feeling at home wherever I went. I could stay in the humblest cottage with a pleasure and ease equal to what I felt in the best-kept castle. Not a single door was closed to me. The Argentier was sure of an eager welcome in the home of a burgher or a prince, and I was received with equal warmth, and far more naturally, at modest inns in the countryside. My name quickly became very well known, however, and this obliged me to take some precautions. All I needed to do was to introduce myself in order to gain entry to the richest of homes, but I had to hide my identity carefully if I wanted to continue to be treated with simplicity by the common folk.

Sometimes it was impossible to dissimulate, and my secret was revealed. One evening, not far from Bruges, I was joined by Jean de Villages who happened to be traveling in the vicinity. Unlike me, he had chosen to flaunt his power and prosperity at every moment of his nomadic life. His company of *écorcheurs* were handsomely dressed. In his train he had four carriages loaded with chests that were filled with all the fine things required for his comfort at each stop, as well as outfits for himself and his whores. Depending on the season, two or three of these ladies would frolic alongside him riding sidesaddle. As for Jean, he wore a golden chain around his neck, to which he had attached a figurine that looked from a distance as if it might be the Golden Fleece.

His arrival in the village where I was staying that day was preceded by a small vanguard of mercenaries. These insolent men had demanded that the main street be cleared, and in doing so they had not hesitated to kick Marc in the buttocks. In return, Marc had mobilized a group of peasants who, had he not intervened, would merely have bowed in submission. When Jean de Villages appeared, wearing a fur hat with feathers and accompanied by his trunks and his retinue of tarts and assassins, he encountered a veritable pitched battle. We had arrived the night before, very late, and I was still half-asleep in my room when I heard shouts in the stairway. Just as he was about to attack, Jean recognized Marc. Now both of them had come to get me out of bed.

On learning of my presence there, Jean had immediately alerted the entire village. The burghermeister, the apothecary, and a canon, with the stammering innkeeper in their wake, came to bow to me respectfully. The revelation of my name had, according to Jean, a miraculous effect. It was, in any event, something he frequently used to his advantage, introducing himself wherever he went as the partner of Messire Cœur. What this meant for me was an end to ease and tranquility. I could never bring Jean to understand that this aspect of wealth was abhorrent to me. These good folk in whose presence he flaunted my power could, in any case, not offer me anything finer than what they already possessed. My down pillow and horsehair mattress would remain the same. The only thing I stood to gain by revealing my identity would be the awkward homage of a handful of burghers, quite prepared to bring me their daughter, when it wasn't their wife, in the hopes that I might let a tiny crumb of my prosperity fall upon them.

*

The only place where I could not cast off my role as Argentier and powerful merchant was my good town. Macé had continued the social ascension begun at a time where our wealth was still quite modest and, so to speak, conceivable. In the early days, she kept her expenses within the limits of our means, which in turn prevented any excess. But now there were no more reasonable limits to her ventures. This new situation brought on a dizziness, which she treated by retiring for a time to a convent.

She came back with a decisive plan. For herself, nothing would change. She would continue to dress simply, even if the fabrics, jewels, and powders she used were of the best quality. All the power we had acquired would serve the family, and therefore our children. She planned brilliant careers for them, almost hoping to encounter numerous obstacles on her path simply for the pleasure of undertaking to remove them.

As I expected, she also demanded that we build a new house. Initially I thought she wanted a comfortable family home. While I was prepared to build the finest of houses for her, I did not think it would go very far. We had a friendly discussion about it before the Christmas season, in keeping with our new relationship, which was respectful if somewhat chilly.

Then Macé made it amply clear what she wanted: we had to have a palace.

At first I protested. Ostentation was everything I had sought to avoid. I still reasoned as an upstart: others would tolerate my success provided my triumph remained modest. Any form of pretension with regard to appearance would provoke an angry reaction from all sides, the king to start with, the kind of anathema that could destroy the fragile balance of my endeavor. Could the king not simply revoke my position as Argentier as easily as he had granted it? All the duties I fulfilled for him, particularly in levying taxes, I presented as tasks, services I agreed to perform for him. If I were to draw attention to my income, it would become clear to everyone that the king's attention, far from inconveniencing me, was serving to make my fortune, and many voices would be raised to demand it be taken away from me. More than anything, if I am honest, I feared the king himself. I knew that he had a malicious streak, filled with meanness and envy. To display too much luxury and power would be dangerous, particularly when that power depended so directly on his goodwill. Moreover, if we built a palace it would signify we were trying to be equal with the princes, whom he despised. Macé swept away all my arguments with a wave of her hand and I realized that she would not yield. After all, one advantage of an ambitious construction was that it would take time. From the acquisition of the land to the completion of the palace would take years. I might hope that in the meantime my situation would become stable and that everyone, starting with the king, would have become used to my fortune and thus tolerate the external signs of it.

I mentioned earlier that under the Romans our town had been surrounded by a high wall. The town had now spread far beyond that enclosure. New constructions were built up against the wall and at its foot. There were some sections where the wall was in ruins and was being used as a quarry. On the south side, a fine section of the ancient rampart was still intact, and I decided to purchase it. It included a tall tower at one end. This property did not look like a bare plot of land, but rather a self-sufficient construction. Now anyone who went by the tower said, "That is Cœur's future house." This would suffice to appease Macé's worldly impatience, and I did what I could to encumber the formalities of purchase. As I was never there to sign the deed of sale, the matter was taking a very long time and I was free, provisionally, from the threat hovering over me.

The strangest thing was that at the very time I was doing what I could to postpone Macé's extravagant project, I became the owner of an estate without either desiring it or planning it. In truth, the event was anything but fortuitous. By dint of opening my purse to the advantage of so many impecunious nobles, it was inevitable that sooner or later one of them, driven to the brink by creditors less accommodating than myself, would let go of his property to avoid prison. Clever lenders would seize his lands, which are always worth something. As I was sheltered by the king's warranty, I would not be so demanding: thus, they handed the old dwelling over to me—that is, a property no one wanted because it brought nothing and cost a great deal. In this way I acquired my first castle.

There would be many others. It is impossible for me to remember them all, and there were some I never even had time to visit. But the first one I remember because it was the first; I will never forget it.

There was no risk that it might arouse the king's envy. No one could accuse me, with regard to the castle, that I had wanted it in order to flaunt my fortune. It was a country estate, hidden in the hollow of a damp valley in the Puysaie, far from any town. The building consisted of four tall towers, huddled together like Siamese twins. Long arrow slits marked the blind façades like gashes received in battle. It became clear as one came up the path leading to the drawbridge that the castle was not known outside the region. Surely no sovereign had ever stopped there, or even bothered to try and attack it. It had sprouted in the undergrowth like a mushroom in damp earth.

It was a relic of the bygone era of chivalry when it had stood there to protect the prosperity of the local countryside. I could picture serfs, not very different from the free peasants who now peopled the region, and in their midst a lord who was unwashed and brutal, courageous, sensual, and pious, doing what he could to defend them. The serfs had transported cartloads of stones and built the four towers for the lord to reign over them.

It was a way of life that had lasted for centuries. There was no better place than this castle to feel the immobility of time—the turning of the seasons, the passing of simple lives, preserved from all temptation and hardship by this immutable order. There was not even any sign that these lords had taken part in the Crusades. The castle and its surrounding fields and vineyards had lived far removed from the turbulence of the world. However, one day the world became so unsettled that its violence reached even this far. Echoing the king's madness, order collapsed. The serfs, now free, hired out their labor to their master—while he was more interested in the town, and wished to acquire superfluous things, for without them the merely necessary seemed insipid. The world burst in with its looting and pillaging and the lord was incapable of protecting his people. Finally, he went to join the court, where he fell into debt, and had to sell off the estate in order to pay what he owed. Abandoned, betrayed, and in deepest misfortune, now the peasants watched as this merchant—me, the son of a nobody, perhaps a usurer—took possession of their castle, a sign that the old days were truly in the past and that anything was possible.

I stayed at the castle for three days. I toured all its rooms, wandered for hours in the attic opening old trunks, striding from one room to the next in search of memories, odors, unusual objects. The debtor had left everything, a sign that he had left in haste, or the proof that he really no longer cared for a place too burdened with boredom and the past. I built a roaring fire in the huge fireplace of the main hall and I stayed alone, looking at the shadows dancing on the walls, as if they were ghosts parading before me. This experience was almost as powerful as the one so long ago at the edge of the desert, outside Damascus. Once again I was on the threshold of another world, but this time I most definitely could not go there, because it belonged to the past. It was nostalgia for a time before, for that chivalry I had so often imagined during my childhood, that period of harmony from before the reign of the mad king. The same energy found in the dreams which had led me to the Levant now made me drift toward other lives that were located in an inaccessible past. And yet there was one major difference. When I dreamt of the Levant, my life had not yet taken a clearly defined course. Anything was possible. Whereas now I had come quite far along a certain path, and had already obtained more than I dared hope for. Yet, I was still tempted by other lives. It was then, I believe, that I became aware that no life, however brilliant or happy it might be, would ever be enough for me. There always comes a moment when the dreamer, who ordinarily thinks he is happy because his dreams constantly take him elsewhere, becomes fully aware of his misfortune.

Fortunately, Marc had noticed my melancholy. He brought to it the only remedy he knew, and which he deemed, not without reason, a very good remedy for all ailments. The second night, up the long winding staircase from the dungeon he brought a fresh young peasant woman, who hardly seemed surprised to be singled out for the pleasure of the lord. She did her best to restore me to the present. But what I saw in this scene was a return to ancient seigniorial rights. So much so that, far from distracting me from my dreams, she enabled me instead to immerse myself in them completely.

I never went back there.

In the years to come, I would receive several other estates in payment of debts. Each time, I tried to visit them, often after having acquired them, not to inspect their worth but rather to renew that disturbing experience which allowed me to linger in the unsuspected recesses of the past.

I eventually told Macé about the existence of these estates. She never showed the slightest desire to visit them. I understood that she would not be drawn to these seigniorial abodes for themselves; what interested her was having a palace in her town, a palace that would consecrate her triumph in the eyes of the people who mattered to her. Over time my collection of castles took on considerable, almost ridiculous proportions: not satisfied with merely obtaining property in payment, I began to buy them myself. I was shown the plans and if they triggered a shiver of desire, I paid cash for the property in question.

I have never been able to live without having some sort of passion to free my mind from the tyranny of the present. For a brief time, when I first met Macé, this passion was love. The same feeling then nourished my desire for the Levant. Then came these collections of fortified castles. I perceived this compulsion as a sort of secret but necessary illness, above all delightful, which helped me to love life. I envied my companions. Jean de Villages knew how to find contentment in the moment, and coveted nothing other than real and present material pleasure. As for Guillaume, he derived no satisfaction from things. He lived as a peaceful burgher. His activity drew him toward abstract pleasures—buying, selling, speculating, importing, investing—but they made him happy. Neither one of them understood my passion. Jean appreciated the fortunate opportunity my castles gave him to organize feasts. He often asked me to lend him this or that estate, and he took his merry company there. Guillaume admired my capacities as a businessman, without understanding my intentions for all that. He reckoned that I must have good reason to speculate on these seigniorial properties, rational reasons naturally, that is, comparable to his own.

The king himself got wind of my acquisitions. Far from taking umbrage, he made it a pretext for mockery. The old feudal dwellings I was collecting inspired neither desire nor envy in him. He conveyed his pity, and he was pleased to have discovered my vice, my weakness, the probable consequence of my modest birth. The king liked nothing so much as to be privy to our secrets, for that made us vulnerable. In this way he could go on displaying his own weakness without fear, in the knowledge that at any moment he could unveil our own.

*

In the five years that followed the truce with England, and until his complete victory over the princes, the king was constantly moving. The council meetings were often held in faraway towns where he had just established his authority. I tried to combine my own travels on behalf of the Argenterie with these congregations around the king, but I rarely managed to do so, and consequently did not meet him often. One time, however, he expressly asked for my company on his travels. He had to go to the Languedoc, and he knew that I had business in that region.

We left from Blois. This was not a military campaign, because the provinces in the South had always been loyal to him. The king was in a hurry to return, and he wanted to make quick progress. He had ordered a light escort for the journey, just enough men to protect us from any *écorcheurs* we might meet along the way. In short, I was virtually alone with him.

We spent these two weeks together in a closeness I would never again experience with him. I sometimes forgot who he was when we laughed at the stories he told, when we set our horses at a gallop across the moors, when we wrapped ourselves in sheepskin blankets at night around a campfire. Summer was coming; the nights were warm and scattered with comets. We washed in streams that were scarcely cold. Because I alone was allowed in his company when we washed, I had the privilege of seeing the distortions of his body through childhood deprivation—his stoop, and his clammy blue skin. I was also aware that my observation of his physical wretchedness, which on the surface did not seem to bother him, was a grave transgression for which he would someday hold me accountable. In exchange, I laid bare the secret of my sunken chest, but I could tell that such a small gesture would not redeem my crime.

As I came to know him, I could sense the danger implicit in his person—he was a wounded, jealous, mean man, who allowed no one the leisure of escape. And though I had already known this, and had a premonition of the danger, I was incapable of protecting myself.

There was one thing I discovered during the voyage, and that was Charles's capacity for listening. His ideas were not born solely from personal reflection or intuition; they also stemmed from a slow deciphering of the innumerable words he heard. When the subject interested him, he took the reins of the conversation, asked questions, and guided one's testimony. This maieutic method had a considerable effect on me and I was astonished, as I spoke to him, to find in myself the new ideas he had knowingly inspired, perhaps even conceived.

For example, one evening we had a long conversation about the Mediterranean, which lasted almost until dawn. I remember it perfectly. We were in a town in the Cévennes. We had stopped at a fortified house halfway up the slope. From the terrace, which the present owner had added, we could see the valley of the Rhone, and in the mist in the distance the first foothills of the Alps. It was an ideal place to envisage grand prospects. Charles's tongue was loosened by the sweet wine, and he was comfortably installed in a wicker chair. I was sitting at the stone table where we had dined. I had shoved aside the plates and glasses and was leaning forward with my elbows on the table. When the semidarkness crept over the hillside the king refused to have the candles lit and we went on talking in almost total obscurity. He gazed at the billions of stars in the deep and moonless night. We were no longer a sovereign and his servant; there was only the vessel of dreams on which we had both embarked and which was driven by a great wind of hope, like the one that arises from one's own body when one has rested and eaten one's fill.

It was he who asked me to talk about the Mediterranean. I began by describing the shore in our parts and was quick to remind him that he was one of the four masters who shared its coast.

"Four! And who are the others?"

Still smiling, I gave him a suspicious look. With him it was always difficult to ascertain whether his questions concealed traps. What exactly did he know about the Mediterranean? It seemed impossible to me that he did not already have some notions about the situation. At the same time, he had devoted his attention so exclusively to the war with the English, had so many problems with Burgundy, Flanders, and so many other provinces in the north, that perhaps he did in fact have some serious gaps in his knowledge of the way matters stood in the south.

"Imagine," I began cautiously, "if we were to continue on our way toward the sea in that direction."

I pointed southward, to where the valley opened out. Night had not yet fallen at that point. The king held his eyes wide open as if to dissolve the purplish mist enveloping the river.

"Once you reach the coast, imagine that if you were to turn right, you would enter the home of the Catalan, for whom you have no great affection: Alfonso, king of Aragon and Sicily. He has his merchant fleet for trade, but also his corsairs who attack and pillage whomever they meet."

"More wine!" shouted Charles.

He drank little, taking tiny sips, but I had already noticed that nervous tension increased if not his pleasure at least his desire to resort to drink.

"And to the left?"

"To the left, you will find first of all the port of Marseille, which belongs to the Duke of Anjou, as does all Provence."

"René."

"Indeed, King René."

Charles raised his shoulders and hissed, "*King* René. Do not forget he is my vassal."

"In any case, on these seas, he behaves more like your rival. He may sell his feudal homage to you, but he continues to compete with you mercilessly in the commercial domain."

"I am not obliged to let him push me around."

"To be sure."

I knew he liked the idea. Charles was not a feudal lord. He despised the order which made him the foremost of princes but refused him the means of becoming a king. His alliance with burghers like me, his desire to undermine the great barons, his urge to have a financial instrument at his disposal, to be powerful in trade, and to have his own army—it was all that which I admired in him.

"And the fourth?"

"Beyond Provence, farther along the coast, lies Genoa."

"Genoa," he repeated pensively. "Is it a free city? I have never understood anything about Italy."

A typical reflection for a king of France. The Duke of Burgundy would never have spoken thus. Of all Charlemagne's heirs, the one who reigned in Dijon had always looked to the south and was abreast of everything that happened on the Italian peninsula. The king of France, however, kept his eyes on England. But Charles's question showed that this state of affairs might be about to change. If he managed to rid himself of the English threat for good, the king of France might at last turn his gaze to Italy. I fervently hoped so. I have always thought that France could play a great role in this region. Absorbed by my idea of making the realm the new center of the world, I could not conceive of that center without Rome. Italy was divided, and open to our conquest. The Catalan prince was much less powerful than Charles VII, but had he not conquered Sicily and the kingdom of Naples? I refrained from explaining this too clearly, for fear the king might be alarmed. I merely took a first step in that direction.

"Genoa has always needed a protector. There are some in that city who would be pleased if it were you, sire."

From the way the king, in his unmoving severity, blinked his eyes, I understood that he had grasped perfectly the thrust and impact of my remark. As usual, he concealed his interest, but I was certain that he would bring it up again.

"And what lies beyond Genoa?"

"Nothing that matters on this sea. Florence has no fleet and in Rome the pope pays little attention to his port. Genoa's only rival is located on the far side of the peninsula, on the Adriatic. That is Venice."

The king asked many more detailed questions about the four fleets that shared the coast from Barcelona to Genoa. He questioned me at length about the ports of the Languedoc. I told him about Montpellier and its canal, which in my opinion had no future, as far as Lattes. He was curious to hear the glorious history of Aigues-Mortes. But he changed the subject when I described how the port was silting up, as if this evocation of the work of centuries and, perhaps, the memory of

Saint Louis plunged him into melancholy. This was not the first time I had noticed his visceral fear of time. He could put up with deprivation, failure, and betrayal, but yielded to utter panic at the prospect of death. In hindsight, I see a certain coherence. His strength lay in waiting, and placing his hope in the changes the future might bring. But the moment he became aware of his finite nature, time was no longer on his side. Deprived of this ally he became vulnerable, and what he had accepted as provisional now became unbearable, since he would no longer have the time to free himself from it.

It was completely dark out by the time he turned the conversation to the Levant. The serving woman who had brought our wine was still there. I could just make out her form in the semidarkness. It seemed to me that she was standing next to the king, and while he spoke he was stroking her leg.

"In the Levant," I said, "there are four of them as well. They are all enemies, two by two."

"Explain yourself."

"It's very simple. Most people will tell you that in the Holy Land Christianity is confronted with the Mohammedans."

"That is generally the significance ascribed to the crusades: you are not of this opinion?"

"Yes, of course I am. But by describing it in this way, one is neglecting another rivalry that is just as violent."

"And what might that be?"

"The one that divides each camp into two groups."

"The Mohammedans are divided?"

"Deeply. The Sultan of Egypt, who reigns as far as Damascus and Palestine, has no worse enemy than the Turks in Asia Minor."

"Are you implying that we could use one against the others?"

"Incontestably. The merchants who come from Europe are given a warm welcome in Cairo."

"And is it not true that the Christians who are still in the Holy Land are subject to all sorts of harassment?"

"The Arabs distrust them, that is true. But it must be said, without excusing them, that the partisans of the crusades have not given up, starting with your cousin Burgundy. And they continue to mistake their enemy. They believe the Turks are friendly and they are angry with the Arabs for occupying Jerusalem. However, it is the Turks who prevent the pilgrims from going to Palestine, and they are the ones who are going deeper into Europe, advancing through the Balkans."

"And are the Christian kingdoms also divided in this way?"

"Of course. Anyone who speaks to you of 'Christianity' and its struggle against the disciples of Mohammed is thinking of Byzantium and the Turkish armies camped all around it."

"And is that wrong?"

"Not wrong. But this propaganda suits the Basileus first and foremost, for he likes to present himself as the final rampart against Islam. The truth is that he spends just as much time fighting other Christians."

"And who dares to attack him?"

"Our Latin friends, Genoa and Venice. And if the Catalans do not join them it is because they are waiting to lend a hand by means of their corsairs."

The moon had not yet appeared in the sky, but our eyes had grown used to the darkness. Now I could see the serving woman, standing behind the king. He had guided her hands and she was massaging his shoulders. Several of his mistresses had told me in confidence that he had great need of such manipulation. Only in this way could he find relief from the terrible tension that twisted him in every direction. I understood that, far from distracting him from my words, the servant's gestures enabled him to cast off the burden of his pain, and left him free to listen to me with the utmost attention.

"While Constantinople is threatened on land by the Turks,"

I continued, "it suffers constant setbacks in the islands due to the Latins."

The king asked for many details about the commercial and territorial rivalry between Constantinople and the Italian city-states. His questions were so precise and, at times, so trivial, that once again I was under the impression that this was an amusement for him. My own assurance in the matter was a challenge to him, and no doubt he was trying to put me on the spot. And he managed to, on several occasions, when I had to confess that I did not know the answer. Then he would give a little laugh of satisfaction. After one of these lapses, he stood up, thanked the serving woman with a caress on her cheek, and went to bed.

For the two weeks that our journey lasted, he went on questioning me. In Montpellier he asked to see a galley, and even went on board to inspect the cargo. The town gave him a welcome worthy of a sovereign, but he curtailed the ceremonies, thus increasing the time at his disposal to see the trade facilities, to converse with the ships' captains, with merchants, and even with the oarsmen on the galleys, whom he questioned about their work. This was before the era of galley slaves, and oarsmen were still free, although it was easy to imagine they were not of the most upstanding sort. They often signed on in order to avoid a prison sentence, or worse; the law would spare them provided they stay on their bench and at their oar for several crossings.

I came back from this journey feeling I had grown closer to the king. But through some effect of his personality, the more the distance between us diminished, the greater my incomprehension. Everyone assumed that I must now belong to the coveted inner circle. But I myself was certain I had entered a zone of danger, like a man who in order to uncover a secret goes so deeply into an underground passage that any return is blocked, and he finds himself at the mercy of perils that are all the more dreadful for their unpredictability and strangeness. Nor did I have the impression that our time together had induced him to listen any more closely to my opinions. Regarding the situation in the Mediterranean and the Levant in particular, I came to the conclusion that the king had found it amusing to make me talk. He had piled on his questions until he could reveal my ignorance but, after that, never brought up the subject again.

*

Upon our return, I took part in the first Council without knowing what the king intended to discuss. Imagine my astonishment when he enumerated a series of measures that derived from the very conversations we had had. He painted a precise picture of the situation in Italy, and the subject surprised everyone, as they had long been accustomed to hear only of England or sometimes Flanders or Spain. He set forth the basis of a policy he would implement methodically in the years to follow, and to which I would contribute. With regard to the Mohammedans, he affirmed that we must place a great price on obtaining the sultan's good grace in our regard. This element was the result of his conversations with merchants in Montpellier who had met the Arab sovereign in Cairo. The other counselors were impassive on hearing these declarations. After all, the embargo on trade with the Moors, which the pope had proclaimed, was riddled with exceptions, and the Languedoc, for a start, enjoyed a limited right to trade with them. Still, the idea that the king of France might establish cordial relations with the infidel occupying the Holy Land was deeply shocking to those in attendance. The king added that he was putting me in charge of the construction and fitting out of the French galleys that would be trading on behalf of the Argenterie. And he ordered that the recruitment of oarsmen for the galleys would now be a matter for the law. No longer would it suffice for a convict's sentence to be commuted if he chose to embark; the courts must now include the galleys among the punishments to which the accused could be sentenced, and this in ample number.

Once again the king was showing us that he had vision. He was opening France to the Mediterranean and the Levant, and involving the country in Italy's affairs. These decisions confirmed that he had listened to me and understood my point, and they surpassed even my own expectations.

I set about eagerly implementing the king's wishes. I called on Jean and Guillaume as well as my most important agents from the Argenterie to inform them of these revolutionary changes.

By opening the route to Italy, the king was endorsing a project we had often spoken of at the Argenterie but had feared we would not be able to implement any time soon. As merchants, we were well aware that we depended on those who produced our goods. If we could become manufacturers ourselves, it would be to our great advantage. And for the most precious substance, which was silk, and which we were now buying in great quantities, we must follow the example of the Italians. They had discovered this material in China, and for centuries had been bringing it from there at great expense and with significant losses. One day they uncovered the secret of its fabrication, and now they were producing it locally. Florence had become the greatest silk making city in all of Europe. If we in turn could enter the closed circle of silk producers, we would no longer be dependent on others to supply us. We could control the quality, the quantity, and the prices.

In order to obey the king's political desires and, at the same time, pursue the interests of the Argenterie, I turned to Italy. In the spring I left for Florence.

This time I would have to make an impression on people I did not know, and win them over. I had only a few contacts in the milieu of moneychangers. Guillaume had dealings with two major Florentine merchants regarding a cargo of spices, but he had never been there. Therefore, contrary to my usual habit, I decided to arrive in grand style and flaunt my titles. From what I had heard, the Italians were less inclined toward simplicity than we were; rather, they considered it belonged elsewhere. Politeness, for them, meant maintaining one's rank, and what seemed like ostentation to us was to them merely a convenient signal one gave so that others would immediately know where to situate one's role in the great comedy of society. Once this was established, affable, natural behavior was possible, and even appreciated. In France the process was often just the reverse. Notables might put on a show of simplicity, but to make sure their importance was acknowledged, they sprinkled their words with insolence and marks of vanity.

As soon as we had crossed the Alps, I adorned myself in splendid garments. My horse was groomed and harnessed in velvet, with a host of gold curb chains and sparkling pompoms. My escort of ten lansquenets were wearing identical livery of tawny leather. When we came in sight of Florence, we displayed our banners. One bore the coat of arms of the king of France and the other my personal blazon, featuring three hearts and scallops. I had taken the precaution of providing for an interpreter. He was an older man who had once served a Lombard banker in Paris, before the Armagnacs expelled all the Italian financiers from the capital. He had accompanied his master to various towns all over the peninsula and he provided me with useful descriptions of Florence.

I was prepared for what I would see. However, it was still a shock to discover the city. I could even say that my surprise and wonder were equal to or even greater than what I had experienced in the Levant. I found myself in a city that expressed harmonious development, that had been spared by the wars that had ruined France. The beauty of her palaces and churches, beginning with the marvelous Duomo of colored marble, was stupefying. The same refinement I had appreciated in the Levant could be found here in this gentle, sunny climate, but instead of the arid deserts that surrounded the cities of the Levant, Florence was encircled by verdant hills. Wherever one looked there were ancient relics to remind one that civilization had existed here for centuries. It is true that civilization in the Levant also had distant origins, but now it seemed frozen in its refinement, whereas in Florence it was alive, constantly evolving and improving.

The city was overflowing with energy, activity, and novelty. In every street one could hear the sound of new construction. Stone masons, brick masons, roofers, and carpenters were constantly adding new palaces to the already tight warren of buildings. I rapidly understood that there was no difference in this free city between what at home we defined as noblemen and burghers. One could see this constantly reflected in the customs governing fortune and construction in particular. In France, palaces and castles are primarily the legacy of nobles, who in fact have neither the means to maintain them nor to build new ones. As for the burghers, their ambition is more constrained than their finances: they are always fearful of rising to a height forbidden by their birth. In Florence, wealth knows neither modesty nor prohibition. The only precaution taken by those who display their wealth is to ensure that it wears the appearance of art. Beauty is the means whereby the powerful share their wealth with the people.

I had never seen so many artists, and they were widely celebrated. Crowds would gather around to admire every new statue on squares and crossroads. You could see workers rushing all over town carrying the huge paintings intended for new palaces, and everyone stood respectfully out of their way. Believers hurried to church not only to say mass but also to admire the new retable on a high altar or hear the latest oratorio composed for a choir. I discovered that several of the city's renowned artists had come from Constantinople or fled the cities of Greece and Asia Minor. The link I had made intuitively between the splendors of the Levant and those of Florence was not, therefore, altogether fortuitous. The movement of civilization from the Levant to the West was not a dream: it had already begun. All that remained was for France to be inspired, too.

Oddly enough, there were not many Frenchmen in the town. While trade had induced the Florentines to travel abroad quite readily, even as far as China, it would seem that their city did not attract many foreigners. Initially I feared that this absence might indicate that it would be difficult for a stranger to settle in the city. But I soon found out the opposite. Provided one did not act in an arrogant manner, or strive to hide one's wealth or power, one was given a warm welcome. In short, all that was necessary was to adapt to the customs of this city of merchants and bankers. The master here was money, and one's power was in proportion to the means one had at one's disposal. My position at the court of France, my profession as a merchant and financier, and above all the lifestyle I decided to lead from the moment of my arrival, opened every door. I stayed only four days in a hostelry, the time it took to rent a palace, at an exorbitant price, from a widow who could no longer afford it since the death of her husband and the ruin of his activity. I modeled myself on Ravand and Jean and arranged my own little court, and I began to receive visitors.

Wherever money reigns, it never stays still. Everyone is trying to acquire it, and all you need to do is display it and you will have all sorts of people rushing up to you and offering their services. In no time I understood that everything was for sale: objects, of course, but also bodies and even souls. In the air I caught the same whiffs of corruption I had smelled in Paris; here, however, there was a certain good humor and, might I say it, sincerity in fraud, which immediately endeared the place to me.

The interpreter, who was also working as my steward, instantly received offers for the services of several cooks, a dozen chambermaids, and suppliers of all kinds. He sorted through these proposals and in less than a week the house was bustling with servants, the cellars were filled with wine from Asti, and the kitchens were overflowing with ham and fresh victuals.

By then I had already perfected the method I would always use in business. My part was minor, but essential: I chose my men myself. For as long as I can remember, that is the way I have done things. A vision carries me toward a project. This project presupposes a number of daily activities, and an aptitude for counting, surveying, and ordering, which I have only in very limited supply. The solution is to find a man and to infect him with my dream, the way a plague-sufferer infects those around him, thus allowing the illness to develop inside him. This is what I had done everywhere in France, from Flanders to Provence, from Normandy to Lorraine. In truth, my enterprise comprised a troop of madmen, all contaminated by my ideas and sparing no effort to make them reality. All the more so abroad, and in the unknown milieu that was Florence: it was out of the question for me to enter alone the thorny forest of laws that had been drafted to be corrupted, of rules burdened more with exceptions than classic examples, of merchants connected to each other through mysterious ties of kinship, allegiance, or intrigue. I needed a partner.

There were weeks of dazzling suppers, receptions, and feasts, where I met all sorts of people in my trade. What was new was to discover a society that had no bearings, because it had no sovereign. In France, no matter the king's misfortune, his supremacy was never questioned. The court is ordered around him, and everyone shines with the brilliance this central star casts on those in his proximity, even to the darkest corners of the realm. In Florence this was not the case: great families ruled, the highest ranking being the Medici, followed by an infinite number of greater and lesser noblemen, whose hierarchy was anything but obvious. For a person to be illustrious, there were several prerequisites: lineage and relations, to be sure, but also, and perhaps above all, property and fortune.

This mixture was all very new to me. I came from a world that had long been dominated by the land, by those who own it and those who work it. Feudal tradition fixed every person to his place within the three orders of land, labor, and prayer. Beyond that, nothing mattered. This was why for so long merchants and craftsmen had occupied such a lowly position, devoted to the base activities of exchange, usury, and manufacture. Gradually, the burghers and those who worked with money had become established, particularly under Charles VII, until one day they found themselves being granted the most eminent positions. However, among the merchants there did remain an aspect of the old days: the vague certainty that we did not belong to the order of God's chosen subjects.

Now, in Florence, it was a revelation to see that these two worlds, rather than excluding each other, could be united. The Florentine aristocracy does value its feudal order. They possess castles and fields, they have roots in the earth. But at the same time, they do not know what it is to scorn work. They do not forbid themselves from working in trade or industry. Far from disdaining wealth, they have seized upon it. This curious mixture, in its way, has reconciled me with the two orders I had always held to be incompatible.

Yet in mingling, these two qualities of nobility and wealth are altered. They have given rise to a singular breed of humanity that resembles neither the lords nor the merchants one meets in France. I felt at ease with these elegant, affable people, but at the same time I could not rid myself of a disturbing impression: I could understand them no better than they themselves understood me. I needed an intermediary whom I could trust.

This has always been a decisive step in the expansion of my business. How many times have I stayed for days or even entire weeks in strange towns, surrounded by people who are eager to oblige me, offering me their relations and their fortune simply because they hope to become part of the "Maison Cœur" and serve as my agent? I can make my choice as soon as I arrive, and on occasion I have been resolved, or forced, to do so. But most of the time I wait. I don't know what I am waiting for, still less for whom. I only know that at a given time, a sign comes to show me in whom I can place my trust. Now and again I have been mistaken, still more frequently deceived. Now that I think back on this, I was always deceived by those individuals whom I was most reluctant to employ, and their sign in my consciousness had been weak, or nonexistent.

In Florence the sign was clear, and I did not hesitate.

*

Nicolo Piero di Bonaccorso arrived at my house with his youngest sister on his arm. I never knew who had invited them, and even today I suspect it might have been some little ploy of Marc's to lead the young beauty to my bed. He was wasting his time. In Florence, perhaps because I had introduced myself in grand style and using my true identity, I did not intend to leave myself vulnerable because of some feminine intrigue. It seemed to me that in this society the women were even more dangerous than the men. It did not take me long to notice that they were the ones who reigned over this city of jealousy and pleasure. It required some effort to keep to my resolution, because the Florentine women were charming and clever, their great natural beauty enhanced by the finery of gold and silk that had made the fortune of their city. The young girl escorted by her brother was no exception. She seemed modest and reserved, quite incapable of making a man lose his head. Since my adventure with Christine in Paris, I had come to view such qualities as even greater reasons to be on my guard.

I do not know why the feature I found worrying in the sister—her simple, natural manner—intrigued me in the brother. As I talked with Nicolo, before long the thought occurred to me that he was certainly the one whom Providence had chosen for me. He was at least twenty years younger than I, but behaved with far greater composure than I had at his age. On his mother's side he belonged to the milieu of silk manufacturers. He was also indirectly related to the Medici. And, unlike some older men who had been informed of my arrival and knew of my position with the king, he knew nothing about me. When I informed him of my plans, he seemed genuinely enthusiastic. He gave me a great deal of advice, and he could already picture silks from Florence spreading through France. He dreamt of going there one day.

I decided to make him my agent for Florence. And a wise decision it was, too. It took not even two years for him to arrange my enrollment in the most powerful silk guild, the Arte della Seta. I took my oath there, as would both Guillaume and my youngest son, Ravand, later on. Our firm never became as great as that of the Medici, but we occupied an honorable place nonetheless. Our cloths of silk and gold were almost immediately exported to France, conveyed on horseback over Alpine passes to our branches in Lyon, Provence, and, naturally, the Argenterie in Tours.

Demand was enormous. The truce with England was lasting, and there was no limit to people's hunger for happiness. I was struggling to satisfy the orders that came in at the Argenterie. People were thankful when I managed to honor their requests, and when I delivered a gown it was as though I were saving a life. As the buyers often lacked cash, I gave credit, and before long everyone of importance at the court of France was in my debt.

Florence had transformed me. Upon my return, it occurred to me for the first time that not only could I increase my wealth, I could also put it to use. Prior to this, money had merely been the product of my activity; I was not governed by the desire to obtain money and, as I have said, my daily life, with a few vital exceptions, remained simple and frugal. In Florence, something else had been revealed to me. It wasn't a sudden liking for comfort or the lure of luxury; in truth, it was yet another dream, but one whose time had come, now that my other projects had been fully realized and were beginning to lose their hold over me.

How can I explain this revelation? I could sum it up by giving it a name, and say that Florence showed me what art truly is. But that is not enough. I must be more precise. Until then, I knew only one form of art, that of the craftsman, as practiced by my father, for example. Mastering the means to transform a rough-hewn object into something useful that was also solid and pleasing to the eye—that was what furriers and tailors did, or masons and chefs. That art could be perfected, but on the whole, it was a hereditary art. It was handed down from master to student, from father to son. In Florence I learned to distinguish between the art of artisans, which was extremely refined, and the art of artists, which reflected something else altogether: genius, exception, innovation.

I met a great many painters there. As I observed them, I learned to distinguish between two orders: technique, and creativity. When mixing their colors, and preparing their materials to paint *a tempera*, on frescoes, or with oils, they were still only craftsmen. Some of them remained so, producing conventional work inspired by well-known models. But others, in the moment of their creation, moved away from those references, and went beyond the techniques they had mastered, to give free rein in their work to something more. And I recognized that something more: it was the immense realm of dreams. Dreams confer nobility upon humankind. We are human because we have access to what does not exist. These riches are not given to everyone, but those who do make their way to that invisible continent return laden with treasures they then share with everyone else.

I am referring here to painters, no doubt because I was particularly sensitive to their genius. But I could also mention architects, musicians, and poets. These artists were far less numerous than the simple craftsmen. But their activity was like a motor driving the entire city. This was a major difference from the Levant. I understood what I had felt in Damascus. All the refinement, all the wealth converging toward that city merely settled there in an inert fashion. Nothing new appeared. The city must have known a golden age; it seemed to be over. It was subsisting on the accomplishments of that bygone time. In Florence, however, innovation was everywhere. The city had gone far afield to find wealth and competence, as with the culture of the silkworm, imported from China. And the city did not stop there. It had to go on transforming, surpassing, creating; it was a city of artists.

I went back to France convinced not only that we must amass wealth, but that we would never truly have a chance to become the center of the world unless we also reached the sovereign domain of art and creativity. Today this is a common idea. But at the time it was novel.

It is difficult to grasp how much has been accomplished over the last ten years. At the time of the truce with England we were emerging from nearly a century of war and destruction. We knew only two states, poverty or abundance. By emerging from one, our only desire was to cast ourselves into the other. And this gave us an extraordinary appetite for quantity: ever increasing amounts of jewels, finery, victuals, palaces, feasts, dances, and love. During the time of violence, our meager resources had been consumed by a feeble flame, but that fire was burning out of control now: countless delights were being tossed its way by the armful, delights that had become easy to acquire thanks to the stability of peace. However, our taste remained vulgar.

I had become one of the purveyors of extravagance. In Florence, I had passed a milestone: not only was I dealing as a merchant with objects that came from elsewhere, but as a member of the silk guild I also took part in their creation. I was one of the rare individuals in France who was also thinking of manufacturing. I brought Guillaume and Jean together to inform them of my plan. We would no longer import arms, but produce them; we would no longer sell fabric wholesale, but make it ourselves. I decided to acquire money not only through commerce, but also through my own production. To that end, I bought mines in the hills around Lyon, and I brought in Germans who were skilled at extracting metal from the ground.

Under the influence of the Florentines, I gave the concept of creativity greater scope. The idea was not merely to reproduce what was being made elsewhere, but to seize the very power that was the principle behind these discoveries. My aim was to innovate in every domain. I liked the idea of employing every form of the imagination, in order to inscribe its effects in matter. I now knew that artists would be at the summit of this new form of manufacture. There were very few such people in France. Our musicians peddled tunes that had been handed down to them by tradition; painters copied conventional religious subjects. Only our poets, perhaps, moved about in the original space of their thoughts and feelings. But they were also those who had the least purchase on things. When I came back from Florence, I set myself to the task of bringing together the talented people I met and giving them free rein to create new finery, new buildings, and spectacles of a kind never seen before. After the long fallow period of war, it was not at all certain that we would even manage to do this. However, this land, which only a hundred years earlier had given birth to builders of cathedrals, was certainly not arid where the arts were concerned. What was needed was to find new talents, and provide them with the conditions necessary for their growth and the blossoming of their creativity.

*

I was given the opportunity to contribute myself, by means of building the palace I had promised Macé. Before I went to Florence, I could not conceive of this building as anything other than what was in keeping with my notion of supreme luxury: the château at Mehun-sur-Yèvre. Built long ago by Duke John, it was the king's residence when he was in the region. It was a fortified building surrounded by round towers, and its only novelty, albeit a very tentative one, but which was what made it so attractive, were the tall windows set in the walls, which offered an admirable view of the countryside.

The land I had acquired, with its Roman foundations, was to serve as a foundation for a construction similar to Mehun, or at least that is what Macé and I had decided. To that end, we decided to flank the tall Roman tower with a twin, which would give the building the air of a fortified castle. But when I came back from Florence, I realized that this was a ridiculous idea. In Florence I had seen palaces blossoming without a single trace of war, and for good cause. They were tall, airy buildings, whose only towers were used to contain spiral staircases. The architects vied with each other to beautify these dwellings with an elegance and lightness that made our fortified houses seem barbarian. On the walls, frescoes burst with color, and stained glass filtered a living light.

I decided to follow these examples and rethink our project completely. Alas, the moment I arrived in our town, I saw that in my absence Macé had already started construction work. The Roman wall had been reinforced and redesigned, in such a way that one could already see the two towers rising on the lower end of the plot, in a smaller imitation of Mehun. Macé toured the site with me, delighted to show me how diligently she had worked in my absence. I was in despair. I did not dare show her the plans an architect in Florence had drawn up at my request.

I had a quick journey to make to Le Puy. All through the trip I could think of little else than the palace. I had tried to put on a good face in Macé's presence, and, given her enthusiasm, I had acted satisfied. But the moment I was alone I felt overwhelmed with despair. For what obscure reason? I had other properties, and the means to build whatever I liked elsewhere, more in keeping with my Italian taste. I had just purchased the land to build a house in Montpellier. Neither Macé nor anyone else could tell me what to build. And yet these thoughts were no consolation. The palace in Bourges, which hitherto I had paid so little attention to, and had only decided to build in order to please Macé, had now come to occupy an unexpected place. In truth, since Florence, I could think of nothing else. It seemed vital that at the heart of my life, in the place that was both my family home and the center of my business, I should build a palace that would be a testimony to the future, that would be in keeping with my desires and a fulfillment of my dreams. It would be ridiculous to build a pale copy of a seigniorial castle in its place, like some pathetic symbol of noble pretension that would fool no one. In short, the image I would project would be that of an upstart. For years or even centuries, this monument would be the source of a terrible misunderstanding regarding my person. It would show me as a man who was hungry for power and money, who wanted to conquer his place in the feudal world. Basically, I cared little what people in the future would think. But the misunderstanding would start now, with my own family. And to Macé, to our children, and to the king, I wanted to show my true face and my deepest motivations. Money, titles—none of that mattered to me. What drove me was my dream of another world, a world of light and peace, of trade and work, a world of pleasure where what was best in man could be expressed in other ways than simply through the invention of new methods for killing his fellow man. A world where all the finest things from every continent on earth would converge. That was the world I had caught sight of in Florence, and I wanted my palace to resemble it.

When I came back from Le Puy, I was so distracted by these thoughts that I had an accident. I was riding an old black horse that had accompanied me in Italy, and I knew it to be a placid animal. The road climbed steeply up to where a chapel was visible on the edge of the forest. Just as we were halfway up the hill, two dogs ran at my horse's legs. The old gelding swerved to one side, and would not have thrown me had I been more attentive. I fell heavily from the left side, hard onto my shoulder. I was taken to a farm and a surgeon arrived two hours later from the neighboring town. The break was not serious. He bound my arm and I was able to get back on my horse and finish the journey.

This accident had a strange effect on me. Through an unexpected association of thoughts, it gave me an idea regarding my future palace. I thought about this new difference in the two sides of my body, one in good health and the other immobilized, and all of a sudden this suggested a solution. The land where we were building was, as I have said, situated on two levels: a lower level at the foot of the old Roman rampart, and above it an upper level located at the height of the former oppidum. But thus far the work had only affected the rampart, that is, they had hardly touched the upper section. It would therefore be possible, without changing what Macé had already built, to give the future palace two distinct façades. On the side of the rampart, by continuing the work already begun, it would look like a fortified castle. But on the side toward the top of the town, there was still time to build a façade that would follow the Florentine plans. That way, each of us would be satisfied.

Macé could show everyone the imposing wall of a castle that was worthy of our status and proof of our new power. But when arriving from the other side, along the small streets leading down from the cathedral where I had spent my gray and gloomy childhood, I would have the pleasure of knowing I had built an image in stone of the future, and that it was proof that life could be different, and not only elsewhere. The moment one went through the door on this side—a modest door like the ones on palaces in Italy—one would enter a courtyard, and I imagined a cheerful dwelling, with numerous immense openings, and where the few walls that were visible would be decorated with sculptures, fine columns, and frescoes.

The moment I arrived, I shared my plans with Macé. She agreed to it, without fully understanding how this would change her plans, for she had never seen the houses in Italy. She only understood that my intention was to bring a number of innovations to our palace, features I had discovered during my voyages. I am sure she had no idea of the anguish this episode caused me. She insisted I get some rest, first and foremost. From the bed I could see the leaves of springtime in the garden, and the pale sky full of fluffy, white clouds. The linen sheets were soft, and there was a printed canvas on the wall representing a scene from antiquity. I felt immensely relieved, and for three days and nights I did nothing but sleep.

Looking back, I think my mind and body were preparing for the great turmoil they were about to undergo. A great love, when it draws near, is preceded by signs that are initially impossible to decipher. They only become intelligible after the wave has receded, once it has laid bare on the shore the confusion of memories and emotions. And then we understand, but it is too late.

*

I had only just recovered when the king sent for me. Charles never stayed in the same place. In the old days, it was because of the war. And now he continued to do so because it pleased him. In his message he told me that he would be in Saumur very soon, and he summoned me to join him there to take part in the council.

My arm was less painful now, and the physician authorized my journey, provided I was prudent. A few drops of an elixir I had brought back from the Levant eased what remained of the pain, and brought waking dreams full of sweetness and bliss. I set off on a calm mare that the grooms had provided with a deep pommelled saddle. Marc walked alongside to prevent any mishaps. We made our way slowly through the renascent countryside. The fruit trees were in flower and hawthorn blossoms whitened the hedges. The peasants bent over their labor no longer seemed fearful. The treaty had not yet been signed, but peace was already perceptible in the countryside.

Marc, as always, was well-informed, and knew what to expect in Saumur. He spoke to me at the length about the changes in the king. It was true that because of my long voyage in Italy I had not seen him for several months. The truce with England had been confirmed, and there was great hope of turning it into a lasting peace. It was said that Brézé was negotiating a matrimonial alliance to seal the new understanding. In all probability, it was the daughter of René d'Anjou who would be chosen to marry the king of England. It was hoped that this would erase the sinister episode of the failed marriage between Henry V and the daughter of Charles VI, which had rekindled the war thirty years earlier. Charles had reason to be pleased. Marc, however, did not attribute the transformation in the king solely to this favorable outcome. For him no explanation could be valid unless it was rooted in the king's deepest secrets, and such deep satisfaction in his success must be tied to a carnal passion. While he was not generally forthcoming about the political situation, Marc could talk forever about the king's emotional life. The entire matter, in his view, could be reduced to this: Charles had a new mistress.

One of Marc's favorite subjects was to describe the misfortunes of Queen Marie in detail. The poor woman had been overwhelmed by one pregnancy after another. The way Marc reckoned it, the child she had just given birth to was her twelfth. The king's ardor was remarkable, all the more so in that he seemed to have plenty to spare. While the Queen was pregnant or recovering from childbirth, in other words more or less all the time, he directed his attention to other women, of whom there was always an ample supply. I had already had the opportunity to observe the man's vitality, surprising in someone who the rest of the time seemed so downcast, gloomy, and sickly.

In itself, the rumor that said he had a new mistress would have been neither incredible nor astonishing had there not been profound changes affecting the king's personality over these last months. Charles had not been the same since the end of the English peril, or since victoriously leading the country against the princes, with his reforms to reinforce his power. Those who knew him well felt that the two sides of his personality—dark and light, ardent and lethargic, proud and modest—were in the process of reversing their roles. Now the king emerged from the dark recesses where he usually hid, and showed himself in public. At the head of his armies he was valiant, almost reckless; at his council he was energetic; and with women he was gallant.

Until now his liaisons had been furtive and purely carnal. The fact that he had a mistress and that everyone knew it seemed to indicate that in this aspect as well he had decided to bring out into the open something he ordinarily kept hidden. Or, at least, this was my conclusion, on hearing Marc's gossip. I could scarcely have imagined how the king would surprise us.

I arrived in Saumur early on a Monday morning. The castle was asleep, and we met no one in the hallways. A few sleepy valets were limply employed at clearing huge long tables of the remains of a banquet from the night before. As I wandered through the empty rooms, I thought about this king's destiny, and how far he had come since I had first met him at the château in Chinon, alone and fearful. The chair where he had been sitting during the meal was tipped over backwards. Cutlery, napkins, and dirty glasses were strewn everywhere; scraps of food littered the table and the floor around it. I could imagine Charles staying up late, laughing, perhaps singing, complimenting the women and jeering at his companions. Where was the man we used to see who hardly ate, who was so afraid of his fellows that he only entertained a few at a time and at a distance? What had become of the voracious, inconsiderate lover who, according to a few of the women subjected to his assaults, used all his energy to satisfy his desires without a single word of kindness to them?

And yet I could not believe that the king's shadow side had completely disappeared. The evil instincts, which until now had been easy to uncover because they were fully visible on his face and in his behavior, had given way to more complacent virtues. But I suspected those evil instincts were still there, hidden, and that one should be more careful than ever.

I came back at the beginning of the afternoon. The king was up and about. He was standing in a workroom with three young men from the court, whom I knew vaguely by sight, and who were responsible for organizing feasts and banquets. The casements were open. I could hear the wind rustling in the poplar trees and faraway cries rising from the village. The room was filled with sunlight. Charles was holding his face toward the rays of sun, blinking slightly, as if succumbing to the warmth of a caress. He started when he saw me come in.

"Jacques, what a joy to see you at last!"

The others arranged their features in an expression of cheerful contentment, just like the one on the king's face.

He bade me sit down next to him and called for something to drink. Each of his gestures triggered something like an echo of the supposedly joyful agitation in the others around us. Valets came and went, wearing broad smiles. The general atmosphere was good-humored, but the effort everyone was making to conform was clear proof that they were obeying an order.

Charles had summoned me to prepare the upcoming celebrations. The most important, though still some time in the future, was the wedding of his vanquished rival, the king of England, to the daughter of René d'Anjou. But first there were other festivities to plan. I had drawn up a statement of the Argenterie's reserves, in order to be ready for any pertinent questions he might ask. The king seemed pleased with my replies. I added, although he had not asked, that I was at his disposal to contribute financially to the celebrations if need be. Charles shook my hand and let out a laugh, which the others echoed.

I, too, feigned gaiety but remained watchful. Once he had finished with the subject of the celebrations, Charles banished his table companions from the room with a wave of his hand. They left, noisily, jostling each other with jokes and peals of laughter. The king acted as if he shared their good mood. But no sooner had the door closed behind them than his features fell and his expression was doleful once again.

He went over to the window, closed it, and drew the heavy curtain partway, so that the room no longer had the direct light of the sun. Then he dragged his chair over to the wall in the darkest corner and motioned to me to sit down opposite him. This brutal return to our former manners should have alarmed me, but strange as it might seem, it reassured me. On seeing the king revert to the self I had always known, I felt I was treading on firmer ground. At the same time, I knew I should be doubly vigilant. In the old days, when he showed his worst side in public—indecisiveness, weakness, envy—it was to hide his best side deep within: his energy, his firmness, and through all the ordeals, what one must call his optimism. When he displayed cheerfulness, majesty, and gallantry, it meant he was concealing his worst side, and once the door had closed on these spectators, I should expect grave danger.

After a long silence he gave me a sidelong glance and said, "I need a great deal of money for the war."

I shuddered. Ever since the financial reforms the council had been instigating over recent years, the king had employed a permanent personal income to ensure the country's defense. This was one of his principal victories over the princes, the fact that he was no longer obliged to solicit them before starting a campaign. In the new order of the realm, wealth belonged as much to the burghers as to the nobles, and they contributed generously through taxes to their sovereign's expenses. If, in spite of that, he still needed money, this meant that the revenue he received from the treasury did not suffice. Thus there was something more, something of a threat to the king's words.

This revenue depended greatly on the loyalty of those who collected taxes in his name. The king had gratified me with the taxation of the states of the Languedoc, and various levies, in particular on salt. With the same men who represented my company in these regions, I had implemented a very efficient system of collection. Regarding the salt, Guillaume advised us to take charge of transportation and sales all along the Rhone valley. As I was a person both paying the taxes in my capacity as a merchant and collecting them in the name of the king, I could make a considerable profit. I was not stealing from the king. In those territories and activities where I collected taxes on his behalf, the yield was excellent, far superior to what it had been when he was represented in these parts by local noblemen, who tended to keep everything, or almost everything, for their own profit. But, obviously, once I had paid what was owed to the king there was still a great deal left over. I wondered if I should see in his allusion a criticism of my newfound wealth. In any case, if the king felt that the sums amassed were not sufficient, he would certainly ask me to contribute more.

Nor could he ignore the fact that my other activities were extremely lucrative. I had the distinct feeling that, either of his own accord, or under the influence of the many people who envied me my fortune, the king now begrudged me my wealth. His words in that semidarkness, with his sidelong glance, evil, insistent, and the sudden reemergence of his familiar and basic meanness and envy, made it clear that an era had just come to an end.

"The immense consideration which your Majesty has shown leave me eternally in his debt. May I ask your Majesty what exactly is required?"

As I uttered these words, I suddenly found myself again with my father, in the presence of his rich customers in Bourges. Once again I saw him at their mercy, trembling, subjected in advance to their iniquitous decisions. And at the same time, as always, a vision of Eustache the butcher's apprentice flashed through my mind, declaring war against the arbitrary behavior of those in power.

"I want to lay siege to Metz."

"Metz?" I said.

"You know that my brother-in-law, King René, is Duke of Lorraine through his wife," answered Charles grumpily, avoiding my gaze. "His subjects have rebelled, and I am obliged to come to his assistance."

The king's obvious reticence to reply confirmed that this campaign in Lorraine was not strictly necessary, and he knew it. It was merely another concession granted to the house of Anjou. The king had never before seemed so subservient to the influence of his in-laws. Yolande, the mother of Queen Marie, had had him under her thumb for years. Some had even seen her hand behind the providential visit of Joan of Arc, who had been born in Lorraine on lands belonging to Anjou. Yolande's death two years earlier had not released the king from the Angevin influence, far from it. His brother-in-law René lived in his kingdom in grand style, and it was his daughter who had been chosen to marry the king of England. René's brother Charles reigned over the king's council ever since La Trémoille had been eliminated. As for the king's new mistress, people said she was lady-in-waiting to René's wife . . . Thus, behind the king's new strength was the same old weakness that left him dependent on a clan. And he was as subservient to Anjou as he had been to other clans before. In this respect, nothing had changed.

I was suddenly made aware of the limits of my method. I had decided to ally myself with the king in order to eliminate the arbitrary power of princes. I had thought I would be able to establish a relationship of mutual interest. Yet I had managed no such thing. I had merely positioned myself, along with all those who, like me, produced and traded, in absolute submission to a single man.

Our exchange on the issue was very brief, and everything I have just described went through my mind in a flash. We added a few words, to determine the amount of my contribution, and that was all there was to say on the matter. Then the king seemed to relax, and he kept me on for a long while to speak about Italy.

I gave him a detailed description of Florence. But caution had returned and I refrained from telling him that I planned to register there as a silk manufacturer. He would surely have seen it as another attempt to shelter a part of my business from his authority. And he would not have been mistaken.

From the other questions he asked about Italy I understood that he had not abandoned the idea of expanding his influence in that direction. I again mentioned Genoa. But his immediate concern was the pope.

We sat like that for a good hour, and in all that time he never shed his grave demeanor. He was as I had always known him to be: impenetrable, with his twisted mind, enlivened by an evil curiosity that betrayed his envy and vengefulness. For the first time I thought that if he had liberated his country and practically vanquished the English in spite of the constraints of his initial situation, perhaps it was not out of a concern for his kingdom, but rather to assuage the more base desires of revenge that childhood humiliation had nurtured in him, as invasively and painfully as a forest of brambles.

Suddenly the shrill chiming of a church bell rang out in the garden. The sound seemed to wake him up and distract him from his malicious political dreams. He wiped his face and looked all around him like a man who has suddenly regained consciousness. He stood up and opened the curtains wide. The sun had moved. The clear air had a slight chill to it. He pulled his shirt closer, taking a deep breath. Then he came back over to me and sat sideways on the corner of the table.

"What would you advise?" he began.

His features had changed completely. One would have looked in vain for any trace of bitterness or gravity. His anxiety was like that of an adolescent.

"Have you received any rare items at the Argenterie lately,

something precious . . . I would like to find a gift for a lady, the finest gift to be found, or, better still: a gift that cannot be found."

He seemed to delight in the turn of phrase that had come unbidden into his sentence, and he laughed noisily. I stopped and thought for a moment.

"My associates have informed me that a merchant from the Levant recently sold us a diamond of exceptional size."

The king's eyes lit up.

"A diamond! That would be perfect, but it must be truly extraordinary."

"It is. I have heard it is as big as a pebble from the Loire."

Charles's eyes were shining.

"Bring it to me!"

"The problem, sire, is that it has not yet been set, or even cut. As it is, it is a mere gray pebble."

"Never mind. The person for whom it is intended knows what a diamond is. She will have no difficulty imagining . . . "

I promised to have it delivered to him in three or four days. The king took my hands and thanked me. Then he called out, and a troop of servants and stewards immediately appeared. I took my leave. Before walking out of the room, the king held me back for a moment. He leaned closer and whispered, "I am happy, Jacques."

His eyes were proof that he was telling the truth. But in a glance I also noticed the black stubble on his cheeks, his large graceless nose, his twisted limbs and the overlong torso on which his garments hung so awkwardly, no matter how the tailors tried to adjust them. And I told myself that, without a doubt, this man had more charm in misfortune.

Only two days later I would meet Agnès . . .

IV.

Agnès

When I reached this point in my memories, I was overwhelmed by emotion and could no longer continue serenely. I stopped writing for an entire day.

According to Elvira, there is no water on the island where I was hoping to hide. So escape in that direction is impossible. I greeted the verdict less despondently than I would have expected. It is bad news, however. I am doomed to stay here, whatever happens. At the same time—and it is probably for this reason that I was not completely annihilated—the news did have one favorable consequence: I won't be obliged to give up my writing. Now that I have come this far, my desire to open the next door to memory, the one through which Agnès can at last be seen, is so great that I would not have liked to postpone the completion of this project.

So I will stay here, since needs must, but I am conscious of the great risk I am taking. The tranquility of the island, that nothing has come to disturb since the visit from the podestà's man, seems more deceptive than ever. In that way lies danger, and I even have the impression it is coming nearer. I lost my temper with Elvira, who assures me that I have nothing to fear. If she does not feel the threat, it is perhaps because she is too naïve. Most of the time that is my conclusion, and it allows me to be as tender and carefree with her as possible. But there are times when I see her quite differently. I tell myself that while she may be a peasant girl, a daughter of the sea and the vine, she is also a woman who grasps things, who calculates and nurtures hopes I am unaware of. And that is when I become convinced she is betraying me. Now that she knows I am hunted and doomed, and she can no longer obtain anything from me, perhaps she hopes to obtain something from my enemies, if she were to hand me over.

It disgusts me to think like this. I have lived for so long in the midst of intrigue, and in spite of myself I have had the irrefutable proof of human baseness and duplicity so often that I carry the stain of it with me everywhere. Even to this island, where everything seems simple and pure. The only person I have known who kept her soul intact and noble even when surrounded by the worst corruption was Agnès. Elvira and Agnès are as far apart as can be. And yet something makes them similar, and even, in my mind, unites them.

Now that I know there is no escape, there are only two solutions: to stay hidden in the house or make the best of the situation. After I first heard the news I did not sleep all night, and I reached my decision. Since fate has given me this island for a prison, I do not wish to live here as a recluse. If it has to be my cell, I may as well wander here and there and enjoy its beauty. I have begun taking long walks, careful to avoid the town and the harbor. But there are many other things to see. Yesterday, along the trails through the interior of the island, I almost reached the other side. The groves of mastic trees are fragrant in the heat; men come to gather the tears of resin that trickle from the trunks. They greet me, and invite me to drink with them. On the slope leading down to the sea, on the side where the sun sets, I have found lemon orchards, and I enjoy taking an afternoon nap under one of the trees. Their golden apples give me the illusion, when I wake, that I am in the garden of the Hesperides. Here am I, who dreamed of making my country the center of the world, and now I am on the very edge of that world, perhaps even outside it. And in the end, I do not suffer. My ambitions for France were no more than an illusion, and my true country is that of dreams. Is that not where I am now?

Agnès has been haunting me, ever since I wrote of my meeting with her. All these years I had placed her in a recess in my memory, beneath a shrine I have not opened since her death. All my memories are there, intact, fragrant like her body. It was enough for me to say her name for the vial to be broken. Her face, her perfume, her voice have invaded everything. I can no longer find sleep beneath the lemon trees, and I have hurried back here to continue writing. If they came for me now . . . I would have only one regret: if they kill me before I have time to relive my years with Agnès.

I came home at sunset. Elvira had set out olives, ewe's cheese, and an entire basket of fruit. We dined in twilight. There was no moon. Night was falling and I could hardly see Elvira's naked arms crossed on the table. I could hear her breathing. I ran my hands through her heavy mane of hair. As the night gradually caused her singularity to vanish, she was transformed into an indistinct presence made of the smell of her skin, the silkiness of her hair, her short, light breathing, so typical of a woman. All through that long evening until sleep, which came only at dawn, I was with Agnès again. The words took shape inside me and the images came with them. And this morning, all I had to do was sit down and begin for everything to follow.

*

Ten years have passed, but I keep a precise memory of the moment I saw her for the first time. It was two days after my arrival in Saumur. I was giving instructions to one of my shop boys, who had come urgently from Tours. Above all, I had to organize the quick and safe shipment of the rough diamond I had recklessly promised to deliver within four days.

I am not the sort of man who can sit in an office. And even if I were, life would never have given me the leisure to do so, because I am in constant movement. My papers follow me around in a chest. I work wherever chance sets me down. I have been known to confer with my agents from my bed. I sign letters on my lap while they stand before me, hat in hand. But what I like best of all is to work outside, weather permitting. Those days in Saumur, a southerly wind was bringing warm air laden with sand. The shade in the castle gardens was delightful, evocative of moments in Damascus. I had asked for a writing case to be taken into the orchard. In my shirtsleeves, without a hat, I was pacing to and fro and dictating while my agent took notes. He did not want to remove his coat. Sitting on a stone bench, he mopped his forehead and moaned.

Suddenly we heard peals of laughter. We were hidden in the shade, and the young women coming toward us did not see us there, blinded as they were by the sun and absorbed in their conversation. They were still at a distance from us, in the sunlight. They made a tight little cluster, perhaps five or six of them. However, I saw only one of them, and all the others seemed to circle around her like nocturnal insects around a flame. The group followed her wherever she went, and their winding path through the garden was subject to her whims. When they were not far off, her foot struck a pear that had fallen to the ground. She stopped, and the others did likewise. With her toe she kicked the bruised fruit, then, casting her gaze up at the grove of trees where we sat, she cried out, "Look, there are some more!"

She went over to the pear tree, but almost immediately, as she entered the shadow, she saw me and froze. And though I did not know her, I was instantly sure of her.

She cannot have been more than twenty years of age. Her blonde hair was pulled back and arranged simply in a chignon. She had no eyebrows, and her temples were shaven quite far back, which gave her an admirable forehead, as smooth and round as an ivory ball. Sculpted from such a fragile, precious substance, her features were extremely fine. That morning, with her followers, she had not arrayed herself to any effect. Her beauty came from no artifice. It was the brute handiwork of the gods.

Surprise gave her a grave expression, and it was with that expression that I would always remember her. Later I would come to know her laughter, astonishment, fear, disgust, hope, and pleasure. Those were the thousand and one harmonics that the heavenly instrument of her face could produce. The fact remains that, for me, her truth was always that bass note she showed me the instant we first found ourselves face to face.

Her gravity allowed a glimpse of the tragic nature of her beauty: such perfection, envied by all, is for the chosen woman a painful fatality. Beauty of this degree is an image of the absolute to which nothing can be added. And yet the woman who wears it knows how ephemeral it is. It gives her a natural authority, an unequaled capacity for power, but only through a disarmed and fragile body, which can so easily be broken. Beauty of such intensity separates a woman from other mortals, and arouses their jealousy and desire. For the one man she might satisfy, she will leave behind untold victims, who will transform the pain of their disappointed love into a dangerous vengefulness. A king, to whom one can refuse nothing, will see such beauty as an offering of choice, which nature has reserved for him. Thus, the woman who owns such beauty will most often have to forfeit her own desires and follow the exalted destiny to which her perfection has condemned her. At that very moment, I thought of Charles, with his bad breath, his twisted limbs, his rough beard, and I imagined his graceless hands on that diaphanous skin, his mouth on those pale lips.

Accustomed to mistrusting her own feelings and those she aroused in others, the young woman paused hesitantly in my presence. As she knew she was destined for royal favor, she was fearful of any other attachment that she would be obliged to reject, whether she wanted to or not. Later, she would tell me that when she first saw me, she, too, had shared that trouble I felt as she walked toward me.

Yet I did not possess the same qualities as her. I was twenty years older, and could make no claim to beauty. I was dressed like a farmhand bringing in the hay, and there was nothing about me to indicate my identity to her; I had neither the power nor the artifice to make an impression. And yet, I know in that moment she felt something deep for me. We would have numerous opportunities to speak about it later. The explanation she gave me hardly enlightened the mystery. If I am to believe what she said, she immediately recognized me as her "double." It is a strange word, I will grant you that, and never was any double more dissimilar. But she lived in her own world, and the real world had little to do with it. No doubt it was a refuge she had built for herself as protection against life's aggressions. In any case, the only people allowed to enter that world were those she secretly chose, and I had the painful privilege of occupying an eminent place in that world from the moment we met.

The other girls came forward in turn into the leafy shade, and once their eyes grew used to it they stared at me. These were all maidens from the entourage of Isabelle of Lorraine, the wife of King René. Several of them had seen me from a distance when I was attending the king and their mistress was in our presence. Now one of them, less restrained, cried out and put her hand in front of her mouth, "Master Cœur!"

Thus Agnès learned who I was. For nothing on earth would I have wanted for that knowledge to change her attitude. So I stepped forward and, bending my knee, greeted her, never taking my eyes from hers.

"Jacques Cœur, mademoiselle, at your service."

I placed the accent on Jacques, and she immediately resolved to adopt the same intimacy.

"Agnès," she said in a clear voice, and added breathlessly, "Sorel."

None of the others told me their names, as if they had all understood that the scene unfolding was between myself and Agnès. The moment I noticed this fact, I saw a shadow of alarm pass over Agnès's face. No matter the strength of what we were feeling—all the more so, as it was powerful—we must hide it at any cost from these little women. They may have been acting obedient and joyful, but no doubt beneath their finery they concealed daggers of espionage, jealousy, and betrayal.

Agnès took a step back and curtsied.

"I am a faithful customer of your Argenterie, Master Cœur."

Her eyes, as she spoke, looked at each young woman in turn, thus showing that she was not speaking to me alone. Her followers nodded, confirming that things were as they should be. However vaunted my profession, I was still an employee of the king, and a woman of Agnès's position must have only distant relations with me, cordial but lightly tinged with scorn, of the sort one has with a purveyor.

"I hope you are pleased, mademoiselle. You may count on me to do whatever I can to fulfill your desires."

There was a discreet flash in Agnès's eyes in lieu of a smile. In that moment I understood that two registers of expression, like those of an organ, coexisted side by side in her: the first, quite obvious and even exaggerated, was that of social mannerisms, which caused her to share her fits of laughter, astonishment, or sorrow with those she spoke with, as easily as if she were tossing scraps to her dogs. But beneath that, almost imperceptible, as faint as the ripples of a gentle breeze on the surface of the sea, were signs of suffering, hope, tenderness, and genuine love.

"As it happens, I do have several orders in mind, which I will not hesitate to speak to you about. As you know, there are great celebrations in store. We will need to show ourselves there."

She burst out laughing, as did her friends. Everything became joyful, hurried, and frivolous. They left again, in a group, saying goodbye with a nonchalance that verged on insolence.

*

This encounter left me in utter turmoil. In the hours that followed, the most contradictory thoughts went through my mind. I must admit that, in those days, I was becoming more aware of my extreme solitude. The last time I had visited my town I had been able to gauge the indifference I now felt toward Macé. She lived in her dreams of nobility and piety. None of the things that mattered to her—honor, position, the subtleties of social hierarchy in the Berry—had any value in my eyes. At the same time, I met all her demands. The entire family, moreover, seemed to have modeled their expectations on Macé's. My brother was now a cardinal, and he had always gotten on well with his sister-in-law; he surrendered to the same passions as she did, under the guise of his red hat. Our children had also completely adhered to their mother's opinions. My son Jean had finished the seminary. He seemed to have learned more about how to serve himself through the church than how to serve God. My daughter was preparing to make a fine marriage. Only Ravand, my youngest son, seemed interested in following in my footsteps. But it was from a liking for money and not, as with me, in order to pursue his dreams. So much the better for his sake: it would be easier for him to find happiness. I had apprenticed him to Guillaume, and he was doing well.

No one in the family seemed to expect anything from me other than that I keep the riches flowing in. And no one seemed to imagine that I, too, might have desires, needs, and suffering of my own. Ever since my adventure with Christine, I had continued to make use of women without ever trusting any of them. These were brief, carnal, relations, governed by two forms of violence: the cupidity inspired by my fortune, and my mistrust of sentiment. Nothing inclined me in the slightest way toward love, and my solitude was further enhanced by such brutal commerce. In addition, there was my perpetual uprooting. I lived on the highway, and any relations I might establish in the towns I passed through were perforce ephemeral. My friendships were all sealed with the cement of interest. The immense fabric of my business was becoming ever more solid and widespread. But I was all alone in the multitude, trapped like a spider in its own web. There were days when, caught up in the flow of activity, I did not think about it; but other days, as I jogged along on my horse on the open highway, I surrendered to daydreams where my solitude evaporated. But when activity was sluggish, or the news was bad, or I was in the presence of the king and felt physically threatened and endangered, the pain of being alone was overwhelming. This was precisely my state of mind when I met Agnès.

No doubt that is why the desire to see her again, to be with her and to open my heart to her, was so strong. In a split second she had allowed me to glimpse the forgotten delights of love. It was absurd, far too hurried. And yet, ever since I first met Macé, I have known that for me, when true love comes, it is immediate, the instant I set my eyes on the loved one. Moreover, I am sure that certainty, in this matter, does not come with time. It is not habit that creates it. It appears fully armed and unannounced. The letters that love traces in us are never easier to decipher than on the white page of an unprepared mind.

Whatever the case may be, I was in love. At the same time and with the same intensity, I evaluated the horror of this realization. Agnès was the king's mistress. I was entirely dependent on that man and knew only too well his jealous, cruel nature. For a moment I thought of fleeing. After all, my presence was required everywhere by my business, and no doubt I would find some urgent matter somewhere to justify my departure.

It was late afternoon and I was lost in these distressing thoughts when suddenly a messenger came to inform me that the king would be holding council the next day and was counting on my presence. Any retreat was cut off. I had no other choice than to try to remain calm.

So I stayed at court and did not leave except on a few short missions. It was the beginning of a new stage in my life. All at once I found myself parted from my business. Over the last few years I had lived solely amid the frenzy of orders, convoys, and transactions, and now all of a sudden I was instantly handing everything over to Guillaume. This was now possible because we had established a solid network: I had over three hundred agents representing me all over Europe. The movement of money and merchandise was unceasing. Everything radiated from the nerve center of the Argenterie in Tours. The kingdom of France had been reinvigorated through her victories, and in just a few years we had managed to make it the new center of the world, on which the most enviable riches were converging. Once the movement was launched, all that was needed was to maintain it. Guillaume and a few others, all of whom had come from the Berry and were connected to me through greater or lesser ties of kinship, got along perfectly.

Thus, for the first time, freed from the responsibilities that had constantly kept me elsewhere, I immersed myself in life at court.

This world, which until now I had only glimpsed in passing,

was a revelation. To begin with, I was dazed by the luxury. The endless processions of carts that accompanied the king from one town to another were filled with treasures. I took the full measure of this when, not long after my arrival in Saumur, we left again for Tours. There, we joined the queen. The negotiations for the king of England's wedding were being finalized, and the duke of Suffolk was awaited, to conclude the final agreement with great pomp. I was in constant demand at these celebrations. Orders to the Argenterie came pouring in, and I agreed to a good number of loans.

This was all quite usual. But once the time for the ceremonies had come, I suddenly saw beneath the vaults of Plessis-lès-Tours all the riches it had become possible to acquire because of me. Fine cloth, embroidery, jewels, weapons, equipages, fragrant trays of spices, bowls filled with exotic fruit—all of this was the glorious, living aspect of the contracts, commitments, letters of credit, and inventories that went to make up my everyday life. Until that moment I had lived inside the clock's mechanism, and all at once, looking at the clock face, I could admire the harmonious ticking of the hands and the precise chiming of the bell. I became aware of how far my heart had traveled during these years of labor. In the pursuit of my dreams I had ended up losing sight of them, for they were hidden by the monotony of numbers and the petty striving of commercial activity. All of a sudden I was once again standing at the heart of my dreams—dreams that, in the meantime, had become reality.

I was grateful to Agnès for having brought about this transformation. After our first brief meeting, I did not see her alone for a long time. Strangely enough, this state of affairs suited me. The feeling she had aroused was so strong that initially I succumbed to panic and wanted to flee. Retained by the king's summons, however, I was obliged to remain in her proximity, and realized that being near her, catching sight of her across a room, or speaking to her in public all brought intense pleasure, and, in a way, this sufficed. I was afraid that if we were brought any closer together, the power of her attraction would become too great and would lead us to disaster.

I observed the king in her company. His love was never bold, and he was careful never to display the slightest gesture of affection in public; as a result, his passion was expressed only through jealousy. I noticed the expression on his face whenever Agnès spoke to another man. His thoughts distracted him from conversation, and his gaze followed her with a mixture of pain, fear, and malevolence. I was careful not to arouse any such feelings in him. And I was grateful to Agnès for never placing me in such a delicate and dangerous position. Given her great tact, she had long before grasped how cautious she must be in the king's presence. Had he been cleverer, he would have understood her game: in fact, it was those she sought to destroy to whom she showed favor in public. Charles d'Anjou, for example: he was the one who had introduced Agnès to the king, since he held not only the official position as head of the king's council, but also the more dubious one of purveyor of young flesh. With him, Agnès was openly affectionate. He was weak enough to find it entertaining, never realizing that she was preparing his disgrace. Brézé, on the other hand, my friend Brézé, always bold, ambitious for the kingdom, and generous to his friends, was someone whom I knew Agnès appreciated greatly. And yet she showed him nothing but coldness when she met him in the presence of the king.

And so these shining, happy weeks went by, and I waited expectantly for the event that would bring me closer to Agnès, knowing neither its nature, nor when it might come. It was enough for me to see her, hear her, and know that she was near me.

*

I was suddenly very busy with the council, following the king in his majestic wanderings from castle to castle. This was, in truth, the first time that I was completely involved in life at court. I was astonished to see that it consisted of almost equal parts boredom and festivity, two conditions which hitherto I had scarcely known. Boredom reigned over the castle for hours on end. My life had accustomed me to rising early; yet now I discovered motionless, silent mornings where everyone was shut away in their apartments. The space was given over to valets and chambermaids. They maintained this silence in order not to compromise the freedom it gave them. Afternoons were equally languid, either because they were filled with the gloom of a downpour, or, as the season progressed, because sunshine and warm air instilled in people's drowsy consciousness a desire for naps or whispered conversation. But in the evening everything came alive, and the premises were filled with feasting. The brilliant chandeliers, the intoxicating perfume, the shimmering colors and powders all converged to create an excitement that began before supper and ended late at night.

I learned to gauge the refinements of the house of Anjou, now in the ascendant. Charles of Anjou was at the head of the council; René was the future father-in-law of the king of England; Queen Marie, however unfaithful her husband might have been, still gave birth to multiple heirs; and wherever one looked there were Angevins. King René, the head of this house, I did not know well. He was a mediocre politician who had lost all the property he had inherited in Italy, and who was king of Jerusalem only on paper. But one must pay homage to the fact that he knew how to live. Until this point I had served luxury like no other man; the paradox was that I had rarely enjoyed it myself. Since childhood I had been dreaming of palaces, but, as in the old days with my father, I still approached a palace as a stranger, and never stayed for long. It took my meeting with Agnès and my brutal conversion to life at court to experience what it meant actually to inhabit such luxurious dwellings, to feel I had a right to be there, and to live to the rhythm of the festivities.

This conversion, although the causes were very different, was fairly similar to the one the king had known. Prior to this, his life, and his family's, had been austere. Public events were limited to the four plenary courts, at Easter, Pentecost, All Saints', and Christmas. The king gave presents to his courtiers and attended a solemn mass. Then a feast was held, at the end of which valets tossed coins, crying, "Largesse, largesse." It was simple, short, and basically quite dreary. Now that the king had shown he was open to pleasure, certain customs that were in fashion at other courts had been introduced into his own.

The great organizer of these new festivities was incontestably King René. His energy in such matters commanded admiration. Circumstances were particularly favorable for him, and when we joined him in Nancy he offered us a veritable apotheosis of divertissements of all sorts. Through his travels, his widespread family ties, and his own curiosity, King René knew everything there was to know about festivities in Europe. He did not want to be the last one to indulge. He paid for troupes of artists and impresarios. He was the one to introduce in France the custom of the *pas,* which had long been current in Burgundy. These *pas* were knightly tournaments whose complicated rules had been established in Germany or Flanders. During these celebrations, the old warlike and courtly foundations of chivalry were combined with all the artifices of modern luxury: chiseled weapons, magnificent gowns, and grandiose spectacles preceding the tournament.

The king seemed to enjoy himself greatly during these festivities. After the surrender at Metz, he went to Châlons, where

René had organized a *pas* in his honor lasting eight days. Charles was acclaimed when he broke lances with Brézé, who manifestly had let him win. It was clearly Agnès whom the king intended to dazzle. He greeted her conspicuously. For the occasion, she was wearing a silver gem-encrusted suit of armor. This exceptional piece, like almost all the finery, adornments, and saddlery that made the assembly so brilliant, came from the Argenterie. In the preceding weeks I had received all the most illustrious courtiers, and I had done my best to give all of them, even the most impoverished, the means to maintain their rank. Agnès had come to see me in person. She cannot have failed to notice that I was disturbed by her presence. However, she was not alone, and the conversation was limited to practical questions concerning her requirements for the *pas*. Our encounter left me puzzled and somewhat melancholy. This was the first occasion I had seen her on her own since that first time, and so many weeks had passed. Even if I took into account the reserved manner required by the presence of her ladies-in-waiting, I could no longer sense in her those feelings I had once intuited. Not a sign, even the most discreet; not a gaze, let alone an ambiguous word to provide purchase for my feelings. I began to wonder whether once again I had been carried away by dreams that belonged only to me.

Her attitude during the *pas*, which I observed attentively and with no need to dissimulate, because she was the object of all gazes, showed me that she was in love with the king more than ever, and more than ever beloved by him.

When one's heart is sad during such celebrations, one is sure to cast a cool eye upon the events. I had eight full days, therefore, during the festivities, to form an opinion about King René and the nature of the luxury and enjoyment he had introduced to the court. I was richly attired, as was befitting, for the king constantly sent for me to accompany him here or there, or asked me to see to some material details. I wore a smile for the occasion, to make everyone think that I, too, took part in the general merrymaking. In reality, my mood was glum.

These tournaments seemed ridiculous and inappropriate to me. They were an attempt to revive a bygone era. If at last we were about to triumph over the English, it was because we had created a modern army, which Bureau provided with artillery and I was financing. It was this new army we should have been celebrating, not the chivalry that had ruined the realm.

And if only this evocation of the customs of the past had been humble and modest! When I acquired my fortified castles, it was the muffled echo of that long-ago time that I heard, and it filled me with a pleasant nostalgia. But during these tournaments, on the contrary, chivalry claimed to be alive still, whereas I knew very well that it was dead. And I knew what was going on underneath it all. I had an exact accounting of the lands that had been sold, the castles let go for nothing, the loans under contract. I knew how much poverty went to pay for this debauchery of riches. Chivalry was alive when it was founded on the possession of land and the submission of men. Now it was money that reigned, and there were no more lords.

One of the highlights of the spectacle, in Châlons, was the gallant demonstration by the paragon of knights, the illustrious Jacques de Lalaing, who was known all over France to be the epitome of the valiant knight. He was a hero straight from the legends of King Arthur. His gestures of piety were known to all, and he shone with the halo conferred by the reputation of his exploits in single combat. He made of his chastity a virtue and a paradoxical tool of seduction. I was curious to meet this prodigy who claimed to be keeping the discipline of chivalry alive and at its most rigorous level.

What I saw was a pretentious and virginal young man, crude and actually quite ridiculous. His chastity was clearly not the result of a vow but rather of timidity disguised as virtue. His manners were so unlike those of the time that it was as though he were acting a part. Spectators eyed him with the same curiosity that had caused them to applaud the comedians performing before the *pas*. During the tournament, Jacques de Lalaing turned his experience to good advantage as he went from combat to combat. While ordinary gentlemen rarely indulged in such activities, for this professional knight they were a familiar routine. He owed his success more to the awkwardness of his adversaries than to any talent of his own. However, he glorified every one of his acts with so much affectation, he sacrificed so scrupulously to the most complicated and old-fashioned rituals, that his victories seemed to be the logical consequence of a nobility, the appearances of which he painstakingly maintained.

In reality, the little man was a perfect imbecile. Conformity was taken to the extreme, in lieu of originality. I had proof of this when, between two jousts, I had the opportunity to converse with him. Wandering in the vicinity of his valets, I realized it would be better not to look too closely at the knight's equipment. The leather of his harnesses was dry and split, fabrics were patched, and his horses, once they were stripped of their showy battle gear, were scrawny, underfed beasts. These details reassured me somewhat. They made the knight more human, and above all more representative of the caste he claimed to incarnate. Like everyone else, he had no money. The world he thought he belonged to no longer had anything in common with the errant knights of yore. No matter how much he hurried from one combat to the next, luxuriously received each time, he was finding it difficult to survive. In the course of our conversation I urged him to speak of material issues. He looked at me with horror. I realized that his aim to live a life of heroic, eternal chivalry was not an act. He obstinately refused to see the world as it was, and he looked on people like myself with the same scorn his ancestors had lavished on our kind. If I had not seen Agnès showing him so much admiration, casting loving gazes on him, perhaps I would never have been so cruel as to hound him into a corner during our conversation. But I could not resist the pleasure of watching him squirm. He knew of my role in the king's entourage and could not treat me as disdainfully as he would have liked. His defense, when faced with my impertinence, was to mumble some confused words.

I was accustomed to behaving quite naturally around all the noblemen at court, and thus was acting perfectly normally when I offered him new mounts and leather imported from Spain. I prodded his battered armor shamelessly, while cruelly vaunting the quality of our Genoese breast plates, and informed him that all he had to do was come by the Argenterie to have one made to his size. As he was choking on his words, desperately seeking a pretext to run away, I aggravated his distress by offering him payment facilities for any amount he might deem necessary to spend. Absolutely terrified by now, more disarmed than if a fire-breathing dragon had attacked him in the forest of Brocéliande, Lalaing climbed back into his saddle without waiting for help from his valet. His armor rattled like old saucepans and he had to make three attempts to get his leg over his horse's rump. He did not stop shouting, "Thank you, thank you," and trotted away sitting sideways and blinded by his helmet, which, during these acrobatics, had slipped down over his eyes.

This entertainment left me with a bitter taste, and in any case did not suffice to reconcile me with this merrymaking that to me smelled of death. I pondered my rage all through the remainder of the festivities. I had come to a decision: I would leave the court. I had been totally mistaken with regard to Agnès's feelings, and moreover, what could I dare hope for? This brief interlude had been absurd, sheer madness, one of the manifestations, no doubt, of that melancholy that grips men in midlife and makes them imagine, mistakenly, that they can begin a second life, enlightened by the experience of the first one. All that remained was for me to find a way to announce my decision to the king and to persuade him to accept it.

I do not know whether it is to be regretted or seen as an opportunity. In any case, my resolution was broken in the weeks that followed, when Agnès sent for me from Beauté.

*

The king, whose frugality had long verged on miserliness, now liked to spend. He expressed joy or gratitude by giving gifts. Every time she gave birth, the queen received a superb gown. And as I mentioned, Charles found it equally natural to buy a huge diamond for his mistress. His victories over the English gave him opportunities to make many other, even more generous gifts, since they consisted of land seized from the enemy. In general, this war booty was used to reward his most valiant captains or other notables at court.

The king combined the practice of bestowing gifts of affection with the royal privilege of granting prerogatives when he decided to give Agnès an estate. I doubt he picked it out himself, because his basic stinginess would certainly have compelled him to choose a more modest dwelling. No doubt it was Agnès herself who asked for Beauté. And she got it.

Did she already know the place, or had she been charmed by the castle's name? In any case, she made an excellent choice—too excellent, even, for it caused a scandal. Built by Charles V, the domain of Beauté, near Vincennes, is one of the most beautiful castles in France. Charles's grandfather had made it his favorite residence. It had been recaptured from the English by Richemont five years earlier.

The nature of this favor suddenly revealed what everyone knew but pretended they didn't: the king was in love. By taking possession of this royal domain, Agnès rose above the status of a mere mistress. And yet no one was prepared to envisage her entry into the royal circle. Jealousy was rampant, and the courtiers' expressions now gleamed with hatred.

Neither the king nor Agnès gave these envious courtiers the satisfaction of paying attention to their moods. Charles was certainly sincere: he was far above such base considerations, and if he did happen to notice the scowls of jealousy on others' faces, his natural cruelty must have rejoiced in it. As for Agnès, she understood everything. But with the exertion of a constant effort she managed not to let anything show, and was even more considerate with her worst enemies.

She did not let her new title as Dame de Beauté go to her head. However, the name was doubly provocative because it was both a sign of nobility and a compliment. She wore it the way she wore her gowns: perfectly naturally, and with pleasure, neither seeking to shine nor depriving herself of the means to do so.

The celebrations at Nancy and Châlons required her presence, and gave her no time to settle into her estate. It was only after the *pas* that she decided to go there. And, to my astonishment, she took me with her.

Thus, I had a first opportunity to observe how clever she was. She had indicated her indifference and even coldness toward me all these weeks so conspicuously that the king, no matter how jealous, made no objection to my presence at Agnès's side for the voyage. Moreover, as there was talk of refurbishing and renovating the castle, it was logical that I go there myself to see what would be needed.

We set off with an armed escort, but there were only four of us with Agnès. She had brought only one of her ladies-in-waiting, and I was accompanied by Marc. I had hesitated to take him. I knew I would have to put up with his knowing smile and suggestive glances. If Agnès happened by chance to intercept one of these signs, she might take me for a vulgar individual. In the end, I did take Marc, but ordered him to trot behind us and keep his distance.

It was a fairly short journey, because Agnès was a good rider and preferred to cover as much ground as possible. We had two days of bad weather. She loved galloping through the storm, causing the escorts to panic. In their efforts to keep up, the men were encumbered by their weapons, so I often found myself alone with her. It was as though I were seeing another individual emerge from under the noblewoman's mask, an exalted, almost reckless woman whose gaze at times burned with a disquieting flame. Her hair was ruined by the rain, and her powder was running. She emanated a wild energy. The looks she gave me at times, her peals of laughter, and the way she would run her tongue over her lips, wet with the cold rain, were all deeply disturbing. Once again I felt the powerful familiarity of our first encounter. But, for all that, I did not know what to think or, above all, say.

We went through Vincennes on a fine sunny day. But we arrived at Beauté before we had a chance to recover from the ravages of the storm. Consequently, we looked more like a gaggle of gypsies when we crossed the drawbridge over the castle moat.

At the end of the afternoon I went with Agnès on a tour of Beauté. The English had not kept it up, but at least they did not pillage it. The rooms were already dark, and I held a torch in my hand. In Charles V's library, thousands of neatly aligned books shone in the glow of the flames, sparkling gold in the darkness. The square tower in the middle of the castle consisted of three stories. The room of the Evangelists was decorated with monumental paintings. The room "above the fountain" had not been altered since Charles V had died there. His son liked to retire to the castle with Isabeau of Bavaria, in the days when the madness had not yet alienated his mind. He had closed up the austere and tragic rooms where the old king had ended his life, and had arranged one floor where he could live with his lover. Agnès took one of the rooms on this floor for herself and gave the other to me, which was separated from hers by a landing furnished with a large oak wardrobe. She decreed that the staff would stay on the ground floor, as had been the custom under Charles VI. Her lady-in-waiting was a tall, silent, smiling girl. Agnès seemed to have chosen her deliberately from among the others, because there was little that was spiteful about her. She did not object to being apart from her mistress. Marc seemed delighted to be lodging near the young woman—now it was my turn to give him a mocking smile.

Before night fell, Agnès led me up to the top of the tower. We could see far into the distance above the forest, and even make out the smoke above Paris to the west. We stood side-by-side with our elbows on the rough stone of a large crenellation. The peacefulness of twilight did little to calm the turmoil inside me. I could hear Agnès's breathing, slightly quickened from walking up the stairs—unless it was from emotion, and I thought I was mad to hope that it was. However, she did nothing that might let me guess her feelings, and I remained as cautious as ever. When it was dark we went back down. Marc served us supper in a room on our floor that must have been used for councils of war in the time of the English. The table in the middle was small. It must have dated from the time of Charles and Isabeau's love affair. All around there were the chairs that the English had set out for their war meetings.

Agnès and I had already talked a great deal during the journey. While she was from Picardy, and I from the Berry, we discovered we shared a passion for Italy. She had lived there for several years with Isabelle of Lorraine, and, thanks to her, she had met many artists with whom she corresponded.

Our conversation, as we rode along in the open air within earshot of her lady-in-waiting, could not be very private, although every word Agnès said seemed to carry a weight of feeling which extended its meaning. I learned a great deal about her background and education. She was the daughter of a minor lord from the region of Compiègne. He belonged to the House of Bourbon, and, through the intercession of the Duke, who had allied himself with the House of Anjou, Agnès had been sent at a very young age to attend to Isabelle of Lorraine. Isabelle was an energetic and cultured woman, and she had a great influence upon Agnès. Agnès told me what I already knew: that after the defeat of her husband and his capture at Dijon, Isabelle had united René's vassals at the castle in Nancy, and had made them take an oath of loyalty to her. When, subsequently, through the random nature of succession, the unfortunate captive had found himself king of Naples, Sicily, and Jerusalem, Isabelle had left for Italy to take possession of this legacy while waiting for her husband's release. She had valiantly defended his property, selling jewels and silver to raise an army against the king of Aragon. And she had been far better at it than poor René, who, once he was released, had hastily proceeded to lose everything. The episode was well known. The most interesting thing was to see the impression it had made on Agnès. In addition to high culture and a good education, Isabelle of Lorraine had left her with the model of a bold, free, strong woman. Agnès particularly admired in her the mixture of deep, total love—for she had known true passion with René—and independence, which meant she could act on her own. Circumstances had not left Agnès with similarly favorable conditions to follow Isabelle's example. But I could sense, and the future would prove this to me, that she nurtured the same qualities in herself, and would find the means to express them.

That first evening at the castle we dined in near silence. The last leg of the journey had been long. This place—so rich in royal intimacy, these rooms which had witnessed death and love, defeat and renewal—made us uneasy. In spite of the small dimensions of the room and the tapestries that stifled noise, we felt strangely intimidated, as if we were dining beneath high, echoing vaults.

After supper, we wished each other good night and withdrew to our separate chambers. I had Marc bring up some water and I spent a long time washing, to remove from my skin the dust of the road and the mingled odors of sweat and horse. I could hear footsteps coming and going across the hall, which told me that Agnès was doing the same. Then the servants went down to their floor. Agnès's lady-in-waiting let out a laugh in the stairway, a probable sign that Marc had not waited to be all the way downstairs to intercept her.

At last the castle fell silent.

Fatigue came, and with it, sleep. However, once I had stretched out on my bed, I stroked the linen sheet pensively, and could not bring myself to snuff out the candle. I revisited all the details of the voyage, and Agnès's expressions. I wondered how I should interpret this voyage, the trust she was showing me by accommodating me so near. Her position as the king's mistress, the attraction I felt to her, the idea that my feeling might be shared, and the fear of breaking the spell if I were to go further all formed in my mind a tight knot of contradictory and disturbing thoughts that Agnès alone could have unraveled.

Which she did, somewhat later during the night, by coming into my room.

*

Ten years have passed since that night, seven without her. I have never spoken of that moment with anyone. And yet everything is etched on my mind with perfect clarity. I remember every gesture, every word we exchanged. To bring it all back to life now in writing is causing me a curious mixture of extreme delight and pain. It is a bit like reliving those moments with her but also, and forever, in her absence.

I was hardly surprised when she opened the door. Without knowing it, I was waiting for her. And everything happened in a similar fashion, through an unspoken agreement, barely conscious but total. She was holding a copper candlestick. Her face was golden in the light, and her forehead seemed bigger than ever. She had let her blonde hair loose and I was surprised to see it fell almost to her shoulders. She did not say a word on entering, but smiled and came over to my bed. She sat on the edge and put the candle down on the night table. Matching her boldness with my own, I lifted the sheets and she slipped in beside me. Her body suddenly seemed very small, like that of a child, perhaps because she curled up against my shoulder. Her feet were icy and she was shivering.

We stayed like that for a long time. Everything was silent outside. We could hear a shutter banging in the wind on the floor above. I felt as if I had rescued a hunted doe who was slowly recovering her calm after a long pursuit in which her life had been at stake. She seemed so vulnerable, so fragile that, despite her sweetness, the exquisite smell of her hair, the feminine lightness with which her body embraced mine, I felt my desire ebbing. The urge to protect her was too great. It crushed any urge to possess her, as if taking anything from her, let alone her entire self, would have been an unbearable betrayal.

Finally she sat up, took hold of a pillow for support, and, holding herself at a slight remove, she looked at me.

"I immediately knew I could trust you," she said.

Her eyes were open wide, staring at me and studying my face for the slightest expression. I smiled. She remained grave.

"And why?" I asked. "I am a man, after all. A man like any other."

She laughed suddenly, with a clear laugh that showed me her flawless white teeth. Then she regained her composure and with a tender gesture arranged a lock of hair falling on my brow.

"No, no. You're not a man, in any case not a man like any other."

I did not know whether I should take offense at this remark. Was she mistaken as to the respect I showed her? Perhaps she believed I was incapable of desiring her. I had no time to act offended or prepare any denials: she suddenly held out her arms and, with a smile, looked straight ahead into the darkness of the room.

"I had heard about the Argentine. That is a very serious title, and I imagined that the man with such a title would be an austere gentleman. And then . . . I saw you."

She turned back to me and began to laugh again.

"Instead of an austere gentleman, I found an angel. A stray angel. That is truly what you are: a creature who has fallen from the moon, on whom fate has played a curious trick by placing him in high office. And you make a great effort to make others believe you are where you should be."

"Is that how you see me?"

"Am I mistaken?"

I protested as a matter of form, arguing that I had worked hard to obtain what I had acquired, trying to convince her that I was in earnest. But I did not bother to argue for long; she had seen me as I was. No one had grasped more quickly or more deeply the discrepancy between my official role and the world of my desires and my dreams.

"I'm afraid," she cried out all of a sudden. "Do you know how afraid I am?"

She leaned toward me, put her arm around my neck and placed her head on my shoulder.

"It is good to be able to tell someone. I have no one, do you understand? No one I can trust."

"The king?" I ventured.

She sat up abruptly.

"Even less than anyone else!"

"Do you not love him?"

This was not exactly our subject, but the urge to ask the question was stronger than anything. Agnès shrugged.

"How could I?"

Terrible, unknown images blurred her gaze for a moment. Then she regained her composure and went on in a more confident voice.

"I have to fight everyone all the time. That's the way it is. You cannot imagine how good it is for me to be able to lower my guard for a moment and speak freely. With an angel."

She gave me a mischievous look and we began to laugh. I felt incredibly at ease with her, as if I were in the presence of a sister. I told myself that she, too, was a stray angel, and no doubt we came from the same planet, somewhere in the ether.

Then Agnès began to explain her plans. Everything was perfectly coherent and she had thought it through. Behind the young courtier who gave the impression she could not see the hostility she provoked, behind the mistress who showed admiration and tenderness for the king, behind the fragile creature from the Anjou clan, there hid a lucid, determined woman who had a powerful instinct for survival and was exceptionally intelligent when it came to inventing the means to defend her interests.

"Now that I have come this far," she said, "I have no choice. I have to remain the mistress of the king and exert undivided authority over him. The women he had before me were not on the same level. In their time, the king was timid and his liaisons were, if not secret, at least discreet. Now he has changed. He has placed me too high, and I am too visible to survive any repudiation. If he puts another in my place, my enemies will find me without protection and they will kill me."

"But why would he put another woman in your place?" I said to reassure her.

That was indeed my conviction: the joy of having such a woman as one's mistress must surely fulfill a man. At the same time, the thought that anyone but I had that good fortune filled my heart with bitterness.

"I do not trust him at all in that regard," she said curtly. "And I know that Charles of Anjou, who is constantly seeking to ingratiate himself with the king, will not fail to introduce other women in order to supplant me."

"It would be an error of judgment on his part. Are you not, in a way, a member of his house?"

"Less and less. The king's passion for me makes me independent. I have my own means, my own land now, so I am no longer subjected to the house of Anjou. They did what they wanted with me long ago. That is over now."

This evocation of her troubles seemed to distress her, and her tenderness faded. Then she sat up and said, "I'm hungry. Come with me to the dining room."

"Do you think they've left anything?"

"My lady-in-waiting knows that I get up every night to eat something, and she always leaves me a bowl of fruit or some cakes."

She stood up and I followed. We were in our nightshirts, and walked cautiously through the dark rooms like children. Agnès held me by the hand. We opened the door to the small dining room. And indeed, on a sideboard, a pewter bowl was waiting, full of Pippin apples. She bit into one and I did likewise. We pulled up two chairs so that we could sit side by side. With one elbow on the table, Agnès pivoted and rested her legs on my thighs.

"I am pregnant," she said distractedly, reaching for another apple.

"That's a fine thing. It should attach you even more to the king."

She shrugged.

"On the contrary. He has the queen to give him children. My condition will only make things awkward, and I must hide it from him as long as possible. The only consequence at the moment is that I must take action sooner than ever."

"Take action?"

She tossed the apple core onto the table and wiped her mouth with the back of her hand. With her hair down and her throat uncovered, sitting sideways with her elbows on the rough table, she looked like a tavern wench, a raw and sensual little savage. Her courtly restraint had totally vanished. Far from being horrified by this transformation, I was delighted. It made me aware that I was in the presence of the real Agnès, the one she hid from the rest of the world. She confided in me as she would to herself. And although I, too, was accustomed to dissimulation and solitude, I had the strangest certainty that I could tell her everything and reveal to her the truth of my soul.

"Yes, take action. Everything is ready, my Cœur."

She laughed suddenly and took my face in her palms.

"Well, that is how I shall call you. I do not like Jacques. You will be 'my Cœur.'"

She came closer and kissed me on the lips. A chaste kiss.

"You were saying, you must take action?"

She stood up and went to open the door to a cupboard in the wall behind us. She took out a jug of water and two glasses.

"It is time to restrain the influence of the Anjou clan," she said, like a judge peremptorily handing down a sentence.

Then she added, "And besides, Pierre de Brézé agrees with me on this matter."

I knew she was on good terms with the seneschal. I felt a sudden sting of intense jealousy. Did she share the same intimacy with him? While her intimacy with the king only caused me sadness, a relationship with Brézé would have filled me with rage. She smiled and, guessing my thoughts, she sat down again next to me and stroked my hand.

"No, my Cœur! Pierre is a friend but I have not recognized him as a brother, like you. That's because there is nothing of the stray angel in him. He is a fine, upstanding man, but he is a man all the same, no more. He can be brutal, as he has proved in the past. Our friendship is sincere, but it is his fervor as a soldier I must restrain. That does not prevent us from being in agreement. My own interests and Brézé's regarding the well-being of the king and of the realm are in accord. Charles has defeated the English, and subjected the princes. One final obstacle remains for him to be completely free, and a great king: he must remove the Anjou clan who are reigning in his place."

"But Brézé owes everything to the Angevins."

"He shows more loyalty to the king than to anyone. His opinion is that the House of Anjou has become dangerously powerful. They are weaving their web, and when they remove their veils it will be too late."

"So what are you going to do?"

"I am leaving it up to Pierre to choose the time and the manner. It is he who a few years ago rid the king of that dreadful La Trémoille. He is clever at this sort of brilliant maneuvering, and the king fears him."

"And when will he lead the offensive?"

"He's waiting for the right moment, and it will come soon. In the meantime, each of us must encourage the king's mistrust of the Anjou family. Our best ally is poor René. The more he displays his wealth and struts about, the more he annoys Charles and gives him reason to fear him."

I was fairly convinced by Agnès's arguments, and knew myself that the influence of the princes, even when limited to one family, must be curbed at any cost. Nothing shocked me about Agnès and Brézé's change of heart. The Anjou clan had used them unscrupulously and would not hesitate to do away with them if need be. They acted only to protect themselves. But one thing did bother me, with regard to the trust I wanted to show Agnès: how could she betray Isabelle of Lorraine so callously, a woman to whom she owed everything? So I asked her quite openly. She reacted vigorously, like an animal being forced.

"When the men of that family introduced me to the king," she spat, "when they sold me to him like an animal, and I was still innocent, Isabelle tried to defend me. There were terrible scenes between her and her brother-in-law. But her husband was a weak man, and he disowned her, forcing her to yield. We wept all that night. She held me to her and made me swear to obtain my revenge some day. At the time I did not know what she meant, but I swore. And now, the time has come. Not only am I *not* betraying her but, in fact, I am obeying her!"

On these words she stood up and took me by the hand. We went back to my room. Once again she nestled close to me.

"When did they introduce you to the king?"

"Over two years ago. I was nineteen when I saw Charles for the first time, in Toulouse. I was very different then. I have learned a great deal in two years."

A silence fell, and I sensed she was getting drowsy. But before she fell asleep I wanted to ask her one more question.

"So," I said hesitantly, "what do you expect from me?"

She laughed.

"Nothing, mon Cœur. Above all, do not get involved. You have brought me something irreplaceable: you are the only person to whom I can speak freely. With Brézé we may have this plan in common, but otherwise there are very few things I can trust him with. I remain on my guard. You are my brother, my friend."

"And what makes you think I will not betray you?"

She stroked my cheek.

"I know you as well as I know myself. We are two pieces of a star that has split apart and fallen to earth. Don't you believe in that sort of thing? And yet it is God himself who has told me."

"God?"

"He answers me when I pray."

She raised herself up on her elbow and gave me a stern look.

"Do not tell me you have no faith!"

"To be honest—"

"Be silent. You are proud and ignorant."

She smiled, then put her head back on my shoulder. I could tell she was falling asleep.

"If we are caught like this—"

"My lady-in-waiting has orders not to come until morning unless I call for her."

With a yawn she added, "And besides, we have nothing to fear from her."

A few seconds later she was sound asleep. I lay awake for a long time, troubled by the sudden appearance in my life of this little woman who was so determined and so tender, so familiar and so mysterious. I fell prey to hurried thoughts, unable to pin any of them down. Contradictory feelings divided my heart. I was afraid of desiring her, and thus of betraying not only the king but also the trust she had placed in me. At the same time, rather foolishly, I felt guilty for not seeming enterprising enough; would she not take my coldness, as a man, for disdain? Eventually I cast off this ridiculous torment and surrendered unrestrainedly to complete happiness. After all, I had had no lack of carnal opportunities, and they had never fulfilled me. What was lacking, above all, was a friendship of the sort a man and a woman can have only when they are well matched. Agnès brought me the trust, truth, simplicity, and love that I needed as much as she did. I allowed myself to succumb to the delight of this unexpected relationship, and decided that, whatever happened, I would place this trust above anything else. As for the rest, the shape this friendship would take . . . we would see.

*

We stayed at Beauté for five days, five whole days and nights where we were constantly in each other's company. Agnès talked to me about everything, about her childhood, her fears, and her dreams, and I, for the first time, was able to open my heart completely to someone. I could never have revealed to Macé my doubts and my peculiar ideas. Agnès understood everything. If there were certain things that I kept silent, it was because I was sure that she had already understood them.

Thus began the strange affection that in those years made Agnès the most precious creature on earth for me. It was not that the flesh was completely absent from this relationship, because we did love to feel our bodies touching, and the tenderness between us took the delightful form of kisses and caresses. However, for a very long time, and until those last grievous moments, which I hope I will have time to evoke, we were not lovers. It was as if we knew that to cross that boundary would have caused us to enter another space, where all the rest of our relationship would have been taken from us. Thus, our unfulfilled desire, rather than being limited to one act alone, radiated through all our gestures and all our thoughts, and gave that which, in spite of everything, I dare to call "our love" an unequaled intensity, and an inimitable coloring.

It was now out of the question for me to leave the court. I needed to be near Agnès, to be able to share with her, even if it was only a brief look. Life with the king obliged us to be extremely cautious. We were careful never to arouse Charles's suspicions, although he was quick to take offense. We feigned indifference, long days where we never went near one another. And we had to plan well in advance if we wanted to meet. I had let Marc in on the secret, which was unnecessary because he already knew everything. Agnès used the same lady-in-waiting, a woman from Picardy like herself, a girl who was trustworthy and from a village next to the one where she was born. There were times when we were able to spend two or three long spells of an afternoon or evening together in the same week. But a month or more might also go by when we were unable to meet. I am referring, naturally, to private meetings; there was no lack of official occasions to see or speak to one another.

These opportunities became all the more frequent once the revolution Agnès had foretold took place, not long after our discussion at the castle at Beauté. Brézé was wily enough to determine when the time had come to move beyond clever appearances. When he judged that the king was ready, he removed his mask. He asserted that a new plot was underway, led by the Anjou clan, that he had proof of it and that it was urgent to act. The king, at his request, banished several lords who were close to the Angevins, and enjoined René to withdraw to his estate. As for René's brother, Brézé was able to persuade him that if he showed his face again at the council, he ran the risk of being assassinated. Anjou knew what the seneschal was capable of, and he did not come again.

Thus, the king was rid of the Anjou clan, quietly and bloodlessly, and in only a matter of days. He suddenly found himself with a new coterie, and the great lords were now absent.

Because of this upheaval, my own position changed. Thus far I had been tolerated at the council, like the other burghers, because of the services I provided. Now that Charles of Anjou was no longer there, I found myself surrounded by other burghers and minor noblemen like Brézé. He was now the strongman of the Council. We formed a group around him recruited on the basis of competence, rather than birth. What we could not bring to the Council in the way of illustrious family origins we compensated for in numbers: thus we had the Juvénal brothers, the Coëtivy brothers, and the two Bureaus.

Agnès gained doubly through this change of affairs. On the one hand, with Charles of Anjou gone, she was rid of the man who had first handed her over to the king, and then proceeded, with the same offhand cruelty, to provide him with new girls. Moreover, the men who now sat on the Council were primarily her friends. Combined with the influence she had over the king, she was now in a position to play a leading role. This did not shelter her from danger. Her power elicited still more jealousy than in the early days of her affair. The Dauphin despised her, because he saw her, quite rightfully, as a rival who had even greater influence over the affairs of the realm than he did himself. But the greatest danger threatening Agnès, which she well knew, remained the king.

He may have changed his manners, but deep down he was still every bit as mean and inconstant. In spite of her quick wits and painstaking daily scrutiny of Charles's moods, Agnès could never be completely sure of him. She made a constant effort to be charming and surprising. As she had told me, she dreaded nothing so much as pregnancy. It made her heavy, and however she might try to hide them, her pregnancies always necessitated a brief and dangerous absence, the time required to give birth. Unfortunately for her, the Valois temperament Charles had inherited gave him a vigor and appetite that kept Agnès pregnant almost as often as the Queen. The difference between the two women, however, could not have been greater. The queen made a public display of her gestation periods. She went from bed to chaise longue in a perpetual complaint of nausea, edema, and cravings. For her it was a triumph to give birth; it was the moment when the entire court seemed to take notice of her existence, and the king himself brought her a splendid gift. For Agnès, pregnancy was an invisible state where she must intensify her activity and care for her own person. She hid the rosacea on her cheeks beneath plaster of ceruse. She made the most of the other effects of her condition, particularly the swelling of her breasts. She had duly noted that the king found this detail interesting. Her seamstress shamelessly emphasized her attributes with décolletés that opened with laces that could be loosened as the weeks went by, revealing the increasingly prominent curves of her breasts.

As for the actual birth, I never knew where it took place. Agnès would disappear for a short week, and when she came back everybody would compliment her on her complexion. Her children were daughters, and immediately after their birth they were placed with families who were friends. The Coëtivys took in two of them.

We were constantly moving about. The king did not like Paris, as we knew, and he never wanted to make it his capital. He preferred to travel all around the kingdom. This incessant movement filled our lives with constant novelty. We would go from one place to the next, never settling in: in that way our surroundings never had time to succumb to the wearing of routine. We lived in a state of perpetual surprise. We got lost along unfamiliar corridors, and we knocked on four doors before finding the room we were looking for. Nighttime feasting was an opportunity to restore life to dull dwellings.

In spite of the jealousy and fear which still lurked in people's minds, we lived in constant good humor, and clearly Agnès had something to do with this. It was obvious that the king had exchanged his timidity for a boldness that verged on provocation, and he had placed his mistress among the ladies of the queen's retinue. This close proximity could have caused turmoil; on the contrary, the two women found it suited them. The queen, too, had changed. Now she was rich, and she had asked me to advise her in her affairs. She had set about trading in wine, dealing in fabrics from the East, and she bought precious gems with her profits. She took great pains with the castles where the court stayed, and showed considerable taste in decorating buildings and gardens.

Agnès's presence had freed her somewhat from Charles's attentions, which, in fact, had brought her little else than suffering and grief, for many of her children had died very young. She seemed to have reached an age where the woman behind the mother and spouse was revealed at last. Agnès, in her way, had contributed to this. The queen, therefore, had no reason to complain of the situation.

It has to be said that this new life coincided with a period of luxury and plenty, which made everything easier and more pleasant. Obviously I was called upon to fuel this great blaze, into which I tossed armfuls of the Argenterie riches. And these riches were increasingly significant. Our commercial endeavors were beginning to yield their fruit on a grand scale. It had taken time to establish our networks and turn the flow of merchandise in our direction, but now the movement was well underway. By ensuring a core of regular orders, the court supported our activity. The result was unequalled wealth, even though that wealth was founded on the credit I extended.

The women used every opportunity to appear in public to display their latest finery. Horn-shaped headdresses had become gigantic, the trains of their gowns were endless, and there was no limit to their décolletés. Even the most ordinary gowns were made of silk, and their jewelry was magnificent. Agnès was very eager to be at the forefront of all such novelties. This made the king's task very difficult, but gladdened my heart. For in order to give her presents, which was a weekly obligation, Charles had to find a new idea, an exceptional item, some never-before-seen finery which alone could meet his demanding mistress's expectations. And, naturally, he turned to me. I applied all my skill, which the king expected, and all my love, which he could not suspect. When Agnès received a rare jewel, a silk from the Orient, or an exotic animal from the king, she knew that I had chosen them. It was a minor betrayal, to be sure, but one which caused no harm and kept us all content.

*

The other activity which gave me an opportunity to be close to Agnès and safely establish a complicity with her in the open was our patronage of the arts. Now that peace and wealth had come, the French court was caught up in a frenzy of creativity and beauty. Hitherto, only Burgundy had been prosperous and peaceful enough to foster the arts. Charles eventually understood that he too must take up this challenge. It was an additional reason for him to look toward Italy and the East. He had been much preoccupied with England, but that barbarian confrontation had brought only brutality and ruin. For refinement and new work, he must look elsewhere.

Agnès, with her Italian culture, guided and encouraged him. I used my network of agents to import works of art and even, if they were willing, the artists themselves. A painter called Fouquet, who had just returned from Italy, had received the welcome and protection of a member of the council, Étienne Chevalier, whose portrait he had painted, featuring him next to his patron saint. I had gone to meet the painter, and when Agnès found this out she arranged for me to introduce him to her.

This Fouquet was a fairly young man, short in stature and always scruffy, who gladly whiled away his time in taverns and swore like his drinking companions. His hands were splattered with paint and his clothes were torn. All of these details should have made him repulsive, and yet he projected irresistible charm and power from his eyes alone. They were light green, shining feverishly, incredibly mobile but capable at any moment of staring intensely at an object, swooping down, and making off with it the way a raptor would have with its talons. I wondered what sort of effect he would have on Agnès. One day, when we had settled in Tours, I set about organizing the promised meeting. This fellow only suited himself, and he refused to go as far as the castle. At best, he agreed to receive us in his studio. Agnès liked this idea and mentioned it to the king as if it were a fine joke. For a moment I was afraid he might want to go with her. But he refrained, and we set out on our own. We spent an afternoon of bliss. In those days Fouquet had his studio in a hamlet down by the Loire. He employed two companions to prepare his canvases and mix his paints.

Agnès took an immediate liking to him. It must be said that to find Fouquet surrounded by his paintings was the best way to make his acquaintance. It was strange to see such works coming from such a dirty, untidy personage—luminous works of calm beauty, precise execution, and a delicacy of colors and shapes which were totally lacking in the artist himself. His portraits, in particular, set his characters in another world, as if he had removed them from their reality in order to restore them in the décor of their dreams. He and Agnès had a shared ability to understand human beings beyond mere appearance, and to unveil their secret affinities. They immediately liked one another, not the way lovers would—she would have leapt up in indignation at the idea—nor as brother and sister, a kinship she reserved for me. They saw one another, rather, as fellow magicians, creatures who, in a less cultured place, would have been treated as witches. Fouquet compounded friendship with his veneration of beauty, which left him paralyzed with admiration in Agnès's presence.

Obviously, he dreamt of painting her portrait, and was prepared to do anything to that end. When she asked him to paint the king's portrait to begin with, I was stunned to hear him accept. And although he hated all venues of officialdom, he followed Agnès to the castle. That was where he painted Charles's portrait, which everyone has had the opportunity to admire—or, at least, of which everyone has heard. Fouquet behaved well in the king's presence, so that he would not embarrass Agnès, no doubt. But while he hid the aversion he felt for the sovereign, his portrait confessed it openly. It shows Charles in a climate of sentiments that were typical of him: jealousy, fear, cruelty, distrust—it is all there. Fortunately, one of the particularities of Fouquet's works was that they always pleased their models, even when he depicted them in an unfavorable light.

I arranged a stipend for Fouquet so that he would stay at court. This was the beginning of a patronage I discussed with Agnès at great length. Like me, she knew how things were done in Italy, and she wanted to implement the same practices in France. King René's way of doing things, where a troop of artists was attached to his person and paid to enliven his feasts, seemed to her as old-fashioned as it did to me. We both agreed that art should be allowed to live for its own sake. We had to encourage artists to follow their own path, and not create solely to please us. Her judgment of the queen was severe on that point, for she reproached her for keeping a painter in her home solely in order to illuminate her book of hours. Agnès was of the opinion that if we gave artists our dwellings to decorate, our evenings to recite their verse, or our ceremonies to play their music, it was because we cared to place our means in the service of their art and not the other way around. We had long discussions about this, which gave me inspiration for the palace in Bourges. Construction was progressing and very soon it would come time to decorate it. Macé would leave me in charge of choosing the artists and commissioning their works. She trusted me on this point not because she thought I had particular taste in art but because, since I spent most of my time at court, I was in a better position to know what was in fashion.

It is true that I had become a regular courtier. My duties in the service of the king, while still attached to the Argenterie, were less and less restricted to it. Guillaume, as I have said, had taken over the running of our enterprise. He and Jean were expanding the web of our agents all across northern Europe. They kept me fully informed of their activities and I trusted them completely. I remained in charge of the delicate question of commercial expansion into Italy and the Levant. And because I was in contact with the king, my role was becoming increasingly political.

Charles delegated to me the responsibility of keeping abreast of Mediterranean affairs for the council. Regarding the Levant, he encouraged me to enlarge the fleet of galleys and to establish regular trade routes with their ports. In keeping with my recommendations he had decided to bring about a political rapprochement with the Sultan of Egypt. I sent him several letters accompanied by rich gifts, and from him I obtained all the facilities required to trade in the lands under his control. I also sent samples of everything we could provide him with, including items the Mohammedan desired more than anything, and which no Christian was authorized to sell him: weapons. I had no trouble providing him with them, given that he was not our enemy and was not in danger of using them against anyone except the Turks, who had set about invading Europe. Nevertheless, I knew that by delivering weaponry to a Saracen prince, I was taking a risk and giving my enemies arguments against me. However, I did so with the king's approval (although later on he would pretend to forget this), and I thought that was enough.

In order to maintain good relations with the sultan, I was obliged to make other dishonest compromises, which contributed to the enmity against me. Thus, one morning in Alexandria, a young Moor jumped into one of our galleys and asked to embrace the Catholic faith and come to France. The captain of the ship consented. I found this out after his return, and summoned the captain to demand that the Moor be sent back to the Sultan, who had conveyed his displeasure about the abduction to me. It was a difficult decision to make, though I disguised my sorrow and weakness beneath a mask of anger and brutality. I met the boy: he was not more than sixteen, and when they brought him to me he fell at my feet, trembling all over. The captain of the galley explained that if I sent him back to Egypt I would be condemning both his body and his soul: he would certainly be put to death, and before that they would oblige him to abjure the true God, who had now, through baptism, taken him into the fold. I stood my ground. The young man was sent away. I wrote to the Sultan to advise clemency, but I do not think he took any notice.

That was one of the most painful moments of my life. I would be reproached later in life for my part in this affair, but those reproaches never equaled the ones I made myself. In dreams long after I often saw the boy's black eyes, and his cries still woke me from my sleep. This was something I had not anticipated: I did not think I would ever have to pay such a price for my ambition.

Whatever it cost me, I maintained excellent relations with the Sultan. I was able to establish a regular route to the Levant. Our favorable understanding with the Mohammedan sovereign also procured me other connections in the Mediterranean, particularly with the Knights of Rhodes. These soldier-monks had disembarked in Crete and aimed to remove the island from the Sultan's influence. The Sultan had reacted by sending a powerful fleet, and the Knights found themselves in a very difficult position. The Grand Master of the order asked me to intercede on their behalf, which I did successfully. I earned the precious support of these knights, with whom one must reckon when sailing in the Levant.

To deal with these matters, I sought to avoid exposing myself once again to the dangers of a maritime passage, and the king did not want me to be absent for too long from the court because he had grown accustomed to my presence. Therefore, I had to act through the intermediaries of messengers and delegations. To that end, I employed a young man from the Berry named Benoît, who was connected to me through his marriage to one of my nieces.

As for Italy, however, I would have to go there myself.

*

The king had asked me to keep abreast of affairs in Italy, and the situation in Genoa to begin with. For a long time there was nothing, but one morning a messenger came from Provence with surprising news. A ship transporting a group of important personages from Genoa had arrived in Marseille. Among these Genoese was a member of the powerful Doria family. The man leading the operation was a certain Campofregoso. He wrote to the king to solicit his help. He wanted to obtain the means to set up an army for the reconquest of Genoa. He pledged that he would then place the city under the authority of the king of France.

I had informed Charles, already long before, of the unrest in the city of Genoa. He had grasped the significance of a potential French conquest of the city. The Genoese had trading posts all through the eastern Mediterranean, and were renowned for their industry. It was an opportunity not to be missed.

The king reacted enthusiastically to Campofregoso's proposition. Alas, he had no experience of these Italian condottieri, and he took their pretentiousness for importance. The letter from the man from Genoa was excessively vain, and implied that he was in charge of a veritable court in exile. I urged the king to beware. I knew such adventurers only too well. In all likelihood they were a gang of misers, and one must treat them with caution, but they were far from deserving any princely protocol. Charles would not listen. He put together a mission, led by the Archbishop of Reims, which included old Tanguy du Châtel, his chamberlain, who had rescued him thirty years earlier from the massacre in Paris. I was ordered to go along with all these grave individuals. We went to Marseille, and anyone who saw our procession pass by might have thought we were on our way to an audience with the Byzantine Emperor. The Genoese, no doubt informed of our arrival, put on their finest attire and welcomed us in the grandest style at the house of an Italian merchant. The Archbishop of Reims was well accustomed to confusing power with its conventions. He was deceived by the elegance of the Genoese, and took their boldness for nobility. Better informed than he was regarding customs in Italy, I had immediately seen them for a bunch of imposters and scoundrels who were trying to obtain from us not only the means to conquer their city, but even to fill their own plates, no later than the very next morning. I tried to warn the Archbishop, but I soon realized it would be impossible for me to make him change his mind.

What followed was a ridiculous negotiation. It led to a very solemn treaty between the king of France and . . . no one. For the people who signed the treaty were only representing themselves. They agreed, from the moment they came to power, to place Genoa under the authority of the king of France. Our plenipotentiaries walked away satisfied once again. They left me behind to provide the conspirators with the means to recruit soldiers and lead an expedition.

Campofregoso sensed that he had not fooled me with his theatrics. As soon as the emissaries had left, he was friendly and direct with me. In any case he could not hide the truth for long: the conspirators needed everything. The man was pleasant, jolly, generous, and a bon vivant. However, I no more trusted his natural good humor than I did the mask he had worn at the start. In Italy I had met a great many of these enterprising, voluble, charming people, who were always disconcertingly inconstant. Betrayal, in these cities that have known so many revolutions and changes of allegiance, is a weapon like any other. Perjury is worn proudly like a bandolier, the way in other parts one hangs one's sword from one's belt. To me it seemed that Campofregoso would stop at nothing, and what happened next proved this was so.

While the Genoese set up their headquarters in Nice thanks to the funds I advanced them, I went to Montpellier for my business. When I returned, they had not made much progress. I reckoned it would take many months before they would be able to attack their city. I left an agent with them, one who represented me in the region, and I returned to the court at Chinon.

The time has come, no doubt, to explain the events which later would be held against me as proof of betrayal. It is true that at the same time as I was helping to arm Campofregoso's expedition, I was corresponding with Alfonso of Aragon, who supported the party in power in Genoa, the very same one which the emigrants were determined to overthrow. I have already mentioned the fact that I had long prided myself as a friend to the king of Aragon, who was now the king of Naples. This friendship assured that my ships could navigate freely in the waters infested by his corsairs, because King Alfonso regularly provided me with safe conduct.

I needed him, and I needed Genoa just as much. Over time I had gained a clear vision of what I must accomplish in the Mediterranean. It was the same vision I had tried to share with the king. My most important connection in the Levant was with the Sultan, and to make sure that my ships would reach him, I had to rely on the support of the entire chain of powers located along that route—Naples and Sicily, the lands of the king of Aragon, Florence and Genoa, the pope, and the House of Savoy—for free passage over the Alps.

If Charles VII were to take over and manage to extend his influence into these regions, so much the better, and I was prepared to help him in any way I could. But if he did not, I must preserve my own alliances. Thus, in Genoa, I honestly did everything I could so that Campofregoso and his friends could honor their commitments. However, I never broke off my ties with their adversaries. Much good it did me, in the end. For the emigrants whom I had helped to arm did indeed eventually conquer their city—only to declare at once that they were in no way bound by any commitment to the king of France. I loyally attempted, during a final voyage, to overturn the situation. I begged the king to deploy his troops. Campofregoso would have taken fright and yielded. But Charles was busy elsewhere and did not follow my advice. Genoa was lost to him. Fortunately, thanks to the alliances I had preserved on both sides, with Campofregoso who liked me well enough and knew what he owed me, and with the partisans of my friend the king of Aragon, I went on doing an increasing amount of business in the city.

When the time came for me to explain myself, I know that no one understood my opinion. The fact that there were some individuals who viewed my position as a betrayal affected me more than any torture I had to undergo. In truth, I was angry with myself for not finding the words to express my convictions. For a man who in spite of everything is still imbued with the chivalric ideal, the interest of the lord is more important than anything. In serving Charles VII I should have broken off with Genoa the moment the city refused to pledge its allegiance to him. And to them it was inconceivable that someone could maintain friendly relations with the enemies of one's king. Such conceptions, to my mind, were the cause of much misfortune and ruin, and should no longer be obeyed. It is my conviction—but who shares it?—that a superior bond unites all men. Trade, that trivial occupation, is the expression of that shared bond, which, thanks to the exchange and circulation of goods, unites all human beings. Beyond birth, honor, nobility, and faith—all things invented by man—there are humble necessities such as food, clothing, and shelter, which are obligations of nature and before which all human beings are equal.

I allied myself with the king of France to support my enterprise and fulfill my dreams. He served me and I served him. But his reign will only last for a certain time and in a certain place, whereas the great movement of mankind and things is universal and eternal. That is why, while I sincerely desire to please the king, when he goes against something that seems useful to me, I take care of it myself, with other means and other people, among whom there might happen to be some of his enemies.

*

It is strange for me to be writing about such grand matters when life has now deprived me of everything. There are storms brewing above the island, and I felt a few drops of rain earlier coming through the trellis. I went into the house to go on writing. An idea came to me as I was moving so pitifully inside. It contradicts everything I have just asserted. And I am wondering whether my detractors were not right after all, and whether the king's mistrust of me is not justified after all. Do I not have an inadmissible but deep penchant for what others call betrayal, and which I fail to see as a flaw?

The truth is, I feel absolutely incapable of devoting myself completely to one cause. That same impetus which troubled my mind during the siege of Bourges and enabled me to view everything as from a great height, like a bird, is no doubt the most characteristic feature of my personality. Most of the time it is a strength, in particular when I'm called on to negotiate, when putting oneself in the other's shoes is essential. It is also a profound weakness, which all my life has kept me not only from bearing arms, but even from behaving like a loyal combatant. When I see that poor Dunois, entirely devoted to his hatred of his adversary and who has no other choice but to defeat him or die, I take the measure of my own weakness. In his position, at the moment of assault I would be overcome by thoughts for my adversary. Considering the righteousness of his cause and seeing the situation with his eyes, I would ask myself whether it is truly legitimate to exterminate him. And in the time it took for me to ponder this, I would already be vanquished and dead.

If I consider my life in this light, the evidence is blinding. I have never ceased—although it was not my intention—from betraying everything and everybody, even Agnès herself.

Depending on my mood, I might not call it a betrayal, and I might find good excuses for having behaved in a certain way. But now that I have been stripped of everything and have no more indulgence for myself, I cannot forgive my cowardice.

The instrument of my felony was Louis, the Dauphin. Agnès had no more formidable enemy. She had managed to win over nearly the entire court, even the queen, and she knew how to render inoffensive the hatred of which she was the object, if not to suppress it entirely. But with Louis she never succeeded. He saw Agnès and Brézé as obstacles between himself and the king, depriving him of the power to which he aspired. After multiple intrigues in which he had associated himself with the king's worst enemies, he had begun to come up with audacious schemes for foreign alliances, in order to give free rein to the energy he felt inside and, perhaps, to acquire enough power so that some day he might defy his father the king. That is the way he was, constantly involved in complicated projects where common sense, in the end, was not altogether absent. We had been long acquainted. I helped him financially in some of his enterprises, provided they were not directed against the king. He showed me his esteem, but respected the secrecy of our relations, in order not to put me in a compromising position. I hope that the day he becomes king he will have it in his heart to spare my poor family.

Finally, the first day of January in the new year of 1447, he considered that everything was lost, and threw a fit. I do not know what his father had said to him. In any case, he left for his lands in the Dauphiné and as of this writing he is still there. He began to launch unremitting attacks on Agnès and Brézé. If the situation had been reversed, I am absolutely certain that Agnès would have made my enemy her enemy, and would have violently opposed the Dauphin. But I have never been capable of that integrity of feeling which gives combatants their conviction and delivers them from doubt, so I have sought to reconcile contraries, to reunite enemies and, with hindsight, I see that I proved myself disloyal to both in the end. Louis knew nothing of the nature of my ties with Agnès, and did not even suspect them. As for Agnès, I do not know what she would have thought if she had known that I went on maintaining close ties with her worst enemy.

There are those who might view my attitude as simple mercantile logic. The Dauphiné is located along the route to the Mediterranean and the Levant. By discreetly intervening, against the king's wishes, to facilitate Louis's remarriage with the daughter of the Duke of Savoy, I was making two essential allies and opening the Alpine route to our trade with the Levant.

However, if I am altogether sincere—and in the position in which I find myself today, I have no other choice than to be sincere—I should admit that my secret loyalty to the Dauphin was never based on any mercantile considerations. I am prey to deep personal attachments that nothing can explain or, at times, excuse. The antagonism between Agnès and Louis did not seem sufficient reason to me to break off our friendship. There are some loyalties that lead to treason.

It must be said that in those days, ever since I had met Agnès, duplicity informed my entire existence. It was less reprehensible only in that my happiness was founded on it. I was betraying the king by having a relationship with his mistress—a relation that, though not one of lovers, would have seemed to him, had he learned of it, a savage betrayal of his trust nonetheless. However, this relationship gave me greater serenity in his presence, for I was certain that Agnès would be working to obtain his kindly support where I was concerned, which made me less fearful of his moods and the effects of calumny.

Similarly, I was betraying Macé and my entire family. The carnal relations I had enjoyed on occasion until then were solely infidelities of the body. In this instance, while the body did not partake, it was my soul that was forsaking my legitimate spouse and surrendering in its entirety to someone else. However, a new serenity in my relations with Macé emerged from my betrayal. I accepted our insurmountable differences, her thirst for respectability, her love of appearance. It had become pointless for me to desire or regret everything this woman did not offer me, since now I found it with another.

In addition, it was a period of repeated triumphs for Macé. Through Guillaume Juvénal, acting in the name of the king, our son Jean had been introduced to the pope, and the pontiff had agreed for him to succeed Henri d'Avaugour as archbishop of Bourges. For Macé this was a double triumph. She could be immensely proud, personally, of her son's great advancement, and doubly so because it had occurred in the only place that mattered to her: our town.

Not long afterwards there came another crucial event for Macé: the marriage of our only daughter, Perrette.

This episode sent me to extremes of guilt, as far as betrayal went. Perrette was marrying Jacquelin, the son of Artault Trousseau, viscount of Bourges, and lord of the château at Bois-Sir-Amé. The wedding was held at the castle, to Macé's great delight. However, that same year the king, who had acquired the castle, had given the property to Agnès. Thus, circumstances placed Bois-Sir-Amé at the crossroads of the two irreconcilable parts of my life.

Agnès loved the castle and we stayed there often to oversee its restoration, as we had done at Beauté. Every visit to Bois-Sir-Amé granted us the happiness of an impossible union. This place, more than anywhere on earth, united memories of the two great bonds in my life, although they were so different from one another. My wife, my daughter, and all my children walked over this same ground where Agnès had run barefoot in the summer to come and kiss me. Thus, the four walls of the old castle brought together everything I was incapable of uniting in myself.

Agnès was always in my thoughts, even when I was not by her side—particularly when I was not by her side. I did my best to curtail the missions entrusted to me by the king. The affair in Genoa, however, kept me longer in the south than I would have liked, and I took the opportunity to attend to my business in Marseille and Montpellier. In both those towns, particularly the latter, I built houses that, while they did not match the wealth of my palace in Bourges, were nevertheless magnificent edifices. I did not need this luxury, as I rarely stayed in these cities. But it served as a sort of compensation. By representing me, and allowing passersby to imagine me inside as they walked past my imposing doors, these grand houses functioned to make others forget my absence. In truth, the same applied to the house in Bourges: the price of my freedom not to be with Macé was my gift of a palace.

As for Agnès, the king could offer her the sort of estates I would have found difficult to obtain for her. But I performed in secret a strange comedy for myself alone. I have already mentioned that I took pleasure in buying ancient fortified castles. This useless expenditure had not ceased, and since I had met Agnès it had even taken on the proportions of a veritable vice. I astonished myself, during my trial, when I discovered how many estates I owned.

The fact is, the fairly mysterious passion of the early days had been replaced by a sort of amorous madness which, in order to be assuaged, demanded ever-increasing numbers of offerings, like some cruel god. The time I had spent at Bois-Sir-Amé had left me so nostalgic and with such a memory of great happiness that I sought, pathetically, to reproduce it. Every time I bought a new estate, I imagined myself living there with Agnès. It was, obviously, a fantasy. There was no reason for her to come to these damp, remote backwaters in the Puisaye or the Morvan. Even if she had agreed to accompany me there, we would have had to explain to the king the purpose of our visit . . . Yet, like a sick man who sets aside any objection that might prove the contrary and surrenders to the delight of believing he will recover his health thanks to some providential remedy, I seized the opportunity of every new acquisition to dream of living there with Agnès.

These dreams lasted only a short while, and sooner or later they vanished. I had to find something else, to acquire a new place. All the same, whenever these dreams had me in thrall, I was happy. Thus, during the days spent riding along the dusty roads of Provence, or the never-ending discussions with those rogues in Genoa, or while I listened gravely to my agents as they reported on their transactions, my mind took flight and cloaked itself, as though with a warm and precious cloth, with the endless and glorious name of some old estate lost in the forest that I had just acquired, and flew to Agnès to take her there. My interlocutors would see a faint smile come to my lips, and were disconcerted. There was no way they could begin to imagine what I was thinking, and for good reason, so they interpreted as irony something that was no more than bliss. And, convinced I had seen right through their lies and their miserable scheming, they were unsettled and confessed the truth.

But sometimes when I was in this mood I could also fly into a terrible rage if my orders were questioned, or if grievances were laid too forcefully before me—in short, if someone forced me to leave behind the sweetness of my dreams and return altogether to the present. Thus, on the basis of these deep misunderstandings, my reputation grew, quite unfairly, as a cunning, implacable, and occasionally violent man.

Although I was not aware of it at the time, such reactions earned me lasting enmities, occasionally verging on hatred. I discovered this much later, when the time came to take stock of my resentment and incurable wounds. But that time had not come yet, and for now, everything seemed to be going my way.

*

In Montpellier, and along the coast of the Languedoc, I could see how our trade with the Levant was prospering. We no longer had to entrust our cargoes to other ships: our own fleet of galleys ensured the transport. New vessels were being built, for our needs far surpassed what our existing ships could satisfy.

We could sail where we liked throughout the Levant. I had sent Jean de Villages to the Sultan, and his mission had been a resounding success. The Mohammedan had signed a treaty that was very favorable to our trade in his lands, and he sent magnificent gifts to the king of France as proof of his friendship. During my last stay in Genoa, I had learned of Campofregoso's volte-face, for he refused to honor his commitment and ally himself with France. But the friendship I had formed with that scoundrel, together with the trust shown me by the king of Aragon, now master of that city, gave me the confidence to go on doing fruitful business there. I went to see King René in Aix and he opened the markets of Provence to me. The Dauphin and the Duke of Savoy were my clients and, dare I say it, my debtors. In short, in the course of only a few years, trade in the Mediterranean had begun to flourish. Silk from Italy, taffeta from Baghdad, weapons from Genoa, mastic from Chios, crepe from Syria, and gems from the Orient were all delivered in great convoys, and there was never enough to satisfy the appetite of the court, or all the needs that the cessation of hostilities had revived. Cloth from Flanders and England, furs, finery, and cut gemstones all went the opposite direction to the courts of the Levant, where people were eager for such things.

These successful transactions enabled me to return to the company of the king, and thus to Agnès. I was very active on the Council. Charles acted pleased to see me. Above all, he was grateful that I had been able to meet all his demands, and he did not hold me accountable for all his favors: he had helped me to build my fleet of galleys and he had appointed me steward to the states of the Languedoc, and the contributions of those states had enriched me beyond the sums I was obliged to transfer to the king. To show that he was pleased, in addition to all the other favors, that year Charles appointed me Collector of the Salt Tax. Our relation was one of mutual profit. By entrusting me with such a responsibility, he knew I would make it prosper. And likewise, in any business, I undertook to set aside the part that, in one form or another, must be reserved for the king. Everything was going well, and all I wanted was for the situation to stay as it was.

Alas, the king's satisfaction in my regard, although it had flattering effects, also disturbed my peace of mind, because he sent me back to Italy. He had appreciated my intervention in the affair in Genoa, even though it had ultimately failed. Charles was beginning to understand what a mission must consist of. Prior to this he had been far too susceptible to the influence of the princes. For those great lords, representing the king meant bringing together a group of bishops and marshals, men who had great names and were rigid with their own self-importance. As a rule, the result was catastrophic. Such worthy notables listen to no one, have great difficulty getting along, and in the end they can be taken in by anyone—if, as is often the case nowadays, they are not received by men as noble as themselves, but rather by scoundrels.

With me the king had discovered another method. In Genoa I spoke with everyone and without any prior protocol. With my interlocutors I used the new universal language, which, alas, had replaced the codes of chivalry: money. Some can be bought, others must be paid, promises are made to this one, credit extended to that one: it is a language that everyone understands. Just as Charles had finally defeated the English by abandoning the methods of chivalry and using the weapons of the villeins, now, in similar fashion, he intended to exercise a new form of diplomacy, particularly with the myriad small states clustered around the Mediterranean. And unfortunately for my own tranquility, he made me his diplomat. The affair with which he entrusted me was, in its way, even more complicated than Genoa, because it had to do with the pope.

I have never had much appetite for matters of religion. During my childhood, because of the Schism, we had multiple popes. The papacy was such a comfortable position that there were two, even three of them who claimed the right to fill it. My mother suffered greatly from these papal turpitudes and she prayed that the church would recover its unity. My brother devoted himself to that cause, pacing up and down the corridors of Rome. As for me, I nurtured secret, insolent thoughts. Today I can reveal them without fear that they might wrong me, any more than I have already been wronged: I believed that God must know best how to tidy up his own affairs. If he was not capable of deciding who should represent him on this earth, no doubt it meant that he did not wield the almighty power one attributed to him. Later on I would always comply with the customs of religion, but without seeing it as anything more than an obligation.

Although we never discussed it, Macé had always understood that I did not share her faith, and she did not hold this against me. What she would not forgive, however, was my mistrust of prelates. She had always been fascinated by their unctuous piety, their serene authority, and she was dazzled by their sense of pomp and luxury. Their great expenses were justified by the fact that they were incurred in God's name, and this removed any remaining scruples Macé might have had to be sensitive to their ostentation.

As for me, I like the raw power that nothing can hide, the raw power of kings and wealthy merchants. That power, at least, speaks its name. It shows its true face, and it is up to each individual to decide what he intends to do with it. Ecclesiastical power makes it way beneath the mask of humility. It never acts or strikes without invoking the submission of those who exert it to a superior force, to which they claim to be the slaves. In short, when one is in the presence of a man of the cloth, one does not know with whom one is dealing: a master or a servant, a weak man or a strong one. Everything in their world is uncertain and secret, concealing hidden traps that one discovers only once the ground has already given way beneath one's feet.

I had always taken care to avoid venturing into their presence. To be sure, at the time I was appointed to the Argenterie, I had taken part in the assembly at Bourges that had prepared the Pragmatic Sanction. Since the pontiff had left Avignon and returned to Rome, he had become, as far as the king of France was concerned, a foreign power, whose intervention in the internal affairs of the realm could not be tolerated. Through the Pragmatic Sanction, the king now asserted that his sovereignty over the Church of France could safeguard it from any abuse on the part of the pontiff. I was in agreement with Charles on this point. Together with the struggle against the princes and the financial reform, this text would give the king absolute power over his country. But I could not go too far in showing my support for the king's initiatives, on pain of displeasing the pope in Rome, whom I needed for my business. Through the intermediary of my brother Nicholas, I regularly obtained dispensations from the pope authorizing me to trade with the Muslims.

The religious quarrels became even more complicated when the Ecumenical Council met in Basel and set about curtailing the pope's powers and limiting his excesses. One could not help but subscribe to such a praiseworthy program.

Alas, the Council rebelled so thoroughly that it elected another pope. The old schism had been reignited. I told myself that there was really nothing to expect from the clerics. It so happened that I knew the antipope of Basel quite well, since he was none other than the former Duke of Savoy, with whom I had long had business relations. He was a pious and humble man who had abdicated in order to shut himself away in a monastery. Circumstances dictated that such peace would not be granted him. The delegates of the Council had come to drag him from his retreat and inform him that he was the pope. With him, at least, the position would be filled by a man of faith and great integrity. Charles saw him as a lesser evil and I agreed with him, all the more so in that at the time the pope in Rome had neither scruples nor morals. Nevertheless, in our Italian affairs, between northern Italy where France sought to play a role, and the kingdom of Naples, which had been lost by the Angevins, it was absolutely essential to consolidate the power of a pope over these states, and that this pope should be in our favor.

For all these reasons, the king opined, and I agreed with him, that it was time to finish once and for all with the Schism, and send the unfortunate duke who had become the antipope back to the monastery he should never have left. I attempted a first mission to Lausanne. The old duke wanted nothing more than to be persuaded, but he was surrounded by a court of canons and clerics who refused to listen. They were too gifted at scholastic controversy for me to attempt to confront them on their own terrain. I went home empty-handed.

But not long after that, the situation changed. A new Roman pontiff was elected, under the name of Nicholas V. He was a cultured and reasonable man. The majority of cardinals recognized his authority, while the Council of Basel had been discredited due to its stubbornness and excess. As a result of this election, Charles decided to act.

He ordered me to negotiate with the two popes once and for all, using all the financial means at my disposal to convince them. While I was attempting to bring this secret diplomacy to a successful conclusion, he would send an ordinary mission to Rome. Its purpose would be to greet the new sovereign pontiff and thus to let the world know where the king of France's preference lay. The antipope would understand that he had lost his most important support. To make the message clear and unambiguous, it was necessary to pull out all the stops. The mission to Rome must be brilliant: significant in size, a lavish display, an event to resonate all over Christendom. I would travel with the mission, and my primary role would be to ensure its desired brilliance.

*

Agnès was always sad to see me leave, and told me as much, but she had a very different reaction when she found out I was going to Rome. I knew her devotion, which she displayed through her luxurious offerings to her parishes. But I had been unaware of how genuine her faith was, and we had never spoken about it. Because of this pending mission, I discovered the depth of her piety. Agnès's religious fervor in no way resembled Macé's. There was no room for ostentation, even if her kindly deeds to the church, given her position at court, were public knowledge. The Collegiate Church at Loches had received several of her offerings, in particular a golden altarpiece, which contained a fragment of the True Cross brought back by the crusades.

Agnès took no pleasure in seeing her gestures made public, however. On the contrary, she made every effort to conceal the acts of charity or piety that she initiated. Prayer, for her, was a private affair. It was an opportunity for her to allow her pain, remorse, and sorrow to surface. I found this out later. But the moment she left behind her private meetings with God, alone or at the private masses where no one else took part, she came back to the court and was gay and in a good mood. Unlike Macé, she fled from the company of sinister prelates, and went as little as possible to high mass.

When she found out I was going to see the new pope, she entrusted me, blushing, with a private mission. She made her request in the presence of the king, so that he would know what she had asked me to do. But as we had the opportunity shortly thereafter to meet for three long days at Bois-Sir-Amé, she subsequently explained her reasons to me, once we were alone.

Agnès's goal was straightforward: she wanted to obtain from the Pope the right to own a portable altar. Such an instrument, with all its accessories—ciborium, patera, cruet, and so on—makes it possible for the believer to celebrate mass outside of a consecrated building. As always with Agnès, this request was proof of both immense pride and great modesty. It required great boldness for a young girl twenty-four years of age, whose only eminence was the fact she was the mistress of the king, to solicit a favor to which only high notables had been hitherto entitled. But this was not for appearance's sake, far from it. Agnès did not want anyone to know about this favor, if it was granted to her. On the contrary, it would enable her to practice her faith in a more complete withdrawal from the world.

When we were alone, I questioned her further about these practices. They were so foreign to me that I found it impossible to believe they were sincere. I was particularly eager to understand. Agnès lived in such obvious sin, and seemed to take a great deal of liberty with her body, as well as partaking in affectionate relations like our own, something which the Church would have found difficult to define, let alone condone: how could she embrace the rituals of a religion whose principles she so rarely obeyed? So, over two long evenings, sitting side by side, our legs entwined and my arm around her shoulder, we spoke about God.

Far from contradicting her, let alone making fun of her, I listened at length to her reasons for believing, or, rather, I was given the proof that she was inhabited by faith of the sort which knows no reason and which even goes against all reason. Christ, for her, was a sort of companion who protected her and called to her in his martyrdom. Whence the blend in her character of insouciance and tragedy, of an unprecedented gift for the joy of the moment and the resigned certainty that fate would grant her only the smallest of favors. Jesus put her to the test, then helped her to find joy in her pain.

This was also the first time that we spoke openly about her feelings for the king. She had been brought before him by the Anjou clan, and had felt immense horror at being handed over to such an individual. Everything about him was repulsive. His appearance repelled her: the big sleeves that hid his shoulders were too narrow, and his tights were often dirty and emphasized the deformity of his legs. She did not like his manners or his ideas. His voice and even his breathing, when he dozed off, filled her with violent aversion of an almost animal nature. And yet, she did not rebel. She called to Jesus, for hours on end, to give her the strength to face the ordeal He had set before her. And it was during that time that she felt closest to Him, the Crucified. He listened to her, consoled her, and gently showed her the way to a sort of resurrection.

If she had learned to live with Charles, it was because Christ had given her the strength to overcome her disgust, to drown her aversion in the cheer of festivities, to delude her repulsion with the help of a great deal of perfume and priceless fabrics. So much effort had to go into it. In the beginning, beneath the sweet sauce Agnès could still taste the bitterness of the dish. And yet, gradually, the miracle came about. Beneath the twin influences of his love and his armies' victories, Charles changed. To be sure, she was under no illusion, any more than I was, that beneath his new appearance the same man continued to exist. But at least life with him was becoming more bearable. And she rendered thanks to God for this transformation. At last she had understood the words of her confessor, to whom she had been careful never to divulge her most secret thoughts: salvation comes through the trials sent to us by the Lord. This thought prevented her, should she ever be so tempted, from acting ungratefully toward her Creator. Christ had saved her, but she had no doubt, since He wanted what was good for her, that He would send her further trials. So she continued to nourish a generous fear, the certainty that she was in imminent danger, and the hope that Christ would help her to overcome any new obstacles along the path to wisdom and salvation.

With the king's transformation, her fear changed in nature. In the beginning Agnès feared his presence, and dreaded that the situation fate had imposed on her would last for a very long time. Then she was afraid of the contrary: that he would abruptly cast her off, a fear she had shared with me in private at Beauté. Now that the Anjou clan had been eliminated, her fears were more diffuse, but just as strong. Now I know that she had a premonition of her fate.

I confess that at the time I did not fully understand her fears. They seemed to stem from a worldview that was not very Christian. Everything Agnès saw was a sign, and only had meaning in another reality known to her alone. For example, as I have said, she identified me as a sort of twin in the world of her dreams or of her origins. On the other hand, some people were bearers of curses, by virtue of the role they played in the invisible. These ideas could have led her to madness but, oddly enough, on the contrary, they gave her great strength and cunning. Certain people she was wary of, others she trusted; she protected herself from the former and opened her heart to the latter, guided by her intuition and memories. However astonishing it might seem, she was rarely mistaken.

Reincarnation, spells, curses, and superstition filled her thoughts, and, though she was not aware of it, these notions led her far away from Catholic concepts. If anyone had pointed this out to her, she would have protested: she was convinced she was an exemplary believer. And indeed, next to her strange ideas—or, if you like, above them—her great respect for all the institutions of Christianity predominated. She truly revered the pope, the heir to St. Peter. It is true she was born during the period where there was only one pope, before the Council of Basel imposed a second one.

I was touched to learn more about Agnès through these revelations. She must have been a tragically solitary and unhappy child. That day we went for a walk by the ponds surrounding the castle, the sky over the Berry was dappled with clouds. Laughing, Agnès picked dry grass and moss. I watched her, frail and joyful, running across the russet moorland. A thought occurred to me then, unexpectedly, and which seemed grotesque at first: she was like Joan of Arc. I had not known the Maid, but Dunois and so many others had told me about her. She and Agnès were two similar young women, obedient to their solitude and capable of drawing great strength from it. One had become the king's mistress, the other his general, but beneath these differing roles lay hidden a similar capacity to seize power in order to bend it to one's will. Charles was sickly and indecisive, so he latched onto this kind of energy to overcome insurmountable obstacles. But he could not bear to follow and be dependent on others for long. He had made no effort to save Joan, so obviously so that some people wondered whether her death had not freed him from an ally who had become burdensome. I suddenly had the painful premonition that he would abandon Agnès in a similar way.

She handed me her dried bouquet and asked me why, when I looked at her, I had tears in my eyes. I did not know what to say, so I kissed her.

*

I would like to have the time to finish this story. I must find a way to tell of my love for Agnès, to the end. To follow the path right to the last moment, to cross the meadows full of flowers until I reach the frozen fields . . . It seems to me that my life depends on it. It will only ever be truly fulfilled and, dare I say, happy and successful, if I manage to do this.

Thus, I find it even harder to forgive myself for yesterday's carelessness, for which Elvira has harshly reproached me. The fact that nothing had happened since the visit of the podestà's envoy, over two weeks ago, had given me the impression that I was no longer at any risk. I became bolder, and during my walks I went closer and closer to the town. Yesterday, I even thought I could go into the town without danger. I do not know what force compelled me to venture as far as the harbor. I am so thoroughly inhabited by the memory of Agnès that I walked on without thinking of anything else. I found myself sitting on the wooden bench near the fish market and for a long while I gazed at the boats rocking gently by the pier. This was incredibly foolhardy.

It was late afternoon and the shadows in the harbor were beginning to lengthen. I don't know how long I sat there dreaming. Suddenly I was roused from my torpor by a furtive movement behind the pillars of the covered market. I came to my senses and looked around. A moment later I saw something move: a man was leaping from one pillar to the next, coming closer to me. Between each leap, he hid behind the stone column, but I could see him peek out and look hastily in my direction. By his third leap, I had recognized him: it was the man I had seen upon my arrival, the assassin who was after me.

I came to a decision in a split second: was it really the best, under the circumstances? I jumped to my feet and ran around the corner of the house next to which I had been sitting, on up the street, and then I turned twice and began to walk normally again. My pursuer, given the time he had been in the town, was surely better acquainted than I with the labyrinth of its alleys. I constantly changed direction to be sure I had lost him. So great was my effort to cover my tracks that I eventually did reach the edge of town, but on the opposite side from the path that led to Elvira's. After walking for some time I realized with terror that my pursuer had been joined by two more henchmen, and was still on my trail. I made the most of my head start and began running again, recklessly, now that I was out in the countryside. Night was falling, but far too slowly for my liking. I hoped that the moon would not rise too soon. When darkness fell they had almost caught up with me.

Finally, after great fright and an entire night of wandering,

I managed to shake off my enemies. I arrived at the house at dawn, all in a sweat. Elvira had not slept a wink, worried sick.

This incident upset me greatly. It convinced me that from now on I must work twice as quickly to finish these memoirs, because clearly my days are numbered. It also convinced me that I must ask for Elvira's help. Until now, I had never sought to clarify my situation to her. Now I explained as best I could the threat hanging over me. She is going to try to find out more about my pursuers. Before now, I didn't want to get her involved in this, but it seems I no longer have the choice.

She left for the town this morning, determined to get to the bottom of the matter. I no longer allow myself to go for walks or indulge in disordered daydreaming. As long as I have daylight for writing, I stay at my table and continue with my story.

*

I left for Rome in the spring, taking Agnès's requests, and many others, with me. It must be said that, by virtue of my lengthy stays at court, I was now in contact with an infinite number of people. Naturally, I knew all the members of the council and the royal entourage; I was acquainted with the noblemen who gravitated around the sovereign, but there was also a multitude of merchants, bankers, magistrates, artists, and the teeming crowd of those who came to solicit a purchase or a loan. I maintained a lively correspondence with our agents and the various relays in our possession, for purchases or payments, from Geneva to Flanders, from Florence to London. To be sure, Guillaume de Varye saw to the everyday business, together with Jean, Benoît, and now many others. But there were some tasks only I could fulfill, when it was a matter of a major decision or an important client. Which meant that even though most people at court were idle, I was constantly busy. The rare moments I spent with Agnès were exceptions in my life, but they gave meaning to all the rest. It was during those moments of idleness and tranquil communication that I could take the full measure of how little my life belonged to me. My dreams of long ago had been so fruitful that they were now buried beneath a stifling everyday life of documents and meetings. Others might envy my success, but for me it was a servitude. With the exception of the freedom I sometimes stole with Agnès, all I saw around me were constraints and obligations. An invisible whip lashed my sides and I was hurtling forward at ever increasing speed. I could no longer count my fortune; I was the king's right-hand man, and controlled an immense business network. And yet I never gave up hope that some day I would be my own person again.

The Argenterie had become the instrument of royal glory. We worked wonders, in particular for grand ceremonies, an opportunity we were given regularly through the capture of new cities, where the king must make a majestic entry. Horses, weapons, cloths, banners, costumes: everything must shine, and ensure that anyone who had just joined the realm would never wish to leave it. Diplomatic missions were also opportunities to display to foreigners the king's newfound power. I deployed all my accumulated expertise in such circumstances to confer unequaled brilliance on the mission to the pope. Eleven ships left Marseilles for Civitavecchia with everything that was vital for the mission on board. The tapestries destined for the pope had been shipped down the Rhone with the help of King René. Three hundred richly harnessed horses would serve as mounts for the plenipotentiaries and their suite upon their arrival.

Our ambassadors—the likes of Juvénal, Pompadour, Thibault and other dignified prelates or scholars—did not rely on their prayers to preserve them from danger. They refused to embark, and made the voyage over land. The only intrepid voyager who deigned to accompany me on my ships was Tanguy du Châtel. He was nearly eighty years old, and had little choice remaining in his life, only the place of his death; thus, he was not averse to the idea of perishing on the open sea. He was not granted that satisfaction. Our crossing was without incident: we met neither corsairs, nor tempests, nor accidents. A warm wind carried us to Civitavecchia. I spent many a delightful hour conversing on deck with the old swashbuckler from the Armagnac; we were in our shirtsleeves, our heads sheltered from the sun by huge straw hats. Tanguy regaled me with hundreds of anecdotes of the early years of Charles VII, when he was still no more than a precarious Dauphin, or a king without a territory. Du Châtel despised the Caboche rebels, for it was from them that he had rescued the young sovereign one night. His story recalled Eustache, whom I had forgotten, and this in turn brought back my own thoughts from those days, when I, too, wanted to be liberated from those in power. We spoke openly of the assassination of John the Fearless on the bridge of Montereau. He confessed that he had been one of the assassins. It was his idea to kill the Burgundian leader during that meeting, and Charles was not informed. Given the series of misfortunes the assassination had unleashed, Tanguy was filled with remorse for having conceived it. But now that a more beneficent monarchy had eventually emerged from the web of events, along with the defeat of the English and the surrender of the princes, he reasoned that in the end he was right to trust his intuition and slay Charles's rival. This thought, as he approached death, brought him much peace of mind.

He had a deep affection for the king, of the kind one has for those one has known since they were unhappy children. His love found greater sustenance in the kindness he had shown him than in any favors Charles might have granted. For in return all he had received was disgrace and ingratitude. He saw the king for who he was, neither misrepresenting his character nor hiding his faults. After several days of such confessions we had established a certain intimacy, and he gave me a solemn warning: to the best of his knowledge, there was not a single example of someone who had risen under Charles VII who did not, eventually, go on to arouse his jealousy and suffer the consequences of his cruelty.

I looked in silence at the ships bending to the canvas. Surrounded by white seabirds, the squadron sailed across a sea stained violet by the shallows. Nothing could give a greater impression of power than this convoy laden with gold and royal gifts. That was the nature of the Argenterie: it was a peacetime army, but the king, indeed, could still fear it. Tanguy's warnings had a greater effect on me than all of Agnès's impetuous terrors, because they were based on a long acquaintance with the monarch and numerous personal disappointments. At other times when I was alone, I gave much thought to how I might protect myself from an eventual reversal of the royal favor, and I secretly made a number of decisions I promised myself I would implement upon my return.

Upon our arrival, we met the plenipotentiaries who had come by land, and who were growing impatient. The pope was receiving an English mission at the same time, and our legates were eager to quash their influence by a show of strength. When we unloaded the treasures the ships contained in their hulls, they were reassured.

Our delegation's entry into Rome made such an impression that even five years later it had not been forgotten. Luxury was necessary to emphasize the importance the king attached to this mission and the respect he showed the pope. But to go so far as to believe that this debauchery of power would impress the pontiff and induce him to act in a conciliatory manner during the forthcoming negotiations—that was another matter altogether.

*

Pope Nicholas V was a frail little man, slow in his movements. He seemed to hesitate before making the slightest gesture. To reach for a goblet and lift it to his lips he would start over three times. Before walking from one corner of the room to the other, he would evaluate the distance, and any eventual obstacles. Was it the danger inherent in his position that had forced him to act so cautiously or, on the contrary, had he attained his position by means of an inherently cunning nature? I cannot say. The only thing of which I could be certain was that the apparent hesitation of his body hid a great firmness of mind. He was a thoughtful, determined man who made his decisions very wisely and implemented them without accepting the slightest concession.

He was clearly pleased to see our mission arrive. The support of the king of France was a great asset to him. However, in the discussions he held with the plenipotentiaries, he purposely showed himself to be demanding and inflexible, particularly with regard to his rival, the antipope appointed by the Council. He expected his abdication, pure and simple, without compensation.

Nicholas knew that I was not the head of the delegation and that his official discussions would be held with others, in particular Jean Juvénal, the Archbishop of Reims. However, he was well-informed, and a letter from the king further clarified things: he was aware of my true role and my preeminence in financial matters. He was a Tuscan who had once worked as a tutor to the Medici family. He knew that the essential value nowadays was money, and that everything, whether one welcomed the fact or deplored it, was subordinate to money, even nobility. Thus, our discussions had neither the luster nor the official stamp of the forthcoming diplomatic talks, but they were every bit as decisive.

In order to have me accommodated in his palace, he resorted to subterfuge so that we could confer tranquilly and in private. One day, when we had all been convened to an important audience, he suddenly stood up, came over to me, and, stretching my eyelid with a hesitant finger, he cried, "You are ill, Master Cœur, I must warn you. Beware of malaria, which is rampant in our region and kills a great many healthy men every year."

A shiver of terror went through the archbishops and theologians, and they all stepped away from me. When the pope offered to have me examined by his personal doctor ("He works wonders for that illness in particular."), they nodded their approval. And the relief was obvious on their faces when, as a practical conclusion to his offer, the pope, with no further ado, invited me to stay in a wing of his palace.

Thus two parallel negotiations were under way. One was held in the afternoon, in an official hall decorated with imposing frescoes. The ambassadors expressed themselves one after the other, swelling their voices and employing interminable circumlocutions. The pope responded unctuously, but remained inflexible.

With me, matters were different. Most often we met in the morning, in a small dining room, with windows open wide onto a flower garden. Fruit juice, bouillons and pastries adorned the little round table shining with silver dishes. The pope wore a simple chasuble, which left his forearms uncovered. In these private interviews, he left off all the compunction that hindered his gestures in public. Instead, he used his hands to illustrate his words, and often, when speaking, he stood up, went over to the window, and came back to sit down. Our dialogue was simple and to the point, of the sort to which my commercial activity had accustomed me. We were doing business and, as I had sensed right from the beginning, we soon struck a bargain that satisfied both parties.

Nicholas V repeated to the plenipotentiaries that he expected the unconditional abdication of the antipope. He did not want it said that he would accept the slightest concession in order to obtain it. With me he was more realistic. Through his legates and an efficient network of spies, he knew his rival better than anyone.

"To convince the antipope to leave," he said, "we must negotiate . . . with his son—that is, the Duke of Savoy."

Before devoting himself to religion and becoming pope, Amadeus had transferred the Duchy of Savoy to his son Louis. Louis was very ambitious: he wanted to take possession of the Duchy of Milan. To do so, he would have to assert his rights regarding this inheritance, and above all do battle with the condottiere Francesco Sforza. This all required a great deal of money, and the support both of the king of France and of the House of Orléans, who were heir to the Viscontis' rights to the Duchy of Milan. An expert on Italian affairs, the pope advised me how best to proceed. If we provided the young duke of Savoy with the means to go to war—on the condition that his father give up the papacy—it would no doubt be possible to sway the elderly Amadeus.

I followed his advice and was satisfied. The subsequent missions I undertook with the antipope, directly or indirectly, were far more fruitful now that they were founded on money and not on something far less central to the situation: theology.

To conclude the negotiations with the antipope, moreover, particularly on the issue of the conquest of the Duchy of Milan, on the strength of the information I relayed to him the king thought it fit to appoint Dunois. Dunois knew how to speak to Amadeus using the raw language of war, and helped the duke of Savoy to organize his army. He was definitely the man necessary to put an end to the Schism.

Thus, the trip to Rome was profitable to me thrice over. I found the means to help solve the crisis of Christianity, and indeed, early the following year the antipope abdicated. I consolidated my relations with the House of Savoy by offering them a loan whose conditions were very favorable to me. Finally, and most importantly, I befriended the pope.

Pleased with our meetings, and with the knowledge that I had adhered to his suggestions, Nicholas V granted me all the favors I asked of him. I obtained permission for Agnès to have a portable altar, and I ordered one in gold, encrusted with rubies, from the craftsmen of the Trastevere. The pope honored my intercessions in favor of a number of protégés. Finally, and I would say above all, he renewed and extended the indult authorizing maritime commerce with the Sultan. The clearance now contained neither expiration date nor limits to the number of ships. It also gave me permission to transport pilgrims to the Levant. At my request, the Pope added the right to export arms, in the form of a gift from the king of France. Alas, either through caution or a misunderstanding, Nicholas V never published a bull regarding this matter.

But our relations were not limited to these exchanges of good procedures. We both knew what to expect in these matters. People in positions of power have simpler relations with the notion of interest than ordinary people do. At this level, you cannot help but be aware that anyone who approaches you will be asking for something, and there is no reason to be offended. For ordinary people there can be no friendship, love, or even trust when the shadow of an interested expectation looms. For the powerful, on the other hand, the only way to establish true relations is to deal openly with the subject of interest. First and foremost, they will ask: what do you expect from me? And the possibility of moving to a higher level of intimacy will depend on the frankness of one's reply.

Pursuant to our plain discussion of serious matters, Nicholas V and I were able to relax and indulge in conversation that had neither purpose nor profit, but which enabled us to become better acquainted. Moreover, the ailment of convenience with which the pope had diagnosed me did truly and thoroughly infect me. I had to remain longer in Rome than the plenipotentiaries, and during my convalescence I was the pope's guest. As I saw him every day, I eventually got to know this man of multiple faces well. He is dead, and I am nothing now; I can speak the truth, both about him and about myself.

He belonged to that group of Italian prelates for whom religion hides above all a great passion for antiquity. Nicholas was a learned scholar of the Greek and Roman philosophers. In Rome he had taken in a number of scholars fleeing Byzantium as it was about to fall. He had always maintained that he was acting for the good of the Catholic Church by taking in those who were heir to the Eastern church, as well as struggling against the Schism in the West. And it is true that during his pontificate Rome became once again the only center of Christianity. However, as I followed him around his library, I quickly understood that the passion he nurtured for ancient culture had very little to do with religion, that it even went against it. Unlike others, he made no effort to prove that Plato and Aristotle had merely been paving the way for Christ through their ideas. He read them and respected them for themselves. He even confided to me that every day, like the followers of the philosopher, he put into practice the teachings of Pythagoras summed up in the "Golden Verses."

He had set about building a new pontifical palace in Rome, whose majesty would exemplify the new and, he hoped, eternal unity of the Catholic Church. This Vatican is still under construction; I had the opportunity to visit it before embarking for Chios. To design the building the pope commissioned two architects who were steeped in ancient learning. He went with them to visit the remains of temples, and did not hesitate to climb among the ruins himself to measure the proportions of pediments and colonnades.

One day he made an astonishing confession: if he earnestly hoped to convince the European monarchs to launch a new crusade, it was primarily to save the cultural treasures of

Byzantium. His primary reproach to the Turks was their lack of consideration for ancient works.

"In addition to which," I ventured, "they are Mohammedans . . . "

He looked at me and shrugged.

"Yes," he said.

The clever smile that spread slowly across his face, and the gleam of irony that I could read in his eyes, convinced me once and for all: he had no faith. He must have discovered my own weakness long before. This secret bound us more closely than an oath. Later, he would have the opportunity to prove it to me.

*

Italy, the Mediterranean, the Levant: now our gazes were turned in that direction. Perhaps we forgot about the English a bit too hastily. To be sure, the new king of England hated the thought of going back to war, and his wife, the daughter of King René, usefully apprised him of the advantages of peace. But not everyone in England was of this mind. When I returned from Rome, the five-year truce was coming to an end. Incidents had broken out with the English garrisons still present in France: they were no longer being paid. Fougères had been attacked by an adventurer in the employ of England. The city had been looted down to the last spoon.

The court was in an uproar. Over the last five years, everyone had forgotten the English peril, as if the sum of the horrors that endless war had accumulated had blocked the entrance to memory and prohibited any thought of fighting. The king himself had reverted to his former despondent and indecisive attitude. It was as though the English peril took him back to the distant, hateful past of his childhood. His change of appearance and his new manners had been valid in every respect except that one. His indecision was the despair of his warriors, and I shared their dismay. For five years we had been striving to build a powerful army. The *compagnies d'ordonnance*, the *francs-archers*, the artillery detachments: everything was ready. The truce had brought us prosperity, and quickly, and however fragile that prosperity might still be, we were now favorably positioned to resume fighting and conclude the war to our advantage.

I found Agnès in a state of extreme anxiety. She was very pale, and was at pains to hide a great weakness. She informed me that a month earlier she had once again given birth to a daughter, who, like the two previous ones, had been sent away at birth. Agnès had lost a great deal of blood and had suffered from a fever, which had only just abated. But this time she had not been able to hide her condition from the king. He had not said anything, but he had done nothing to alter his festive lifestyle during Agnès's absence. A thousand gazes, in the dangerous shadow of the court, had been observing the first station of what might become a way of the cross. Agnès had one knee to the ground. Beautiful young women were complacently shoved in front of the king. Nothing had happened yet, and Agnès was back on her feet. But everyone was waiting for the next ordeal.

She feared it herself. It was taking her a long time to regain her usual energy. She was particularly languid, which was not usual for her. However, Brézé, Dunois, the Bureau borthers, and all her protégés on the council begged her to intercede with the king to persuade him to go to war. She could not bring herself to do it; my return encouraged her.

I had come home filled with enthusiasm, exalted by my stay in Rome. On my way through Bourges, I was pleased to see that the work on my palace was progressing. Inspired by my visits to various houses in Rome, I ordered a few modifications. I also had the idea of building a steam bath like the ones I had visited in the Levant. I had some difficulty persuading Macé. But this was a private fantasy of my own, invisible to anyone outside, and it would not affect our reputation in any way. On that condition, she accepted.

I then went through Tours, before returning to court. Initially I had to devote myself to various meetings related to my work at the Argenterie. But as soon as I had a moment, I went to see Fouquet to tell him about the painters I had discovered in Rome. And it was he who first brought Agnès's condition to my attention. During my absence he had met her fairly often, and had achieved his purpose: she had agreed to sit for her portrait. He had made a number of studies but did not yet know how to portray her. He was still fascinated by her beauty, but as a man who was used to staring at people's faces, he had noticed a new gravity in her expression. In truth, this was merely an exacerbation of a quality he had always noticed in her. Until now, however, these tones had been in the background and hardly showed through, hidden as they were by the bright colors of her gaiety.

Now, that gravity was there for all to see. Agnès's efforts to act cheerfully served to dissipate the clouds for a short while, but they soon came back. All the sketches Fouquet showed me depicted her with her head slightly tilted forward, eyes downcast, mouth closed.

He had laid the sketches out on a table and we looked at them silently. The unease I felt on seeing the pictures was vague and inexplicable. And suddenly I understood: this was the face of a recumbent statue, a death mask. I looked up at Fouquet and saw that his eyes were filled with tears. He shrugged his shoulders and picked up the sheets of paper, muttering to himself.

When finally I returned to court and saw Agnès again, I understood she was glad of my presence. But she did not show it in her usual way. Even alone in her apartments she seemed afraid that she would be found out. As we conversed, the awkwardness was perceptible. To make things easier for her, I moved quickly from a personal register to the question of war. I told her that I thought the looting at Fougères was providential. We must use it to our advantage to finish the work of reconquest, and have done with the English peril once and for all. Initially my enthusiasm seemed to arouse her own. But very quickly her eyes glazed over. She reminded me of the Dauphin's attacks on Brézé the previous year, perpetrated by a miserable spy called Mariette, whom I had had imprisoned. According to Agnès, the Dauphin was continuing to lay his diabolical traps in order to discredit her. For him, the best way to undermine her was to target those she supported. Was this business with the English not simply yet another provocation? I could not see how, from his faraway Dauphiné, Louis could be attempting to revive the war with England, nor to what end. Agnès admitted that I was right, but in the very same moment almost burst into tears. She was nervous, and saw danger everywhere, even when it was most unlikely. Finally, we agreed that we must act, each of us with the means at our disposal. She told me that in her opinion, the best thing would be to persuade the queen to begin with, and they would go together to exhort Charles to engage the enemy. It was not a bad idea. It would avoid making the war seem like the intention of one party—Agnès—which would have had the effect of driving all those who were jealous of her into the opposite camp.

As for me, I went the very next day to see the king and we had a long conversation. I related in detail my exchanges with the pope. We also had a thorough discussion about Italian affairs, and he inquired about Jean de Villages's mission to the Sultan. It fascinated him, and his face lit up with delight when he spoke of these subjects.

So his displeasure seemed all the greater when I took the initiative to steer the conversation onto the subject of England.

It mattered little that the June heat was coming through the window with the brilliant sunshine: Charles began to shiver. With one hand, he pulled his collar tight, and slumped in his chair. He listened as I enumerated my arguments, then he protested weakly, speaking about the king of England.

"Henry is our relative now. René's daughter has been working wonders, it would seem, to prevent him from going back to war."

"Indeed, and many people there blame him for that weakness."

"The English have kept their commitments in spite of everything. The truce has been lasting."

"Do not forget we had to send Dunois and an army to reconquer Le Mans, even though they had agreed to evacuate."

"The English Regent of their provinces in our region has presented his apologies regarding the matter of Fougères. It was a roughneck from Aragon who took the liberty—"

"Sire," I interrupted, seizing his hand, "the reality of things matters little. The pretext is there, just waiting. You will win. Now you have the strength, the arms, and the money."

Charles drew his hand away and paused on my last word.

"Money, you say?"

There was a long silence. His searching gaze burned into me.

"Such a campaign would cost a great deal of money," he continued. "Even if I now have the means to maintain a permanent army without calling upon the princes, it would be something else again if I have to pay for their campaign . . . "

He was still staring at me.

"Money," I answered at last, perhaps a bit too late, "is not an issue. You know that everything that is mine, is yours."

These hollow formulas, which one can use fearlessly in the Levant because no one would venture to give them credit, ring differently in the ears of a man like Charles. He nodded, and I wondered if I had not poured a poison into his mind that would someday prove lethal to me. He looked away from my face and let his gaze wander into the opalescent clarity of the window.

"How much could a campaign like that cost? Let us suppose we invest all our means, and the affair lasts until winter . . . Three hundred thousand . . . No, no . . . I would say, rather, four hundred thousand écus. Would you give them to me, Messire Cœur?"

He had again turned his gaze to me, as if awaiting my reaction. This was the worst question anyone had ever asked me. If I said no, I would be rebelling against my king and he would never forgive me. If I said yes, the sheer enormity of the sum would instantly reveal the extent of my fortune. The king was poorly versed in matters of finance. However, they were touched upon at the Council, and his quartermaster general kept him regularly informed as to the state of his treasury. He knew that I was rich and he was certainly aware that it was in part due to the duties he had conferred on me. But now for the first time, what we both knew, without ever having spoken of it, was about to appear in broad daylight, through my reply: I was richer than the king, richer than the state.

"Yes," I replied, and bowed.

The moment I uttered it, I knew that this word was sealing my fate. It is not a good idea to contest the power of such men. He did not bat an eyelash, but I got the impression I was hearing my words fall into the darkest depths of his mind. He thanked me, with a cold smile. Then he told me that he would think about it.

In the days that followed, he was once again in a good humor. When the queen, accompanied by Agnès and other women from her retinue, came joyfully to urge him to shine before the ladies, by leading his army to vanquish the English rabble, he laughed in a rather vain manner. It was obvious in any case that he rather liked the idea of the challenge. We removed to Roches-Tranchelion, not far from Chinon, for it was there that the king had decided to hold the great council. Opinion was unanimous, although one could discern two groups of individuals in the assembly. Some of them, friends of Agnès for the most part—but also some who were close to the Queen, minor lords who had been despoiled of their property in Normandy due to the English occupation, and even a few disinterested and sincere men—recommended war, out of a sense of conviction and honesty. The others rallied merely to please the king, for as good courtiers, they had discerned the signs, however discreet, of his change of heart.

*

Once the decision was made, everything happened very quickly. Scarcely three weeks after the council, Charles VII left Touraine at the head of his troops. King René, who had been keeping to his lands, in a constant bad temper ever since his brother had been banished, now forgot everything and rushed to join in the combat.

By joking about how valiant the king was, about the impression he would make on the ladies, the Queen had intended to prick her husband's self-esteem. But she had no intention of going with him to witness his exploits. Agnès, on the other hand, would have gladly begged for that favor. Perhaps she did ask the king. She said nothing to me, but she seemed greatly vexed to be staying behind. I had convinced the king that I had to stay for a few days in Touraine in order to make arrangements for campaign supplies. I would join him later, on the battleground. He consented. I was also given permission to stay alone with Agnès. When we met, I tried to understand what was making her so nervous. She did not usually suffer in this way from the king's absence. It is true that since she had met him, there had been no actual wars in the land, at the most a few localized skirmishes. So she had not had the opportunity to show her support for him.

And yet I could not get to the bottom of the reasons for her anxiety. Was she afraid for him? When he had been confronted with Talbot, who was commanding the English army, and though he was not yet twenty-four, the risks of a reversal had been considerable. Agnès could still recall the chivalric wars where the lords, with the king at their head, fought hand-to-hand and died in the hundreds or were captured. She could not imagine any better than I could the new forms of warfare that were about to be deployed, transformed by the action from a distance of culverins and bombards, the archery corps and the infantrymen.

I had the feeling that she was also afraid for her own sake. The queen's words, when she enjoined the king to "shine before the ladies," had upset her. Perhaps Agnès pictured Charles in his glory, exalted by victory, and eager to prolong the reconquest of his provinces by other, more intimate conquests, where swooning women would open their hearts and bodies to him without hesitation.

She had always feared her pregnancies, and had undergone three of them without the majority of courtiers knowing a thing, and now she pleaded with Charles to stay with her the night before his departure. She made a strange confession to me: she hoped that the gestures of love during that last night would plant (for the first time with her willing approval) a royal heir in her womb once again.

By virtue of struggling to overcome the repulsion that the king had initially aroused in her, and fully aware of the persistent flaws in his character that meant that he was not to be trusted in the least, she had finally grown attached to him. This bond, over time, had become so vital to her that she could not conceive of life without it. In short, she loved Charles.

I tried to calm her. I promised to keep an eye on the king

during the campaign and to let her know if anything at any moment might indicate she had reason to be alarmed.

Two weeks later, I went to the scene of battle. There was hardly any fighting; there were only victories. The towns rose up, encircled the English in their quarters, and opened their gates to the soldiers of the king of France. Pont-Audemer, Pont-l'Évèque, Lisieux, Mantes, Bernay, all fell. On August 28, when I arrived, the town of Vernon surrendered to the king. Dunois hoped to be given the place, but Charles decided to offer it to Agnès. He demanded the keys to the city and sent them to her at Loches by messenger. I was pleased for her. Two days later, we entered Louviers and for the first time the king held council in Normandy. It was decided we would march on Rouen immediately.

I left again for Tours, while waiting for the capture of the city to be organized. Obviously, I could not resist going to see Agnès in Loches. The gift from the king had reassured her. Her wish had been fulfilled: she was pregnant, and for the first time she was not hiding the fact. Her condition gave a faint pink glow to her cheeks, and her expression was livelier. She was laughing, and seemed to have regained her spirits. But I knew her well, and I could sense in her a deeper anxiety and dark thoughts. The slightest noise startled her and the slightest alarm gave her eyes the frightened brilliance of a hounded doe's.

She had me tell her at length about the war, and never tired hearing of the king's triumphs. I insisted on his valiance, but as I depicted it to her I was careful to show that he was in no danger. She listened thoughtfully. Her gown was so tight that it revealed the slight swelling of her womb. She was wearing the type of décolleté she preferred, and the stretching of the laces indicated that her breasts were full and taut. I do not know whether it was the news of her pregnancy, the shape it had given her, or the sudden presence of fecundity among all her other assets of charm and beauty, which hardly needed it otherwise, but for the first time in her presence I felt an intense, almost painful surge of lust. She was too intelligent not to have noticed. We exchanged a smile, and then immediately, as if to ward off the spell, she led me into the garden to show me her roses.

I left her the next morning, reassured about her condition. Unfortunately, what I knew of the king caused me to fear that she had reason to remain on her guard. And when I returned to Rouen in mid-October, what I discovered confirmed my fears, and even horrified me.

Negotiations to limit the bloodshed were underway with the English garrison. Emissaries from the populace of Rouen came and went between the camp of royal troops and the city, keeping the assailants informed about the situation inside the city and receiving instructions for those civilians who wished to take part in their liberation. Charles was biding his time. But the waiting was making everyone nervous, given the succession of almost daily victories since the beginning of the campaign. Everyone, starting with the king, felt the end was in sight. At the same time, these final hours of war, incensed by the memory of years of atrocities committed in the region, were also full of joy, restrained now but just waiting to burst forth. The result was an almost continuous debauchery. The faraway sound of the cannonade brought wild exclamations from the royal camp. Charles displayed a forced and vaguely anxious cheer, drinking from morning to night with his courtiers. The serious men—Brézé, Dunois, and the Bureaus—kept well away from such excess: they were waging war. However, around men of power there is never any lack of volunteers prepared to deal with petty tasks and adjust their facial expressions to suit the mood of those they court. The enviable position of king's pimp had been empty ever since Charles of Anjou had ceased to occupy it. Several less illustrious individuals with more vulgar taste were eager to put their energy to good use and take over the position. With the legendary appetite of his Valois ancestors, as well as their poor judgment, Charles now lay siege to the young serving girls or the fine Norman ladies, who put up very little resistance.

Such excess was not worrying in and of itself. Charles had already displayed such indulgence in the past, and the exceptional circumstances of the last days of war could easily explain it. What was in my opinion far more serious, relative to Agnès's fate, was the arrival of several young women from the court. The king had not taken the queen with him because she did not wish to go. But Agnès had pleaded with him, and he had objected, saying that no women were to take part in the campaign. Therefore the presence of this handful of ladies, all young and fresh, naturally took on a particular significance.

My observation of these signs of debauchery was interrupted by the long-awaited news: Rouen had been captured. The rebellious populace opened the gates to Brézé and then to Dunois, each of whom was accompanied by a powerful cavalry. The English were retrenched in their castle, which was being bombarded by Bureau's cannons. Finally, to the great chagrin of the people of Rouen, who would have liked to make them suffer a punishment in proportion to their crimes, the English were allowed to flee with their lives. They left behind a number of other fortifications as the price for this mercy, and now with Rouen all of Normandy was free.

Now all that was needed was a consecration, a ceremony to illustrate for all time this ultimate victory. I sent for Jean de Villages and several of my young assistants who had some experience in organizing magnificent ceremonies. Convoys traveled day and night, bringing from the Argenterie precious cloth and ceremonial coats of arms. Finally on November 10 our procession entered the city, surrounding the king beneath his canopy.

*

The story of this triumph has often been told, and I have nothing to add other than my own impressions, since I had the great privilege of taking part in it. I rode alongside Dunois and Brézé. We were deafened by six trumpets just ahead of us. All three of us were wearing purple velvet doublets lined with marten's fur. Our horses' caparisons were embroidered with fine gold and silk. Mine was red with a white cross on it, for it had been ordered for the Duke of Savoy, but he had not been able to stay until the procession. There was an immense crowd, and we could tell that this was no ordinary royal spectacle, nor an everyday gathering of simple onlookers, rubbing their poverty up against the irritating but admirable contact of wealth and power. The inhabitants were enjoying their own celebration of freedom and victory, and the king had been invited as a benefactor and a relation. The old men wept with the memory of their suffering, and to honor those unfortunate victims who had not lived to see this day; the women once again felt hope for their children, and could tell themselves that they had not simply brought them into the world to suffer, but also to know peace and happiness. The young men were filled with energy, laughing and shouting the forbidden name, the one which until now they had to whisper in fear, because it belonged to the king of France.

For those of us in Charles's entourage, who were responsible for an entire country, this celebration bore us much further than the city where it was held. For France it meant the end of a century or more of war, misfortune, and ruin. To be sure, we still had to drive the English from Guyenne. But there they were far from their home base, and surrounded by hostile forces; it was only a matter of time. There had been at least one advantage to this endless war: it had ushered in the demise of the world of princes, who exchanged land and people as if they were inert things, the way a woman might bring a mill, a pond, or a forest to her marriage as part of her dowry. The man who had delivered these people from their yoke was the king of France; they were no longer the property of the local lord, but the king's subjects.

I glanced over at Charles from time to time. He was wearing a full suit of armor, with a hat of gray beaver fur, lined with vermilion silk. To the front of his headpiece I had attached a little fermail set with a big diamond. The king seemed to be nodding off on his horse, his eyes half closed. What was he feeling? I would not have been surprised, if I could have asked him, if he had answered: boredom. Before we mounted our horses, while the procession was being prepared, he had ordered white wine to be brought to his campaign tent. If he had drunk four or five glasses, it was not to calm the impatience anyone in his place might have felt, but rather to give himself the courage to confront an ordeal he would have gladly done without.

When I had gone to find him to inform him of the order for the ceremony, he had asked trivial questions about the supper, for he wished to spend it in the company of a select few, those same ladies whose arrival we had witnessed several days earlier.

This king truly had a strange destiny, tossed as he was into the world, so weak and humiliated, the scorned sovereign of a ravaged, occupied, divided land yet who, through his will alone, had overcome all the obstacles, putting an end to a war that everyone had thought would be eternal, terminating the Schism of the West, witnessing the fall of Byzantium and rescuing part of its heritage by opening his country to the Levant. And while he desired and organized all of this, it was not in the manner of an Alexander or a Caesar. Such men, in a moment of victory, would have ridden out bareheaded, borne by the crowd's enthusiasm, and it would be clear to all that their armies had followed them because they were inebriated and adoring. But Charles had prepared everything in silence, like a thwarted child plotting his revenge. The great things he accomplished were merely the projected shadow of his petty calculations. His weakness meant that men of worth attached themselves to him, felt sorry for him, and he used them like lifeless playthings, never hesitating, should his feelings toward them change, to smash them to bits. And now that the hour of victory had come, now that the capricious child had had his revenge, he had none of those other ambitions which true conquerors always nourish, which grow and increase until they can grow no more; Charles's rewards were selfish and petty: drink, entertainment, and lust. In short, a void.

In the midst of great events there are often men about whom poets and dreamers will say, "Oh, if only I were in their place, what an unforgettable harvest of emotions I would reap!" And in comparison to this supposed turbulence, the calm of great figures passes for self-mastery. But these victors are often men without dreams, and for them hours of glory are monotonous and fastidious; to endure them they focus their thoughts on insignificant objects. An aching corn on their foot, their unassuaged appetites, the ill-timed memory of a kiss refused or awaited: their mind bathes in this lukewarm, stagnant liquid, while the crowd acclaims them.

It was an endless day of festivity and emotion. Charles attended mass in the cathedral, and received endless tributes. People's cries could be heard everywhere, even from out-of-doors. Drunken bell-ringers took turns at pulling the bell-ropes. The wine, food, and clothing that had been hidden from the English poured out into the street. Fortunately for the king, November days are short, and that one, in addition, was bitter cold. An easterly wind hurled icy gusts at the populace but could not subdue them: the feasting continued indoors. After making an appearance at various official sites, the king withdrew to the intimate supper he was expecting.

I spent a solitary evening surrounded by revelers. All those to whom I had lent money were eager to invite me, as if to prove the good use they had made of my funds. Their cordiality was unbearable. I refused to look on them as my debtors and, in general, to judge them in proportion to their fortune. I did not however, go so far as to view their debt as sufficient reason to appreciate their company. I was overcome by melancholy, and that me made me drink; the wine contributed further to my sadness. I finally made my escape from a house where the feasting was still at its height, and I began wandering through the streets.

I happened upon Dunois. He was sitting on a guard stone, holding his head in his hands. When he saw me, he let out a hoarse cry of joy. There was nothing left of the cheer we had felt that morning. He too, with the help of the wine, was drifting on a flow of dark thoughts. This man who, thanks to an impressive pyramid of victories, titles, and lands, had managed to make others forget his illegitimate origins, was now, with the ebbing tide of triumph, once again the bastard of Orléans, that same man who had welcomed me to the court, who had gone looking for death and found glory, until this day we had just lived through and which, by fulfilling all our desires, had annihilated them. We pulled our hoods down over our brows, to keep our faces in shadow, and we wandered through the streets, speaking at length about the past, as if we refused the proof that it had abandoned us. Then Dunois began a soliloquy about further conquest. His forced enthusiasm did little to mask the fact that, if there were more battles, they would lack the invisible albeit essential uncertainty as to their outcome.

Finally our steps led us back to the castle where we were staying. We presented ourselves to the sentry and walked into the great courtyard. From the keep, through the open windows of the king's apartments, there came the sounds of music and women's laughter. Dunois stopped, looked up toward the lighted rooms whence these joyful sounds were coming, and suddenly turned to me.

"Beware of him," he whispered, pointing with his chin in the direction of the king.

His breath made it clear to me that he was speaking under the influence of alcohol, but while until now his words had seemed confused, and his mind fuddled, at that moment he seemed to master himself perfectly.

"You saved him, and now he no longer needs you."

"Did he say anything that might have led you to think . . . ?"

But lucidity had already faded from Dunois's face. He shook his head and made a painful grimace.

"Goodnight!" he called.

And he disappeared down the corridor leading to his room.

*

I slept poorly and woke the next morning shortly before dawn. The intoxication and feasting had left the castle in a stunned silence. Marc was nowhere to be found. He was surely out enjoying the festivities as well. I went myself to the kitchen to try to find something to eat. Two baker's boys were sleeping on the chopping table near the warm oven. I went through the cupboards and found a jar of butter, and a crust of bread at the bottom of a bin. I took a stoneware bowl from a mountain of dirty dishes and wiped it on the apron of one of the sleeping baker's boys.

I went back upstairs with my provender and cleared a space among the bottles scattered across a stone table on the castle's flower-decked terrace. The sun had returned and covered the city with warmth, much welcomed by those who had fallen asleep in the street or on their doorstep. I had been there day-dreaming for an hour or so when a man stood in the entrance to the great hall. In one hand he was holding a pitcher and in the other a dish of salt meat covered by a red-and-white checked cloth. It was Étienne Chevalier. We had hardly seen each other during the ceremonies: he had been part of another group, riding behind King René. I could see from his demeanor that he had slept no better than I had. His beard, which ordinarily he kept close-shaven, blackened his face, and his eyes were bloodshot and swollen. He sat down next to me, removed the cloth from his terrine and began digging into it. He too must have rummaged to see what he could find in the kitchen.

We began talking about the celebration, and we both remarked on how long ago it already seemed. We were both surprised, despite our experience of life, at how our exaltation could have subsided so quickly and so thoroughly.

Sleepy valets were drifting down the corridors. They seemed to be headed to the king's apartments. Chevalier and I were thinking the same thing, I am sure. He knew Agnès and loved her, too, though in a very different way, with greater distance and respect.

"I have been told that one of those ladies has precedence over all the others," I ventured, repeating something I had heard somewhere during the night.

"Antoinette de Maignelay," murmured Chevalier, and he cast a dark look at the king's windows.

There was a long, awkward silence. We were not well enough acquainted to confide further in each other or speak freely of the king's behavior.

"I could scarcely have believed," he continued, seeming to come back to his senses, "that I would live to see this day. To think I would be here one day, with you, in Rouen, with the city liberated . . ."

He sniffed noisily, grabbed a piece of terrine and, before lifting it to his mouth, said with a sudden exhalation, "And I never would have thought that such a moment would leave me feeling so unhappy."

I stayed three more days in Rouen on business for the Argenterie. We had to seize the opportunity offered by the return of the city to the realm as quickly as possible: Normandy, its products and its maritime trade were now wide open to us. I met the king only once during my stay. He sent for me on the perfectly trivial matter of an embroidered doublet he had ordered from the Argenterie and which did not fit. I was used to having him refer to me for all sorts of things, from the greatest to the most insignificant. This time however, I sensed an ulterior motive behind his summons. While he was questioning me regarding this minor issue about which I, obviously, knew nothing, Charles stared at me with an enigmatic smile. The interrogation was held in the presence of several courtiers and some of the women who had joined the court during the campaign. I tried to determine which one might be Antoinette de Maignelay. But the king did not leave me the leisure of such a discovery. He began to reproach me for mismanaging the Argenterie. Without looking at me, he called on all those present as his witnesses. Clearly he felt a sinister joy in humiliating the man who had provided him with the means to his victory. Thus, my premonition had been correct. By advancing the four hundred thousand écus, I had inflicted a deep wound on him, which might prove mortal for our understanding. This first blow dealt in public was a harbinger of further ordeals and greater danger.

I left Rouen, trying to put a good face on things. No one could imagine the turmoil in my thoughts. At least there was one advantage to my alarm: it aroused my spirit, made dull by the languor of victory. I was now certain that something had been set in motion. I must find shelter before the king's vengeance came to strike me. My only chance was his predilection for complicated maneuvers and cold revenge. While he played with me, and grew annoyed with tormenting me, I could act. Thus was I reduced to the woeful extreme of hoping that my ordeal would last a long time.

I headed first to Tours, where Guillaume de Varye was expecting me on business. We had made good progress by nightfall and had already stopped at a postal relay on the road to Tours when I called to Marc in sudden haste and had him saddle the horses again, though he had just groomed them and led them to the stable. We went back the way we had come, galloping furiously as far as the crossroads for Loches. It was a moonlit night and we continued on our way, in spite of the darkness and cold, until by dawn we were in sight of the castle where Agnès was staying.

I had dreaded seeing her again, for fear she might question me about the king's behavior and I would have to lie to her. But such cowardice was not worthy. I had made her a promise; now I must honor it. I lay down to rest on an embellished chest, near the big fireplace, and that is where Agnès found me in the morning. She was as I loved her, unaffected, her hair on her shoulders, wearing a simple chasuble with fine straps that both hid her body and revealed its curves. I soon understood, however, that this relaxed appearance was not a good sign. Her eyes were swollen and her nose was red. Her hands were trembling slightly and her gestures were so abrupt as to be—something which was rare for her—awkward. She almost knocked over a candlestick and somewhat later she broke a glass she was trying to raise to her lips. Above all, she seemed chilled to the bone, as if some invisible protection had been taken away, leaving her vulnerable to everything, including the biting damp air of the old castle.

The huge chimney in the room where I had slept spread its warmth easily enough for me. But Agnès led me to her room, shivering. Around her bed she had hung a tapestry of Nebuchadnezzar that the king had given her. I had had it made, and for several months I had followed its execution at the weavers'. I was pleased to find it there and, above all, to see that Agnès liked it and was glad to have it there. As soon as we were in the room she climbed onto her bed and motioned to me to sit next to her. This nest kept the damp at bay and preserved the body's gentle warmth, and she seemed to relax. It was as if her energy could now leave her limbs and enter her mind. She began speaking, so sharply that sometimes she choked on her emotion.

I realized she already knew everything: I had been afraid she would question me on the king's behavior, but it seemed someone had already related it to her down to the slightest detail. When she saw that I was surprised, she told me that Étienne Chevalier had passed that way two days earlier, and had told her everything he knew. It was not the king's unfaithfulness that grieved her. If she had learned that he sported with whores during the campaign, she would have understood and not felt alarmed. But she could not bear what she conceived as a double betrayal: Charles's, and her cousin's. For Antoinette de Maignelay was directly related to her mother, and it was Agnès herself who had introduced her at court. As for the king, it was a typical betrayal, concealed beneath the appearances of a favor. In fact, at the very moment he sent her the keys to the city of Vernon, he was taking another woman to his bed.

I tried to calm her down, telling her that the incident would be short-lived, and that the king would come back to her.

"Short-lived? You do not know Antoinette! She is ambitious, and a schemer. She has come this far, and will be determined to stay there."

Now that I know the rest of the story, I have to admit that she was right. Not three months would go by before Antoinette de Maignelay officially became the king's mistress. But at the time I thought Agnès was exaggerating. When I told her as much, she reacted angrily. Then, very quickly, her anger subsided and gave way to a sorrowful weariness that was infinitely sad to see.

She looked at her belly, already swollen with the pregnancy, which for once she had desired. Her hands were swollen. She played nervously with an amethyst ring the king had given her and which now would not slide onto her thickened finger.

"I am confined here—heavy, ugly, weak, and far from him. Whereas she is there, sharing the finest moments of his life, and being with him in his pleasure."

I held her in my arms. She placed her head on my chest and began weeping quietly. I could feel her tears trickle onto my right hand. She was shivering. I had never seen her so weak and disarmed. She had always shown such extraordinary energy in every circumstance, and particularly in adversity, but now she was despondent, all her strength gone. No doubt it was also the effect of her condition and probably, already, of illness. I felt immense tenderness for her and a desire to do everything I could do attenuate her suffering, or, at least, not to make it any worse. I felt no pity, because I knew that pity was something she despised, and she would not have liked to arouse it at any cost. For the first time, however, I consciously felt a veritable hatred for the king. The way he had taken possession of Agnès, compromising her by displaying his favor, keeping her in the hopes of a shared love—only to humiliate her publicly and expose her to general scorn: it was despicable. My judgment on his behavior was all the more harsh—although the circumstances were different—in that it resembled the attitude he had adopted with me.

Our shared experiences seemed to reinforce each other—although I still had the means to escape from the king, and sufficient fortune to find support and protection from others in high places, if I could no longer rely on his patronage. Agnès had nothing. She had been handed over to him, had forced her nature in order to form a sincere attachment to him. He could take everything she owned away from her again. Judging from his behavior toward those he had repudiated or banished, one could not expect him to behave generously toward her if she was disgraced, and particularly now that he might be under the influence of a rival who would set about erasing the very memory of the woman who had preceded her.

These turbulent feelings tormented my mind, and led me to seek a way to escape their violence. Agnès lay abandoned at my side, and our bodies were closely entwined. We both knew how vulnerable we were despite the protection of the warm sheets enfolding us: all of this conspired to bring us closer than we had ever been. Physical desire overwhelmed the modesty of our usual friendship. I reached for her throat and began to untie the delicate veil of satin covering her. She protested, and this token refusal was all that was needed to convince me that my passion was not coercion. Had she not opposed my gesture I would have been reluctant to take advantage of her weakness. Whereas by showing me her will, even if it was contrary, she proved to me that her lucidity was intact: her consent, should she show it, would be fully valid. And indeed, before long I felt that the gestures with which she opposed my caresses merely served to prolong them. By acting as if she were pushing my hands aside, she guided them. I had often held her body, but chastely, so that this time I felt as if I were discovering it. I was surprised to find how fragile she seemed. At the same time, however delicate her limbs might be, her breasts and belly were full, bursting with life, more burning than I had expected. In such close proximity, the familiar smell of flowers and spices no longer veiled the slightly tangy perfume of her fair skin, but brought my desire to a peak. She could no longer ignore the proof of this, and if this time she refrained from crying out it was because her desire was equal to mine. It was pointless trying to hide it. She stared at me, squeezing my hands tightly, then with a delicious slowness she placed her lips on mine. After this long kiss, she pulled up the covers and, in the darkness of the linen sheets, as they formed a wild and gentle cave, we united our bodies and our pain, our caresses and our rebellion. In a brazier of sensual delight, for the time that love lasts, all our wounds and rancor, our disappointments and disillusions blazed together, melting our souls, uniting them.

I would like to make one thing clear: the inestimable value of this moment had nothing to do with the satisfaction of conquest or any other form of male vanity. If for me this instant, even with the distance of time and perhaps all the more so because of it, constitutes the turning point of my entire life, it is because it was caught, or should I say crushed, between two contrary forces with an intensity I could never have imagined. On the one hand, our affinity, even to the extremes of carnal union, turned out to be perfect. Everything we had ever imagined turned out to be true, and our mutual attraction was neither an illusion nor a mistake, but indeed the sign that we had been destined for each other from all eternity. But the moment it became reality, our union was soiled by its original sin. We had just destroyed the distance that had allowed us to remain close. Once we crossed that line, everything could come crashing down upon us: the king's anger, Agnès's remorse, the fact of my age, and the precariousness of my present situation. It was as if we had broken a vial filled with blood, and our bodies were suddenly splattered and stained by imminent punishment.

We should have fled. We should have left everything behind at that very moment. But love only gives the strength to maintain its own fire, and the delight of the senses left no energy for anything other than renewing our carnal embrace. The proof of the danger surrounding us engendered only one desire, that of loving again. The more we felt that this beginning was an end, the greater the grip of a desperate desire to prolong its life.

In a moment when pleasure gave me respite, the only thing

I was conscious of was the thought that, until then, I had never loved, and that Providence had bestowed a great favor on me by allowing me to know, even just once, such happiness.

We stayed like that until nightfall. A serving woman knocked on the door to bring the candles and Agnès called out to her to come back later. The pale remnants of the day filtered through the thick glass windows. Agnès opened the curtains wide and went quickly to wrap herself in a nightgown. I dressed hastily, searching awkwardly for my clothing, scattered on either side of the bed. We were suddenly overcome by embarrassment. Like Adam and Eve leaving the Garden of Eden, terrified to discover their nudity, we were suddenly both aware of what we had done. A strong sense of remorse ordered us to erase any trace of those moments when we had freed ourselves from all restraint and the laws of modesty.

Either because the act of love had revived the energy she had been lacking, or because she wanted to be active and put her moment of abandon behind her as quickly as possible, as soon as we were dressed and groomed once again Agnès began to speak in a determined manner, and set before me the principles of her future conduct.

"I will not allow them to trample on me," she said as we went down to the salons. "I am going to fight. I will go shortly to find the king. He must yield to me, or explain himself."

I was happy to see she had regained her firmness and confidence. But I did not really believe she would act on her words. Beyond the excitement of the moment I could still see the fatigue in her features, and even that which I did not yet know I must call her illness. In the rooms which Marc, at my request, had kept warm with a continuous blaze of elm and birch logs, it was easy to talk of traveling and riding off to see the king. But winter had come to stay, and promised to be harsh. I hoped that Agnès, when it came time to act, would think about the dangers of the climate and the bad roads.

After supper, she kissed me chastely and went back up to her apartments. I made arrangements with Marc for my departure the next day, and I went to sleep in the room I normally occupied at Loches. I left the castle midmorning. Agnès had risen early. She was wearing a red velvet gown with a collar of marten fur. She wished me a safe journey, and showed every consideration, making sure we had enough food and drink with us. Unbeknownst to me, she slipped into one of my pockets an ivory statue representing St. James. It is an item that the richest pilgrims take with them, hoping for the saint's protection. I have often wanted to take the way to Compostela and, in consolation for never finding the time to go, I have offered help to many penitents asking for my support. It is not that I believed in these so-called relics. But it has always seemed to me that my fate had a secret and powerful bond with the pilgrimage to Compostela. Was it not St. James who started the movement of peoples all across Europe, instigating trade, forcing the peasants to leave their glebes, and those from the North to discover the South, or from the East to discover the West? Along with war, pilgrimages are the most ancient cause of human migration. I have devoted my life to the movement, everywhere, on land and on sea, of merchandise and merchants, and so I feel I am his heir and, so to speak, the successor to the labors of a saint for whom I am named. Perhaps Agnès sensed this. In any case, I felt her choice of gift was not fortuitous. Of all the things I would lose, later in life, the statue is the only thing I sincerely regret.

The sky that morning was heavy with cloud, yellow beneath an invisible sun. The freezing air smelled of plowed fields, and crows circled above the castle walls. Agnès stood slightly back from the door, no doubt so that the faint shadow would hide her face and not show her lingering discomfiture. Our transgression had broken something and we both knew it. I was even more upset than she was. Unlike me, she must have known that this misunderstanding would be without consequence, for the simple reason that another event would soon come to occult it and remove all its substance. She waved goodbye and before my horse had left the courtyard she had already gone back inside. The door closed behind her. I would never see her again.

V.

Toward Rebirth

What came thereafter is a matter of record. It belongs to History. The king regarded Agnès's death as an event of considerable importance, almost equal to his victories. But the mausoleums and royal endowments, the low masses said twice a week for the salvation of her soul, and even the ducal crown which Charles granted to her posthumously perpetuate the image of a woman who was not the one I had known. For me that woman vanished the moment the door at Loches closed behind her: who will ever know what her last feelings were? Her last thoughts? What we know of her is her path through life and a few dates. We know that she left Touraine not long after my own departure, at the beginning of January, in wintry weather. She braved the cold and the danger of the roads, which were still not safe from lurking rowdy soldiers formerly allied with England and now left to their own resources. The king was again at war, and the women who had joined him to celebrate his triumph in Rouen had departed. The few fortifications that remained to be reconquered put up very little resistance. Charles could parade in full regalia and even lead the attack without great risk to his person.

Agnès had faced greater peril, and yet she was the one who admired him. He enjoyed having her near him. All the witnesses have told me that these few days were happy. Did she complain to him about his infidelity, or was she content merely to have her place again, for everyone to see? I think she was too clever to risk resorting to reprimands. And she must not have felt sufficiently irreproachable, given what we had experienced together, to pose as the virtuous one. Those who were close to Charles and Agnès during these last days insist on the harmony that seemed to reign between them. I have every reason to believe they are telling the truth. Agnès was sincerely happy to be with the king again and to share his glory, so much so that she would be blind to his vainglorious posing as a great leader, and above all she would ignore the fact that he had complacently received tributes from another woman.

Agnès and I shared the same paradoxical feelings regarding this strange individual. We knew that he was capable of betraying us or even surrendering us without a qualm to our worst enemies, that he could contemplate our annihilation without lifting a finger, as he had done with Joan of Arc; and yet, at the very thought that we had been unfaithful to him, we were crushed with the fear of making him suffer even the slightest bit.

In any event, there were those days of happiness. Her ladies-in-waiting later told me that, after the hardships of the journey, and surely already weakened by illness, Agnès had used up every ounce of strength remaining to respond to the king's enthusiasm, to stay up late and laugh with him. When he left again on a new campaign at the beginning of February, the moment he was out of sight Agnès collapsed.

People have often described her dying days, in terms destined to honor her piety. Among the various other gifts the pope had given me for her there was a plenary indulgence, which assured her of absolution in her final hours. The document had stayed behind in Loches, but her confessor took her at her word. Now in this time where I myself have need of such a viaticum for the hereafter, I realize how great the gulf between myself and my religion has grown. However, it is with infinite tenderness that I think of the deep, naïve trust which

Agnès placed in such promises, made by men in the name of a God whose very existence—and, above all, desires—they knew nothing of.

Everything happened so quickly that I did not hear of this apotheosis or of her death. On February 15 a messenger came to inform me, in Montpellier, where I had come on business, that Agnès had died and that she had designated me, along with Étienne Chevalier and her doctor, Robert Poitevin, as one of the three executors of her will.

All through the months that followed Agnès's death, I continued to live and to act so that anyone who met me in those days would think nothing had changed. However, deep inside I felt empty and cold. The circumstances of our last meeting had stripped from any mention of Agnès the peace I had known prior to that. When I thought of her, it was to feel the pain of our misunderstanding, and to wish to the verge of insanity that we could go back in time, cancel certain gestures, and find again our lost innocence. But not to think of her was to abandon her and kill her a second time.

Nothing could take my mind off this dilemma. I threw myself into still more travel and activity, trying in vain to escape.

One of the effects of Agnès's death was to enhance the danger that hovered over her friends. Brézé, whom she had always defended and even saved on more than one occasion, was the first to pay, only a few weeks later. On the pretext of granting him a grand-sounding title in Normandy, the king removed him from the council. This was yet another reason for me to fear the worst. However, Agnès's death had another consequence, which, in the case in point, proved useful: it had killed all feelings other than those connected to her memory. I no longer felt either joy or sorrow or, in this case, fear. To be sure, I went on as previously, preparing to shelter my business and, before long, myself from the king. But I did this methodically and without passion. The torment of uncertainty, the nightmares that used to wake me in a sweat, the fear at the most unexpected times at the thought of disgrace, or the memory of the king's icy gaze when I had lent him the four hundred thousand écus: all of that had disappeared. An abnormal but convenient indifference caused me to greet every event with equal detachment. I prepared for the worst but I no longer feared it.

Moreover, the circumstances during the spring following Agnès's death were indirectly favorable to me, and for a time they warded off any risk of disgrace. A strong English contingent had landed in Normandy to join Somerset's troops, who had stayed behind after their defeat in Rouen. The war had resumed. The king was alarmed. Dunois was retained at another front. He hastily appointed a commander in chief whose experience was not as great. He reckoned that the lack of a commander would be attenuated by the quality of the troops and materiel. He needed money more than ever, and a great deal of it. Once again he turned to me. I no longer dreaded revealing the extent of my fortune to him: he already knew. I paid up. The outcome of the battle, uncertain to begin with, was in our favor. Although it was not what anyone wanted, the fighting took place in the village of Formigny. It was a complete success for the armies of France, and it was England's last offensive.

All that remained in English hands in Normandy was the fortification at Cherbourg. The king absolutely insisted on taking it, in order to remove once and for all any chance of a new invasion. Alas, Dunois and the other men of war maintained that there was nothing to be gained by besieging the city, as our fleet was not powerful enough to blockade the port. They had to find another way. There was one, and once again it was through me.

The Englishman in command of the garrison at Cherbourg had a son, who was held prisoner in France. According to custom, by virtue of the value they represented, the king would allocate these captives to some of us in reward for services rendered during the war. My financial assistance had earned me the right to receive several of them, including the son of this English captain. The king then ordered me to negotiate with the father in order to obtain the surrender of Cherbourg in exchange for the prisoner's release. There were other details to see to, and we could be sure that the English would not concede anything easily. They demanded payment for the return of their troops to England. Which I provided, obviously—a considerable amount. It all ended well. Father and son were reunited, and Cherbourg was liberated on August 12.

I knew I could contribute to this type of intervention for some time. After Normandy, the royal offensive against the remaining English presence turned to Guyenne. Every campaign was an opportunity for me to buy some time and keep the threat at bay. And yet I knew that this was a fragile interlude. One episode, in case I had forgotten, came to remind me that royal lightning could strike anywhere, at any time: the conviction of Jean de Xaincoins.

Xaincoins was younger than I, and he had spent his entire career in the king's closest circles. Still, we had many things in common. He was also from the Berry and from a modest family; he was in finance, as a treasurer and tax collector; he was the king's steward to the states of the Limousin, as I was to the Languedoc; and for the last two years he had also been a member of the Council. He was disgraced pursuant to base denunciations. The legal proceedings left him no chance. Of all the things to which he was sentenced, it seems that the most significant was a fine for sixty thousand écus that he was to pay to the king.

As soon as I got wind of this affair, without waiting for the verdict I decided to expedite my preparations to protect myself from a similar adventure. My request to be registered as a burgher in Marseille was taking too long. I pressured my agent there to hasten matters to a conclusion. I could not suddenly abandon Montpellier for Marseille without attracting a great deal of attention. But I arranged for our ships to stay in port for longer periods, and I included in their cargo an ever-increasing share for the merchants of Provence.

I even sent Jean de Villages in the utmost secrecy to the king of Aragon and the Two Sicilies. He returned with a safe conduct that enabled me to transfer some of my property to Naples.

*

On the face of things, nothing had changed. The king behaved amiably toward me and even gratified me quite frequently with favors and attention that made everyone believe, even if I did not, that his kindly disposition toward me was intact. There was tension, however, in the atmosphere. Brézé had been sent away, old Tanguy du Châtel was eliminated, Dunois was becoming progressively more vulgar with each of his victories and all the property he was accumulating—all of which meant that the support I used to find in the king's entourage was gone. Other individuals had arrived on the scene and were becoming increasingly influential. Many of them were in my debt, which did not please me either. I saw it not so much as a danger as an inconvenience: I know from experience that sincerity is not compatible with the humiliation everyone feels when they are indebted, with the exception of perhaps a few noble souls who judge neither themselves nor others on this basis.

Most of these newcomers were strangers to me, and my relations with them remained distant. Thus without realizing it, I was exacerbating the wound to their self-esteem. It was not scorn on my part, only a sign of weariness. I no longer felt I had the strength to establish the sort of complicity, trust, and, if I am honest, friendship that I had shared with those I had known ten or fifteen years earlier and who, today, were far away or missing altogether.

My immense prosperity, together with the somewhat sad detachment that had been my ordinary state since Agnès's death, all contributed to make me a solemn person, and difficult to approach. My very gestures had become slower, my step heavier. This became apparent to me quite suddenly one evening in Tours during the calm of the first winter after Agnès's death.

I had been working all day at the Argenterie together with a new accountant whom Guillaume de Varye had hired. He was surrounded by several shop boys who were young and industrious, and very clever in business despite their age. It was the time of the Epiphany, and I knew that several of them had recently married and that their families were waiting for them for a little celebration. At around six o'clock in the evening, when darkness was beginning to fill the office, I gave them leave to depart. I used the pretext of a letter I had to write to stay there by myself. The night watchman stood by the entrance and would lock the doors again behind me when I left.

Silence fell, and darkness crept into the room, kept at bay only by a single candle. After a few minutes during which I sat motionless, I stood up, took the copper candleholder, and opened the door leading to the warehouse. I walked down among the shelves and clothing racks. My footsteps echoed on the tiles and faded away in the huge space of the warehouse. With the feeble light of my candle I could not see the roof, far above my head, or even the walls of the building, for it was too big. I walked through the obscurity, and now and again I caught a glimpse of something gleaming colorfully in the dark, and I could smell all the particular odors. Bolts of fabric stacked high, the coppery sheen of new weaponry, jars filled with rare substances faded into the heights and depths of the space. From time to time the light aroused the gentle undulation of furs, the metal skin of breastplates, the glossy surface of blue ceramics from China. On I walked, and wherever I went new treasures appeared and gave way to still others. All the world's riches were gathered there, taken from the forests of Siberia and the deserts of Africa. The skill of craftsmen from Damascus was displayed alongside the talents of Flemish weavers; spices ripened in Oriental warmth stood among marvels from the earth—minerals, gems, fossils. This was the center of the world. And it had not been acquired through conquest or pillage, but through trade, the talent of industry, and the freedom of mankind. The energy that had been wrested at last from warfare now spread to all the works of peacetime. It held the weaver's arm, guided the steps of the laborer, gave courage to the miner and agility to the craftsman.

This was the world I had dreamt of. But reality does not have the lightness of dreams. The success of my plans went far beyond anything I could have imagined, and I felt as though I were being crushed beneath the weight of it. Again I saw myself in the procession entering Rouen, and I was stifled by the thick fabrics, sweating in my velvet attire, and feeling how even my horse was restricted by his ceremonial saddlery.

This was what I had become. The freedom and peace for which I had labored were everywhere except in myself. I was invaded by a mad, painful, urgent desire to give up this life, to return to the peaceful enjoyment of a sufficient and modest prosperity. To recover the idleness and dreams, love . . . If Agnès had lived, would she have understood? Would we have decided to run away together? I would have wanted nothing more than to set off with her again on the path to the Levant, to ask the Sultan permission to reside in Damascus, even if it meant leaving him all my fortune.

Agnès was no more, but the desire for freedom remained. That night I told myself that perhaps my fear of the king was providential: by compelling me to flee the kingdom, it would give me the opportunity to put an end to the slavery that all these duties and inhuman fortune had become. What I had shipped to Naples would suffice to settle there. From Naples I could continue to oversee the navigation of several galleys from Marseille. Who knows? Perhaps I could go with them to the Levant. I foresaw a new life. In the heavy darkness, saturated with the odors of new leather and spices, I thought I could see a light, glowing yellow, moving so quickly and nimbly that I could not keep it in my gaze. I kept on walking and still I could not see the end of this cavern of riches. And suddenly I saw a name on the flash of light that was guiding me like a star. The light was not in the objects surrounding me, although the flickering of the candle sometimes gave that illusion. It was buried deep inside me, and it had come back this evening, as at every decisive moment in my life, to show me the way: it was the leopard from my childhood.

*

So I knew what I had to do. However, before I could leave this life and begin a new one, I still had to devote myself to certain obligations. It was a sign of how burdened I had become that I found it impossible to act without things constantly holding me back. It was as if I were maneuvering a cart that was overloaded, where too many people had climbed on board for me suddenly to stop.

My business was a burden, but not the heaviest, particularly if I ceased to add to my fortune and resigned myself to protecting what was strictly necessary. In truth, in those days, the greatest constraints, the ones which drove me to defer my departure, came primarily from my family.

With Macé over the years we had attained a form of attachment and respect which had long ceased to be love but which preserved a certain measure of complicity and would keep me from causing her any displeasure. Her ambitions had been fulfilled beyond her wildest dreams, and she had reached a level where she could act simply even when she was demanding, behave quite naturally amidst ostentation, and exercise restraint even in moments of splendor, all of which are the mark of either an old fortune or an authentic nobility of the heart. She had learned to organize cheerful ceremonies that brought elegant women together with original minds, and they always included a great number of prelates, titled guests, and influential merchants. Everyone felt at ease, the atmosphere was joyful, and the conversation was stimulated by the music and the fine fare. Macé would not have been capable of such generosity toward people had she remained, like in the old days, so eager to occupy the highest rank and be admired for her beauty and her piety, her fortune and her education. But she had changed greatly. These last years had marked her. Two very cold winters had kept her bedridden for long periods. Her hair had turned white. Her teeth pained her and her smile had lost its brilliance. Like so many others, she could have concealed the ravages of time by using artifice. But, on the contrary, without making a show of it, she had accepted them.

Upon my return from Italy I had been struck to find her both older and peacefully resigned to the fact. It seemed to me that she felt she had done what she must do. The two things that mattered to her now were her children and her faith. The time was approaching when the full blossoming of the former would allow her to devote herself entirely to the latter. One day she informed me of her plan to withdraw to the tranquility of a monastery, albeit without taking orders. The last important event regarding the children was our son Jean's nomination to the archdiocese of Bourges. The same year that had witnessed Agnès's death and the complete rout of the English at Formigny, he had reached the required age to enter the priesthood, to which the pope had appointed him two years earlier.

Macé was waiting for the event with painful impatience. She had dreamt of it for so long, had desired it and worked so hard that it had become in her life a horizon beyond which there was nothing left to aspire for, only peace.

The great event was set for the fifth day of September. This time I was entrusted with the organization of the grandiose ceremonies for Macé and our son, something I had hitherto reserved for the king. The entire town gathered in and around the cathedral to honor the event. Jean was handsome in his purple robe, walking down the flower-strewn nave while the choir sang a psalm beneath the high vault, which the September sun illuminated with the dazzling blue of the stained-glass windows.

Our palace was finished, with the exception of a few details, which were not visible. Macé had thought up an ill-advised motto, that ran all around the walls: "For a valiant heart, nothing is impossible." For the occasion I had arranged entertainment worthy of a prince. Foolhardy as it was, it was the last thing I should have done. The king would certainly be informed of the unbelievable expense. Given the circumstances at the time, his jealousy would surely be aroused. But I paid no attention. I wanted to please Macé, and perhaps, through the plenitude of this last worldly event, to atone for all my years of absence, for abandoning her as the years passed, and for the hundreds of betrayals which were without consequence but which prepared the final one, with Agnès—far graver, unforgivable.

I was also doing it for Jean. I had never understood the boy, perhaps never loved him, and he had always taken Macé's side. The only thing he had inherited from me was my ambition, and yet even that was something I did not possess fully; he had placed his ambition at the service of a God next to whom he now stood, and with whom he would soon welcome his mother.

As for the festivities themselves, they brought me nothing but boredom, for in their wake came processions of solicitors. They assumed, quite rightly, that I would find it difficult to refuse them anything on such a day. Fortunately, once the celebrations were over, I was able to stay for a week or more at our new palace. I sincerely loved that house. Of all the dwellings I have built or acquired it is the only one with which I have truly felt in harmony, as if somehow my life and my personality had materialized in the house—the way it was divided into two worlds, the ancient on the one hand, which made it like a seigniorial residence, and the new on the other, with its flavor of Italy and oriental refinement. There were reminders of my journeys everywhere: the door sculpted with palm trees, the ships depicted on the stained glass, and the stone statues of my steward and my oldest serving woman waiting for me, leaning from the window . . .

However, not once during that entire week did the absolute certainty that I would never live there abandon me. Come what may, I had made my decision to leave. My palace was an offering to the future, not in the vain hope that it would remember me, but as a witness to the power of dreams. What the little son of a furrier had once imagined, living two streets away from that site, had become this bubble of stone set in the corner of the former oppidum; those who will go on seeing it when I have disappeared will know how great the strength of one's mind can be, and they will, I hope, take their own dreams seriously. All these things exist outside us. Stones have no need of man to be stones. The only thing that belongs to us is that which does not exist, and which we have the power to bring into the world.

Winter came, and with it, as always, a feeling of numbness and enervation. When I think back on those months, I can see clearly where I went wrong. I wasted precious time. There was not a great deal of business at that time of year. Guillaume de Varye was managing the trade efficiently. Jean had expanded his territory. When he came back from the Sultan, he set off for the extremes of Tartary. And yet the winter went by, day after day, without any impulse that might have aroused me from my torpor.

In the spring, the king revived his plans for reconquering Guyenne. Or, rather, for letting others make plans for him, which he then approved. His character was changing once again. The awakening of his senses, his conversion to pleasure and his delight in the world, in Agnès's time, had assumed a fairly noble form. The king's frivolity seemed to be a tribute he was paying to his long confinement, like the reverse side of a shyness against which he had now decided to struggle. But with Agnès's death he had lost the balance between pleasure and majesty that she had helped him to keep. Charles was now completely given over to debauchery. His new mistress, that same Antoinette who had gone to join him in Normandy, had adopted a strategy that was the opposite of Agnès's, and which was despicably base. She was the one who provided the king with girls who were for sale, in order to assuage his considerable appetite. She need have no fear, as Agnès once had with Charles of Anjou, of the misdeeds of a procurer, since she was the one who assumed that function herself.

I have never been a good companion for drinking or lust. The king, who knew this, did not associate me with his turpitudes. He did, however, continue to solicit me to finance the war and, as before, I consented.

Spring came late. When it did, I gradually emerged from my torpor. However, I had not yet resolved to leave. Perhaps it was because I saw the king less often. The distance gave me the illusion that the danger had receded.

But the reality was something else. I would eventually learn that at the end of the previous year the king had received a visit from several informants who had made grave accusations against me. To jealousy he would now add suspicion and mistrust. The thunder was not far off but I could not hear it. I misinterpreted the few signs that made me think I was still well considered at court. A long voyage to the south to settle some business in Provence further delayed my decision. At the beginning of summer I was still there. And it is generally during this season that lightning strikes.

*

While I continued on my way to the ultimate tragedy, I saw Agnès twice more. The emotion caused by these encounters may have had something to do with the nonchalance I displayed in the face of danger.

The first encounter was in the month of May. The artist Jean Fouquet had sent me a message several weeks earlier to ask me to come and visit him when I was next in Touraine. I was acquainted with him well enough to know that this surely had nothing to do with money. Fouquet had never asked me for any, and if he had been in need he would have chosen poverty over debt. I arranged to go and see him as soon as I could, and at the beginning of May I was in Tours. Marc went ahead to inform the painter that I had arrived, but found no one in his studio, although it was late in the morning. Finally, shortly before noon, the man came walking up the street, dragging his heels. Marc came back to tell me he was waiting for me. The spring sun had come out, breaking through the clouds that on the previous days had brought rain. When I entered the studio, I was overcome by the smells of putty and oil that lay heavy on the air. Simmering on the stove was a mixture of litharge where a black onion was floating. Fouquet came up to greet me and put his arms around me.

All the way at the back of the studio, on an easel, was a rough oak panel. Initially I saw it from the back and noticed only the seams and gnarls of light wood. But when I followed Fouquet and saw the other side, I was filled with emotion. The wooden panel had been carefully prepared and its surface was smooth as a mirror. Already three quarters of it had been painted and while the figures around the perimeter still lacked precision, the one in the center was already complete: it was Agnès. He had drawn her face from the sketches he had shown me, where we had already seen hints of death at work. And now that Agnès had passed away, her features were those of life itself. They revived an expression we had often seen on her face, a sort of thoughtful absence, her high forehead covered with powder, her lips closed, her eyelids lowered and, probably, quivering.

Fouquet had placed her face at the heart of a strange setting. She was wearing an emerald green gown covered with a fine ermine cape. The laces used to close the bodice of her gown were now loosened, and one side of the bodice was pulled down, completely revealing her pale-nippled breast. On her knees the Christ child was looking into the distance and seemed already to be contemplating his sacrificial destiny. On Agnès's head was a crown of pearls and rubies that designated her as queen of the heavens, proof that Fouquet had represented her as the Virgin Mary.

This divine reference, however, as well as the jewelled throne where she was seated, failed to conceal the portrait's other significance: for those of us who had known Agnès, the painting must be a vision of her in her eternal dwelling place. This hypothesis made the picture seen even more ambiguous and disturbing, because this heavenly sojourn evoked hell as easily as paradise. The cherubs surrounding Agnès, who also had their eyes lowered, resembled seraphs and seemed to imply blissfulness. However, Fouquet had painted them in red, the color of demons. My feeling with regard to this vision was that Agnès, in keeping with her sinful life, was truly in hell, but her piety, her gentleness, her charm, and the sincerity she had displayed during her time on earth, disarming even the most hostile people, had enabled her to win the hearts of the Luciferian creatures whom Satan had appointed to guard her, so that in the end she had made them into red angels, as tender as the Christ child, surrounding her in a circle not to torment her, but to protect her from the flames of Gehenna.

I believe this painting is now part of an altarpiece, and there must not be many viewers who would associate it with Agnès. Over time, there will be fewer still, and someday no one will remember her. She will be transfigured forever. I understood Fouquet better now, his despair, and his efforts to drown it in drunkenness. His art gives him a strange power: that of communicating with the realm of the dead, and of leading the living there. He can have no illusions about life. The feeling of eternity, which we all need, is something he cannot enjoy: he knows that our survival can only come from art.

The other time, the last one that I was able to see Agnès, was during the summer of the year following her death. I had already been living for eighteen months in the sorrowful languor in which her passing had immersed me. Rumors as to my possible disgrace had spread beyond the court, to such a degree that even Macé, who had very little to do with royal matters, had heard of it. She sent a letter full of questions, which made her anxiety only too apparent. Using the same messenger, I replied that I had never been in greater favor with the king. A few recent gestures on Charles's part certainly seemed to imply as much. But I did not trust these gestures. The July heat had revived my energy and I had secretly made the decision to leave for Italy at the beginning of August.

In order not to arouse any suspicions, I decided to accompany the king on a visit to the château at Taillebourg, where the

Coëtivy family lived, to see his daughters. Agnès's firstborn had been placed with this family, where the number of children was of little consequence. Madame de Coëtivy liked to hear their little voices echoing down the corridors of the old château. I understood her. Here I was, who had bought so many seigniorial estates, but I despaired when I found them empty and heard nothing but the sinister cawing of crows.

We were due to arrive the next day, but the king was in a fine mood and insisted we depart earlier, so in fact we were in sight of the château a day early. The children had not yet been prepared to receive us. They were running around the garden in a band, playing games suited to their age. There were boys who were already quite grown, and a bevy of little girls. When they saw us from a distance, they came running to meet us in no particular order. We formed a small vanguard around the king, and our servants and baggage followed far behind. Charles dismounted amidst the children. A little girl of the age of ten or so threw her arms around his neck. This was one of the daughters he had had with Queen Marie and who was spending her lovely days at Taillebourg. We began walking toward the château, surrounded by the chattering children. The eldest led the horses by the bridle, others quarreled over who could hold our hands. To reach the moat, we had to go through a small copse, then down an avenue of alder trees. When I reached the last tree I noticed that one of the children was hiding behind the tree trunk. The little rascals around me had also noticed her and I heard them cry, "Marie, Marie!"

The child scurried around the tree to hide. We didn't insist, and continued on our way. The king was already far ahead with most of the little ones, because the older ones had left us to walk over to the stables. I do not know what came over me. Perhaps it was her name, Marie, which set off a secret alarm. Perhaps I had received an invisible signal from much farther away. In any case, I decided to walk back the way I had come.

I motioned to the children who were with me to go ahead and join the group around the king, and I went on my own up to the tree where now and again I could see a little girl furtively peeking out. A simple trick enabled me to go around the trunk and catch her. She hid her face in her hands and protested, laughing.

"What's your name?" I asked, although I knew the answer.

"Marie."

She was not frightened and did not try to run away. Her shyness was a game and it served above all to make others interested in her, not as part of a group, but one-on-one, as if she were a proper grown-up.

"How old are you?"

"Four."

My heart began beating faster. I tried to see her face but she kept stubbornly turning aside.

"What is your mama's name?"

Did she notice that my voice was shaky? Or had she been waiting for my question to open her heart? She didn't answer. But silently, pushing aside a blonde strand that had fallen before her eyes, she turned her head and stared at me, her eyes wide open.

It was Agnès.

There are some children—most of them, to be honest—who resemble both parents, and, depending on their expressions or the particular moment, they will make us think of one parent or the other, or simply alter the features of both, according to some outside influence. Then there are others who, on the contrary, seem to come from a single source, which nothing troubles, and which makes them the reproduction of a single parent, where the only difference is that of time. Marie was Agnès as a child. If her mother had lived, this resemblance would have been merely anecdotal, a touching curiosity. But Agnès had died, and to find her again in the face of this child was like witnessing a resurrection. It was impossible not to imagine, however the mind might rebel against the idea, that the woman who had been Agnès continued to live in this tiny little girl's body.

And although I had no reason to assume that I was right, I was reinforced in my illusion by the sweet tenderness which the child immediately showed me. She held out her little hand and stroked my cheek. Then she gave a hop and with a determined step led me on a tour of the woods. She showed me a squirrel's hiding place, and the bed of dead leaves where a doe rested: she saw her almost every day. She told me gravely about the things that went to make up her life, interspersed with whispered secret references to mysterious creatures that haunted the forest and spoke to her.

We walked for a good hour through the estate right to the edge of the meadows. Once Marie's secrets had brought us closer together, I crouched down before her and dared to ask her the question that had been troubling my mind.

"Do you know where your mother is?"

There was no cruelty in my question, only a desire to find out what she knew, and I had the vague but penetrating suspicion that even if she did not know a great many things, on this subject she must know more than I did.

She looked me right in the eyes and took her time deciding whether I was to be trusted.

"Maman," she said, never taking her eyes from mine, "is no longer in this world."

Then, no doubt considering that I was worthy, and therefore entitled to know more, but that it was preferable not to tell everything all at once, she placed a finger in front of her lips to recommend silence.

Then she took me by the hand and we went back to the château. A bell was calling the children to their dinner. I left her outside the door to the children's dining room, near the kitchens.

Meeting Marie and, through her, her mother, had filled me with contradictory, troubling impressions. Agnès's death suddenly came back to me in all its harrowing reality, as unexpected as when I had learned about it for the first time. And at the same time, even though it had never occurred to me, the fact that she had left this child behind, and two others whom I did not know, was if not a consolation then at least a way to compensate for her absence, and to bear witness to the real world of the woman she had been.

*

I went up the great stairway, preceded by a valet, who led me to my chambers. I was ruminating over a new plan. I wondered if the Coëtivys would agree to let me contribute to Marie's education. After all, was I not her mother's executor? I liked the idea of watching the child grow up and make her start in life, and of seeing whether, even in the smallest way, she would follow in Agnès's footsteps.

It seems no small irony that these were my thoughts when Marc, who had been waiting for me at the door to my chambers, took me to one side, closed the door and, looking very alarmed, insisted on speaking to me right away. The king, he told me, had summoned him to an audience upon his arrival. After touching on various current matters, he moved on to a private council devoted to my person. There had been much vociferous slander against me over recent weeks, and several incriminating revelations had been brought this morning by two delegates from the states of the Languedoc. At that very moment, my fate was hanging in the balance.

This news cast an icy chill over my thoughts, gently warmed only moments before by my meeting with Agnès's daughter, and I exploded with rage. Without making a decision, I retraced my steps, then went down into another wing of the château and, shoving aside the guards who wanted to prevent me from entering, I burst into the council room.

The king acted embarrassed, but I could see in his eyes that the informers had gotten their way. Any affability or kindness he might have sought to express through his gaze had been destroyed by the keenness of jealousy and mistrust. Everything advised caution, but the rush of strength I felt—too late, alas, and which should have compelled me to flee—inclined me, rather, to confront him. I protested, forgetting the usage of deference, and my boldness caused the evil temptation of cruelty and baseness to shine still brighter in the king's eyes.

I could see his weapons, but this time I refused to resort to anything similar to defend myself. On the contrary, out of pure bravado, I suggested they throw me in prison until I could bring them proof that the accusations against me were false.

I do not believe the king was sincere when he said that he accepted my proposal. He let me continue my defense then, as no one put up any objection, I withdrew.

Who would ever believe that I felt reassured once I went back up to my chambers? Everything was clear. I had fended off their blows once again, but this would be the last time. That very evening, I would leave Taillebourg. The days were long at the end of July. We could ride without danger until well after nine o'clock. I figured out where we could stop, and how long it would take to reach Provence and Italy. I would write to the Coëtivys; they were greatly in my debt. There was no need for them to take part directly, but they would turn a blind eye to the abduction I would endeavor to organize so that little Marie could come with me. Like her mother before her, she would come to know Italy and enjoy its beneficial influence.

On my orders, Marc had closed our trunks. I sent for the barber and abandoned myself to the caress of the blade against my skin as he shaved me. I was about to go to supper when a detachment of five men came to my door, commanded by a little Norman nobleman whom I knew vaguely by sight.

I asked him twice to repeat his words when he informed me, his eyes to the ground, that I was under arrest.

*

I felt a surge of hope again this morning. Elvira came back from town bearing news which to her seemed unimportant and which she shared almost in passing when telling me about something else. For me, it is highly significant: my pursuers are not from Genoa but from Florence. What might seem like a detail now changes everything.

If the Genoese had been after me, it would mean that the king of France had ordered it. I still have too many friends in Genoa for anyone to want to take my life of their own accord. But if my pursuers are Florentine, that is something else, and I know who has sent them.

In any case, now I know. If someone had asked on the day of my arrest, I would have been incapable of answering. At the time, I certainly felt surrounded by envy; I had found out that the king was being told malicious slander about me; however, I could not identify a particular enemy. They showed their faces when the time came for my trial.

It is a great sorrow to lose everything and be convicted, but it is an enlightening lesson to be judged, and I might almost say it is a privilege. Those who have not experienced the ordeal of disgrace, destitution, and accusation cannot truly claim to know life. The long months spent waiting while my trial was being prepared were among the most dreadful moments I have ever experienced, and, at the same time, they taught me more about myself and others than had the prior half-century of my existence.

Never before had I been confronted to such a degree with

the truth about the people who knew me. I evaluated the sincerity of those who showed me their friendship, as well as that of those who opposed me, on the basis of my own feelings toward them. But what did they really think? A certain doubt subsisted, and like most human beings I had learned to live with it. Since I had become rich and powerful, it had been even more difficult to see behind the screen of hypocrisy. I myself displayed a surface courtesy, which did not reveal my feelings, and most of the time even replaced them. I had been known on occasion to act abruptly, particularly when I was speaking in the name of the king, in the Languedoc, for example, when performing my duties as tax collector. Impatience, fatigue, and the irritation of having to intervene constantly in transactions and operations that did not interest me had, from time to time, led me to behave ruthlessly. Before my trial, I imagined that my enemies, if I had any, must be among the victims of these abuses of authority.

The investigation showed me that this was anything but the case. With a single exception, those with whom I had behaved ruthlessly had merely gained even greater respect for me. All I had done, basically, was behave the way they themselves would have behaved had they been in my position. They regarded power and wealth as a justification for intransigence and brutality. Moreover, by treating them harshly, I was giving them my attention; in short, I proved to them that they existed, even if it was to trample on them.

My worst enemies, as I would learn during my trial, were those whom I had not deigned to acknowledge.

Among them there were vicious people inflated with pride, and in any case envy would have turned such people against anyone better served by life than they were. I was not sorry that I had offended them. At most, all that one could reproach me for was having given the signal for a war that would have taken place regardless.

But others, on the contrary, were men of great loyalty, eager to serve, who wished to be part of my undertaking. My mistake was in my failure to understand this, often because I simply had not noticed them. Such was the case of a young Florentine by the name of Otto Castellani, who had come to Montpellier ten years earlier, at a time when I was embarking on great projects in the town. There were already many other Florentine merchants in the Languedoc, with whom I had excellent relations. One of them had been my fellow passenger on board the ship that took me to the Levant all those years ago, and we had remained friends.

I hardly knew young Castellani. I was told he had tried everything to come into contact with me. Perhaps he actually had, but had failed to make an impression. And although my disdain would have been quite involuntary, it aroused a hatred in him proportional to the affection he had been prepared to show me.

He was intelligent and enterprising, qualities I would have been glad to honor by employing him. Instead, he placed those qualities at the service of a solitary ambition now goaded by an inextinguishable desire for revenge. He progressed in his career in the Languedoc. His relations with his home country gave him openings for trade in the Mediterranean. But he also tried to expand his activity to the north of France, as far as Flanders. Here, too, my trial was useful in allowing me to trace the agenda of the man who was my most virulent accuser. By the looks of things, unbeknownst to me I had continued to preoccupy him. His ambition, since he could not serve me, was to imitate me, surpass me, and, to reach his goal more surely, destroy me.

He patiently allied himself with anyone in whom he felt a stirring of spite toward me. And he did whatever he could to make the seed he had planted grow and blossom. Soon he was at the center of a web of bitterness and hatred, and was able to extend its influence to the entourage of the king. Among the mediocre individuals who had infiltrated the grand Council after Agnès's death he noticed a certain Guillaume Gouffier, toward whom I had always behaved with polite indifference, and who was mortified by my attitude. Castellani also turned my former misdemeanors to his advantage, such as the business with the young Moor who had stowed away on one of our ships and converted, and whom I had sent back to the sultan. The captain of the ship, whom I had reproached for his part in the affair, had quarreled violently with me. To him, his anger might have sufficed, but Castellani knew how to rekindle it and make it burn with a steady fire, which would be extinguished only by my downfall.

I had viewed the matter of the young Moor solely from the angle of our relations with the Sultan. His friendship was the cornerstone of our trade with the Levant. It was vital not to do anything that might displease him. Castellani saw the other side of the coin: I had restored to the Mohammedans someone who had willingly embraced the Catholic faith. In other words, I had lost a soul who had asked for and obtained Christ's succor. In the ecclesiastical world where my brother's success and my son's exceptionally rapid advancement had fueled bitterness and envy, Castellani found willing allies with whom to criticize my betrayal.

I know now that the Florentine's relentless activity was one of the primary causes of my disgrace. Castellani achieved his ends so thoroughly that, not merely pleased to see me convicted, he successfully plotted to fill the position I would leave vacant. Thus, he became my successor at the Argenterie.

You would think that such a triumph would be everything he dreamed of. No such thing. So greatly did he need his hatred that he seemed unable to imagine his life without it. Long after my conviction he went on seeking revenge against me and my family. When Elvira discovered that my pursuers were Florentine, I understood what should have been obvious to me much sooner: once again it was Castellani who sent his lackeys after me to Chios. This news filled me with hope.

If my pursuers were the instruments of a private vengeance on Castellani's part, my situation would be less desperate than if these henchmen had been sent by the king of France. Thus far, I had avoided any contact with the Genoese potentate who reigned over the island, for I believed Charles had forced him to spy on me and perhaps capture me. If this were indeed the case, it was difficult to understand why I had been given so long a respite: it would have been an easy matter for the Genoese to arrest me, purely and simply. If the pursuit was being led by Castellani for his own satisfaction, this would explain why it was more difficult for my assassins to do the deed. I could make use of this knowledge. Above all, the Genose podestà, far from being an enemy as I had feared, could become an ally.

Yesterday I wrote a long missive to Campofregoso, which Elvira took this morning to the port to a ship sailing for Genoa. I asked him for his help and to intercede with the podestà in Chios to ensure my safety. I just have to hold tight for a few more days while waiting for his reply.

I have regained hope, and the indifference that had made me accept my fate, no matter how tragic, has given way these days to a great anxiety and a desire to ensure our protection. Elvira suggested another refuge, at the center of the island. She has a cousin in the mountains. He owns a sheepfold high in the hills. From there one can see all the surrounding valleys, and anyone who approaches is immediately visible. I had refused because I saw no way out of my situation. If there was no more hope, we might as well end our days with a flourish, in Elvira's house. But now that I have regained a certain optimism, I want to fight. No matter how uncomfortable the sheepfold might be, we will move there in three days' time.

*

In the meantime, I shall continue my story.

I thought that once the time came to evoke my arrest, my enthusiasm would have waned. But this is not the case. Oddly enough, I do not have a bad memory of it. I even have the very distinct feeling, now, that my disgrace was a new birth. Everything I have lived through since that day has been both deeper and more intense, as if I had been given the possibility to discover life all over again, but armed with the experience I have acquired through the years.

I was transported from prison to prison, placed at times under the guard of men who were respectful and even friendly, and at times in the hands of individuals who did not hesitate to show their scorn.

The first days were difficult. The suddenness of the change in my condition almost made me doubt the reality of these events. It seemed as if at any moment someone would come in and say, "Well now, we only wanted to frighten you. Come and sit again at the Council and show your loyalty to the king." But nothing like that happened; on the contrary, my trial began and the conditions of my detention were toughened.

That was when I was overcome by an unexpected, almost voluptuous sensation: I felt something like intense relief. The weight I had carried on my shoulders, the heavy burden that had come upon me as I wandered through the Argenterie, the obvious signs that I was being crushed by my fortune and its attendant obligations, all of that, with my arrest, had suddenly ceased. Deposed, I was delivered, and captivity restored to me to my freedom.

It might seem incredible that such a catastrophe could be at the origin of a veritable sense of relief. And yet that was the case. I no longer had to worry about convoys and orders, calling in debts or agreeing to loans, levying taxes or supplying markets, leading delegations or financing wars. I had been spread as if on a cross, on a path leading from Tours to Lyon, from Flanders to Montpellier, where all my business in France was conducted: now I no longer had to worry about any of that, or about any Italian imbroglios or Oriental intrigues. It could all take place outside of me, and my detention released me from having to take part in any of it. I was able to devote myself to an activity I had not enjoyed in many years: spending hours on my back, daydreaming. Sitting on the stone bench by the window and watching the horizon turn blue as night fell.

My dreams took me first to revisit the years I had spent in action, where there had been no distance for contemplation or for the slow judging of events and men. I was helped in my recollections by the trial itself. Thanks to this trial, individuals whom I had forgotten emerged from the past, and for the first time I heard tell of events I had never been informed of. I was accused of the most varied and often most unbelievable things: of having sold arms to the Mohammedans; of having purloined a little royal seal which would enable me to draw up false documents in the king's name; of dabbling in alchemy and manufacturing gold by means of witchcraft . . .

The only accusation I was truly afraid of was one that might reveal my intimate relation with Agnès. I knew that for such a crime there would be no clemency, and that I would pay with my life. I also feared, perhaps more than anything, that it would tarnish Agnès's memory. After her death, although he almost immediately found consolation with her cousin, the king had shown great munificence toward Agnès. But if proof were administered that he had been betrayed, he was capable of withdrawing his magnanimity and sullying the image of the woman whom he had, posthumously, raised to the status of a saint.

I need not have been so alarmed. On the contrary, and to my great surprise, the accusation against me was that I had poisoned Agnès. The woman who alleged this was half mad. The implausibility of her words, together with her strange manner as she set forth her aspersions, rapidly contributed to her discredit.

There was one good thing about this calumny, however: it enabled me to take the measure of how cleverly Agnès had arranged to hide our relations. So often and so well had we mimed our quarrels, or an icy difference, or our fallings out, that the memory of our conflicts came first and foremost to corroborate these accusations of poisoning. Other testimonies were required, including those of Brézé, Chevalier and even Dunois, in order to convince my judges that I had, in fact, had harmonious relations with Agnès.

During the long months of the pre-trial investigation, I lived in complete solitude, relieved only by confrontations with witnesses who had emerged from the past and had something to say about me. As if learning the final clue to an enigma, I found out what all these people truly thought of me. Hatred and jealousy, which are so common and so repetitive, soon aroused nothing more than weariness and indifference. But when a woman or a man, very sincere and often of very modest condition, came to testify regarding some kindness I had shown them, or simply to manifest their respect or their affection, I had tears in my eyes.

The further the trial progressed, the lighter the injustice of which I was the victim and the heavier, on the contrary, the injustice I had caused to others came to weigh upon my conscience.

In this respect, it was toward Macé that I felt most guilty. I remembered how we had met and our early years together, and I tried to recall how our estrangement and indifference had gradually taken hold. I received news from her regularly but I did not see her again. It was obvious that she was suffering as a result of my fall from favor. Fortunately, it occurred at a time when she had already fulfilled her greatest dream, which was to see Jean enthroned as archbishop. She did not write to me, but I wondered whether she, too, in her way, was not relieved. Rather than lay herself open to vengeance and show her decline to others, she did what she had always secretly hoped to do: she withdrew to a monastery and gave herself up to contemplation and prayer. She died at the end of my first year of detention. I thought of her a great deal, and as I did not have the resources to pray, I simply expressed a wish that she had found serenity at the end.

That first year of detention went by strangely quickly. I was moved, transferred to Lusignan and placed under the guard of Chabannes's men. He was a former *écorcheur*, murderer and traitor to the king, and the sworn enemy of the Dauphin, yet now he had found an opportunity to prove his zeal, all the more so as he was personally interested in ruining me, and coveted a number of my properties.

My attempt to escape a verdict by pleading ecclesiastical privilege came to nothing. It was true that I had been a pupil at the Sainte-Chapelle, but I had not taken orders and the exemption was rejected. The trial continued.

One witness followed another, interminably. It became obvious that the judges did not find this as entertaining as I did. They deemed that this hodgepodge of gossip and ambiguous sins, which I generally managed to explain away, did not constitute a sufficiently damning case against me. It was at that point, and my hand still trembles as I write it, that for the first time I heard the word "torture."

Who will believe me when I say I had never thought about it until then? The trial thus far had been a matter for the mind; now it would be one for the body. It seemed to me that I had already lost everything, and yet I still disposed of this envelope of clothing which, however little that may be, does protect and conceal. First of all it would be removed. I was interrogated half-naked, sitting for long hours on the sinister chair. My judges, whom I had somewhat hastily considered to be my equals, suddenly grew much more powerful, their domination founded not on the soundness of their accusations, but on the fact that they spoke down to me, sitting on a podium while I was on my little bench, and that they were clothed while I surrendered my unprotected skin to their gazes. This was the first time I unveiled in public the deformation that hollowed out my chest, and I felt particularly humiliated. Moreover, I was afraid that this trace of a violence exerted on me from the time of my birth, as if it were the mark of God's fist in my flesh, might lead to others, by virtue of that law of nature which holds that a wounded animal excites his predators.

Although no one had yet struck a blow against me, those initial sessions had a terrible effect on my conscience. I was able to judge how it was not so much the pain I dreaded, but the diminishment. Several accidents had made me aware of the fact that I was fairly tough. But what I cannot bear is to be dependent on others, to be delivered defenseless to the good will or evil instincts of another person. I even wonder whether my entire life cannot be explained by this boundless desire to escape the violence of my fellow creatures. Ever since my childhood and the episode during the siege of Bourges, I had known that the empire of the mind was one way, perhaps the only way, to escape the brutal confrontation which boys resort to in order to establish their hierarchy. My father had never raised his hand against me. The first blow I received and which I still remember to this day was during a schoolboy squabble on leaving the Sainte-Chapelle. They had just finished preaching to us about kindness and loving one's neighbor, and the sudden contradiction went some way toward creating my subsequent wariness with regard to religion. I found myself on the ground in a general tussle. The punch I had received below my eye was less alarming to me than my impression of suffocation while a dozen screaming bodies piled themselves on top of me. For six months I had nightmares and difficulties writing. My hand would freeze on the pen, and the words, cramped by the stiffness of my wrist, were illegible and chaotic. It was only after the episode of the siege of Bourges and my discovery of the power of the mind that my anxiety abated.

Now, on the torture seat, I felt once again that old buried terror, which had remained intact. Being locked up had not brought it on. But to be there before my judges, undressed and unable to move, and to sense on me the voracious gaze of the two torturers standing by the door, waiting for the single word from the magistrates that would authorize them to use the iron instruments hanging on the wall: all of this made me lose any strength or hope I might still have had.

On the third day of this treatment, having not yet received a single blow, to the great despair of the two torturers who were yawning with boredom, I made a solemn declaration to my judges. I told them that it was pointless trying to use force on me. At the very idea that they might resolve to use it, I would sign anything they liked. My capitulation pleased some of them, but aroused objections among the others. They decided to withdraw in order to debate the matter. I could not understand why they disagreed. What more could they ask for than a full confession, no matter how long, circumstantial, or fantastical it might be? While conversing with one of the guards who behaved in a kindly manner toward me, I learned the cause of the judges' confusion. They were of the opinion that torture, given the pain it causes, is the only way to authenticate the sincerity of a prisoner's confessions. Words uttered under the influence of fear did not have the same value as those dictated by the unbearable suffering the torturers inflicted. According to this concept, fear is still a manifestation of human will. And as such, it leaves room for evil, which, it would seem, is peculiar to mankind; one cannot be sure there does not remain an element of ruse, lying, or calculation. Whereas pain causes the divine heart of man to speak, his soul, which when laid bare cannot help but reveal, without artifice, his blackness or his purity.

This reasoning was repellent to me. First of all, I found it absurd, scornful with regard to human beings, and marked with the seal of the most ridiculous bigotry. But as it took the judges two days to reach their decision, before they summoned me to appear again, I had time to think about it at greater length. And to my great surprise, I discovered that a part of me approved of their abominable concept. If I were free from torture, and my fear sufficed to my judges, I could well understand that the absurdity of the sins they would force me to acknowledge would discredit their accusations. Basically, given this hypothesis, any confession I might sign would not be my own, but theirs. They would find in their own minds the crimes of which they were accusing me, and all of this would have little to do with reality. The king, who knew me, might perceive that my confession rang false.

Whereas if they subjected me to torture, whatever came from inside me could only be the truth. Who knows, if I were driven mad by suffering, whether I would not confess to the most important things: my relations with the Dauphin, my friendship with the king of Aragon and, above all, my relationship with Agnès.

In the end, my proposal was rejected.

*

The torture began.

I had the impression that the discord between my judges had not led to a clear decision, fortunately. They did not initially resort to unbearable torture—reluctantly, for their instinct inclined to them to do much more. During the interrogations the torturers merely tied me up in uncomfortable positions, which at length became painful. The torture consisted above all in inducing a physical exhaustion that was meant to incite me to make confessions, and thus bring a hastier end to the session. Aware of this trap, I limited myself to giving trivial information on quibbling commercial errors. I confessed, for example, to my failure to pay the Rhone salt tax in full, a crime of which the king himself was aware and to which he had turned a blind eye.

After several weeks had gone by, the regime of torture intensified. I was beaten, and although the blows were still bearable, they caused me to panic. I reiterated my offer to the judges to confess to whatever they liked.

After ten days during which the drubbing and flagellation increased regularly in intensity, I began to contemplate suicide. Just as I was trying to determine what, in the place where I was held, could be used for hanging, a timely delegation of magistrates came to announce that my request had been accepted after all. The bill of indictment would be drawn up that week and I must agree to sign it. I consented, trying to hide my enthusiasm, which might have been misinterpreted. The end of the year was spent in preparing the bill. As I had committed to accepting everything, it was up to my judges to set down grievances that would be both realistic and sufficiently grave to justify the sentence, which had quite obviously been decided upon well in advance.

I knew that all of this, whatever happened, would culminate in an incrimination of lèse-majesté, which was punishable by death.

However, I do not know whether it was the means used to obtain this verdict, which at times bordered on farce, or whether it was my intuition that the king was more interested in my fortune than in my life, and would not find it easy to make off with the former if he did not spare the latter, but I never believed in the eventuality of a capital execution.

When the commissioners appointed to judge me published their final indictment, the sentence handed down was indeed death. But less than a week later, this sentence was commuted and all that was demanded of me was that I make amends. The punishment consisted primarily of the confiscation of my property and a tribute of several hundred thousand écus. Now I had to find the means to pay it, for I would only be set free once I had discharged this enormous sum. In a way, I was hostage to myself. My life had been spared on condition I use it henceforth to pay a price for my freedom so high that all the days remaining would not suffice to obtain that price.

The king appointed a prosecutor to proceed with the liquidation of my property, starting with an inventory. The man chosen for this difficult task was Jean Dauvet, the same man in whose company I had carried out my mission to Rome. We knew each other well, and as far as I could remember Dauvet had no reason to reproach me. He was a magistrate, however, and as such belonged to a species that I had not known well before my arrest, but which I had subsequently come to know in detail. These individuals, through their profession, have resolved to stand apart from humanity, by embracing the abstract cause of the law. For them there is no such thing as an excuse, an error, suffering, or weakness—in short anything that is human. For them there is only the law, regardless of what injustice it might entail. They are the priests of that God who is devoid of mercy, and to please him, they will unscrupulously resort to lying and violence; they will condone the ignoble brutality of torturers, and will accept on faith denunciations made by the most vile individuals.

And it was thus that Dauvet zealously, competently, and, dare I say, honestly set about stripping me of my possessions. His methodical efforts to take stock of my property stemmed from the sentence handed down against me. For him that was sufficient reason to prove that his activity was just. He cared little that the powerful men in the king's entourage, the very same ones who had set themselves up as my judges, shamelessly helped themselves to my properties the moment he exhibited them. The letter of the law had been respected, and that was enough for Dauvet.

This period of my detention, after the relief that came with the sentencing, was also very instructive. First of all, as I followed Dauvet's progress in listing my affairs, I became more fully aware of just how widespread they were. The development of our company had been so rapid and so continuous, and it had required so much effort, that there had been no place left for contemplation. Moreover, my role in these affairs, most of the time, was to give the initial impetus. After this, others had caused my business to prosper, and for the most part I was unaware of how far they had gone.

It was a great satisfaction to me to measure the impact and range of the network we had created.

At the same time I learned what had made this success possible. It was precisely what neither Dauvet nor the predators sharing my possessions had understood: the company I had created had grown to this degree because it was alive and no one controlled it. It was a huge organism, and freedom was given to every member of it to act as they saw fit. By seizing whatever they could grab, by sequestering my belongings, by dismembering every piece of cloth contained in our stores, Dauvet and the dogs running with his pack were merely ferreting through the entrails of a dead beast. Everything they took was then no longer free and thus ceased to live. The moment it was evaluated, the worth of my erstwhile property became inert and began to decrease, because its true worth came only from the free and unceasing movement of trade.

Dauvet's balance sheets gave me hope, because beyond the

assets the prosecutor had listed and frozen, I could see—without telling him of course—everything he had not yet touched and which escaped his notice. I knew that Guillaume de Varye, who had been arrested at the same time as me, had managed to escape. Jean de Villages, Antoine Noir, and all the others, most of whom had sought refuge in Provence or in Italy, or were hiding in regions that escaped the king's control, were doing what they could to conceal as many things as possible from Dauvet's deadly inventory. In their hands, these supplies and stores and ships continued to do business, and thus to live.

They managed to get messages to me. Thus I was apprised of the fact that the business had been greatly affected but was not dead.

The situation was fairly obvious. Dauvet would never succeed in raising the sums demanded of me simply by seizing the remains. But the rest of my business, which was still beyond his reach and would always remain so, or so I hoped, continued to generate considerable profit. The choice was simple. Could I ask my friends to go on working with a sole purpose in mind: to give the king everything they earned in order to obtain my release? Or, would I give precedence to our business, and let it prosper without me? That would mean bidding farewell to my freedom.

Then there came the terrible ceremony at the Château in Poitiers, to which I had been transferred, where I had to kneel down before Dauvet, who was representing the king, and ask for mercy from God, the sovereign, and the law.

This ultimate humiliation was a dual deliverance. First of all it made me intimately aware that everything had been lost; I did not have the right to ask Guillaume or any of the others to sacrifice themselves in order to buy my freedom. Particularly from a king who had shown he was perfectly capable of committing such an injustice in the first place: he would never grant me my freedom. I sent word to them the very next day.

Finally, as if placing a seal on the end of my trial, this ceremony marked the beginning of a new condition for me which, as I have said, was very much like that of a hostage waiting for his ransom to be paid. In every respect it was a more tolerable condition. As they were no longer hoping to obtain a confession from me, my jailers found it pointless to torment me. The first favor I asked, and which to my great surprise was granted, was to have the presence of my valet Marc restored to me.

In truth, he had never left me. He had been following me from town to town, wherever my place of detention happened to be. As he had not been authorized to see me before now, he generally stayed in a rundown inn where he would quickly earn the deep affection of the cook or serving woman.

As soon as he could join me and speak to me, my first prison collapsed, the one in which I had locked myself. I immediately stopped feeling resigned to my fate, and I banished the quandary that had occupied my mind all through the previous weeks. It was no longer a question of paying for my freedom or of staying in jail until my death. With Marc, one thing became amply clear: I had to set myself free.

*

But the outlook for freedom was not so simple. In Poitiers I was kept locked in two rooms where the windows had been walled up. The door leading to the outside was fitted with iron plates and locked with three bolts. There were a number of henchmen living and sleeping on the other side. The daylight barely filtered through a tiny barred window above the door.

Marc was allowed to come in at the end of the morning with my laundry and lunch. He stayed with me until they rang Vespers at the chapel.

When he first talked to me about escaping, after an initial rush of enthusiasm I was immediately discouraged by the material obstacles we would face and above all by my feeble physical condition. Before I could even begin to plan my flight, I had to regain my energy, my muscles, the health that these twenty months of reclusion had altered. Careful to evade the guards' notice, under Marc's supervision I began a program of physical exercise. My appetite returned and Marc, with the help of his connections in the kitchen, was able to improve my everyday fare, adding meat and seasonal fruit to the menu.

I asked permission, and it was granted, under very strict conditions, to be able to enjoy a walk in the courtyard of the Château every morning. The still pale sunlight of winter helped me emerge from the stupor into which the darkness of my jails had plunged me. Once again, as at the beginning of my incarceration, I felt the lightness of my new condition, where I was no longer burdened with the weight of my responsibilities. This only made detention all the more disagreeable, because it created an obstacle to the full enjoyment of my new freedom. My eagerness to plan my escape was all the greater for it.

Throughout this entire period Marc did not discuss his activity with me, but he was constantly exploring the château and its surroundings, on the lookout for any breaches in the surveillance. At the beginning of the spring, when he saw that I was physically ready to envisage a grab at freedom, he shared his findings with me.

He had learned everything there was to know about the entire populace of the château, and knew in detail the vices, habits, and foibles of the château's garrison, from the head guard to the most insignificant bucket-carrying valet. Marc did not know how to read or write, but his mind had the precision of a carefully annotated almanac. All those on whom my liberty might depend to even the slightest degree had been recorded in his memory and associated with a particular weakness. One might be a drunkard, another a cuckold, a third had a liking for fine food, or yet another might be obsessed with his mistress—Marc knew everything. His world, let it be said in passing, was not an ugly one. For him these foibles were the natural elements of the human condition. He never observed them in order to deliver the slightest judgment, only to obtain his particular ends. In this respect he was not unlike the prosecutor Dauvet. Both of them accepted the law, one of man and the other of nature. In the presence of such people I came to realize how much I had lived in the ignorance and scorn of those laws, determined as I was to escape them. In a way, we represented the two opposite and complementary poles of human conscience: submission to what is, and the desire to create another world. Although I could acknowledge the worth of people who thought like Dauvet or Marc, I remained attached to my dreams. Because I am convinced that those who conform in full with existing laws may have a good life, and obtain high rank, and triumph over adversity, but they will never produce anything great.

However, given my extreme deprivation, I had no choice but to defer to Marc. I was infinitely grateful to him for his efforts.

He did not limit himself to compiling a list of the weaknesses of the château's inhabitants. He subjected them to a subtle treatment that converted each of those vices into a same unit of value: money. Whether they went about it through drunkenness, adultery, or cupidity, in the end they all proved vulnerable to that universal property which in itself is nothing, but is worth everything. Once he had put a price on every man in the château, Marc began, with me, to lay down the precise plans that would enable us to know whom we actually needed. And, therefore, how much money.

*

Yesterday, Elvira and I moved to her cousin's sheepfold and I had to interrupt my story. We left at night so no one could inform the spies watching me of our direction. The island is not very big, but every island always has its surprises. When you see an island from the coast you cannot tell how big is, and above all you have no idea of the geography of the center. We had to follow narrow donkey paths, cross a wooden bridge, and make our way around rocky ridges.

Now we are in our shepherd's hut. It is much less comfortable than Elvira's house. But given the level of poverty to which I have fallen, and if I judge it from the palaces I have known, it's all the same.

The house, as we hoped, has the advantage of being very safe. To reach it, one must climb a winding footpath. It is protected all around by steep slopes covered with thick, thorny bushes. Even if someone were to find me here, they could not approach without making noise, and the hairless dog chained outside will notify us well in advance of any arrivals. There is a cellar where I can hide, and its entrance is hidden by boxwood. This will be a good place to wait for Campofregoso's reply. Elvira sent one of her friends to the port to keep her informed of any ships arriving from Genoa.

Elvira is more loyal and loving than ever. I am ashamed I ever suspected her. Whatever I do, deep down I still find it difficult to trust women: for a long time I believed this was the fruit of experience, but now I know it is, rather, a sign of pride and stupidity. This blindness exempts me from having to show greater nuance in judging them and above all from being more attentive to what differentiates them all. I have been very tender and thoughtful with Elvira of late, to make up for my suspicions. I don't know quite what she thinks of all my shifting moods. In any case, she accepts them with equanimity and changes nothing in her attitude.

*

I will not go into the details of the plan Marc conceived for my escape from the château at Poitiers. It would be tedious and pointless. I will simply say that it had to meet two conditions: it must make my flight possible, and any traces of complicity used to that end must be erased. This requirement stemmed from the fact that several of the key conspirators had consented to being bought, but only on the explicit condition that their betrayal would not be discovered. Consequently, their superiors who were also bought must keep silent. Rather than come up with a plan based on the improbable sacrifice of one or two guards, Marc was able to convince me that it would be better to buy everybody, in such a way that after my disappearance the investigation would not incriminate anyone and would be attributed to a mystery. Had they not already suspected me of being an alchemist and something of a wizard? Marc set about swaying people's opinions by confiding to some of them that I was capable of . . . vanishing into thin air.

Once we had worked out how much we needed to buy all our accomplices, I sent Marc to Bourges to see my son Jean at the archbishopric. Dauvet, out of the goodness of his heart, had allowed him to visit me a few months earlier. Our conversation took place in the presence of a guard, and I had not been able to give him too many details. I had simply advised Jean to place his trust in Marc if one day he should happen to visit. Jean was able to obtain without difficulty the sum we requested, and Marc brought it back to Poitiers.

Once the funds had been distributed among the beneficiaries, it was time to put our plan into action. Autumn had come, and we must not wait until the cold of winter. And yet Marc hesitated. There had been recent changes to the garrison at the château, and there were some new guards he did not know yet and whose participation he could not be sure of, as he had not had time to observe their weaknesses. I pressured him, for while it may have taken me some time to accept the idea of flight, now I was completely won over to it. I could not sleep, and I was eager to act. How deeply I regret my impatience now! As always, Marc had an intuition of what might happen and I should have trusted it. In the end, to make me happy, he took a risk. He had obtained the list of guards on duty, and he chose a day where none of the newcomers would be on watch. He suggested that date for our operation. I accepted enthusiastically.

It was a Sunday morning. All of the men present would be attending mass at the chapel of the château, with the exception of the guards keeping watch at my door. And there were fewer of them than usual. Everything went as planned. At the appointed hour, I saw Marc come in and motion to me to follow him. He handed a purse to each of the guards as we went by: the promised supplement to what he had already given them. We went down the grand staircase without meeting anyone. The entire hierarchy of jailers had been bribed, so that when the time came and they realized I had fled, each of them would answer for those he commanded. No one would have seen anything. Only the supernatural could explain my disappearance.

We walked across the deserted courtyard. I was shivering in the damp early morning air. The guards on duty at the great gate to the château did not appear, and we found ourselves outside. All that remained was to cross the open space around the moat, and reach the labyrinth of tiny streets in the town.

We were beginning to run when a shout stopped us. Two guards on their rounds had come around the corner of the nearest tower and they had seen us. One of them seemed embarrassed and didn't move: no doubt one of Marc's clients, duly compensated for seeing nothing. But his colleague, who, I later learned, had replaced another soldier who was ill, was one of the newcomers who was not in on the plot. He pulled out his sword and came after us.

I tugged Marc by the sleeve and began to run. We could easily have gotten away. But our plan relied on one essential condition: the alarm must not be raised too early. That was why we had decided to leave in the morning, in order to have a full day ahead of us to flee as far as possible. If we did not overpower the guard, he would soon inform the entire castle, and however much the individuals we had bought might be on our side, they would be obliged to raise the alarm, if proof of our escape reached their ears.

Marc had grasped all of this. He turned around and began walking toward the guard.

"My friend, my friend," he said, drawing nearer.

The guard did not trust him. He had already seen me during my walks in the courtyard and he had recognized me. However, he was confused by Marc's friendly tone. He lowered his sword but his expression remained hard.

"Where are you going? Is that the prisoner?"

Marc was now right next to the soldier. He was grinning broadly and his easy manner, in spite of the circumstances, was confusing. The guard let him come too close, at a distance appropriate for sharing secrets or friendly explanations. Marc pulled out a dagger and stabbed him in the stomach. The soldier felt the blow, and could not believe what was happening. But almost at once he realized that the blade had not gone all the way in. He was wearing a coat of mail beneath his tunic and the dagger had not pierced it. And so he returned the blow with his sword, and although he was too close and at an awkward angle, he was able to strike Marc in the shoulder. Marc's reaction was magnificent and will deserve my gratitude forever. He turned to the other soldier and cried, "If you don't kill him, he will tell the king that we bought you all."

This revelation threw everyone into a momentary stupor. Marc used it to his advantage to step back, but not far enough, alas. When the soldier had come to his wits, he raised his heavy sword against him and struck his skull. Blood gushed from the wound and Marc fell down, dead. A moment later, before the murderer had time to turn around, his associate, into whose thick brain Marc's warning had finally penetrated, took his colleague by the neck and with a single gesture slit his throat.

Now that the other guard was on the ground, he motioned to me to run. I found out only much later that he disposed of the two bodies by throwing them into the moat. No one noticed Marc's death. As for the disappearance of the other guard, it was disguised as a desertion. He was a bad sort, a former *écorcheur* and known assassin: no one was surprised that he went elsewhere to make his fortune.

I hurried down the steep little street I had reached. Turning twice to the right and once to the left I reached the inn where Marc's friend the cook was waiting for me. She was a red-faced girl, somewhat plump, who wore on her face the signs of a life of labor and poverty. When she saw me, she stood on her toes to look over my shoulder to see whether Marc was following. She stared at me; I shook my head, and was unable to say anything more. She pressed her sorrow into her heart and made it disappear. She went through the motions to concentrate on our plan, but I am sure that once she was alone she must have wept profusely. This was Marc's great asset: no woman could fail to realize that he was unfaithful, or rather, that his presence was only destined to last a certain limited length of time. And yet he aroused a sincere and deep attachment that had the power of love, even if it could not bear its name.

The cook gave me warm clothing and led me to the stable where two horses were waiting. She looked away from the one that had been meant for Marc. The saddlebags were filled with food and a blanket was rolled tight and fixed on the horse's rump, and I climbed in the saddle. She opened wide the door to the stable. I rode out and took her hand on the way. We exchanged a gaze where gratitude, sadness, and hope were mingled, in a flash. Then I spurred my horse and trotted to the edge of town.

We had rehearsed everything painstakingly with Marc, so

that his absence did not compromise the success of my plan. But I felt his loss deeply. He was the one person who had filled my thoughts over the last months. This escape was an adventure that we had conceived and dreamt up together. It was a great effort for me to return to solitude.

October was already cold in the Poitou region. Gusts of a northerly wind found their way through the hedges surrounding the fields. I followed the road as planned, meeting convoys and horsemen who greeted me without the slightest idea they were speaking to an escaped criminal. The brisk air, the pale colors of the sky where the sun had managed to break through in the early afternoon, the sight of the well-kept villages, the well-fed cattle, the carts full of produce, all banished the sad thoughts of my escape. A new feeling came over me, and it will seem banal if I say it was a feeling of freedom. There ought to be another word to designate exactly what I was feeling. It was not just the freedom of the prisoner who has left his jail behind. It was the culmination of a long journey, which had begun with my arrest, the loss of all my property, and the cessation of all my business dealings. It had continued with Marc's arrival, the restoration of my health and strength and appetite for life, and the long-nurtured project of my escape. And it all combined into a single sensation, that of the cold wind against my cheeks, my eyes misting with tears that no longer came from the soul but were brought by the icy wind. It all came back to me: people, landscapes, colors, movement. I shouted with joy to the rhythm of the gallop. The gray horse the cook had provided also seemed to have stayed too long in his stall. He flew along, and I did not need to urge him. Children laughed as we galloped by. We were an allegory for happiness and life.

*

At around eight o'clock in the evening, it was already dark

in the forest leading to the priory of Saint-Martial, not far from Montmorillon. A friar with a lantern was waiting for me. I found refuge in the inviolable walls of the sanctuary.

I did not know the prior. Marc had certainly made a generous offering in my name, which earned me an attentive but frosty greeting. I must not outstay my welcome. What the clergy feared most was that I might be found on their premises, and no longer be able to leave. And so after a few hours of food and rest for myself and my horse I left Saint-Martial, at dawn.

We had agreed, when planning with Marc, that we should head in a southeasterly direction. I would find salvation initially in Provence, where King René was still master of his domain. After that, Italy.

I now know that once the alarm was raised at last in Poitiers, the first difficulty my pursuers encountered was that of determining which direction I had taken. Some thought I must have gone east, through Bourges, and on to the duke of Burgundy. Others thought I would flee to the north: Paris, then Flanders. But Dauvet had better reasoning. He knew that only two people would be pleased to welcome me: the Dauphin, and King René. He sent missives to Lyon with the order to watch all the crossing points to the north and south of the city, leading to the Dauphiné or Provence. His clairvoyance deceived me. As in the early stages of my flight I met no obstacles, I imagined somewhat too hastily that the coast was clear. From monastery to castle, I kept strictly to the path Marc and I had laid out. Convents were very safe, as they could not be inspected. In carefully chosen castles I found friends, associates, debtors, all of whom gave me a magnificent welcome. It was, in a way, an antidote to the poison of the trial. After the long procession of envious individuals who had come to denounce me, here was this solid chain of affection and recognition. In November the rain battered the routes of the Auvergne. Fortunately my horse was bearing up, and my clothing, which I always hung up to dry by the fireplace in the evening, protected me from the cold. As I rode through the desolate provinces I could still see some traces of pillaging, but the armed bands had disappeared and one need no longer fear any evil encounters. At last I reached the other slope, the one that leads down to the Rhone Valley. The horizon was washed with rain, a gray and green line: the shores of Provence. A wind from the north began to drive away the clouds. I galloped toward the river beneath a white sun that warmed only the soul. I would soon be safe. I thought of Guillaume and Jean, who were waiting for me on the other side.

Alas, the return to reality was a harsh one. In one of the monasteries where I stopped, along the Regordane Way, at the top of the last hill overlooking the river, the monks informed me that soldiers were out looking for me. They had visited the surrounding area and had even stopped at the monastery to ask if anyone had seen me. The friars who went to sell their firewood and cattle at the markets in the valley warned me that all the crossing points on the river were being watched. Patrols were crisscrossing the region, stopping travelers.

The last of my optimism evaporated. Without Marc's help, how would I manage to make my way past this final obstacle? I imagined prison and torture all over again. The cold air I had not noticed as I was riding now gripped me and I fell ill. I had a fever for an entire week. The monks took care of me, but I could tell they were impatient to have me gone. Their monastery was poor and isolated, open to the wind, and if the soldiers came, they would not hesitate to violate the immunity that religious communities enjoyed.

As soon as I had recovered, they advised me to go as far as Beaucaire, where the powerful Cordeliers kept a snug monastery, of the sort no one would dare enter to drag me out by force. I left one evening after Vespers. Monks returning from the market had made sure the coast was clear as far as the river.

I reached the shore at nightfall. The moon was almost full and lit my way. Instead of turning to the right toward Beaucaire, I decided to go cautiously back up to a little port where salt boats were moored. Most of them, in this region, belonged to me. Sailors are a faithful lot, and if I could find one who recognized me . . .

I headed quietly toward a cluster of small boats. The dim light from a few lanterns was reflected on the water and the sound of voices carried on the still air. Suddenly to my left someone cried out. A man was calling to me in a loud voice.

"Hey, you, come over here!"

Now I could see a campsite at the edge of some trees. A few soldiers were sitting around a fire and a halo of light shone on their hobbled horses not far from there.

I immediately turned around and headed south. My gray horse had regained strength during my illness and over the last few days I had ridden him gently. He displayed all his spirit. Although the light was dim, it enabled us to gallop flat out without danger. After roughly an hour I stopped my horse, headed a short way along a path and, hiding in the darkness, I listened out. Everything was silent. I concluded that the patrol had not followed me. They must have received the order to watch a certain part of the shore and no further. I continued on my way at a gentler pace. A few hours before daybreak I arrived in sight of the walls of Beaucaire. I slept in a clearing, and with the first light of dawn I rode toward one of the gates. I nodded to the watchman, who was still drowsy, and headed up to the monastery. The brother at the gate greeted me and I asked to see the abbot. We were acquainted, because I had often come through the town when there were fairs, and I had made substantial donations to the monastery.

Father Anselme ensured me of his hospitality and took me to one of the cells. Later in the day we had a long discussion. His order was a wealthy one, and I could stay as long as I liked without inconvenience. But he warned me that I ran the risk of not being able to get out again. The town was infested with soldiers who checked everyone passing through. The incident on the riverbank would have reached their ears by now. They would logically conclude that I had come here. The abbot, while he would answer for my protection, if asked, could not hide the fact that I was in the monastery.

And indeed, the next morning, men-at-arms came to inquire about my presence. I was safe, but locked up once again. From the window of my cell I could see the river and, so near, the shore of Provence, where I could have lived in freedom. Who knew whether I would be able to reach it one day? The king, in his unbending vengefulness, had just invented a new torture for me.

*

The atmosphere quickly became strange in the monastery of the Cordeliers in Beaucaire. Now that my pursuers had tracked me down, they need no longer cast their net wide, and they could concentrate their efforts on my hideout. The town was watched with the greatest vigilance. At every gate the ordinary guard was seconded by men-at-arms specially warned against my person. Spies were lurking in the streets and at the markets. But before long it was within the very monastery that I began to perceive the danger. Father Anselme was a very old man, and I soon had to face facts: he was no longer in charge of his house. The monks were grouped in secret coteries, no doubt already plotting to prepare his succession. I felt that most of them were hostile toward me and viewed my presence as a grave error, even a betrayal. A number of these monks came from that part of the Languedoc where I had long been charged with collecting the royal tax. That thankless task had been compensated for by the positive benefits I had procured for the region. But by moving our activities to Marseille and Provence over recent years, I had angered the people of Montpellier and many others in the region, so that at the time of my trial many of my accusers were from the Languedoc. Some of these monks would be related to my enemies, or, at least, would regard them with sympathy.

During that southern winter the cold settled under the vaulted ceilings of the monastery, exacerbated by the north wind, which blew for days on end. Not many of the friars would talk to me. I could see their shadows hurrying away down the icy corridors. I had great difficulty communicating even with three or four of the humblest friars, let alone procuring their friendship: a kitchen boy, a lay brother who was terribly cross-eyed, a gardener. This hardly filled my days, but at least these acquaintances were useful to me to keep me informed of what was going on in the monastery, and they enabled me to communicate with the outside world.

The atmosphere was stifling, I could not ignore the fact. Everything seemed mysterious and opaque. Thanks to what I have since learned, I can now piece together what happened inside as well as outside the monastery at Beaucaire, but at the time I knew only fragments.

Inside, though I was not aware of it, my enemies had formed a tight bond. Indeed, unbeknownst to the abbot, who did not keep watch over his flock, two new friars had come to swell the already serried ranks of the monastery. I found out later that they had been presented to the friar at the gate as brothers who were on a simple visit, on their way to Rome where they had been summoned by the pope. Since Macé's death, I had been considered *clericus solutus* and as such I joined in the worship with the monks. It took me a while to identify the two newcomers. It was by chance that one evening at compline I met the gaze of one of them. It was rare, exceptional even, for any of the friars to pay me any notice. The general tendency, rather, was to ignore me conspicuously. But this monk seemed to be watching me. Sitting next to him was another friar: though he was wearing a homespun chasuble, he intrigued me by his build and his demeanor. He looked more like a sturdy soldier, used to life in the outdoors, confined by his homespun trappings. Both of them were incapable of chanting the psalms, even though they moved their lips to pretend otherwise.

Once I had questioned the cook about these individuals, I no longer had any doubts. They were no more monks than I was, and they had found their way here for the sole purpose of spying on me. At the time I thought they must be agents of the king, and only much later would I learn their true identity.

The purpose of their presence, in the beginning, seemed to be solely to keep an eye on me. My pursuers must have feared that in spite of the armed men on guard at every gate I would manage to escape. The two fake monks made sure, therefore, that I showed up for every service, and at the refectory. Gradually, however, I got the distinct feeling that they were trying to get closer to me. Perhaps they were planning to abduct me, but I didn't actually believe they could, because the protection of the Cordeliers of Beaucaire still stood for something, and any attack would have aroused the anger of the entire Church, right up to the pope himself. However, I did not exclude the possibility that they might try to assassinate me, by poisoning me, for example, or by arranging a blow that would look like an accident, or that could be blamed on a prowler.

Where poisoning was concerned, my friend the cook was keeping an eye out. I was careful to eat only from the platters that were used to serve everyone, and I let the others begin before me. To avoid any attack, I always stayed in the middle of a group whenever I moved around the monastery. Once I woke up late, and to reach the chapel to hear matins I had to make my way alone down the corridors. A shadow behind a pillar betrayed a suspicious presence. I began running the opposite direction and sought refuge in the common room, sliding the bolt home behind me. I could hear two people breathing heavily on the other side, and someone tried to force open the door. Then the footsteps receded. I remained alone until the end of the service and only opened the door again when the librarian brother sought to come in. The abbot was informed of the incident and sent for me. I gave him some trivial explanation of my behavior. For a moment I considered informing him of the threat hanging over me, but he would surely not have believed me, and as I was well aware of his elderly pride, I was afraid he might take my remarks as an insult to his hospitality. While he might not be able to protect me, at least he had offered me asylum, and I did not want to jeopardize his kindly disposition toward me.

While I was busy in the silence of the monastery, trying to evade these insidious threats, beyond its walls, unbeknownst to me, great preparations were being made.

Shortly after my arrival at Beaucaire I managed to convince Hugo, the gardener, to deliver a message on my behalf to one of my agents in Arles, where he had to go to buy some rare seeds. He came back and told me he had not been able to find the man. He had merely given my letter to an illiterate farm worker he knew, who from time to time went to my agent's workroom. Obviously I had no way of knowing whether my message ever reached its destination.

In fact, the agent did receive it, and very quickly. The man had immediately informed Jean de Villages and Guillaume de Varye of my presence in Beaucaire. They already knew that I had escaped from Poitiers, because the news had caused a great stir in the realm. But as they did not know what had become of me since then, they had been extremely worried.

Later I found out that once they knew I was in Beaucaire,

they had some lively discussions. Guillaume, in keeping with his temperament, was for using persuasive means rather than force. Among the soldiers watching the town there must be some, perhaps even their leader, who could be financially persuaded to behave in a negligent manner. This was basically the same method Marc had employed, but there was less likelihood it would succeed, because neither Guillaume nor anyone else knew these soldiers in person. In any case, it would require time.

Jean may have aged considerably and put on some weight due to his prosperity, but he was every bit as impetuous as during his youth. Knowing that I was nearby, barred from freedom by a simple river, locked up in a city he knew well because he had often been there, all caused him to seethe with rage. For him there could be no negotiating, dealing, or waiting. The only solution could be an operation using force. Guillaume and several others pointed out to him, quite rightly, that they were only merchants. While they may have disposed of a few men-at-arms to escort their convoys, they could not put together a true army, which was what would be needed to deal with the garrison at Beaucaire.

They came to a compromise. Jean prevailed, and they decided to mount an expedition. But it would be prepared patiently and methodically, according to Guillaume's recommendations. Jean called on two galley captains, each of whom provided a dozen men for the operation.

I had no knowledge of their plans and, lacking news from the outside, I set about organizing my own defense. My pursuers had become bolder and, judging from the sounds I heard at night, I became convinced they were going to try something against me during my sleep. To please me, the abbot had given me a private cell. Now I asked him to move me to the dormitory, under the pretext that he would certainly need my room for other guests. He thought he would please me further by energetically refusing. As a result, I was spending my nights alone in that room I could not bolt shut, and where it would be easy to attack me. I resorted to a subterfuge to protect myself: although there was little space, I began sleeping on the floor beneath the bed, and I put a blanket in my place to make it seem as if I were in the bed. Hugo the gardener had provided me with a tool that could serve as a weapon, a lead mallet that he used for driving stakes. I had cause to use it the very next day. In the middle of the night I was woken by a presence in my room. From under the bed I could see the hem of a monk's habit. Someone was drawing near, noiselessly. No doubt the intruder was waiting to be closer to strike more accurately. I did not leave him the time, and thumped him with the mallet. The man let out a cry and hobbled away, limping.

The incident caused great alarm in the monastery. All the monks were talking about it the next day. I noticed that one of my pursuers had disappeared. He came back a week later, having tended the wounds caused by the mallet, but he was still limping slightly.

*

After their initial failure, the false monks procured the assistance of several of the brothers. It was becoming more difficult for me to protect myself, because now the danger was no longer limited to two people but involved others whom I did not know. Fortunately, my handful of friends were well-informed and gave me warnings. Ten days or so after the episode with the mallet, the good friar cook came to warn me that they were going to try to poison me with a glass of wine. I do not know how he knew this, but the fact remains that the next day I noticed that the monk who filled our goblets from the demijohn was behaving oddly. He grabbed my goblet, turned away from me for a long while, then handed the goblet back to me as if he had just filled it. In fact, he had exchanged it for another that had been prepared in advance and brought to him by one of his confederates.

The meal began. The day's lesson was devoted to the encounter between Jesus and the Samaritan by the well. We ate in deep silence broken only by the words of the Gospel as read by one of the friars. Discreet gazes between friars revealed the perpetrators of my poisoning. Although they paid no particular notice to my gestures, all those who were in on the plot were observing me to see whether I was going to pick up my goblet and drink or not. Toward the middle of the meal, very calmly but very slowly so that everyone would have time to see, I took a long swallow of wine. A shiver of relief went through the group of conspirators. I was dead.

The cook, who most definitely was well informed, had warned me that the brew would kill me within a week. The murderers wanted to make it look like an illness, so they had avoided using any potent poisons that would have killed me almost immediately.

Therefore I showed no immediate signs of sickness, and finished eating normally. The end of the meal was always a relatively agitated time, after the silence and immobility imposed by the lesson. Each of us stood up and cleared the table. I took the opportunity to empty the remains of the poisoned goblet into a pitcher of water: in fact, I had only pretended to drink, and had not actually let the wine touch my lips.

The next day I pretended to feel unwell. The cook had described the effects of the poison to me and I imitated them scrupulously. I was taken to the infirmary. My enemies waited patiently for my end. This would mean I'd be safe for one week, at least.

During this time, the expedition organized for my rescue was on the verge of departing, but a few details delayed them. Jean, Guillaume, and their entire team were struggling as best they could to resolve the last remaining problems. As luck had it, they were ready exactly eight days after my so-called poisoning.

I had left the infirmary that very morning and I went to the church for the first service, to the great astonishment of my poisoners. Judging from their furious gazes, I could tell they would not delay in preparing another attack and that this one would leave me no chance. One clue, however, showed me how I might obtain help from the outside, and this prospect restored some hope.

Brother Hugo had been stopped at the market the day before by an acquaintance who asked for news of me. The man clearly knew that the gardener-monk was on my side; he implied that he had heard about the letter I had sent thanks to Hugo. I later learned that this stranger was none other than Guillaume Gimart, a former galley captain whom Jean had enrolled in his expedition, and who had come to Beaucaire posing as a merchant. In the same conversation, he asked Brother Hugo whether he knew of any weaknesses in the city walls. The monk grew wary, and deferred his answer until the next day, until he had had time to consult with me. I urged him to give all the information he had to this man. We had nothing to fear and everything to hope for, if he was one of us.

Because of his work as a gardener, Hugo was able to go all over the town. He was in charge of keeping a few sheep belonging to the monastery. He led them to graze beneath the walls, which had the advantage of both feeding the sheep and keeping the immediate vicinity of the ramparts tidy. As he was curious about plants, Brother Hugo liked to study the little clumps of simples that grew in the cracks in the walls. He had often noticed the places where the wall's foundations in the silty ground were uneven, and the cracks were growing wider. He pointed them out to the bailiff, who did what was needed to repair the cracks. One month earlier, as he chased after a ewe who had strayed, Hugo had come upon a fairly wide breach, caused by the spring storms. The entrance was hidden by a hawthorn bush. Water had formed a channel beneath the wall and flowed through to the other side. Hugo had not yet had time to inform the town authorities of his discovery. He confessed to me that, without knowing exactly why, it had already occurred to him that this breach, though it was still too narrow for a man to squeeze through, might one day be useful to me. He described it to Gimart, who seemed very pleased to hear the news.

Now that I was aware that something was going on outside, I grew impatient for my release. I was afraid that my enemies might not leave my rescuers enough time. To further stave off any danger, I decided to sleep with the lay brothers, something that no doubt would be relayed to the abbot and arouse his anger. However, by the time he found out, I would have gained more time.

What I did not know was that someone even more impatient than I—Jean—would no longer tolerate any delay. As soon as they learned that there was a breach in the wall, Guillaume called for a scout to be sent to determine its exact location. Jean refused, arguing that they could find out on the spot. Guillaume objected that the moon was still too full; he advised waiting for a dark night, in order not to be seen. Jean completely lost his temper. There was a violent quarrel between them, and I owe my life to it. Because Jean was more stubborn, that very evening a boat carrying the twenty men of the expedition slipped through the reeds on the Provence shore and set out to cross the river.

To avoid attracting the attention of any patrols that might be posted on the king's shore, the boat was made to look like an ordinary barge. The men were hidden under canvas, like a simple load of merchandise. Fortunately, there were no soldiers about when they landed in a cove slightly to the north of the town. They left two men behind to guard the boat, and all the others set off behind Jean, walking quickly to the ramparts. They made for the breach that Hugo had described. They found it fairly easily, because a heavy rain had fallen the night before and there was a stream of water springing up under the wall. They had brought picks and shovels to enlarge the gap and, apart from a large stone they had difficulty removing, the rest of the hole was fairly easy to enlarge. They shored up the wall in a rough manner with a board and four poles. Once the way out had been cleared, they exchanged their picks for swords and squeezed one after the other through the tiny tunnel.

The night was nearly over. The feeble chapel bell rang matins. I left the dormitory closely surrounded by those brothers I could trust, Hugo in particular. The two fake monks arrived somewhat late and I wondered if it was not because they had been plotting something against me in my cell.

The gold on the altar shone in the candlelight. The monks stood in a circle at the edge of the darkness, and those who were in the last rows could hardly be seen. One of them stood up, went to the lectern and began to chant the psalm "Lord, I come unto thee." The male voices took up the refrain, and the chant, which was supposed to vibrate with joy, echoed limply in the damp air. Who could have imagined that beneath the gentle harmonies of this drowsy orison there lurked dreadful plots and murderous passion, and that, far from transfiguring those men who claimed to find inspiration in God, the chant served as a screen for crime and vengeance?

Suddenly, as if the Lord to whom we were calling so plaintively had decided to appear before us, the door to the chapel swung open. A dozen or more men hurried down the nave, brandishing their swords. The candlelight flickered, but almost at once, taking the flame from a lantern, the intruders lit two torches. The monks recoiled and cried out with more conviction than they had shown mumbling their psalms.

In the red light of the flames, a man stepped forward and called out to me. I recognized Jean de Villages. I took two steps toward him and was about to embrace him when a shadow leapt forward and I felt a blow on my shoulder. Seeing that I was on the verge of being freed, one of the false monks had hurled himself at me with a dagger. Fortunately, Brother Hugo had had the presence of mind to step in his way, so the killer missed his target. The tip of his blade tore my habit and scraped my skin. Jean and his men, surprised by the attack, quickly regained their wits and surrounded the assassin as he tried to escape. His associate, who was right by his side, was captured at the same time. There was a brief scuffle, and both men were killed.

The monks, whether they were accomplices or not, watched in horror as the scene unfolded. Jean raised his sword and spoke to them in a loud voice. He informed them that two of his men would be posted outside the monastery for the time it would take us to get away, and if anyone tried to raise the alarm they must expect no pity.

We left in a scramble. I found it awkward to run in my homespun habit. Fortunately, the streets of the town were dark and deserted, and there was not far to go to reach the hole in the wall.

Breathless and exultant, we made it to the boat, shivering in the wind that was cold and damp from the river. During the crossing, Jean took my hands and I embraced him for a long time, weeping. Horses were waiting for us on the other side. Guillaume had thought of everything, and had brought some travel clothing for me. I changed and climbed in the saddle. The sun rose in a cloudless sky. A straight, well-paved road ran between a sea of pale green olive trees. I had an inexpressible feeling of rebirth, but it was not the birth of an ignorant and vulnerable infant but rather of one of those Greek gods who come to earth as adults in the prime of life, rich with experience and pleased to share the pleasures of human beings, about whom they know everything. We rode for two days until we reached Aix, the home of King René.

*

I stayed in Aix for less than a week, but it seemed like a month. I was reunited with all my friends—Jean, Guillaume, the galley captains, and my agents, several of whom had found refuge in Provence to escape lawsuits in the kingdom of France.

I learned everything that had happened in the world during almost three dark years spent in the secrecy of prisons. Coming from their lips, some of the news, which had only reached me in faint echoes, was striking. They informed me that Constantinople had fallen to the Turks, and they described the huge consequences: the exodus of artists and scholars, and an even closer rapprochement with the Sultan of Egypt, who watched with terror as the Turks increased their dominance. They confirmed a lasting peace with the English. This was indeed the birth of a new world. They continued to exploit every possibility that new world offered, and told me they had saved as many assets as possible from Dauvet's inventory. As I had suspected, Dauvet had merely been cutting off dead branches. But the plant was alive and would grow in other directions. Guillaume now had the galleys flying other flags than that of the king of France: Provence, Aragon, and Genoa. The ships continued on their ceaseless voyages. He had placed much of my property under other names, and had used banking transactions to make funds disappear. Dauvet might be able to get his hands on my houses and castles, but that was not the active part of our business.

I even had some news that not only reassured me but restored some of my optimism: while keeping it secret from his prosecutor, the king had authorized certain transactions that

Guillaume had undertaken on behalf of our business. In other words, he seemed to have understood that apart from vengeance, the cupidity of the great barons, and his own desire to appropriate my fortune, it was in his interest to let us go on doing business. Thus, although he had not pardoned me, he showed that he intended to preserve our activity and let it live.

While everyone, or almost everyone, in his entourage still thought they lived in the era of chivalry, he at least, with greater clairvoyance, understood that he could no longer reign over a fixed order; and if he were to be powerful, this could only be attained through movement and trade, an activity that he could never fully control short of killing it altogether. This gave me some satisfaction, and even, I confess, a burst of pride.

Jean and Guillaume had also preserved ties with my family. They did not know much about Macé's death, because, as I said, she ended her life withdrawn from the world. But the news from my children was good. My son Jean, in his position as archbishop, was untouchable, and he protected his brothers and sisters. Only my youngest son, Ravand, had gone through difficult times. He had endeavored to plead with Dauvet, who refused to give him any help. I was sorry that he had lowered himself in this effort, which was as pointless as it was humiliating. Since then, he had received help from my friends in Provence and he was living well.

What touched me most was to see that Jean and Guillaume and all the others had continued to look after our trading house without ever thinking of taking it over for themselves. They considered that it belonged to me, and they very honestly, and in great detail, provided me with an account of the fortune I had at my disposal. In actual fact, they were also motivated by optimism: they knew our business too well to believe that it belonged to anyone in particular. It lived from, and for, everyone. They acknowledged that I had a particular role, but it was complementary to their own.

In any case, despite the predatory behavior of the people at court and Dauvet's persnickety inventories, I was pleased to see that our web was still just as solid, and that we had considerable means. Stimulated by King René's appreciation for fine things, I took great delight in having elegant clothing made up, in sharing good meals, and in visiting palaces. I had had my fill of rough cloth, hard beds, and prisoners' meals. My gaze was weary of peeling walls. I'd had enough of peering at patches of gray sky through tiny, barred windows. I grew intoxicated with elegance, bright sunshine, music, and pretty women.

Alas, my stay in Provence was not meant to last. My companions informed me that suspicious individuals had been sighted coming and going. In spite of King René's autonomy with regard to the king of France, he remained his vassal, and his lands were open to Charles's subjects. Clearly there were agents among them who were trailing me. René very magnanimously refused to hand me over to Charles VII. But I quickly understood that his resistance did not guarantee my safety. I decided to continue on to Florence.

I went through Marseille, where my house was nearly finished. I only stayed two days. Jean had to wait for the arrival of a galley. He provided me with a comfortable escort and I left by the coast. The gardens by the seaside were bursting with color. It was warm, and the sound of the cicadas could drive one mad. We stopped at shady properties perched on outcrops; I could not get enough of looking at the horizon.

Something had changed, which made this journey very different from those I had made in the old days. With my freedom regained, and perhaps captivity, I had acquired an astonishing aptitude for nonchalance. I was once again involved in the business; Guillaume had brought me up to date on everything, and no one disputed my authority. And yet I no longer had—and I now know that I will never again have—the appetite, the concern, or the impatience that once propelled me into the next moment and prevented me from living fully in the present. That agitation had left me for good. I was wholly there, on that dusty road, at the top of that rocky spur overlooking the sea, or in that garden next to a clear fountain. My mind and body were so altered by freedom that I grew drunk on it. I gulped down the beauties of the world like a thirsty man pressing his lips to a cool spring. This was pure happiness.

Jean had found me a new valet. He was only the third servant to accompany me in life, after Gautier in the Levant, and Marc, until his sacrifice.

I only ever had those three, and now, perched high up in my sheepfold in Chios, I doubt that the future will provide me with any others. Three valets, three personalities, three very different periods of my existence. The last one was called Étienne. Naturally, he came from Bourges. Jean and Guillaume had always surrounded themselves with men from their native town. Some of them had even been appointed ships' captains, although they were born as far from the sea as one can possibly be. Their shared origins gave them an instinctive understanding, on which the basic quality of any enterprise is founded: mutual trust. Étienne was a little peasant whose father had been killed by one of the last gangs of *écorcheurs* as they were leaving the region. This loss caused a strange reaction in the child: he could no longer sleep. It was not an illness, nor grounds for complaint or suffering. He simply did not sleep. Perhaps from time to time he would drop off for a moment, but in all the time that he was in my service, whenever I called to him, no matter the time, he was awake. He had no other qualities in particular, he was neither very clever nor very brave, nor particularly talkative or penetrating in his understanding of others, as Marc had been. But at a time when I might still be under threat, Étienne's infirmity (for I could not imagine that being deprived of sleep was not an infirmity) was supremely useful.

One week after we left Marseilles, as we were about to enter Genoa, the head of my escort, an old soldier named Bonaventure, came to warn me that we were being followed.

I decided in the end that we would not go through Genoa. With its rival factions, its intrigues, and its foreign agents, the city was far too likely a spot for an attack. We continued on our way and reached Tuscany. Every day we discovered new landscapes of woods and green hills, fortified villages, and everywhere, like little javelins hurled by the gods onto the silky carpet of fields, thousands of black cypress trees.

Bonaventure had deliberately left a few men behind, and now they came riding up at full tilt: they confirmed that a group of roughneck soldiers had been following us through the villages and stopped to ask when we had been through. We continued on our way to Florence. There I was reunited with Niccolò di Bonaccorso. The young boy had turned into a grown man. He was unrecognizable with his black beard and deep voice, as well as the self-confidence worn in Italy by both those who have succeeded in business and those who want others to forget that they have not. Two things, fortunately, had not changed: his energy and his loyalty. The silk workshop he managed had grown considerably. He employed many workers and sent his cloth all over Europe. And yet, like Guillaume, Jean, and all the others, he continued to view me as his associate, and despite my disgrace in France he had never stopped affirming that I was the founder and the owner of the workshop.

He suggested I settle in Florence. Every year since my imprisonment he had scrupulously deposited my earnings in the bank, and he gave me a precise account of my assets. They were amply sufficient to buy a house in the town and live there for several years. Niccolò opened his home to me, but I preferred to leave him his freedom and keep my own by staying at the inn.

The first two days in Florence, I surrendered to the delight of knowing I had arrived safe and sound. I could easily and happily imagine myself spending the rest of my days in that gentle city, with its hazy sunsets over the river, its hills, and the ever-growing clusters of *palazzi.* Unfortunately, on only the third day, the alarm was raised. While until then my pursuers had kept at a certain distance and were relatively discreet, in Florence the malevolent surveillance became omnipresent and very visible. My first gesture on reaching the town had been to dismiss my escort. In this refined city where everyone, even the wealthy, endeavored to mingle with others in great simplicity, it would have been ridiculous for me to go about surrounded by Bonaventure and his soldiers. So I ventured abroad with Étienne for sole companion. He was the one who first noticed the two men following us. At the corner of the square, two more men were clearly spying on us as well. A bit further along, outside a church, I myself noticed a group of beggars who seemed anything but authentic and whose gazes lingered on us insistently. One of them, limping low to the ground, followed us to the entrance of the silk factory. I sent Étienne to find Bonaventure. I asked him to follow us at a certain distance when the time came for us to go back to the inn, and to keep an eye out. What he noticed was most distressing: the city was infested with spies who were after me. Neither in Provence nor on the way had I ever been the subject of such heavy surveillance. Niccolò suggested contacting the authorities in order to ensure my safety. As long as we did not know where the threat was coming from, this seemed a bad idea. If they were envoys of the king of France, the matter would become political, and it was not in our interest to notify the city officially of my presence . . . Bonaventure came up with a good suggestion: given the number of people who were following me, no doubt it would be possible to single one out and capture him. An interrogation would yield a bit more information about the matter. That day I deliberately took some long aimless walks through the city. Bonaventure counted my pursuers from a distance. He saw that they were divided into four groups, and that one of them included two children whom it would be fairly easy to frighten.

I went back to the inn, and the men in my escort dispersed to begin following my pursuers. They seized one of the children just as he was about to go home, and brought him to the inn. Niccolò came to join us. He questioned the little beggar in his Florentine dialect.

What we learned from his interrogation was extremely instructive. The child did not understand everything, but he gave us a great many names that he had heard. It turned out that those who were threatening and following me were not the king's men, but Florentines . . . At the origin of it all was my dear Otto Castellani, the very same who, after denouncing me, had ended up taking my place and helping himself abundantly during the scramble for my property. So I had two perils to confront: royal vengeance on the one hand, which had political influence but also limits, fortunately, the further we got away from France, and on the other hand the personal vendetta of Castellani and his associates. By seeking refuge in Florence, I had chosen the ideal terrain. Castellani and his brother had maintained numerous ties with the city where they were born. I had, in a way, thrown myself into the jaws of the lion.

To my great regret, and Niccolò's despair, I had to leave the city at once and find a safer shelter. The only place I might hope to find that safety was Rome. The pope's protection was, in principle, a supreme guarantee, although for a scoundrel like Castellani, nothing was absolutely sacred once money and revenge were at stake. However, it would be more difficult for him to act in a city he did not know well, and where I would have no scruples, this time, in moving about with an armed escort.

*

We continued on our way. I did not mind this wandering, particularly because for so long my only horizon had been four walls. It was getting hotter as summer approached and we headed further south. I had made certain to send two men from the escort to Rome with news of my arrival. As we neared the city, we found stopping points prepared for us in monasteries or luxurious villas. Finally, we reached the banks of the Tiber. The pope was staying at Santa Maria Maggiore during the construction of the Vatican. The fall of Constantinople and the Turkish advance had upset his plans and delayed the extension of the basilica.

As soon as I arrived, Nicholas V received me; he had been waiting impatiently. In truth, he had been afraid he would not live until my arrival. The disease that afflicted him was in its last stages. I hardly recognized him. He had lost a lot of weight. Like most people who go through life with a certain plumpness, his roundness had become part of him, and its sudden absence gave me the impression that I was looking at someone else. He had difficulty walking, even with the help of a very simple boxwood cane, which contrasted greatly with the pomp of his apartments. But it was foremost in his mental faculties that his weakness was so apparent.

This man of letters and culture and politics was not made to confront the great ordeals his pontificate had reserved for him. The paradox was that he had succeeded in full: after the end of the Schism in the West and the fall of the second, Eastern Rome, he had no rivals. This unity, however, which others before him had dreamt of in vain, had come too late for him. He had used up all his strength to obtain it. He spoke to me at length about the situation in the world and the ideas he would have liked to defend if he had still had the time and the means. His basic vision had not changed: this reunified papacy must be consolidated and endowed with a center in keeping with its stature; this he was doing by continuing the construction of the Vatican. After the fall of Constantinople, he had preached for peace among the monarchs of the West and their unity in the face of the danger. But they had not listened, and the rivalries continued.

The result was that the pontiff of Rome was now alone to face the advance of the Mohammedans, and having gained everything, he now risked losing it all again. This was why, when taking into account the lukewarm attitude of the European monarchs, Nicholas V thought that it would be best to abandon any ideas of a crusade for the time being. He sensed, however, that most of the cardinals, particularly those from Eastern Europe, who were directly threatened by the Turks, were eager for a confrontation.

At our first meeting, the pope held forth on these topics, even before questioning me about my plans or about what had happened to me in France. Like all men who are hounded by death, he was completely inhabited by the idea of his end, and to all his interlocutors he addressed an anxious monologue no different from that which he addressed in private to the void. More than ever I had the conviction that he believed neither in God nor, under the present circumstances, in eternal life.

We met every day, for a long while. He was taken out into the Vatican gardens, where he could observe the construction work on the basilica. He showed me the vestiges of the Circus of Nero, where Peter had been martyred. The presence of the past all around him seemed to be his only comfort, as if the afterworld toward which he was headed might also be built with these stones that held the trace of those who had gone before, and which now were sheltered by the cool shadow of the pale green pine trees.

As I had hoped, Rome was a far safer refuge. Nicholas V allowed me to move into one wing of the Lateran Palace. It had been deserted during the popes' exile in Avignon, and it needed to be completely restored. I arranged to have the rooms I would occupy repaired, painted, and furnished. Bonaventure provided me with a permanent guard, also available when I needed to move about, and as most of the time I was with the pope, I enjoyed his protection as well. A number of clues seemed to indicate that Castellani's spies were still observing us, but there was never the slightest cause for alarm.

The pope's health declined rapidly. His doctor told me that he had been losing a lot of blood during the night. In contrast to his skeletal limbs, beneath his chasuble his stomach was swelling. He often placed his hands on it, in a grimace of pain. During these last days, he confessed to me that he found more consolation in Seneca than in the Gospels. He was a simple man, devoid of any pomp, infinitely vulnerable and solitary, and he passed away on March 24 at the break of dawn, without a sound.

His end was expected, not to say hoped for, by the council. The cardinals gathered and rapidly appointed a successor, whose name they had probably agreed on long before. This was Alonzo Borgia, Bishop of Valencia, who chose the name Callixtus III.

Nicholas V had introduced me to him a few days before his death. He was an energetic and indefatigable man of seventy-seven. He was completely lacking in Nicholas's ancient culture. Unlike his predecessor, he was inhabited by a natural and sincere faith, which left no room for doubt and rendered pointless or even suspicious any culture that was not conceived according to the dictates of God and Christ. To the perfection of the true faith he opposed the pagan world, which for him consisted equally of savages who went about naked and Athenian philosophers from the time of Pericles. He was completely committed to the idea of a crusade, and was bent on succeeding where his predecessor had failed even to try.

Nicholas V viewed the crusades above all as an opportunity for the kings and potentates of Europe to present a harmonious front to the Turkish threat. This was an unrealistic goal, because no one among those in power was inclined, no matter what he might say publicly, to curtail his own ambitions and eschew vengeance.

Callixtus III asked for much less: he would leave the monarchs to their quarrels, provided they agree to provide him with the means to arm a fleet bound for Asia Minor. What he wanted was fairly simple and easy to obtain: oriflammes and galleys, knights in full array and troops in modest number, since they must be transported by ship. There were, in the kingdoms and principalities, plentiful numbers of *écorcheurs* in want of plunder, and brainless petty nobles who concealed their bony horses beneath embroidered carapaces inherited from ancestors. The ships were more difficult to obtain, and the pope did not find as many as he would have liked. And yet when they were all brought together, they made for an impressive show, and it did not seem ridiculous for the pope to bless the armada from the tower above the port in Ostia.

I was disheartened to see soldiers converging on Rome from all over Europe, men of the likes of Bertrandon de la Broquière, whom I had met in Damascus. In deciding to attack the Turks without the proper means, the pope would incite them to see him as their enemy, and to pursue their conquest of a continent still plagued by internal conflict. Yet I had no choice. Callixtus III had prolonged the hospitality extended to me by Nicholas V. I was now settled in Rome. I lived there in safety, and it was my duty to comply with the requests of the man on whom my safety depended. The pope came to me for funds and he entrusted me with several missions, particularly that of obtaining new ships in Provence and from the king of Aragon.

At no other time in my life did I surrender so utterly to the luxury of existence and the pleasure of the moment as during those six months I spent in Rome. I do not have a very detailed memory of this succession of happy days. The climate itself, always equal in light and warmth, meant I no longer knew what season it was. All I remember are the beautiful gardens, the splendid feasts, and the inimitable perfume which ancient ruins confer on religion in St. Peter's city. I remember a few lovely images of women. But the atmosphere in Rome was very different from Florence or Genoa, not to mention Venice. The Romans want to show that they are worthy of the popes' presence, particularly after the unfortunate episode of the "captivity of Babylon," as they themselves call the departure of the pontiffs for Avignon. Passions and even vices are no less violent here than elsewhere, but they are more carefully hidden. Étienne was not Marc, and I could not count on him to help me tear aside the veils of virtue behind which the women hid their propensity for sensual delight, however transparent they might be. As a result I was bound to rely on appearances, and must have disappointed any number of women by responding to their cold and elegant manners with polite detachment. To be honest, beyond the respect for propriety and a persistent lack of ease in the domain of gallantry, the truth was that I had no desire to embark on any adventures. The death of Agnès, the death of Macé, my detention and torture—all these ordeals emerged, during those brilliant days in Rome, like stains reappearing on a faded cloth.

Suffering and mourning encourage one to seek out pleasure once one is again able to enjoy it. But the experience of suffering seeps into pleasure, and one can never again fully surrender one's mind to sweetness, luxury, and love, because to be enjoyed these experiences must be felt as eternal. The moment dark memories impose limits and remind one that if one indulges in them one is only delaying the inevitable return of misfortune and death, any desire to know them vanishes. I had never been the jolliest of guests, and already at the court of France I was invited primarily for my influence, and for the debts that had been contracted with me. In Rome I rapidly acquired a reputation as a taciturn, serious presence, and some people may have concluded that I was perfectly sinister.

It was my sincere desire to endeavor to appear in a more pleasing light. But I did not succeed. When I tried to unravel the reasons for my inability, I discovered the truth was quite simple, but I had never been aware of it: ever since my escape, I had been unable to put my newfound freedom to good use. My experience in Rome showed me that I did not want to return to the life I had known before my disgrace. To go back to the society of a court, whether it was that of a pope or of a king, to enjoy the favors of wealth and increase them still further—all this would no longer bring what I expected from the unhoped-for reprieve of my escape. On the contrary, it would be a sure way to lock myself up again in a prison that, no matter how gilded, was nevertheless a prison.

And then my daydreaming led me to a strange decision: I would ask the pope to let me embark on the crusade.

*

The idea of leaving voluntarily on the crusade was all the more unexpected in that all through the previous weeks I had been dreading that the pontiff might suggest or even order me to participate.

Why this sudden change of heart? Because the crusade had suddenly become a means, not an end. If I sailed with this ridiculous expedition, it would not be to embrace their goal or even to take part in it to the end. Quite simply, the galleys of the armada would take me back to the Levant, and I felt the call.

Of course, I could have sailed on one of my own ships, but

that would have meant leaving for scheduled ports of call, in the company of acquaintances who would have watched over me and whom I would have been unable to avoid. The crusade, on the other hand, would take me nowhere, since the pope's expedition had no precise destination. Its value was that of a symbol of Christianity, and that was enough to satisfy Callixtus III. This naval army was too modest to confront the Turkish armies on land. At the most, it might be able to come to the support of the Christian islands threatened with invasion. In all likelihood it would merely sail aimlessly here and there.

I had held this confusion to be regrettable, even catastrophic, until suddenly, when I changed my mind, I saw the chance I had not dared hope for. The crusade, in its wandering, would take me into the unknown. And the unexpected goes hand in hand with freedom.

I had been set free from everything—not just the constraint of prisons, but also the concerns of family and, something even more oppressive, the lofty ambitions of glory and fortune, because I had attained them and had now renounced them for good. I would fuel this total freedom with the unexpected, the unprepared, the inconceivable. Once again I pictured the caravan for Damascus, and I told myself that after this long detour through fortune and ruin, perhaps I would at last be able to take my place in it.

I went to announce my decision to the old pope. He embraced me and thanked me with tears in his eyes. If I had been a man of faith, I would have been angry with myself for so deceiving the man who occupied the throne of Peter. But I preferred to surrender completely to the misunderstanding, and I, too, felt sincerely moved, not to be rushing at the enemy Turk, but to be leaving behind this life of splendor to which nothing bound me anymore.

My plan was simple. As soon as I felt the conditions were

favorable, I would disembark, pretend to be ill, and stay on land.

I mingled with the heterogeneous troop of dignitaries preparing to embark. In another era, I would have been incensed by the commerce of these ambitious prelates, so-called knights, and all the fauna of noble Romans seeking through the crusade an opportunity to acquire some illustrious valor for their family. I shared neither the fears nor the overzealousness of this crowd. I only found myself among them because it was my aim to leave them behind as quickly as possible. Nothing could sway me.

The only upsetting incident prior to my departure concerned Étienne. It pains me to say so, because it would be tempting to laugh, but here was this young man who never slept, and on the day before our departure he did not wake up. I found him early in the morning sleeping in a corridor near my room. He was flat on his back, perfectly calm, his eyes closed. I was stunned to see him sleeping. All the previous days he had seemed very nervous to me. I eventually realized that he was terrified by the idea of boarding a ship. Had his terror so upset him that it had laid him low? In any case, after observing him for a long while, I no longer had any doubt. He was not asleep; he was dead.

I was sincerely saddened by his passing, because I had grown attached to him. But I did not see it, as I might have done in the early days of my escape, as a deathly premonition.

Moreover, the safety I had enjoyed in Rome had reassured me. Bonaventure had not spotted any spies in the vicinity for a long time, and I had asked him to reduce his numbers. I did not want to be burdened with him during the crusade, because it would be far more difficult for me to regain my freedom if I was escorted. I had planned only on taking Étienne with me. In the end, I left alone.

I was allotted my place on board a ship. The departure ceremonies were endless, and a huge crowd turned out. After all, herein lay the essence of the crusade: the fact that it would be proclaimed all over Europe. The festivities lasted all day. The pope's blessing gave the signal for departure. The galleys set off first. Our vessel had some difficulty unfurling its sails, and we had to tow it along the quay. It was already late in the day when we finally reached the open sea.

The fleet sailed around Sicily and set its course for the Levant. Our maneuvers were not precise and headwinds often blew us off course. It hardly seemed to matter since, in any case, we did not know where we were going . . .

We called at Rhodes. My ties with the Knights Hospitallers were too close for me to imagine staying on the island. I re-embarked with the others. From Rhodes, the fleet headed due north past the islands along the coast of Asia Minor. Most of them were little islands where it would be difficult for me to disappear. At last we reached Chios, and I decided that the time had come for me to put my plan into action.

First of all, I began writhing with pain, kept to my bed, and stopped speaking. Doctors are fairly easy to fool, provided one deploys the same energy in pretending as illness does in devouring the afflicted. The ship's surgeon quickly proved as pessimistic about my state as I could have hoped. Very soon he declared that I was doomed, which freed him of any responsibility in helping me to recover. Everything went smoothly. I managed to convince the commander-in-chief not to delay the expedition for my sake. My sacrifice, in an adventure where there had been so few, seemed to be one of the only claims to glory such an expedition could make. It must not go to waste. I was taken ashore, with much weeping, and a solemn farewell was organized for me, which I have recorded at the beginning of these memoirs.

It was only a few days later, as I was wandering through the town, that I came upon Castellani's henchmen. Thus the fleet, the way it sometimes returns from the tropics with vermin, had now brought these wretches from Italy, determined to kill me . . . The vengeance I had hoped to be rid of for good was only in abeyance.

*

That is it.

I have been able to tell all of my story, and I feel infinitely relieved. Yesterday, after I finished writing these last lines, I went out to the front of the sheepfold. I am alone here at the moment, because Elvira has gone down to the harbor. The wind, high in the sky, seems to be dragging the clouds by the hair; they pass before the moon at great speed. That is my dream of freedom: to be like those clouds, chasing each other without hindrance.

It is very strange, but against all evidence I feel I have nearly attained that goal. And yet I am hidden away in a tumbledown drystone house, surrounded by brambles, threatened by enemies who are searching for me on an island from which I cannot escape. Why, then, do I have such a powerful feeling of freedom? The answer came all on its own, as I sat on my wooden bench, about to get back up to come and write these lines. This freedom I have traveled so far to find, and with so little success: it awaited me here, in these pages. My life as I lived it was nothing but effort and constraint, struggle and conquest. My life relived, as I wrote it down, has regained the lightness of dreams.

I was a creature; now I am a creator.

*

Elvira came back at nightfall. I saw her from a distance, climbing up the winding path to our sheepfold. She was carrying a heavy basket, which obliged her to stop frequently. The effort caused her to sweat, and she wiped her brow with her forearm. While she was climbing, I thought of the affection I feel for her, and told myself that, in spite of my reservations and all the reticence of the beginning, her kindness, loyalty, and tenderness have made her, in the end, a true love. I was eager for her to arrive so I could hear the news she was bringing, but even more so to take her in my arms. I went down to meet her, running, and as soon as I reached her I relieved her of the basket and put my arm around her waist. We went the rest of the way breathless and silent, holding each other close. It seemed to me that Elvira, who was holding my elbow, was squeezing it more tightly than usual. I had the feeling she was bringing bad news.

Once we were in the house she went to wash her face and arms in the barrel that fills from the gutter, and I waited for her. When she came back, it seemed to me that she had also washed the dried salt of her tears from her cheeks. We sat down on the wooden bench, leaning against the stone wall. She took a deep breath and told me in a trembling voice what she knew. The ship from Genoa had arrived. It did indeed carry a message for me, which the captain had conveyed to her orally. Campofregoso, because of a new political revolution, had lost any influence in the city, and for the time being he was in prison. The new strongman was a young notable who also preached rapprochement with France. But to him I was nothing more than a fugitive whom he would be only too happy to hand over to Charles VII. There was nothing to be hoped for from the Genoese.

I began thinking very quickly. The king of Aragon, the Knights of Rhodes, and even the Sultan: I drew up a list of all the powerful people I might yet turn to for help.

As if she had read my thoughts, Elvira shook her head and looked at me. Her eyes were red, and her swollen lids could not restrain her tears for long. She took my hand. The mountain, she said, was surrounded. Castellani's men had found us. They had the collaboration of both shepherds and hunters. Down below, behind the large boulders scattered across the plain like knuckle bones on a baize mat, several dozen armed men were waiting, ready to begin the assault. They had let her through, but they had ordered her not to stay with me for long, under pain of suffering the same fate.

I stood up and looked out into the distance. Everything seemed calm, but I did not doubt that she was telling me the truth. We had gained some time by hiding up on this promontory, but the moment we were tracked down it had become a deadly trap. The only path that led here was the one Elvira had just climbed. All around, boulders and brambles prevented flight. And the cave behind the house was a poor hiding place that would not stand up to a thorough search. It was all over.

*

I left off my writing one last time to put my affairs in order. We had decided that Elvira would leave in the morning, as the assassins had recommended. In the beginning she would not listen, refused to abandon me, moaned and cried with anguish. I calmed her with long caresses, and we spent the greater part of that beautiful night loving one another. It is rare that one is aware, when loving, that it is for the last time. But anyone who has knowingly experienced the final moments of passion will be aware that such an ordeal, combining the ignorance of what the next day will bring and the power of the moments shared, is more beautiful than anything, more painful and more intensely felt. Elvira had also brought some candles from the market. We lit all of them, to illuminate our cabin. In this light the rough-hewn acacia beams, the harsh surface of the stone walls, the wooden furnishings polished by shepherds' calloused hands gave off a pale glow, a golden sheen. We drank some light red wine from the jar and ate some olives. Elvira sang in her deep voice, and as we listened to the even sound of the Greek words, we danced barefoot on the smooth dirt floor, softer than any waxed parquet in any palace in Touraine. Late in the night, Elvira fell asleep in my arms and I laid her on the rope mattress. Then I went out with a candle, and on the wooden bench I used as a desk to write these memoirs, I composed a few letters. They recommend Elvira to my agents. With the money I still have, she can sail to the first available destination and from there, with the help of those who are loyal to me, try to reach Rome, Florence, then Marseille. A letter for Guillaume instructs him regarding the inheritance of my fortune. Some of it will go to those of my children who can use it and the rest, a considerable amount, will be for Elvira.

I folded these documents and put them in the bag she will take with her. In a moment, I will add these pages. The moon has disappeared. Elvira will leave at dawn, which means not long from now. The day to come will be the day when night will open for me forever. I am waiting for it without fear and without desire.

I can die, because I have lived. And I have known freedom.

Postface

Certain historical figures have been buried twice. The first time in their tomb; the second time beneath their reputation. Jacques Cœur is such a figure. The number of studies that have been devoted to him is incalculable. Some are very general, others extremely specialized.[3] All of them confine him in the fairly unattractive role of merchant, Argentier or, incorrectly, "Grand Argentier," in other words, the minister of finance, something he never was. Given the vast amount of historical research, the fate of Jacques Cœur and his activity has been documented in detail.[4] But when put together, these lifeless fragments, accounting documents, and inventories of property,[5] cannot reconstitute a living man. At best they sketch a lackluster outline of a wheeler-dealer,

[3] Among the most recent are Jacques Heers, *Jacques Cœur*, Perrin; Claude Poulain, *Jacques Cœur*, Fayard; Georges Bordonove, *Jacques Cœur et son temps*, Pygmalion; Christiane Palou, *Jacques Cœur*, Presses des Mollets Sazeray; and Professeur Robert Guillot, *La chute de Jacques Cœur*, L'Harmattan. The present-day mayor of Bourges, Serge Lepeltier, also wrote a biography of Jacques Cœur for the Éditions Michel Lafon. The figure of Jacques Cœur has also been evoked in many more general books, such as those by Jean Favier (in particular *La guerre de cent ans*, Fayard) or Murray Kendall (*Louis XI*, Fayard).

[4] In this respect, the work by Michel Mollat du Jourdin (*Jacques Cœur ou l'esprit d'entreprise*, Aubier) is a truly comprehensive and extremely precise survey, providing a synthesis of the historical research into Jacques Cœur's commercial activity as well as his property, voyages, and personal and professional relations.

[5] Starting with the one made during his lifetime by the prosecutor Dauvet.

intriguer, and courtier who rose too high, too quickly, and who inaugurated a long series of disgraced favorites, such as Fouquet under Louis XIV.

The Palace of Jacques Cœur in Bourges can be visited as a curiosity, the testimony to a pivotal moment where, in the image of its two very different façades, the Middle Ages would give way to the Renaissance.[6] In short, what one remembers is what came before or what came after, and this division between past and future tends to empty the historical figure of his own reality once and for all.

Why did I set out to bring the man back to life, replacing precise but inert images with a novelistic reality, even if it was less realistic? No doubt it was to pay a debt. I spent my childhood at the foot of Cœur's palace. I saw it in all kinds of weather, and there were certain winter evenings when I felt as if someone were still living there. I used to stop outside a certain little door at the bottom, and in the iron door handle I could feel the warm imprint of the owner's hand.

The house where Jacques Cœur was born (or the one where he was said to have been born) is located not far from my own house. What a contrast with the palace! There could be no better description of this man's extraordinary destiny than the comparison between his humble point of departure and the place symbolizing his triumph. And in between the two, the Levant, his journey, the ports of the Mediterranean . . . All through my harsh, gray childhood, he was the one who showed me the way, who testified to the power of dreams and the existence of an elsewhere full of refinement and sunshine. I owed it to him, to pay tribute on the scale of what he had done for me. At one point, I even entertained the project of having his

[6] The Association of the Friends of Jacques Cœur in Bourges celebrates the great man and perpetuates his memory through ceremonies, seminars, and learned publications. See their official website: www.jacques-cœur-bourges.com

remains brought back from the island of Chios, where he died. I discussed it with Jean-François Deniau, who cared a great deal for him, and who, always eager to embark on an impossible mission, was very enthusiastic about the project. But we soon had to face facts: there were no remains in Greece, there was no burial place. The only way to honor Jacques Cœur was through literature.

Thus, gradually, the idea of erecting a novelistic tombstone to him was born. I had the Hadrian of the "Memoirs" in mind, and I began to take notes with a view to creating a work of a similar inspiration to that of Marguerite Yourcenar's, well aware that I could never claim to equal her genius. As always, I began by collecting signs, emotions, and portraits, as I happened upon them during my reading and my travels—anything that might contribute to the construction of this edifice.[7]

I set about my labors, respecting the facts, where they are known.[8] Fortunately, a great many things are missing in the portrait of Jacques Cœur—an actual picture of him for a start. The events are real and exact, and details of his life have been scrupulously respected, including the final adventure of his flight and escape. But for my theater, where the accessories and décor were available, what remained was the essential, to bring the characters to life and describe their roles. What woman could I place in the costume of Agnès Sorel? (She, on the other hand, has left us a face, thanks to the painter Fouquet.) Jacques was close to her, and was the executor of her will, but what was the nature of the ties that brought them together?[9] The lack of any precise information is great good fortune for the novelist.

[7] I would like to thank Madame Mireille Pastoureau and the entire team of the library at the Institute who helped me greatly in my research.

[8] The primary novelistic infidelity concerns the character of Jean de Villages, with whom I took great liberties.

[9] Biographies of Agnès Sorel, in particular the one by Françoise Kermina (*Agnès Sorel,* Perrin), fail to say anything precise about their relationship.

His imagination can take flight without the risk of colliding with the obstacles left by documents. This is true for almost all of Jacques Cœur's life.[10] Before long, I felt him come alive, trembling, thinking, deciding, acting, living.

In this book I wanted to follow him from his childhood ingenuity and on through his adolescent desires, his choices as an adult, and his doubts and errors. This was a journey to be undertaken without any baggage, trusting my character. We do not know what the Middle Ages were like. Nor did he. He would find out only by living in his time, and we would find out by watching him live.

To understand his time, Jacques Cœur was positioned all the better in that his experience would lead him everywhere. There were not many men who had the opportunity to visit multiple worlds, to know everything and understand everything. From the most obscure corner of a war-beleaguered France to the east, from Flanders to Italy, from the Languedoc to Greece, he visited nearly all the territory of what was then the known world. His exploration was compounded by an eminently novelistic social journey. A man of the people, he rose to share the company of kings, and popes, and everything Europe had at the time in the way of great lords. His fall would then take him to the lower depths of prisons, and the precarious life of the fugitive. There can have been no feelings he did not experience at one time: ambition, but success would quickly abolish it; fear, constantly; love, just once, until Agnès Sorel crossed his path and showed him the happiness and sorrow the human heart could attain.

It was not enough for him merely to understand his era: he transformed it. When he came into the world it was a time of

[10] Frequently Cœur's activity is only known to us by means of very old clues or indirect reports, such as the one by Bertrandon de la Broquière, whom he met in Damascus, and whose testimony enabled me to imagine Jacques Cœur's visit to that city.

great upheaval. One hundred years of war with England were reaching their end; the papacy was reunited; the long survival of the Roman Empire finally came to a close with the fall of Constantinople; Islam took its place as the counterpart to Christianity. A world was dying in Europe, the world of chivalry, serfdom, and the crusades. What would replace it was the development of wealth through commerce, the power of money replacing that of the land, and the genius of creators, artisans, artists, and discoverers. Jacques Cœur was the man of that revolution. He radically changed the West's way of viewing the Levant, and replaced the idea of conquest with that of trade.

Obviously, it would be an error to assume that Jacques Cœur was aware of the revolutions that were brewing. He was not a modern. Nor was he a prophet. He was merely inhabited by dreams, and he gave them a beginning of reality. The only way to keep him alive is to immerse him in the turbulent, warm flow of romantic fiction. One must imagine him in his everyday life, both visionary and blind, full of certainties and doubts in equal number, unaware of the future to which he would belong, far more than he knew.

I do not know what he would think of such a portrait, and no doubt it resembles me more than it does him.

I will let the readers be the judge of that, and draw their own conclusions. The main thing, and my only desire, is that this mausoleum of words, rather than enclosing a dead hero, will liberate a man who is truly alive.

About the Author

Jean-Christophe Rufin is one of the founders of Doctors Without Borders and a former Ambassador of France in Senegal. He has written numerous bestsellers, including *The Abyssinian*, for which he won the Goncourt Prize for a debut novel in 1997. He also won the Goncourt Prize in 2001 for *Brazil Red*.